# SIN CITY VOWS

## ZURI DAY

# SON OF SCANDAL

## DANI WADE

MILLS & BOON

First Published in Great Britain 2019
by Mills & Boon, an imprint of HarperCollinsPublishers,
1 London Bridge Street, London, SE1 9GF

*Sin City Vows* © 2019 Zuri Day
*Son of Scandal* © 2019 Katherine Worsham

ISBN: 978-0-263-27175-1

0319

# SIN CITY VOWS

## ZURI DAY

For all of us who've dreamed of vows
Experienced love's oohs and aahs and wows
The journey is worth it but not always pretty
As you'll see in this read that takes place in Sin City

# One

$B$reedlove birthdays were always exciting. As the firstborn son of this close-knit clan, Christian knew that well. But as he relaxed against the company limo's luxurious interior, he had to give it to the family, especially his dad. They'd surprised him at a time in his life when he thought few things could. The gift he'd received just hours ago had been totally unexpected, had humbled the self-confident, almost cocky businessman in him even as it had filled him with pride.

Now, as they passed the family mansion and reached the estate's private airstrip, Christian realized one more surprise awaited him. A slow smile spread across his face, highlighting dimples that more than a few times had gotten him out of trouble with authority and into the romantic crosshairs of the opposite sex. One look and he was mesmerized. What he saw was a thing of beauty. Sleek lines, muted earth tones, curves in all the right places. *Wow.*

Christian looked over at his brother Adam, who was on his smartphone, texting away. "You knew about this?"

Adam looked up. "About what?"

Christian's smile broadened. "Yeah, you knew about it. Ty is here." His best friend had cut short his business trip and come to help the eldest Breedlove sibling celebrate a milestone. And boy, had he arrived in style.

The sound of another car approaching pulled Christian away from the dazzling view. He turned and saw his dad's newest toy—a black Escalade SUV customized with all the bells and whistles—pull up next to the limo that he'd exited. Their driver, Elvis, hopped out and opened the door for Christian's mother, Victoria, while his father, Nicholas, eased out the other back door, grinning as he approached his firstborn.

*They knew about this, too?* That Tyson had flown in to surprise him on his birthday and show off what looked to be a brand-new Gulfstream G600 jet?

"Well, son, what do you think?"

Christian returned his attention to the rare and opulent beauty now backlit by the setting sun.

"I think I owe Tyson money."

"Why?" Adam had finally put away his phone when they pulled up and exited the limo to join the group.

"To settle a bet. After flying in one of those customized babies last year, we put a thousand bucks on which one of us would be the first to get our own." Christian waved his hand toward the plane. "Looks like Ty won."

The door of the plane opened. Christian took a step forward as the airstair lowered and someone moved through the doorway.

"Happy birthday, Christian."

He stopped in his tracks, shielding his eyes against the sunlight to get a better view of the newcomer, convinced that the ethereal beauty before him could not be real. A woman—tall, richly tanned, with curly dark hair cascading over one shoulder—beckoned him with a smile.

Stunned, Christian turned to his mother, who now stood next to Nicholas, her face beaming. "Who is that?"

"You remember Lauren, don't you, dear? Faye's daughter? She was heading this way, and I felt you wouldn't mind that she caught a ride on your plane."

"Wait, *what*? My..." Christian looked from his parents to Adam. Everyone was smiling.

Nicholas slapped Christian's back before placing an arm around his shoulders. "Happy birthday, son."

Christian turned back to where Lauren now descended the plane's airstair. She was dressed in a belted wide-legged jumpsuit that emphasized pert, ample breasts and a small, curvy waist, and Christian noted a casual yet almost regal air about the way she carried herself. The emerald color brought out the golden tones in her skin and highlighted specks of green in the hazel eyes now fixed on him as she neared them.

He whispered to his mother, almost incredulously, "Is that my birthday present?"

Victoria continued to smile at Lauren while coyly replying, "Only the plane, son." Seconds later Lauren stepped into her open arms. "Hello, darling."

"Hi, Victoria." Lauren turned to Christian. "Hi, Chris."

"Hello." He hitched a thumb toward the plane as he looked at her. "So, Tyson isn't in there?"

"Who's Tyson?" Lauren asked.

"Chris's best friend," Adam replied.

Lauren slowly shook her head from side to side. The impish upturn of plump, glossy lips begging to be kissed suggested to Christian that she'd been in on it, too.

He turned sincere, grateful eyes on his parents. "Mom, Dad... I don't know what to say except...wow...thanks."

"You deserve it, son," Nicholas said.

Christian turned back to the plane. "Well, hot damn!" he exclaimed as the truth fully sank in. He reached out and offered Lauren his arm, which she graciously accepted, then gestured for his family to follow them. "Come on, beautiful. Show me around!"

Even in his excitement, Christian noted Lauren's silky skin and caught the subtle scent of something floral and delectably spicy. Gentleman that he was, he stepped back and allowed her to precede him up the stairs. The view from the back was the same as from the front—very alluring. So much so that entering the upscale and stately cabin that had been tailor-made to the specific instructions of his interior designer mother was almost anticlimactic.

Almost, but not quite. As Christian stepped inside the cabin and looked around, the magnitude of his parents' generosity made his chest swell with gratitude. The interior was exactly what he'd imagined while talking with Tyson, as comfortable as any found in the homes on the Breedlove estate. Walls covered in ivory suede. Ebony-stained hardwood floors. Recliners upholstered in jacquard chenille boasting company colors of black, white and tan. Seats on the left side of the cabin could be swiveled to view the flat screen mounted up front or around to the dining table behind them.

Christian looked from Lauren to his mom, his voice raspy with emotion. "How did you know?"

"Your brother, sweetheart. Adam talked to Tyson not long after the two of you had the extensive custom jet conversation and made that wager."

"Tyson knew about this surprise?" Adam nodded. "And he kept his mouth shut, for almost a year?"

"Wonders never cease, bro," Adam replied.

The pilot came out of the cockpit. Christian recognized him at once. "Not you, too," Christian muttered, shaking the outstretched hand of the family friend who'd grown up with his father and now piloted the company plane. "Am I the only one who wasn't in on this secret?"

Nicholas nodded. "Just about."

"Allow me to show you around," the pilot offered. "She's a real beauty. Glad I got to fly her first."

Once again, Christian held out his arm. "Care to join me on the tour?"

Adam hooked his muscular forearm through the one Christian offered. "I'd love to."

Christian moved his brother aside and placed a hand on Lauren's back. "Do you have brothers?"

"No."

"Do you want one?" Her throaty chuckle was music to his ears. Nicholas and Victoria sat on the white leather sleeper sofa that anchored the right side of the cabin while Christian, Lauren and Adam checked out the accommodations. There was a granite bath with a full shower, a compact chef's kitchen, two sleeping bunks along with a master bedroom, and an area set up as a small private office but that had padded flooring and workout equipment hidden behind the walls.

"How'd she do, Chris?" Nicholas asked when the group returned to the front of the cabin. He stood, then turned to help Victoria up. "Your mom get the design just about right?"

"It's incredible," Christian said, moved. "It's everything I imagined and much more. Hard to wrap my brain around. Earlier this week, the promotion to president, I thought that was the gift."

"Speaking of…" Nicholas turned and removed a thin layer of paper covering a platinum plaque with carved lettering: Christian Breedlove, President. CANN International Inc.

Christian took it in with the utmost pride. The acronym, CANN, stood for the names of him and his brothers— Christian, Adam, Noah and Nick—along with the family's unwavering belief that while working together there was nothing they couldn't do. That belief was the foundation of the Breedloves' empire, an international chain of casino hotels and spas that were second to none.

"That's…exquisite." He smiled and swallowed hard. "Where are the twins? Since everyone knew about it, the dynamic duo should be here, too."

"They're handling the second half of the evening." Victoria eyed her watch. "Dinner at the hotel, where we should be heading right about now. Hope you're hungry. Holding in the secret all day left me with very little appetite. Now that it's out, I'm starved."

Christian hugged his dad and mom and kissed her on the cheek. He shook Adam's hand before pulling him into a tight embrace.

"Jesse," Nicholas called out to the pilot. "You're welcome to join us."

"I've got a hot date," Jesse replied. "But thanks."

The group headed down the stairs and over to where the drivers leaned against the gleaming black limousine. Christian placed a hand on Lauren's arm until the others had taken several steps and created a bit of distance between them. He wanted to take a moment and properly thank her for participating in his birthday surprise. He knew with Adam in the limo he'd get in few words.

Adam saw the move and stopped, too. "I'll catch a ride with Mom and Dad. You two can take the limo."

"Thanks, bro," Christian said.

"Only because it's your birthday." He threw a playful punch at his brother and headed to the SUV.

Moments later, Christian and Lauren entered the limo. The driver followed the SUV's circuitous route out of the estate and across to Las Vegas Boulevard, where the CANN hotel anchored one end of the Strip.

"It appears I'm supposed to know you," Christian whispered once they'd settled into the roomy seats. "But that's impossible."

A slight arch of Lauren's manicured brow preceded her response. "Is it?"

"Absolutely. You look…ravishing. There's no way I'd forget having met you."

"Well, you did."

He thought for a moment. "You're Faye's daughter? Faye Hart?"

Lauren nodded. "Yes."

Christian liked Lauren's voice, low and husky. He could imagine how it would sound in the throes of passion as he branded her as his.

"It's been at least two years since I've seen her, so when did you and I meet?"

"When I was twelve, and just so you know, my inner child is wounded."

Lauren feigned a pout. Christian's eyes dropped to pursed

lips now held tightly together. Even though he knew she was joking, he wanted to kiss her until the frown disappeared, and then kiss her some more.

Not sure he could touch those lips, though, and keep the kiss chaste, he reached out and squeezed her hand instead.

"Twelve?" Christian's relieved laugh was genuine. "Did you look then the way you do now?"

"Not quite." Lauren laughed, too. "I was four years younger than my sister, Renee. You were all into her. I was practically invisible." Lauren delivered the last line with a whine appropriate for a jilted preteen.

Christian's head fell back as more laughter erupted. "Renee Hart! Now it's all coming back to me. You guys used to live in California but moved across the country to…"

"Maryland. My dad took a job in Washington, DC. They bought a home in nearby Brandywine."

"Right. That was part of the excuse used for my being rejected. I think she had a boyfriend. I didn't want to visit LA for a while after that. My sixteen-year-old ego was crushed." He placed his hand over his heart. "In remembering my anguish then, I can very much relate to your inner child's pain."

The atmosphere shifted as comfortable interaction morphed into daunting attraction. Christian opened the door to an elaborate minibar. "Would you like a drink?"

"No, thanks. I'm good."

"Come on, it's my birthday. Don't make me drink alone."

"Okay, champagne then."

Christian opened a bottle of pricey champagne and filled two flutes. He handed one to Lauren. Their fingers touched. Sparks. Heat. *Did she feel that?* He looked up. She glanced away.

Yes, she'd felt something.

"To what shall we toast?" he asked.

"You, of course. It's your birthday, and given your gift, it's obviously a big one."

"For a second back there I thought the plane belonged to a friend of mine, Tyson, and had the foolish hope that you were my present."

Her eyes narrowed in a face that became impossible to read. "A foolish hope, indeed."

Christian moaned. "My second try for a Hart girl…rejected again."

"You can handle it." Lauren winked. "You're an old man now."

"Indeed. The big three-o."

"Over the hill," Lauren joked.

"Totally."

"To your birthday," she said.

"And beautiful gifts," Christian added.

They clinked glasses and sipped.

"So…whatever happened to your sister and that guy?"

Lauren shrugged. "He probably got dumped, like all the others. Until her senior year in college, when she met the man who is now her husband and a father of two."

"Good for her." He set down the flute. "What about you?"

"What about me?"

"I don't see a ring."

Lauren's hands flew up in a defensive position. "No, and you won't."

"Dang, girl, you sound even more adamant than me." Christian chuckled and lifted his glass. "To the single life."

"Hear, hear."

"So…why didn't Faye come with you to visit my mom?"

"It's more than a visit. I'll be working here."

"Oh, you've relocated for work. Who with?"

"Victoria. I'm her new personal assistant. As I understand it, I'll work primarily on events for your family's nonprofit organization."

A slightly raised brow was Christian's only reaction. Inside, he felt a pang of disappointment. So much for the thought of a one-night stand with Lauren, or a short-term girlfriend to cuddle with during the cold winter months. He didn't date women involved with family business. Directly or indirectly, anyone working with his mother was no longer fair game. Any other day he would have figured it out sooner. But that week's promotion, his birthday and the shockingly extravagant birthday gift had dimmed his awareness and caused him to be off guard.

However, now Lauren's presence was becoming crystal clear. His mother, Victoria the matchmaker, was at it again. It was no secret that she wanted him to settle down, get married and start a family. All of which were not high on his agenda. And then there was another darker thought. Maybe his mom wasn't matchmaking. Maybe Lauren was manipulating her. It wouldn't be the first time a woman had used Victoria's passion for helping others through the family's foundation as a way to get to him.

He sighed, settled against the car's supple leather seats and thoughtfully sipped his champagne. The possible truth behind Lauren's visit cleared away the ardent desire her appearance had first aroused. The last thing he needed was a potentially messy fling with the daughter of one of his mom's good friends. He'd just been promoted to president of a multibillion-dollar hotel, casino and spa conglomerate with properties on five continents. What he needed in a female companion was someone fun with no ulterior motives or long-term expectations. Right now, he was married to the family business, and for the foreseeable future, CANN International would be his only wife.

# Two

He was sexier and more handsome than Lauren remembered. The teen who'd stolen her twelve-year-old heart and remained her secret crush all through high school. Tall, lean, sporting curly black hair in a clean, cropped cut that was shorter on the sides and fuller on top. The eyes were the same—dark, intense—and his magnetic smile still had the power to render her breathless.

Even after she'd begun dating, and throughout a fairly serious relationship that began in college and lasted four years, Lauren had loosely followed Christian, the Breedloves and CANN International's ever-expanding empire, which was often in the news. A few years ago the company made history by building the first seven-star hotel and casino in North America, a distinction given to them by *Top-Tier Travel Digest*, the bible for agents and others who catered to the wealthy, the world's 1-percenters and the 1 percent of the 1 percent.

Socially, Christian was a paparazzi favorite, often making the gossip columns and the tabloids while attending Hollywood premieres and high-society events with a gorgeous girl on his arm. Last year, when he made the coveted Thirty Under Thirty list, she'd bookmarked the online article and shared it with her sister Renee. Every year, the names were compiled by business industry legends who pegged the next group of savvy, successful businessmen on the rise, the ones to watch.

Christian was not only jaw-droppingly good-looking, but he was a smart, progressive thinker as well. Were she in the market for a boyfriend, the man seated beside her had all kinds of potential. But she wasn't looking, and especially not for someone like the almighty Christian Breedlove. Not wanting to be manipulated by a rich, powerful man was precisely why she'd fled the East Coast.

"How'd that happen?" Christian asked as the limo headed down the crowded Strip toward their final destination. "You deciding to move here to work for Mom?"

"Very quickly," Lauren said, hitching in a breath as they inched toward the CANN Casino, Hotel and Spa, an award-winning steel-and-glass masterpiece whose tallest point brushed the sky at almost fourteen hundred feet. "Just a day or so ago."

"Really, that fast?"

"Yes." She shifted her gaze back to his remarkably handsome face. "Victoria was venting to Mom about a dilemma. Her assistant resigned abruptly and gave no notice, in the middle of planning a Valentine's Day–themed fashion show and several springtime charity events that Victoria says are very important to the foundation's funding. Mom mentioned that she thought I could help, and Victoria called and asked if I could come over ASAP. I understand the fashion show is just a week away and is a very big deal."

Christian nodded, thoughtfully rubbing his chin. "Speaking of abrupt notices, what about your employer?"

"She was totally understanding." To his raised brow, Lauren continued, "For almost a year now, I've worked for myself."

"Ah, I see. What's your specialty?"

"Marketing, promotions, branding and PR. I have a small roster of regular clients and just finished a major campaign for a Southern university. Your mom needed help and I needed…a break…so here I am."

"When was the last time you were in Vegas?"

"Three years ago, for a friend's wedding."

"So you haven't been to our new hotel."

"No," Lauren replied. She looked beyond Christian and out the window. The limo turned into an impressive entrance bordered by marble waterfalls, the word *CANN* bold, shiny and backlit to stand out in the night. "But I've seen pictures. It looks amazing in magazines and now, up close, is even more impressive."

The limo passed the main entrance and continued to a side door. Christian exited and reached back his hand to help her. "It delights me to hear you say that," he murmured as a uniformed employee opened the door and greeted them. "For CANN, our goal for this location is quite simple—to be the most spectacular hotel in the world. We believe it is."

Once inside, Lauren totally agreed. Unlike other hotels boasting casinos on the Strip, the area they entered was elegant, modern and most of all, quiet.

"Where's the casino?" she asked.

"The main casino is two floors down, accessible by a separate entrance," he answered, pulling out his phone to respond to a text. "There's a private one for high rollers on a higher floor. We'll go later, after dinner, if you'd like. It's a whole other world."

Lauren noticed that the employee who'd opened the door still walked behind them, a respectable distance away. As Christian put away his phone, he saw her glance back and looked, too.

"I don't need anything. You can return to your post."

"Are you sure there isn't anything I can do for you, Mr. Breedlove?"

"Absolutely sure."

"I understand it's your birthday, Mr. Breedlove."

He tsked. "Can't keep a secret around here."

"Not with us," the employee responded with a small smile. "Happy birthday, sir."

Christian walked over and shook the employee's hand. "What's your name?"

"Eric, sir."

"How long have you been a part of our security detail?"

"Was just hired a month ago, sir."

"I think our security manager made a very fine choice. Welcome to the team."

"Thank you, sir."

They continued down the hall and past an opening where Lauren glimpsed a vast lobby filled with well-dressed women and expensively suited men. For many reasons, she was glad they'd come through a private entrance. The paparazzi seemed to live for Christian. A splashy spread announcing her whereabouts was the last thing she needed.

A few moments later, they reached an elevator that blended seamlessly with the wall, its doors boasting the same design. She watched him place his thumb on a scanner discreetly located above a chair rail. When the doors opened, Lauren slipped her arm around the one Christian offered and held on, taking in the landscape of neon lights as the elevator ascended to Zest, the Michelin-starred restaurant she'd read about that was housed on the one-hundredth floor.

The doors parted, and the view from the room took Lauren's breath away. Beyond the semiprivate booths and massive crystal chandelier were floor-to-ceiling windows that gave the illusion that there were no walls, that one could walk to the edge of the floor and touch the sky. The atmosphere in the main dining room was fairly quiet, dim and understated. All of that changed when Christian opened the door to the private dining room.

"Happy birthday, Christian!"

"You're the man, Chris!"

Other shouts and cheers filtered through the applause as those who were sitting got to their feet. Lauren looked at Christian, who'd stopped just inside the door, clearly surprised to see the large crowd that filled the room. Two men broke away from the group and approached them. Had she not known about the twins, Lauren may have thought the champagne had kicked in and caused her to see double. They were identical—tall, dark, handsome, sporting the Breedlove dimple in their left cheek and swagger in their stride.

"The dynamic duo," Christian said once they'd reached him.

"Gotcha, old man!"

"We did it, huh?"

"He didn't see it coming."

"Had no idea!"

Lauren stood mesmerized at the twins' rapid-fire delivery, sometimes finishing each other's sentences without a pause in between. Her eyes shifted back and forth between them, trying to find a way to differentiate between the two. They had the same soft black curls as Christian, but while his were close-cropped, theirs were longer, wilder. Studying them reminded her of a favorite puzzle at the back of one of her popular fashion magazines, where two pictures that looked identical actually weren't. The test was to find the differences. There were usually several. Here, she was just trying to find even one. Then she spotted it. The one on the left wore a tiny diamond stud in his ear. The one on the right didn't. *Bingo!*

"The dyno duo strikes again!" The two men high-fived before executing an intricate handshake. Their joy and excitement was contagious. Christian was clearly enjoying their friendly verbal sparring match. Just being around them made Lauren smile.

"Where are your manners, Chris?" Diamond Stud asked.

"Yeah, Chris. Introduce us to this beautiful lady."

"To do that you two will have to quit talking."

"Whatever."

Said in stereo. *Cute.*

"Lauren, meet my annoying younger brothers Nicholas Jr." He motioned toward the twin who'd last spoken, the one not wearing an earring. "Called Nick to differentiate between him and my father."

"Hello, Nick," Lauren said, with outstretched hand.

"And Noah."

"Hi, Noah." Again, she offered her hand.

"Ah, no, Lauren. Shaking is for business. Hugging is for friends."

Noah pulled Lauren into a bear hug.

Christian placed his hand on Noah's shoulder. "Back off."

Nick laughed. Christian looked over as a few others headed toward them.

"Tyson!"

Tyson, a striking blond with clear brown eyes, bore a mock scowl as he approached. "You going to stand here by the door all night?"

"You're a trip," Christian said. The two men enjoyed a hearty embrace. "I can't believe how well you helped pull this off. You remembered everything, bro."

"I'm good like that." He looked at Lauren, clearly impressed. "Hello, I'm Tyson Ford."

"Lauren Hart—"

"Hey there, birthday boy!"

Lauren found herself being pushed aside by a whirlwind of haughtiness wearing stilettos and cloaked in what smelled like an entire bottle of perfume. The woman threw her arms around Christian. Lauren looked on, more amused than annoyed. But if she read his expression correctly, for Christian the opposite was true. She watched as he deftly removed the brunette's arms from around his neck, just as more and more of his friends came over to greet him. Soon he was swept into a circle of admirers, all clamoring for attention. From the corner of her eye, Lauren saw someone approach.

"Come, dear," Victoria said, slipping her arm through Lauren's and walking toward the head table. "That was Chloe, who grew up with Chris. I've seated you with the family, beside me, so that I can offer a play-by-play on this motley cast of characters. In order to do your job properly, you'll need not only an in-depth grasp of the CANN conglomerate but also the ocean of high society here in Nevada and beyond…"

She paused and watched Chloe glide back to her table. "And the sharks who swim in those waters."

The next hour was a blur of names and faces as during dinner Victoria pointed out the movers and shakers of metropolitan Las Vegas and the few who resided in Breedlove, the unincorporated Nevada town founded by Nicholas and a few others more than twenty years ago. Lauren was introduced to some of them, along with many of Christian's friends from across the country who'd flown in for the occasion. Once the last dessert plate was removed, a few tables were rearranged to make room for a dance floor. A famous DJ from Miami fired up the crowd.

Nick walked over. "Come on, Lauren. Let's dance."

She waved him away. "It's been a long day. I'd rather just relax and watch all of you."

"Okay, but if you change your mind…"

"I'll come find you."

When Lauren got up a few minutes later, she didn't head to the dance floor. She'd seen Victoria and Nicholas heading toward the exit and after getting their attention, made a beeline toward them to catch a ride to her new home. In the past forty-eight hours, her already-chaotic life had been thrown into further disarray, and she needed time to try to process everything and figure out what would come next.

She felt eyes following her as she crossed to the door, saw Chloe whispering to another girl as she neared the Breedloves and fell into step beside them. She could only imagine what Chloe and all the other socialites were wondering about the new girl, and whether or not she, too, was vying to become the missus of tonight's birthday boy. They needn't worry. While they may be in a footrace to catch a husband, Lauren had upended her life to avoid one.

# Three

*Am I still dreaming?*

Last night, Lauren swore that was true. After the driver dropped off Nicholas and Victoria, he'd continued on for about a mile until reaching a cul-de-sac lined with exquisite single-story homes, all different architecturally and uniquely beautiful. Her immediate favorite was the very first one on the corner lot, a Spanish-inspired design of tan stucco and adobe brick with a black gabled roof. Even in her exhaustion she'd admired the wrought iron accents and arches on the windows and doors. When the driver had pulled into that home's driveway and announced it as the guesthouse chosen for her, Lauren's jaw had dropped.

"I'm staying here? Are you sure?"

"Positive," the driver had responded with a knowing smile. "You'll find your luggage in the bedroom. The residence has been stocked with everything one might need for an extended stay, but just in case you need anything else the guesthouse manager's card is on the table in the foyer." He handed her a small envelope. "Here's the code for the lock. Can you make it in okay?"

"I'm fine."

"Just checking. You look pretty wiped out."

She had been, but from exhaustion, not from too much drinking as she believed the driver assumed. It had taken her a couple tries to key in the correct code, but upon opening the door, it was like entering the abode of a fairy tale. The decor was straight out of *Architectural Digest*.

And now, awakening on the cloudlike memory foam bed after a blissful night's sleep, the dream had yet to dissipate. She sighed contentedly. The sun was shining. She was well rested. And everything that had happened, all that she'd seen, was real.

Lauren sat up, stretched and reached for her phone. She tapped the face. "Oh my God!" It was after 10:00 a.m. An early riser since college, Lauren couldn't recall the last time she'd slept this late, even after a night of partying. She'd even slept through the telephone ringing, with missed calls from Avery, her bestie, and her mom, Faye. Victoria had told her to come by after she'd risen for a casual visit. Lauren had said to expect her around nine o'clock. Now she'd be lucky to get there by eleven.

After sending Victoria a quick text requesting they meet at eleven, she took a quick shower, pulled her hair into a high ponytail, and hurriedly donned a free-flowing, light yellow maxi dress, silver jewelry that included her ever-present charm bracelet and a pair of ivory-colored sandals with cute yet comfy wedge heels. She arrived at the front door of what could only be described as a mansion with two minutes to spare.

A middle-aged Hispanic woman with coal-black hair and kind eyes opened the door.

"Hello, are you Lauren?"

"Yes."

"The missus is expecting you. Please, come this way."

Lauren entered a wide foyer with art-lined textured walls and slate tile, with hues of orange, tan, blue and ivory, colors that were repeated throughout the home's elegant yet comfortable decor. One hallway flowed into another. To the right was a formal dining room with huge single-paned windows that not only let in loads of natural sunlight but showcased the beautiful and meticulously landscaped garden in the expansive backyard. They turned left down a short hall that ended at ornately crafted French doors, standing ajar. Beyond that was a great room with two-story ceilings, chandeliers and one wall that seemed made entirely of glass.

Victoria was seated on an oversize tan sectional boasting soft Italian leather. She was wearing a short floral caftan and crystal-covered sandals. Seeing her in the bright, natural light of day made her even more beautiful than when Lauren first hugged her last night. Her pixie hairstyle framed a face devoid of wrinkles, one that looked more like thirtysomething than what Lauren knew was actually fifty-plus years. She turned and smiled when Lauren entered, put down the magazine she'd been reading and patted the space beside her.

"Well, good morning, sunshine!"

"Good morning, Victoria."

Lauren sat, then leaned over to accept the older woman's embrace.

"Look at you, all fresh-faced and fabulous. You woke up like that?"

Lauren laughed. "Not quite."

"But you're not wearing makeup."

"No. I hope that's okay. You said this would be a casual meeting, so…"

"Oh, no. It's fine. I'm just impressed. Not many women in my circle would be caught dead without their war paint."

"I do have on mascara," Lauren admitted. "And lip gloss."

"That's all? Must be nice."

"I could say the same about you. You look more like Christian's sister than his mom."

"Not without effort. Our hotel spa has some of the best aestheticians in the country, who are always researching the latest skin-tightening, wrinkle-eliminating, turn-back-the-time trends." Victoria placed a hand on Lauren's arm. "I was just about to have a light lunch. Care to join me?"

"Sure, thanks."

Victoria turned toward the woman who'd opened the front door, standing so quietly Lauren hadn't realized she was still there. "Sofia, tell Gabe we'll have the quinoa and spinach salad with sparkling cranberry orange juice. Thank you."

Victoria watched Sofia nod and leave the room. Her eyes shifted to Lauren. "Did you rest well?"

"The best sleep ever. I barely remember my head hitting the pillow."

"You'd had a busy two days."

"Yes."

"And…somewhat of a tumultuous time before that." Lauren nodded. "Faye didn't go into detail and you need only share what you'd like, but when I mentioned my assistant's abrupt departure and that I needed to replace her ASAP, she all but accepted the job for you. Said time away from the East Coast was exactly what you needed right now."

"She was right." Lauren took a deep breath, on one hand nervous to share the personal dilemma while on the other compelled to confide in someone with an unbiased point of view. "What exactly did Mom tell you?"

"That you were in a difficult relationship, one exacerbated by the fact that he's the son of your dad's employer?"

Lauren's chuckle held no humor. "That's one way to say it." She looked Victoria in the eye. "My dad is trying to force me into a marriage that would be bad on the home front but apparently good for business."

"Force as in…like an arranged marriage?"

"Yes."

"Well, that's just ridiculous. This is the twenty-first century, and while I've known more than one desperate soul who's walked down the aisle for money, I'd counsel any woman who asked to marry for love."

Lauren watched myriad expressions flit across Victoria's face as she processed the situation.

"What does Faye say about it?"

"Basically, she agrees with you, and so do I. But Dad is really pushing the idea, almost desperately so. Being married to the man orchestrating the idea puts her in a difficult position. She wants what's best for both of us, but he can be very persuasive."

"You say this guy's father is your dad's boss?"

Lauren nodded. "Years ago, when Dad sought investors for his accounting firm, Gerald was first in line with an open checkbook. The future looked promising, but in the end, Dad's small company couldn't compete with the intellectual diversity and electronic wizardry of the larger firms."

She released a breath, then continued.

"While Dad had struggled, Gerald's consulting firm had grown by leaps and bounds. When his CFO took an early retirement, he called my dad, who felt he owed it to Gerald, given the investment he'd made and never gotten back."

"Gerald sounds like a good friend. But if your dad is already in an executive position, how would you marrying the son make business better?"

"I don't know." Lauren paused, wondering just how much she should tell Victoria. "Can I trust what we discuss to remain just between us?"

"Absolutely, Lauren."

"Shared with no one, not even my mom?"

Victoria placed a hand on Lauren's arm and squeezed. "Not even Faye, darling."

"Years ago, Ed and I briefly dated."

"The son."

"Yes. I was a freshman in college. He's eight years older than me. I was young, dumb, impressionable and thrilled to get the attention of an older, successful man. Mere weeks into dating, he gave me a ring. A promise ring that we both assumed would lead to an engagement. But it didn't."

"Why not?"

"Because in time I realized that Ed's well-put-together image was a facade hiding a controlling narcissist who was verbally abusive. I gave back the ring and ended the relationship. I don't think he ever got over it. Ed's an only child used to getting what he wants."

"Your parents didn't know?"

"They knew we'd dated but not why we broke up. I never told them about anything—the verbal and emotional abuse, his anger issues, definitely not about the ring. Our parents are friends and I didn't want to cause trouble between them. Anyway, a while back, I heard that he'd been boasting about an upcoming engagement to a young, naive but really pretty girl. Something happened and the relationship abruptly ended. And then…"

Victoria raised a brow but remained silent.

"He tried to get me back, tried to force me into a relationship by reminding me of the promise I'd made and admitting his fault in our not working out. When I rebuffed his overtures, things got ugly."

"How so?"

"He demanded that I marry him, and if I didn't comply, he threatened to make things difficult for my family. Of course I told him hell would freeze over before I got involved with him again." She released a quavering breath. "I don't know what he told my dad, but now two men are trying to force my hand."

"Did you ask Paul why?"

"Yes, and Dad's answers don't make sense, nor does the chummy friendship that seems to exist between them. In the past few months they've really ramped up the pressure. This break is a godsend, so thanks again."

The women paused as Sofia returned bearing a tray of warm homemade rolls, a pitcher of juice and a crystal bowl filled with the spinach and quinoa salad that Victoria had requested. When conversation resumed, the topic shifted from Lauren's personal life to the freelance marketing work she'd handled over the past twelve months and the professional duties she'd take on as Victoria's personal assistant, work that would largely center on the CANN Foundation.

"I'm sorry to overwhelm you," Victoria finished. "But next week's tea and fashion show has become a hugely popular event. That this one takes place around Valentine's Day, focuses on love and features some hunky eye candy along with the fashion has made it even bigger. But between the two of us, I think we'll be fine."

"I do, too," Lauren said, zipping up her tablet cover and placing the computer inside her tote. "It's a lot of work, for sure, but I love being busy and I'm a huge fan of Ace Montgomery, his wife London and the HER Fashion line. I'll do everything in my power to ensure the event goes off without a hitch."

"There's one last thing, Lauren." Victoria reached for a folder on the table before her. "I've drawn up a six-month contract covering from now until July 15. Had I had one before I wouldn't have been left high and dry without help. I hope you don't mind signing it."

"On the contrary, I'd be delighted. That means it's literally illegal for me to return home."

Small talk continued as Victoria walked Lauren to the door, with Lauren commenting on the original art pieces that lined the hallway. They stepped outside to a clear, cloudless sky and a subtle warm breeze. "Where's the car?" she asked.

Along with the guesthouse, a car had been placed at Lauren's disposal. She had yet to drive it.

"I walked here," Lauren replied. "The dry air is a wonderful change from Maryland's humidity, and weather this warm in February rarely happens back east. Plus I haven't worked out lately, and can use the exercise."

"Just so you're sure, because I'd be more than happy to have someone drive you home."

"No, thanks, I'll be fine."

The women hugged. Lauren waved and headed down the circular drive to the sidewalk that cut through an expansive lawn, toward the paved road. The two-mile-long walk was barely remembered, so consumed was she with the amount of work she'd need to handle to help Victoria pull off next week's fashion show. She'd wanted to escape Ed, the pressure from her father and a predictable life, but as she reached the front door of her lovely Spanish-styled home, Lauren couldn't help but ask herself, had she jumped from the frying pan into the fryer?

Lauren entered the home and headed toward the dining room table, pulling the tablet from her tote while crossing the room. She wanted to go over the notes while the conversation with Victoria was still fresh in her mind. Tossing her tote on the couch, she pulled a bottle of water from the fridge, then sat and fired up the tablet. That's when she noticed something missing—her charm bracelet.

A pang of fear seized Lauren's chest as she jumped up from the chair, retrieved the tote and began searching inside it. The bracelet had been her talisman since receiving it as a birthday gift at the age of sixteen. She'd moved cross-country to dodge domineering men and take control of her future. Now would be the worst possible time for her luck to run out.

With no success from a search inside, Lauren reached for the sandals she'd kicked off upon entering the house. She slipped them on and opened the front door. Just before stepping outside, her cell phone rang. *Victoria, maybe?* Had she found the bracelet on the manse's exquisite marble floors? Lauren hoped so, and hurried to catch the call before it went to voice mail.

"Lauren Hart." Her greeting came out in a rush of panicked air.

"I know who I called," a familiar voice answered.

"Oh, Avery. Hi." Lauren headed back toward the still-open front door.

"Obviously not who you were expecting," Avery said. "Which answers my second question after 'How are you?'"

which is 'Have you seen your teen crush?' Is that who you thought was calling?"

"Actually, I was hoping it was Victoria, his mom."

"Oh."

"I lost my bracelet and was hoping she'd found it."

"Your good luck charms? Oh, no!"

"Exactly. I'm trying not to freak out."

"Don't do that. Just think of all the places you've been and retrace your steps."

"That's what I'm getting ready to do." Lauren stepped back inside the home and headed toward her closet for a more comfortable pair of shoes.

"Can I call you back?"

"Not before an update, a short version at least, since my phone calls have not been returned."

Lauren retrieved her tennis shoes, sat on the bed and put the call on speaker. "From the second I touched down, it's been a whirlwind. I was going to call you tonight."

"So you had to start work as soon as you landed?"

"No, but in some ways that's how it felt, and that's after being in transit for almost eight hours."

"Why did you book a flight with that many changes, or such a long layover?"

"To be a part of Christian's birthday surprise. Yesterday was his thirtieth birthday. His parents surprised him with a slew of gifts and I was a part of that package."

"What?" The single syllable held out for several seconds suggested there were many more questions behind it.

Lauren laughed. "Not like that! His parents bought him a private plane and wanted me to fly in on it. So I took a flight to Atlanta, where the Gulfstream was built and customized, and then flew on it from Atlanta to here."

"Ooh la la! Envy has me greener than the wicked witch right now. Your charm search is going to have to wait. I'm going to need a play-by-play from the time you boarded until right before I called."

After changing shoes, Lauren went from the bedroom to the living room as she gave a recap of the past twenty-four hours, including the instant attraction she'd felt for her preteen heartthrob and why with all of the social maneuvering around Christian that she'd seen last night, the party had felt like work.

"Everyone wanted a piece of him," she finished.

"Including you?"

"Avery! I can't believe you just asked me that!"

"Why wouldn't I? You forget you've been your friend for a very long time. It's just a matter of time before you have to act on that attraction. And don't give me the 'no love in the work zone' argument. You've had a crush on that guy since forever. Don't blow your chance to make your fantasy a reality."

"I'll think about it."

"Do more than think. Act. You'll only be there for six months. What do you have to lose?"

It was a good question, one that Lauren promised Avery she'd ponder while resuming the search for something she'd already lost—her lucky charms.

# Four

Christian told himself that going to see Lauren was just about returning the bracelet, that spotting it on the driveway as he pulled up for an impromptu visit was life's way of leading him toward her place.

When Victoria offered to have Elvis or one of the other guys drive it over, Christian told her he was "already heading that way." But the real reason the newly elected president of a multibillion-dollar conglomerate was playing the part of delivery boy, instead of sending any one of at least fifty employees who worked on the estate, was because the only time it seemed he was able to stop thinking about Lauren was when he was talking to her instead.

In spite of his suspicions as to why she was here, thoughts of the sexy siren in that emerald-colored jumpsuit had consumed him since she'd stepped off the plane. He remembered his brief interactions with Lauren all those years ago. She'd been the quiet, leggy kid with adoring eyes who'd watched him when she thought he wasn't looking. The kid he'd brushed off or ignored while pursuing her older sister.

What it was about Lauren that now had him so enthralled Christian didn't know, except that it was something that none of the other women he'd been around lately possessed. It wasn't just her beauty, though she was gorgeous, with features she seemed to have been born with rather than purchased. Christian had been around and dated some of the most beautiful women on the planet. What attracted him to Lauren was a mystery, one he was determined to solve.

Christian pulled into the driveway, cutting off the engine and stepping out in one smooth motion. Ignoring his increased heartbeat, he strolled to the front door and rang the bell. Several long moments passed and he lifted his hand to knock just as the door opened.

"Oh. It's you."

Christian took in Lauren's bouncy ponytail and colorful sneakers, and the way her darkly bronzed skin glimmered against the pale yellow dress draped so becomingly over her curves. She looked absolutely delectable, and he prided himself on resisting the urge to lick his lips or kiss hers.

"Who were you expecting?"

"Um, someone else."

She seemed distracted, swiping an errant strand of hair away from her face as she looked at the floor around her.

"Am I interrupting?"

"Actually, I was just heading out to look for something."

"This, maybe?" He held up a silver link bracelet with dangling charms.

"Yes!" She reached for the bracelet.

Christian pulled back.

"Chris, give it to me. Now."

"Only if you'll be kind enough to invite me inside." He meant that in all ways imaginable.

"Sure," she said, stepping back.

He moved inside, stopped directly in front of her, just a few inches and a wall of heat between them.

"Now give me the bracelet."

"Ask nicely."

"May I have the bracelet, please?" Said through gritted teeth with flashing eyes.

Christian laughed. He unclasped the bracelet. "Here, allow me."

"Where did you find it?"

"At the edge of the circular drive. I saw it just before going up the steps."

She eyed him suspiciously. "Come on now," he drawled, then grinned. "It's why I came over, to give it back."

"Really? I can't tell." She held out her arm and smiled as he placed the delicate silver chain around her slender wrist and looked into her eyes. She returned his stare—bold, unflinching. Obviously the shy, awkward tween was all grown up. He hooked the clasp, then, still holding her arm with one hand, turned the bracelet with the other and reached for one of several charms, this one a heart.

"Each of these has a meaning, right?"

"Yes."

Christian's thumb brushed the inside of her wrist. An unasked question was immediately answered as Lauren's nipples hardened and pressed against soft cotton. She wore no bra. Acutely aware of his gaze, Lauren eased her wrist from his grasp and crossed her arms over her chest.

He observed the move but made no comment. Was she sincerely embarrassed? Playing hard to get? *What does it matter to you?* It didn't, Christian reminded himself. He'd had enough experience with women to know that even if she agreed to a casual affair, emotions could shift and life could get ugly. She could become a stalker or worse, somehow try to trap him. He knew that when it came to temporary liaisons, it was best to keep a safe distance between his lovers and his family and professional life. That wouldn't be the case with Lauren. Their mothers were very good friends. Even more, Lauren was now his mother's assistant. Which meant she was off-limits.

Life wasn't fair.

"A heart, huh?"

"Yep." Lauren fingered the silver trinket, her eyes on him as her headlights dimmed. She'd gotten her body under control, he saw, at least for the moment.

"So since you're wearing it on your sleeve, so to speak, does that mean no one has it yet?"

"That was really bad, Christian." She turned and walked into the living room, toward the couch. "Like something you would have asked my sister when you were sixteen."

"Yeah, it was pretty lame." He pointed to the couch. "May I?"

"Of course. I'm sorry, where are my manners? Would you like something to drink?"

"No, I'm fine."

Lauren joined him on the brushed-suede sofa. He moved to lessen the distance between them. As one hand encircled her wrist, the other fingered another charm on the bracelet. "Does this signify your wild side?"

"If so, I'd be quite dangerous. Bears are strong. That's the mascot of my alma mater's football team."

"Which is…?"

"Morgan State."

"I see."

"Are you into college sports?"

"Not too much, and not football. My games are golf, basketball and tennis. A little pro baseball every now and then. Are you a big sports fan?"

"I like football."

"So if I decided to tackle you, it would be all right?"

"You could try, but I might rise up on hind legs and swipe you with my paw." Christian chuckled as Lauren continued. "Leave a trail of fingernail scratches across your body. But then again, that probably wouldn't be the first time."

"Except for my brothers or teammates, being attacked would absolutely be a first. I'm not a violent man."

"What about the women you date, like Chloe?"

"What makes you think I dated her? Mom told you?"

"You and your life were not a part of our conversation. Chloe's reaction toward me said it all. If evil eyes were daggers, I wouldn't have lasted the night."

"Chloe doesn't like to be outshone, and you were the brightest star in the room," he murmured. "We've known each other for years, basically grew up together, and dated off and on in high school. What about you? What does your boyfriend think about you moving cross-country to take a job?"

"Is that your roundabout way of asking whether or not there's a man in my life?"

"Is there?" he asked.

"No."

Christian quirked a brow. "That doesn't seem possible."

"Perhaps, but it's true. My last serious relationship was a while ago. After that I threw myself into work, networking and building up my client base."

"And you left all you'd built to work with my mom?" he probed.

"Victoria knows I have ongoing clients and believes I can handle the work required for them and help her out, too."

Christian studied Lauren as she talked, knowing she held back much more than she'd spoken. She hardly seemed the all-work-and-no-play sort of woman. Patience was one of the traits that made Christian such an astute businessman. Patience and intuition, knowing when to hold and when to fold. So he held his curiosity for why she'd leave a growing clientele to work for a nonprofit foundation with his mother. But still, he wondered. Was she running away from something? Was she part of his mother's plan to turn him into a married man? Did she have plans of her own?

"How old are you?"

"Twenty-six. I'll be twenty-seven in April."

"You called me an old man last night but you're not too far from thirty yourself."

"Getting older is not the worst thing that can happen, you know."

"But it seems to be harder for women than for men. Don't you want to get married and raise a family?"

Christian had asked the questions casually, but he listened intently as she answered.

"At some point that might be nice, if I find the right man. Why?" She looked at him from beneath long, curly lashes, her smile reigniting the desire that had sprung up when she opened the door. "Are you applying for the job?"

"I already have a wife." He laughed as shock registeréd in her eyes. "Her name is CANN."

"Then—" Lauren leaned toward him "—a mistress, maybe?"

"Careful, beautiful lady. You're about to start a fire."

"You're right. I shouldn't tease."

"No, you shouldn't. Don't poke the bear."

# Five

Lauren said she was teasing, but she wasn't. She *wanted* to poke the bear and stroke the undeniable heat between them into a massive flame, and then spend a night or twelve putting it out. All the while knowing the very last thing she needed was a meaningless fling, a too-close-for-comfort friend with benefits.

But she'd been guarded for a very long time. And Christian was so damn sexy. Being in close proximity to him had caused the embers from her childhood crush to catch a spark. His smoldering gaze and gentle touch on the pulse of her wrist had turned that spark into crackling flames. Lauren's body was on fire, and the man who owned the hose that could put it out was sitting right beside her.

She watched Christian deftly adjust his pants as he shifted his body away from her. It was good to know she wasn't the only one being physically affected in this moment. He checked his watch. The movement brought her attention to his long, masculine fingers and neatly manicured nails. Imagining the goose bumps that would arise if he ran them lightly across her body, she reached for his hand for a closer examination. He pulled it away.

"Really, Christian? If I didn't know better I'd say there was a hint of fear in your eyes. Are you afraid that I might be too much to handle?"

"I can't remember the last time I've been afraid of anything," Christian answered, a comment that sounded arrogant except Lauren had a feeling it was probably true. "There's definitely never been a woman to make me show fear."

"Then what was that? You aren't in a relationship. You

admit you find me attractive. You say you like sex. Wait. Are you experiencing erectile dysfunction?" They both laughed. "Do we need to get you a little blue pill?"

Christian chuckled. "There are no physical problems when it comes to my ability to function sexually. I am the epitome of a virile male."

"Is that so?" He nodded. "Prove it."

Christian's gaze changed, intensified. His irises darkened, dropped to her lips. She licked them, waited, watched the muscles in his arm ripple with tension, like a feral black panther ready to pounce. But he didn't. He stood and reached for her hand.

"Walk me to the door, pretty lady."

Lauren steeled herself. She already knew that electricity flowed when their skin touched, so she braced herself for the shock. What she wasn't prepared for, however, was that after standing she'd be pulled into Christian's arms and seared with a kiss that made her gasp. Or that he'd take that opportunity to deepen the exchange. Skilled and demanding, his tongue was like a sword in the hands of a master—cutting away at her defenses, carving a place for himself in her world.

Lauren wanted more and took a step closer. She slid her hands up and over strong, broad shoulders, heard him groan and felt his hand moving toward her butt. When her hand began a similar journey, she felt him stiffen beneath her touch. He stepped back. The apology forming on her lips was interrupted by his ringing cell phone.

"Still popular, I see."

"Comes with the territory," he said with a shrug. He straightened to a height at least six inches taller than her five-foot-eight frame, tweaked her nose. "Are you coming to the house tomorrow?"

"I don't know. The past few days have been a whirlwind and my job officially starts on Monday, so… I might take the time to get settled, maybe check out the town a bit."

"All right, then. Go easy on these Vegas cowboys. Somebody like you will be hard for them to handle."

"Thanks for the advice, partna," Lauren drawled.

Christian laughed as he opened the door and stepped out. His dimple offered a flirty wink while his taut butt and long, muscular legs gave a final adios. And what a goodbye stroll!

Lauren closed the door and leaned against it. She took a deep breath to calm the flutters in her stomach…and elsewhere. Amazing how unwanted events completely out of her control had landed her in Nevada, the Wild West, in very close proximity to the first man she'd ever desired.

Christian had no need to worry about any other of the town's broncos. He was the only stallion she wanted to ride.

The next morning Lauren's cell phone rang at six o'clock, but it didn't wake her. A restless night had given way to morning. Thoughts of Christian warred with the nightmare of a situation that her dad had created. Bad business choices, the partnership he desired. And the piece of the puzzle she hadn't shared with Victoria—his ultimatum about marrying Ed. When she picked up her cell phone and saw her mom's picture, Lauren felt unexpected tears threatening to erupt. She forced down the emotion and took a breath before sitting up and hitting the speaker button.

"Good morning, Mom."

"It's morning but there's very little that's good about it."

"Why? What's the matter?" she asked anxiously.

"Your dad was under the impression that you were on a weekend getaway. He's furious to learn that you'll be gone for months."

"Which is why I asked you to let me handle telling him."

"I know, but when he asked what time you'd be returning today, I couldn't lie."

"I'm sorry for putting you in the middle of this. But

when it comes to marrying Ed, Dad's encouragement has turned to insistence." She sighed. "Telling him about taking the job with Victoria would have made it much harder to leave. Besides, I told you that I would call him later and explain everything."

"I know, but we've been married for more than three decades. He knew something was going on."

"What did you tell him?" Lauren demanded.

"That you were working with Vickie and—"

"Mom! You told him I was here, in Vegas? The next thing you know he'll be showing up on the Strip!"

*Or even worse, Ed will.*

"Better that I told him rather than he find out on his own," her mother reminded her. "Now everything's aboveboard and it doesn't look like you're running away."

She huffed out a breath. "But that's exactly what I'm doing!"

"You can't run forever, Lauren."

"I can't marry Ed, either, and I'm sick of being pressured about it."

Her mother released an audible sigh. "Hopefully whatever business deal he and Ed are working on can proceed without you being in the middle."

"Business deal? What are you talking about?"

Faye's voice lowered. "We'll talk more later. I've got to go. Call your father."

Her mother's calling had roused Lauren from sleep, but any chance of reclaiming her snooze fled with Faye's unintended announcement. *What kind of deal could Ed have that would involve Dad?*

Lauren rolled out of bed. After a quick turn in the bathroom, she pulled on a pair of baggy shorts, a white tee over a striped sports bra, and a pair of tennis shoes. After placing a pair of earbuds into her cell phone's jack, she slipped the phone into an armband, grabbed an apple from the bowl of fruit on her bar counter and headed out the door.

The sun had risen but the sky was hazy, providing a cool breeze for the beginning of her run. She looked in the direction of the mansion and pointedly ran the opposite way. With what her mother had shared fresh in her mind, she wanted to avoid seeing any of the Breedloves—especially Christian.

Mortification swept through her. What had she been *thinking* yesterday coming on to him like that? Their families had known each other for years, but what did that matter? They'd known the Millers a long time too. She'd thought she knew Ed. He was good-looking, with a brooding disposition that she'd at first considered sexy but now knew hid a jerky personality. Who was to say that Christian wasn't an ass, too? That a phone call had interrupted her attempt at seduction was probably the best thing that could have happened. It might have helped her dodge a bullet headed straight for her heart.

Lauren stilled her mind and focused on running, her steps rhythmic, measured, her breath paced as evenly as her steps. The surroundings were beautiful, vast stretches of green grass that had to have been specially planted, a stark contrast to the browns, blues and grays of the mountain range and brightening sky. She followed the road, kept time with the beat and let herself get lost in the rhythm of the world around her. Time fell away. So did her problems, as she chose not to focus on the conversation with her mom, or why she'd left Maryland.

She took in the mountains and the pines and…*cows*? Lauren slowed her pace. The farther she went the more cows she saw. Dozens? Hundreds? And then she saw him. A ranch hand? A cowboy? Indeed, and galloping straight toward her.

Lauren slowed to a walk, then stopped and watched the rider approach, noting the darkly tanned forearms tightly holding the reins. *Christian?* Certain body muscles clenched at the mere possibility. So she changed focus and looked at the horse instead. A Thoroughbred from the looks of it, black and majestic. Like Christian. It had been years since she'd gone riding, but her love of horses came back with the magnificent creature's every stride.

Rider and horse reached a fence that was jumped and cleared by at least two feet. He pulled on the reins and the Thoroughbred slowed. Finally, the rider took off a worn cowboy hat.

"Good morning, gorgeous."

"Adam, good morning! I wondered who was hiding under the hat."

"I see you're an early riser. A runner, too."

"Guilty on both counts," she confessed. "That's a beautiful horse."

"Do you ride?"

"It's been a while."

"Would you like to? You'll want to change into jeans or long pants first, then I can put you on a filly. They're tamer than the stallions all day long."

"So it's a stallion, huh?" Lauren took cautious steps forward, her tone soothing as the horse watched her with apprehensive eyes. "What's his name?"

"Thunder."

"Of course. It suits him. Hello, Thunder." She slowly moved her hand toward his mane. He bobbed his head but didn't back away. "There you go, beautiful fella. No need to be afraid."

Lauren continued talking, her tone soothing. She remembered the apple in her pocket and pulled it out. She looked at Adam. "May I?"

"No, thanks, I've had breakfast."

Laughter burst forth at the unexpected comment. "Not you, silly, the horse."

"Oh, sure."

She noted Adam's eyes had the same twinkle as Christian's. One thing about those Breedlove men, they were a roguishly handsome bunch.

Lauren waved the apple under Thunder's nose. "Would you like a bite?"

Thunder nodded, opened his mouth and took the apple from her.

"Okay, you've paid the price of entry and made a friend. Ready to ride?"

"Sure, why not? I am in the Wild West, after all."

"Here, take my hand."

Lauren mounted the horse in one smooth motion and settled in behind Adam. As he steered the horse toward the guesthouse where she could change clothes, his phone rang.

"Chris!"

A familiar voice came through Adam's cell phone speakers. "What's up, bro?"

He guided Thunder into a soft trot. "Out riding, like I do most mornings. What are you doing?"

Lauren held on to Adam's shoulders. Hearing Christian's voice increased her heartbeat. If she was unable to quell these physical reactions at the mere sound of his voice, she decided, then working for Victoria was going to be challenge.

"Golf? Right now? Sounds boring, buddy. I'm heading to the mountains, going to show Lauren the view from Breedlove Peak. Yeah, she's with me now." He paused for a moment. "She was out running so I invited her for a ride. Listen, let me holler at you later. We're headed to Lauren's house so she can change clothes and then to the stables to get her saddled up. Thunder is getting restless and wants to run. All right, cool. Talk to you later."

"That was Chris," Adam said as Thunder ate up the distance with his smooth, increased gait. "He said to tell you hello."

"I couldn't help overhearing that it was him on the phone," she replied, raising her voice to be heard above the horse's clomping and the wind. "I heard his voice but not the entire conversation. He's on his way to play golf?"

"No, he's headed to my house."

"How do you figure? I heard what he said."

"Because I told him you were with me. So, trust me, he's on his way."

# Six

"Helen," Christian called out to the house manager who'd been employed by the family for almost twenty years. He felt just as he had years ago as a teenager, when he'd been caught sneaking into the house past curfew. More than once Helen had been a lifesaver, fussing at him for disobeying his parents while warning that she'd keep his secret of coming in late only if he maintained a grade point average of 4.0. Christian graduated at the top of his class.

Helen turned around, her face scrunched as she squinted to see who'd called her. "Chris? Goodness gracious, boy, what are you doing coming in over here?"

"Because I knew it was where you'd be." He flashed a charming smile and wrapped his arms around the diminutive woman, lifting her off the floor.

"You're so full of it, and too grown to be sneaking into the opposite wing. What are you after?"

"I could never fool you. My riding boots. I think the last time I used them I left them here."

Helen smiled, her eyes twinkling with mischief. "What, no golf today? That's how you usually spend Sunday morning."

"Thought I'd try something different," was Christian's casual reply.

"Wouldn't have anything to do with the pretty girl Adam took out on the range now, would it?"

"Absolutely not!" He hoped he looked appropriately insulted.

It cracked Helen up, and she swatted at his broad shoulder and barely missed. "You forget that I've known you since you were a kid."

"You're right, Helen. Hard to get anything past you."

"Even harder to try to slip past your mother." The house-keeper crossed the hallway, reached just inside the door of a room on the opposite side and pulled out a pair of worn black leather cowboy boots. "After talking with Adam, she thought you might be motivated to take a ride and had me retrieve them from your old bedroom."

Christian feigned annoyance and snatched the boots from Helen's hands. "Be careful!" she called out behind his re-treating back.

"Love you, Helen!"

Christian hopped in the SUV he used to tool around the grounds. He couldn't help grinning at the whole situation, even though he was also chagrined. Helen was right. There was no getting around Victoria's motherly intuition. He'd rarely been able to keep something totally hidden from her. The saying that moms had eyes in the backs of their heads? From the time he was a kid, Christian knew this to be true.

A few twists and turns later, opposite the parcel of land that housed his five-thousand-square-foot bachelor pad, Christian drove through the iron-and-brick gate announcing one's entry into Breedlove Beef, the award-winning busi-ness that Adam and his partners had built from scratch and made profitable in four short years. He continued down the road, past Adam's innovatively designed ranch house with interlocking pavilions that seamlessly combined indoor and outdoor living, traveling along the ruggedly landscaped ter-rain to the horse stables behind the barn.

Turning off the engine, he reached for the cowboy boots he'd retrieved from the house, smiling at the weathered face coming to greet him.

"Well, I'll be damned!" was the gruffly voiced greeting from a man whose taut, wiry frame belied over six decades of hard cowboy living. "What brings you down from the crystal tower to wallow in the mud with the rest of us?"

"Shut up, old man," Christian said, pulling the grandfatherly figure everyone called Rusty into a hearty embrace.

"Wait a minute, I know. It's that fine filly I just saddled up. The one whose bass drum is full and plump and made to both sit in a saddle and ride at the same time."

"Lauren's a lady, Rusty. Show some respect." Christian shook his head, still smiling. "You haven't changed a bit."

"Too old to change." Rusty pointed out a bench just inside the stable. "Sit there and pull your boots on. You need chaps, too?"

"I'm going for a ride, not a roundup."

"Shit," Rusty answered, holding out the word far longer than four letters required. "Tell that to somebody who hasn't known you since you were knee-high to a gnat. You're about to round up that sweet darling who trotted out of here on the back of Old Glory."

"You put Lauren on that old nag?"

"That old nag, as you put it, can hold her own against any young filly any day of the week. Push come to shove and a situation needed escaping, I'd put my money on OG."

Rusty disappeared inside the stable. Christian pulled on the well-worn boots and then strode over to a wall of saddles and pulled down a lightweight, dark brown leather one embellished with silver tacks, conchos and corner plates. He reached into a wooden box and after feeling a few, decided on a brightly colored Navajo blanket over the more expensive pads. The sound of softly clopping hooves caused him to turn. He came face-to-face with a young palomino standing regal and strong, eyeing him intently.

Christian's tone was gentle, soothing as he made proper acquaintance, patting the horse's coat before saddling up and mounting the frisky steed. Christian immediately tightened the reins, gently pressing a heel into the horse's side to direct him and establish control. The palomino dipped his head in agreement, as if to say "you're the boss."

"Good boy, Biscuit. You and I will do just fine."

"That's a load of power you've got there," Rusty said. "You sure you don't need me to take you on a turn or two inside the corral before you ride him across the prairie?"

"Thanks, but I've got this." Christian steered the horse toward the stable exit, as comfortable in the saddle as in a boardroom chair. "Which way did they go?"

"Ah, so you *are* on a roundup."

"Rusty…"

"Toward the mountain," the old man answered, amid the enjoyment of a good guffaw. "She's worth riding for, my boy. Go get her."

Christian intended to do just that, and with the wide-open landscape, Lauren and his brother weren't hard to find. He spotted them on the winding trail leading to Breedlove Peak, where the boys had spent countless hours as children, target shooting, catching prey and roughhousing.

With his goal in sight, Christian allowed the palomino to run freely, quickly closing the gap between them. Adam was the first to see him approach. Christian watched as his brother led his horse closer to the one Lauren rode. Seconds later, she turned and waved. Christian ignored the tightening in his groin as he led the horse toward the mountain trail.

"Look who's up before noon," Adam said as Christian approached. "You really are getting older, big brother. I would have thought you'd have partied the whole weekend."

Christian pulled up alongside Adam. The two enjoyed a hearty handshake. "Ty and the rest of the guys are on their way to the airport. Felt a bit of fresh air would do the body good." He looked over at Lauren, his eyes quickly scanning her from head to toe. Rusty was right. She sat the hell out of that saddle. Again, his groin tightened, this time making it harder to ignore. He shifted in the saddle in order to covertly adjust himself.

"Good morning, beautiful."

"Good morning, Chris."

Damn if those eyes and sultry voice didn't make him want to lift the blanket from his horse's back, throw it on the ground and lay her on top of it. Just the thought of her here, in the sunlight, naked and wanton, required him to make another adjustment. He needed to do something quick, before he embarrassed them all.

"Hey, brother. Is the cave still there?"

Adam nodded. "Of course."

"Cave?" Lauren asked curiously.

"Depending on the day," Christian explained, "as kids it was everything from a science lab to Matrix headquarters to our hideout after getting in trouble with Dad. Want to see it?"

"I'm game for whatever," she replied.

Christian's eyes darkened as he digested her words. "I'll keep that in mind."

The trio continued to a plateau near the top of the mountain. They dismounted their horses and continued over rocks and small bushes to a side of the mountain away from the sun.

"Do you remember where it is?" Christian asked.

Adam looked over his shoulder at him, smirked and kept walking. He reached a crevice in what appeared to be a large boulder.

"Do you see it?"

"Here, let me help you." Christian reached for Lauren's hand as he walked toward Adam. "See what?"

He stepped to the rock, ran his hand along a narrow seam. His eyes sparkled like the ten-year-old he was when they'd discovered it. "The triple *S.*"

"The secret silver sliver. Yes, indeed."

The two brothers grabbed a large slab of rock and watched Lauren's expression go from skepticism to amazement as the cave entrance came into view and Christian pulled her inside.

"Stay close to me," he whispered, sliding a hand around

her waist and coming precariously close to her delectable backside. "The bogeyman might get you in the dark."

"Are you the bogeyman?" Lauren retorted, gripping his waist to keep her balance over a dirt floor strewn with potholes and rocks.

Glad for the opportunity her unsteadiness presented, Christian slid his arm around her and pulled her closer. "Woman, haven't I warned you? You're about to get in all kinds of trouble."

"Promises, promises," she cooed.

"I can't believe they're still here..." Adam said into the darkness before setting fire to a huge glob of wax that at one time had been a group of individual candles now melted into a ghostlike creation. Soon the space was illuminated enough for Christian to make out Lauren's luscious lips. The flickering candle brought them in and out of focus. He felt her hand fall away from his body as a web of undeniable desire began to wrap itself around them until he and Lauren were the only ones there. Her lips, her body, the heat drew him closer...

"...since the last time we were here. That was what, Chris, about ten years ago?"

The sound of Adam's voice penetrated the fog of need, lust and almost primitive hunger stirring in Christian's gut.

"Um, yeah, even further back than that. I think my last time spending the night here was when I was fifteen, sixteen years old."

Sixteen...the last time he'd seen Lauren until two days ago. When his testosterone was in overdrive and she was still a kid. That was then. This was now. Lauren had grown into a sexy-ass woman who clearly knew how to go after what she wanted, and she'd made it clear that what she wanted was him. The feeling was mutual and in this moment, while he knew that he shouldn't cross that line, the truth of the matter was he couldn't help himself.

He wanted to taste more of what Lauren so freely offered, wanted to give his body to her so she could ride him all night long. It was time to cut short the trip down memory lane and land squarely back in the present. Fortunately, Adam was thinking the exact same thing.

"All right, guys, enough time in the dungeon." He blew out the candles. "Let's get out of here."

They walked outside and though they'd only been in the cave a few minutes, the weather had warmed under a sun-drenched sky. The trio headed to the horses and untied the reins that had been looped over a well-worn iron hitching post on the plateau embedded in stone.

Adam placed a foot in the stirrup and swung up in a graceful motion. "Ready to head to the top of the mountain?"

She shook her head. "No, it's getting hot. I think I'll head back down."

"I thought you liked the heat," Christian murmured. The way Lauren's eyes swept over his body proved she'd gotten the double entendre.

Adam had finally gotten the hint, too. A wagon of romance was starting to roll, and he was the third wheel. "On that note, big brother, it appears that my job is done. I'll see you guys at brunch." He turned Thunder and guided the horse past Christian, stopping to let Lauren turn Old Glory around. "You follow me and let Christian bring up the rear," he instructed. "When it comes to us and horseback riding, coming in last is familiar territory for him."

"See you at the stables." With that, a sure-footed Thunder headed down the sloping landscape, Adam's boyish laughter trailing behind him.

"Show-off," Christian grumbled, edging Biscuit forward. "Don't mind him. Let's you and I take things nice and easy."

"Come on, OG," Lauren cooed to the horse, gingerly rubbing her sleek and shiny chestnut coat. "Let's go, girl."

Christian followed Lauren down the gently slanting hillside, enjoying the backside view. The sloping gave way to a vast expanse of flatland, and Lauren gradually increased OG's pace. Christian stayed just behind her. With each gentle jostle from the horse's gait, her ass lifted from the saddle, plump and rounded, accented by her tiny waist and bobbing ponytail protruding from beneath a cowboy hat.

In the middle of his borderline-inappropriate daydreaming, a series of quick movements caught his eye. A long, fast-moving whip snake slithered across the terrain. Old Glory sidestepped the snake and rose up. Her hooves pawed the air. The horse came back down with a vicious jolt and almost unseated Lauren.

"Lauren!"

In an instant Old Glory shed her years and ran like the wind. Lauren screamed as her body was jostled from side to side.

"Lauren, hold on!"

Christian spurred Biscuit on, trying to catch OG and grab the reins. Old Glory shifted right. Lauren's body went left and into the air, then landed on the ground with a sickening thud. Christian pulled Biscuit forward and missed her head by mere inches. He halted the horse, jumped out of the saddle and rushed to Lauren's body, motionless and twisted, beneath a clear blue sky.

# Seven

Lauren felt as though she were in a tunnel far beneath the earth. In the distance there were voices that she heard but couldn't make out. Slowly, she came out of what felt like a fog and heard the words more clearly.

"Lauren, come on, beautiful. Wake up," Christian said.

Lauren heard hoofbeats, and then the muted sound of what she imagined was Adam dismounting Thunder and his handcrafted cowboy boots connecting with the hard earth.

"What happened?" Adam asked Christian.

"OG got spooked. It was a snake. Call the doctor, Adam," Christian said, pulling the blanket from under Biscuit's saddle and making a cushion for Lauren's head. "Have him meet me at my place."

She felt errant strands of hair being swiped away from her face as Christian spoke to her.

"Lauren, baby, please wake up."

She slowly opened her eyes. Squinting against the bright sunlight, she tried to focus on what was now a blurry view of Christian's concerned face. *What in the heck happened?* She tried to get up.

"No, don't move," Christian rasped, gently wiping damp tendrils off her forehead. "You may be hurt."

Lauren pushed away his hand, coughed and rose to her elbows. "I'm fine, just got the wind knocked out of me."

"Are you sure?"

"I think so." She moved her leg, which was not fine at all. "Ow!"

"I said don't move!" And then more calmly, "Where are you hurt?" Christian coddled her as gently as a swaddled babe, her head shielded in the crook of his arm as he helped her sit upright.

"I think my ankle is broken. It hurts like hell."

"We've got to get you out of here, sweetheart. I'm going to lift you up, okay? Place your stomach on the saddle. Then I'll pull your healthy leg around so we can lessen all movement of the other one."

He placed an arm beneath her legs. "No, Chris! Wait!"

"Trust me, I've got you. Okay?"

Lauren nodded. "Okay."

"Put your arms around my neck and hold on tight."

She did as instructed. Christian lifted her gently and laid her across the saddle. "I've got to steady your body while moving your leg, understand?"

Lauren acknowledged his question through gritted teeth.

"So you won't think that I'm trying to cop a feel."

She laughed and braced herself for his touch. Christian's hand splayed across her behind made her almost forget the pain. That she seemed unable to control her feelings had her convinced she'd already lost her mind.

Once she was safely mounted, with the blanket serving as padding for her injured ankle, Christian swung up behind her, pressed her back firmly against his chest and spurred Biscuit into action.

Lauren grimaced against the throbbing pain in her ankle that kept time with each instance that the horse's hooves touched the ground. She was going into a state of delirium. Had to be. There was no other way to explain that at a time when the ache in her leg was so severe she felt having it amputated without anesthesia would be less painful, she was keenly aware of the hardness of Christian's chest against her back, the feel of his arm on the side of her breast, and the way long, strong, sure fingers gripped her waist and held her firmly against him.

A flood of warmth pooled in her core, danced with the flames of pain shooting up from her ankle and set her entire body on fire. Why fight it? she thought as Adam's ranch house came into view. She closed her eyes and relaxed into Christian's embrace.

Seconds later, Lauren felt herself being gently lifted away from Christian's chest, while a sure pair of hands steadied her legs and ankle. She opened her eyes as Adam secured her legs with his arms and Christian effortlessly slid from the saddle while still maintaining a hand on her back.

"Careful, brother." The concern in Christian's urgently muttered command caused a pitter-patter in Lauren's heart. "Is the doctor—"

"Headed to your house right now. Not Dr. Simon, though. He recommended an orthopedic specialist. She's on the way."

"Let's get her in the car. Open the door and then go over to the other side to help me ease her in. Don't touch the right ankle. It might be broken."

Lauren wrapped her arms around Christian's neck and burrowed her head into his shoulder. The pain had ramped up considerably. Yet in the moment, her nostrils had the nerve to catch a whiff of Christian's cologne, a musky, smoky, spicy combination of sandalwood, bergamot and... was that patchouli? Damned if Lauren could help but reason that had she known this was the fastest way to end up in Christian's arms, she would have broken her foot Friday night!

Safely ensconced in the back seat of his SUV, Lauren felt the car turning around and speeding down the long road. From her visit to Victoria the previous day, she knew they were heading in the direction of the main house. Yet when the car pulled to a stop a few minutes later and she rose up to look around, the home-slash-architectural-wonder was one she hadn't seen before. One of three garage doors rose. Christian hopped out of the car and opened the back door, just as another car pulled up beside them.

"Where are we?" Lauren asked.

"My place," Christian said, scooping her up and effortlessly carrying her as though she weighed nothing at all. "The doctor is here, baby. You can relax now. Everything will be fine." He turned to the woman exiting a white sedan. "Doctor?"

"Yes. Dr. Burman."

"This way, please." With strong, sure strides Christian ate up the distance between the driveway and the side door inside the garage. As they neared it, the door opened.

"Mr. Breedlove!"

"Hi, Tara." And then to the doctor, Christian ordered, "Follow me."

As he passed by the woman holding open the door, Lauren took in the kind, worried eyes of a short older woman with long black hair. They continued down a hallway and up a short flight of stairs to the first-floor landing. Lauren caught glimpses of slate tile, marble, stainless steel and large paneless windows before they entered another hallway leading to a set of exquisitely carved black African wood double doors.

After placing his palm against a panel on the wall, the doors opened into a master suite the size of Lauren's condo back home. He strode through a sitting area to a four-poster bed on a raised platform. As he gingerly laid her on a silky soft spread, she looked up, closed her eyes quickly and looked again. Instead of a luxurious beamed, vaulted or tray ceiling one might expect, the master suite's ceiling was made entirely of a tinted glass that let in the cloudless sky and the sun's colorful rays while shielding the room from its heat. If she died and went to heaven, she hoped she'd end up in a room like this.

"What can I get you, Doctor?" Christian asked.

"Only privacy," Dr. Burman responded, with the slightest of smiles as she placed a black bag on the bedside table and opened it.

"Oh, of course. I'll be right outside if you need me."

Dr. Burman began speaking before the door closed. "Hello... Lauren, correct?" She nodded. "We're going to have a look at that ankle, okay?" The doctor pulled out a pair of scissors. "I hope these aren't your favorite jeans. I'm going to have to cut them away to have a look."

"It's fine," Lauren replied, her jaw clamped tight against the pain.

The doctor's tone was casual, conversational, as she reached for the pants leg hem and began to cut. "On a scale of one to ten, how bad is the pain?"

"About a nine, I guess."

Lauren felt the doctor's gentle touch on her foot and calf. "The ankle is swelling quite a bit and beginning to bruise. Now, this is going to cause a bit of discomfort but I need to apply pressure on the affected area to determine the severity."

The doctor was quick and efficient. Once she finished examining the leg, she checked Lauren's vitals, as well. "At the very least you've experienced a severe sprain, and there may very well be a fracture of sorts. We'll need to get you in for X-rays to determine how extensive the damage is. Until then, I'm going to do a compression wrap of your ankle to provide stability and support and cold therapy packs to help decrease swelling. I'll also give you something for pain relief. Keep these pillows beneath the ankle so that it can remain elevated at all times. Other than that, stay off your feet as much as possible and get some rest. Do you have any questions?"

"If fractured, how long will it take to heal?"

"That depends on your body. In some cases a fracture can actually be better than a sprain because then you're dealing with bone instead of muscle, which can heal faster and easier. It feels as though your ankle is badly sprained. For now, just focus on staying calm and positive, knowing that with the Breedlove family you will receive the best possible care. If the condition worsens—more pain, fur-

ther discoloration, continued swelling—we'll get you in
for an X-ray tonight."

After wrapping the ankle and activating the ice pack,
Dr. Burman disappeared to another part of the room and returned with a glass of water. She handed it to Lauren along
with a pain pill and after briefly leaving the room, returned
to Lauren's bedside. She helped remove the cut jeans and
sweaty tee and provided her with a clean extra-large T-shirt
from Christian's wardrobe room.

With the doctor's reassuring pat and a quiet goodbye,
Lauren fixated on the colorful prisms on the glass overhead created by the sunrays as they danced their way west,
and fell asleep within minutes. Hours later, groggily coming awake, she was filled with Christian's scent and the
feeling of him in bed beside her—naked, hot and hard.
She moaned, her arms encased in his embrace, something
wrapped around her legs. She shifted to push the cover away
from her foot and…

"Ow!"

Lauren's eyes flew open as pain shot through her body.
Brow scrunched, she looked around as the sensual dream
faded and cold, hard reality dawned. She was alone—not
tightly ensconced in Christian's arms—and the bedsheets
had somehow wound themselves around her.

Gingerly sitting up, she placed a pillow behind her and
leaned against it while looking around. The lavishness and
exquisite attention to detail in the room's design that she'd
missed earlier were now breathtakingly evident—grays,
tans and ivories, burnished metals, sleek, clean-lined fur-
nishings and abstract art. There appeared to be several
rooms; one she knew contained his wardrobe. Another she
assumed was the master bath.

But there was more. Turning left, a profusion of color
greeted her. On the bedside table was a bouquet of vibrant
flowers: yellow calla lilies, orange roses and hot-pink dai-
sies. Amid the blossoms and Hypericum berries was a small

white envelope, her name scribbled across it. She pulled it from the holder and retrieved the note inside.

*Hello, sleeping beauty: I hope you've rested well and are feeling better. Push the button beside you for whatever you need. Your pain medication prescription has been filled. The doctor sent along crutches. Don't use them. You'll heal faster by staying in bed. Tara is waiting to assist you with food, drink, whatever you need. I'll be home later.*
*CB.*

She read the note twice, frowning at his presumptuousness in issuing orders even as she ran her finger over the authoritatively delivered promise that he'd be home later. Discreetly placed beside the table was the button he mentioned, one that she imagined would bring servants running, ready to attend to her every need.

What was it like to live this way, she wondered, with everything at your fingertips? A part of Lauren felt appalled at the idea, the other part could quite get accustomed to it. She nestled against the pillow, remembering her dream, imagining a lifetime with Christian beside her. She shifted her leg. A jolt of pain shot up from her ankle, reminding her why she was there. She sat up and consciously shut down the wistful meanderings.

She reached for the pad and pen on the table beside her and replied to Christian's acts of kindness. Then, after deciding what actions to take, she pushed the bedside button. Tara magically appeared. She carried a small plastic container that she set on a table. She removed a small pill cup and crossed to the bed.

"Are you in pain, Miss Lauren?" The housekeeper held out the small paper cup. "Here is your medication."

"Thank you, Tara, and please, just Lauren is fine."

"Oh, no, Miss Lauren. I couldn't. The title is a sign of respect."

Lauren shrugged. "Okay." Let the lady have it the way that she wanted. After today she'd likely not see her again. She reached for the glass of water on the nightstand and downed the pills.

"Are you hungry? Thirsty? Would you like help with a bath?"

"I'm fine, thank you. All I need is something decent to put on and a ride back to my house."

Tara's eyes briefly widened. "Oh, no, Miss Lauren. Mr. Breedlove gave explicit instructions that you are to remain here to be properly attended to."

Lauren's brows rose as images of how properly he could probably attend to her flashed through her mind.

"Thank Mr. Breedlove kindly, but it's only my ankle and it already feels better. I left a note so he'll know it was my call. Is there someone who can drive me, or should I call a cab?"

"That won't be necessary."

Both ladies turned as Christian sauntered into the room with the air of a boss and an expression that brooked no argument.

"Mr. Breedlove!" Tara stuttered. "I didn't expect you back until later."

"There was a change in plans." He moved to the edge of the bed and lifted the cold pack, now room temperature, from Lauren's ankle.

Tara hurried to the container she'd brought into the room. "Here is the new cold pack, Mr. Breedlove. I was just about to change it."

"Thank you, Tara." He spoke to the housekeeper but his eyes were on Lauren. "I'll take over from here."

"Yes, sir."

Once the housekeeper left the room, Christian walked over to place the used cold pack in the plastic container.

After gently placing the fresh one on her ankle he said, "I thought my instructions for you were very clear—to remain here, in bed."

"And I thought my dad's name was Paul."

Lauren watched his eyes narrow and darken, the message within them unreadable. She kept her face neutral, but her insides shivered. This was her first encounter with his presidential persona, a man undeniably in charge, used to giving orders and having them followed. His autocratic demeanor and commanding tone were traits she was sure had felled lesser men. They moved her, too. But he wouldn't know it. She lifted a defiant chin and met his smoldering gaze.

The atmosphere in the room snapped, crackled and popped.

Christian's eyes held a devilish glint when he raised them to her. "You're being a lousy patient."

"A lousy houseguest, maybe, but I'm following the doctor's orders, Dr. Burman's instructions," Lauren emphasized, "as best as I can. She has an exceptional bedside manner."

"And I don't?"

A flippant answer died on her tongue, replaced by a quiet intake of breath that matched the slow, steady trail Christian made with his finger, from ankle to knee and back again. He walked to a chair, sat, and began removing his shoes.

"Are you saying my bedside manner needs improving?"

"I…"

Again, words failed her. Lauren could only watch as he rose from the chair and erased the distance between them. Without removing his khaki shorts or polo shirt he eased up on the bed and against the headboard and pulled her into his arms.

"Perhaps I'm out of practice," he whispered against her temple, before planting a kiss there, and then another. "Perhaps you being here is just what I need to…refine my skills."

He placed a finger beneath her chin. Lauren's head fell back against the arm that supported her. Since it had happened before, she thought she was ready for his explosive kiss—those pillow-soft lips and super-skilled tongue. But she wasn't, couldn't have been, or else the earth would not have tilted on its axis, along with her body as her tongue danced with his. A sigh of contentment escaped her lips as he brushed his cushiness against hers, kissed her cheek, then her neck. His hand moved down to her breast and cupped it. He flicked his thumb across her sensitive flesh and stroked her nipples, making them harden and her entire body yearn for more.

Her mind was willing, her heart open, her body oh so ready to receive everything that he had to give. But the pain medication was strong and chose this inconvenient moment to begin taking effect. She felt him ease away and off the bed.

"No…" She tried to pull him back to her, but he resisted.

"Not like this, my love. When we come together, I want you to remember everything that happens, and for the only haze to be that of our ardent desire. Right now you need rest and food."

"I'm not hungry."

"You need sustenance. I'll have the chef prepare and deliver a meal, and get someone to drive you home."

"Why not you?" Lauren mumbled through her fogginess.

He smiled, walked over and kissed her forehead. "Trust me, if I take you there, you'll get no rest at all."

A last kiss to the lips and Christian backed away. "Feel better, baby."

Tara helped her dress. A short time later, Lauren arrived at her front door, aided by a collapsible crutch and one of the estate's many employees. On her kitchen counter was a well-stocked basket from which wafted something delicious. She'd wanted nothing more than to stay in Christian's bed and have him rejoin her in it. Had it not been for the pain medication, it would have surely happened. Moments away from making love and once again, life had intervened. Maybe the universe was sending signs that a dalliance with Christian was not a good idea.

She already had one serious man problem. Perhaps she should focus on solving that issue before jumping into bed with another. Whatever the case, here, in her temporary abode, she'd have the space and the time to think more clearly. Because if she'd stayed in his home, the pain would have dissipated, her appetite would have returned, and Christian would most definitely have been on the menu.

# Eight

Before leaving home and heading to work, Christian tucked Lauren and the events of the weekend into a mental box that he then pushed to the back of his mind. Compartmentalizing and single-minded focus were skills he'd unconsciously honed as a kid, ones that allowed him to master whatever challenge he faced and developed him into a brilliant businessman. Having just been promoted to president of CANN International, Christian was determined to stay focused on the myriad of moving parts in the family's ever-expanding empire. Even though Nicholas would continue to be a vital voice in the business, Christian knew that from now on the buck would stop with him.

So as he turned his pricey sports car into the private executive entrance of the hotel, his mind wasn't on yesterday when he'd returned home and found Lauren ready to flee. It wasn't on the mixed emotions he'd felt at having Lauren in his bed—hot, waiting and ready—and then realizing she'd just taken pain medication. He couldn't help but remember that had he not come home when he did, his bed would have been empty. Which brought up a few questions. Was she sending mixed signals, being a tease? How much of the desire she displayed was real, and how much was part of a grander scheme, perhaps the real reason she'd moved to Vegas to work with Mom? And maybe the most important question of all, why did he care?

Passing a mirror on the way to the boardroom, Christian stopped and took in his reflection with a critical eye. Today he wore an original design from his good friend Ace Montgomery's HIS collection. The tailored navy suit had been paired with a pale yellow shirt that highlighted his bronze skin and the blue, gold and silver patterned tie that bore the CANN logo. His jewelry was platinum but under-stated—square cuff links with a matching tiepin and a de-ceptively simple watch.

Christian straightened his tie, ran a hand over his silky curls and then, convinced that his look was perfection, con-tinued down the hallway. He wasn't vain, and while he'd walked the runway a time or two, he wasn't the style-con-scious clotheshorse that fashion magazines often pegged him. But he was his mother's son. From their youth, Vic-toria had preached the importance of and connection be-tween looking good and feeling good. Christian had listened and learned.

He reached the closed boardroom doors and, mentally pushing the on button, entered his first executive meeting as the corporation's president.

"Gentlemen, good morning!"

Hearty claps and a chorus of greetings followed him to the head of the table. He nodded in acknowledgment but didn't let the outward show of approval go to his head. He knew that at least two of the smiles were half-hearted at best and one was an outright lie. He was now the boss to men older, wiser and no doubt in their mind more deserv-ing of the position.

"Thanks, everyone. I appreciate the support. Especially now, as I unfold plans for a vigorously ambitious building project, one that will be our most innovative and expensive to date. Let's get down to business."

He opened his laptop and connected it to a port on the table.

"As all of you know, CANN UAE was built at the onset of that country's push to become a playground for the wealthy. However, the window of unlimited opportunity and un-bridled growth is quickly closing. For the past year, my advisers and I have been scouting the world for the best location of the next man-made paradise for the superrich, and I believe we've found it. More accurately, we've found the land where we want to create it. Any ideas?" He looked over at the adviser sitting at the table. "Not from you," he jokingly admonished.

The names of several locations were thrown on the table—from Sydney to Madagascar, to islands everywhere. As he listened, Christian pushed a button that turned the wall behind him into a screen and pulled out a pointer.

"All excellent ideas, guys, but none that are close. How about this choice?" He tapped his keyboard and on the screen came the outline of a country and one word, Djibouti.

"Where in the world is that?" half-hearted number one asked.

"Africa," another man answered.

"You've got to be kidding," said half-hearted number two, his skepticism and dislike for Christian barely concealed. "No one's going on vacation to that part of Africa."

"A few years ago," Christian calmly countered, "that's what was being said about the Middle East, specifically the United Arab Emirates. Yet Dubai became a rich man's playground. In the next hour or two, the team leading this international effort and I will lay out the vision for this admittedly ambitious endeavor. I have not only faith in this vision but months of research and analysis behind me, and believe as did one wise farmer, and I paraphrase, if we build it correctly, the wealthy of the world will come. Why does the team so fervently believe this?"

Christian's nearly onyx eyes sparkled as he looked around the table. "Because we're CANN."

Back in Breedlove, Lauren also believed she could. She was confident in her abilities to properly assist Victoria, to make the upcoming fashion show the best that Vegas had ever seen. Even with a severely sprained ankle, as had been the news from her nine o'clock appointment with the podiatrist that Dr. Burman had recommended. It was a second degree sprain. The doctor assured Lauren that she'd be back jogging in four to six weeks.

Meanwhile, she'd gotten permission from Victoria to work from home and turned her dining room into an office. Sitting at the table, she fired up her laptop and opened a spreadsheet to chart out the tasks that needed completion and a timeline for making them happen. She'd just hobbled from the kitchen to the dining room with her microwaved tea when someone laid on the doorbell.

WTH?

"Coming!" She put down the mug, picked up the second crutch and crossed the room. She looked through the peephole. It was no one she recognized, but knowing how tight security was on the estate, she opened the door and would later pride herself on maintaining a solemn expression.

"Yes, may I help you?"

"Probably, Lauren, but I'm here to help you. Miss Vickie sent me over, said you could use an assistant, and from that muumuu-looking thing you're wearing, girl, I can see that she was right!"

"Excuse me?"

"I shall, and gladly, because when you got dressed this morning you didn't know me yet. Now can you let me in, because otherwise trying to work together with a screen door between us is going to be problematic."

Lauren listened to this rapidly delivered comment while taking in a man at least six feet tall, sharply dressed and flipping a perfectly coiffed shoulder-length bob away from a stunningly made-up face. As the teen girls she'd once mentored in DC would have said, his hair slayed and his face was beat. He stood in his truth with such confidence and authority that instead of being offended, she was humored and a little impressed. She unlocked the outer door and stepped back. The gentleman entered with a big smile and wide-open arms. He bent to embrace her.

"Hi, Lauren! I'm Frankie. It's so nice to meet you!"

"Me, too, I think." They both laughed. "When I spoke with Victoria this morning, she didn't mention anyone coming by."

"She told me I'd surprise you. Do you need help back to…" Frankie looked around. "Wherever you're sitting? This is nice," he continued without taking a breath, walking farther into the room and proving that if Lauren did need help she was on her own. "Miss Vickie's style is all over this place.

"Oh, I'm sorry," he continued as Lauren neared him. "Look at me seeing beauty and getting all carried away."

"Thank you, I'm fine." Lauren continued past him, noting the six-inch Louboutins giving Frankie extra height. "And what's wrong with my caftan?"

"Nothing that a Goodwill donation bin won't cure."

"Ha! You're funny."

"Laughter is the best medicine, child, and I'm trying to stay healthy. I see you're setting up shop in the dining room. How are you going to use those poster boards?"

"In lieu of a whiteboard, taped to the wall. Organizing projects on the board helps me stay organized in my mind. What is your skill set? By looking at you I'd guess it's the fashion world."

"That's one set, but don't let all of this fashion fabulosity fool you. I type eighty-five words a minute and can file papers better than my manicurist files my nails." He set a tote he carried on the table and pulled out a small laptop. "But yes, fashion is my passion. I love me some Ace Montgomery, honey. I don't know him personally but I have several friends in the industry, designers and models, male and female."

"Do you know London?"

"Ace's wife? Not yet. But if she comes to the show this weekend, I expect she and I will become the best of friends."

"That wouldn't surprise me at all. Would you like some tea?"

"No, thank you. Caffeine causes wrinkles."

"It's herbal, but thanks for the health information," Lauren finished sarcastically.

"Always grateful to be of service."

Said by Frankie so sincerely that Lauren laughed out loud. She took a seat at the table.

"Sit."

"Yes, ma'am."

Lauren wanted to get better acquainted with Frankie, who was *quite* a character, but later for that. There was a fashion show to finish coordinating. She'd promised Victoria an update at the end of the day, and with her newfound friend here to help her, Lauren was sure the report would be as good as her uplifted mood.

# Nine

The week was a whirlwind of tweaking, adjusting and putting out fires. By Saturday night, Lauren and Frankie were best buds and as they stepped into the grand ballroom, redesigned as a Valentine-themed fashion fantasy, both knew the long hours and sleepless nights had all been worth it.

Grand chandeliers anchored yards—perhaps miles—of snowy white and fire-engine-red tulle covering the mass ceiling. Textured silk fabric adorned the walls. Five hundred cushioned chairs at tables for ten had been draped with designer organza tied with satin bows. Special risers had been installed to give each donor attending an unobstructed view. Dividing the room was a T-shaped runway that ran twice the length of a bowling lane, outlined with red Ecuadorian roses. Tucked in one corner was a ten-piece orchestra underscoring the fanciful scene with the classically romantic renderings of Tchaikovsky and Chopin, Puccini and Liszt. Lauren was almost moved to tears but couldn't be sure whether it was from the room's stunning beauty or lack of sleep.

"You did it, mama," Frankie whispered. Clearly, the room's beauty had moved him, too.

"*We* did it." Lauren turned toward him. "Seriously, I could not have done this without you. Which is why as of this moment you are officially off the clock and ordered to take your seat at table number two."

Frankie's jaw dropped. "Girl, don't play with me."

Lauren laughed. "I'm not."

"But what about you? I can't know you're still working and enjoy myself."

"Don't worry. I plan to join you. I'm just going to take one last walk-through and make sure everything's set."

Frankie gave Lauren an enthusiastic hug. "Thank you, girl. This feels like Christmas and the Fourth of July at the same time." He looked beyond Lauren's shoulder. "And Lord help me if I couldn't have some fireworks with that fine man right there!"

Lauren turned, expecting to see Ace or one of the male models. Instead, it was Christian heading her way.

"You go on and handle that, girlfriend," Frankie whispered. "I'm going to take my seat."

Lauren braced herself against the onslaught of desire guaranteed to erupt when their eyes connected. Now thankful for Frankie's earlier insistence that she dress to impress, she felt girlie, almost beautiful, in the silky kimono mini that draped her body and teased her skin. An unbidden image flashed through her mind—Christian's full, masculine lips replacing the fabric that kissed her flesh. As quickly as it appeared, she shut her mind against it. Christian was a tempting morsel. He was also Victoria's eldest and unlike her father, Lauren had reversed her plans to get entangled with a boss's son.

"Good evening, Lauren."

She nodded slightly. "Christian."

"You're looking stunning and a bit...uncomfortable?"

"No, not at all. I just...didn't plan to see you here."

"Where else would I be? The foundation is my mother's passion but very important to all of us." Christian paused, looked around. "Is this your handiwork?"

"I had help."

His eyes narrowed as they shifted from the room's decor to Lauren's face. An expression as tantalizing as it was unreadable sent a blast of heat to her core. What was it about this guy, she wondered, that lit her body up like a match?

"When it comes to glorious achievements, one should never be coy."

"That's not my intention. I believe in giving credit where it is due. A lot of people helped pull this day together, with Frankie, my assistant for the show, topping the list."

Lauren finished speaking but Christian's eyes remained on her lips.

"What are you doing?"

"Remembering..."

One word drew dew from her feminine flower as Lauren was immediately transported back to last Sunday and his master suite. His kiss. Those touches. A promise waiting to be fulfilled, but one that couldn't, shouldn't happen. For the umpteenth time she'd flip-flopped back to her original position. Christian was off-limits. It wasn't what she wanted, but being the professional that she was, she knew it was the right thing to do.

"Yes, about that..."

Before Lauren could finish responding, they were interrupted by a harried assistant.

"Excuse me, Lauren. The social media campaign is crazy. Operators can't keep up. Can you come help us sort it out?"

"Sure." She turned to Christian, glad beyond words to be leaving his fine but mentally disruptive presence. "Enjoy the show."

Two hours later, the fashion show was over. Every piece of the puzzle had been placed to perfection. Wearing a heart-shaped dress made out of candy, celebrity model London Drake Montgomery had made the finale a showstopper, and Lauren's idea to auction off lunch dates with the male models had exceeded all expectations. Within minutes of the show ending, Victoria relayed great news. The show had set a record by raising more money than any other charity event to date.

Lauren was exhausted but giddy with excitement, not only because of the considerable buzz that had been created due to a social media marketing campaign she'd de-

signed but also because Victoria had been gracious enough
to fly Lauren's mother out for the event and put her up in
one of the hotel's suites. Earlier there'd only been time for
a quick hug, but they would spend the next two days together. Lauren had her luggage delivered there and had
broken away from the crowd of well-wishers long enough
to go and freshen up before joining Victoria, her mom and
a few others for a late-night dinner.

It was the first time she was visiting Taste Test, one of
ten restaurants spread throughout the CANN Casino, Hotel
and Spa. She was more than ready. With her stomach having been in knots all day, Lauren hadn't been able to eat
a thing. But now, with everything over and labeled a success, her appetite had come back in full force. Not even the
throbbing ankle could wipe the smile off her face. The pain
medication made her sleepy, and she didn't like taking drugs
anyway. So she'd distracted herself from the ache with delicious food. Taste Test had received amazing reviews. She
was about to judge for herself.

It was hard to be sexy on crutches. By the time she'd
taken the elevator and navigated through the crowded hallways, Lauren almost wished she'd taken Frankie's advice
to arrange for a blinged-out wheelchair and be chauffeured
around. Lauren reached the hostess stand.

"Good evening! Bless your heart, can we get some as-
sistance for you, a wheelchair perhaps?"

"No, I'm fine. I'm here for dinner with Victoria Breedlove. I'm Lauren Hart."

"Yes, Ms. Hart. Right this way."

Lauren followed the hostess down a hallway opposite
the main dining room. There were a series of closed doors.
She stopped at the first one on the right, gave a light tap
and opened the door.

"Enjoy your evening."

"Thank you."

"There you are!" Victoria said, rising to greet her.

"I knew I should have gone up to help her," Faye said.

"No way." Lauren hugged Victoria. "Mom is staying for such a short time. I wanted you two to catch up."

"Sit there, darling," Victoria said, pointing to one of two empty chairs between Victoria and Faye.

Lauren complied and after a quick hug greeted the designer Ace, his wife London, and two foundation board members she'd met earlier in the day.

"Where's Frankie?" she asked, with a nod at the empty chair beside her.

"I have no idea," Victoria said.

"Perhaps trying his luck at a blackjack table," Ace offered.

"Not Frankie," Lauren countered. "He'd never spend money gambling when there are designer shops nearby."

While the rest of the table continued to chat, Lauren folded her crutches. She bent over to place them under the table, out of the way of the other guests, then heard the door open. Frankie, she thought, glad that Victoria had invited him to join them. Like Lauren, Victoria also knew he'd been a generous contributor to the show's overall success.

"My man!" Ace exclaimed.

She straightened, ready to laugh at Frankie's response, and her breath caught in her throat. It wasn't Frankie. It was the one and only man who could enter a room and change her temperature.

"Not this evening. You're the man," Christian replied, offering Ace a fist bump before kissing London on the cheek. "Good evening, everyone."

He waved at the board members, spoke briefly to Faye and continued around the table to Victoria. "Hello, gorgeous," he said, as he leaned down and kissed her cheek.

"Hi, son. Gorgeous is the one you're sitting beside. The most beautiful woman walking on crutches that I've ever seen."

"I agree with you," he replied, drinking in Lauren with his smoldering dark eyes.

"I have Ace and the HER collection to thank for that," Lauren said, referring to her kimono. "He and Frankie, who insisted on covering my bandage with the crystal-covered bootee."

"I'm kind of digging the bootee," London said. "You just might start a trend."

"Hello, beautiful."

*Is it my imagination or did the room and everyone in it just fade away?*

"Hello, Christian," Lauren answered.

He gave her cheek a whisper of a kiss, brushing his warm lips across her skin. Wreaking havoc on her body, as always.

"Congratulations on a job well done. The show was amazing."

"Thank you," she murmured softly. "I'm glad you enjoyed it."

"I wouldn't have missed it. Ace is my favorite designer."

Victoria feigned a cough. "I thought it was because mine was your favorite foundation."

"That goes without saying."

"Were you aware that tonight's fund-raiser was our most successful so far?" his mother asked.

"Really? Even more so than last year's golf tournament?"

"Absolutely," Victoria replied. "And we have Lauren's innovative and highly progressive marketing skills to thank for that."

"It was a team effort," Lauren said.

"To put on the affair indeed took a village. But your ingenious auctions for dates with the models and jewelry sold on social media allowed us to raise almost as much money from those who weren't in attendance as we did from those who purchased tickets and clothes."

"Interesting," Christian said, curiosity and a hint of admiration in his eyes. "Tell me more."

Lauren explained how after finding out about London's new jewelry line, she got the idea to present those items on social media, in limited quantities, to the highest bidder. Because of the short setup time frame, bids were limited to those within the United States. "Had it been opened internationally," she finished, "we would have easily doubled what was made."

Christian nodded. "I'd love to see the video."

"I'll send it to you."

"Perfect timing," Victoria announced as several servers arrived with the group's first course, each carrying two plates, and placed them down simultaneously. "Enough about CANN for one day. Let's talk about something really important."

She looked at London. "Like how someone who just had a baby four weeks ago can look absolutely fantastic!"

"Not to sound chauvinistic, but that sounds like a conversation for ladies' night out." Ace laughed at the immediate looks of indignation and hurried on to escape rebuttals. "Let's talk about something we can all participate in, like a trip to Paris by private plane. I heard someone at the table just got one."

Christian sat back, a smile barely concealed. "That's the rumor."

"More than a rumor," said one of the board members. "My husband shared pictures with me last week. He'd gone online and found the model. Very nice."

"Thank you, Ally. It was an incredible gift and you're all invited to join me on a trip I'm taking next week. It's not Paris, though."

"Where?" Ally asked. "Italy? I've never been but always wanted to. I hear it's so romantic, and with my divorce almost final…"

She let the sentence fade as imaginations took over and the titters increased.

"Not sure that where I'm going next week you'll find romantic," Christian said, pausing for dramatic effect. "I'm going to Djibouti."

"Da-booty?" Faye repeated, and the table laughed.

"Ja-booty, Mom," Lauren corrected with an indulgent smile. "It's a small country in the Horn of Africa, strategically positioned to be a commercial, military and shipping hub."

Christian wasn't the only one looking at her with amazement. Lauren wasn't used to being the center of attention but when in her wheelhouse of business, PR and marketing, her confidence soared.

"Last year I worked for a client doing business there," she explained. "I was hired largely because I could create his marketing materials in French, one of the country's three official languages."

"Have you been there?"

Lauren shook her head. "No, Christian. Just lots of research online."

"Did you hear that, Christian?" Victoria interjected. "Lauren speaks fluent French and is an expert on the country that you're scheduled to visit."

"Yes, Mom. I heard. And yes, that is impressive."

"I wouldn't exactly call myself an expert," Lauren demurred.

"Perception is reality," Victoria countered. "And from where I'm sitting, you have assets that could greatly benefit not only the CANN Foundation, but the corporation as well."

The servers returned with the evening's second course, and the conversation went in another direction as London and Ace regaled the table with untold tales of the fashion world.

While all eyes were on them, Christian leaned over and whispered, "You can run, but you can't hide."

"Who's running?"

"Earlier, it appeared that you were."

"I didn't run. I was called away. Why would I want to run from you?"

"That's what I'm trying to find out."

"I'm not running," she repeated, more forcefully this time.

His chuckle, soft and deep, made her core quiver.

"I'm beginning to think that you're a tease, Lauren Hart."

"I am not."

"Prove it."

The very words she'd used the day he returned the bracelet came back to haunt her. London saved Lauren. She asked a question about DC. Later, Lauren would have been hard-pressed to remember anything else talked about at the table, her body in sensory overload at Christian's nearness. His scent, that deep, husky voice, the way his leg casually brushed against hers when he shifted, the manner in which his eyes floated over her body with a subtle intensity. How did he do that? How did he manage to at times look totally uninterested and in the next moment fix her with a quick, ardent gaze that got her wildly aroused?

She sighed. The only thing more delectable than him at the table was her third-course choice of a grilled cedar plank swordfish. The roasted zucchini and cherry tomatoes that accompanied the dish caused a gustatory orgasm, and the black-and-white truffle creamy wild rice on which the fish rested was so decadent she could have licked the plate. Still, when her mother begged off dessert citing fatigue, Lauren was grateful. It had been a long day, and trying to maintain a casual indifference toward the hottie beside her was like another job. Besides, her mother was leaving soon. She needed mommy time.

Christian reached for his phone and passed it to her beneath the table. "Type in your number," he commanded in a low tone meant for her ears only. When she hesitated, he continued. "For the video link," he explained. "Unless you're afraid of how much you want me, knowing that one night together might not be enough."

Lauren snatched the phone, hurriedly typed in her number, hugged Victoria and said goodbye to the table. Christian's parting words played on mental repeat. She was chagrined at how accurate his arrogant assessment was. Yes, she wanted him. Yes, she was afraid. But Lauren ran from wannabe fiancés and desperate fathers, not from his type of danger. Christian had asked her to prove that she wasn't a tease. Soon, he'd get just what he asked for.

# Ten

Once out of the private dining room, Lauren finally acquiesced to the use of a wheelchair, which Faye insisted on pushing. They reached the suite and while she'd been in it earlier, Lauren was newly impressed. Earlier her focus had been on a quick change and food. Now she had a chance to take in and appreciate the room's simple grandeur, if there could be such a thing. While being wheeled to the suite where her mother was staying, Lauren's phone dinged. Christian.

Let's link up. Starting with the video...

She smiled, sent the promotional video from the fundraiser and set her phone to silent. The next several hours were for her and her mother alone.

"This suite is truly beautiful," Lauren said from the living room. She rose from the wheelchair, tossed one crutch down and used the other to walk over and take in the view.

"I told Victoria not to make a fuss over my visit, but she insisted I stay here."

"Next time you should plan to stay longer, and at my place."

"Your place?"

"Well, technically the home belongs to the Breedloves, but it's mine for now."

"Yes, Victoria told me. You're under contract until mid-July."

Faye joined Lauren and peered out floor-to-ceiling windows that showcased the length of the neon-lit Strip. Then she turned to her daughter.

"You look good, dear. Las Vegas seems to agree with you."

"Getting away from the stress of Ed and Dad's demands sure does."

"Is that it? The miles between here and Maryland?"

Lauren ignored her mother's knowing smile. Since the women were best friends, she was sure Victoria had told Faye all she thought she knew about what was happening between Lauren and Christian. She peeked into one of two spacious bedrooms before hobbling over to a low-slung tan couch and plopping down. She reached for the remote and turned on the television. Several local stations had covered the fund-raiser. She was curious how it would be shown on the news.

Faye followed her over. She sat in a matching chair, ran her hand over the deluxe silk velvet and lovingly eyed her daughter.

"You must be exhausted."

"I am, and happy my first event as Victoria's personal assistant is in my rearview mirror."

"It was fantastic, darling. Victoria went on and on about how well you did. You should be very proud."

"I never could have done it without my assistant, Frankie."

"Perhaps he can take over when you leave."

"Or perhaps this temporary move will become permanent."

"You can't really mean that."

"Yes, Mom, I do. For the first time in months I'm not being badgered. I can't tell you how good that feels."

"That's largely because your dad believes you'll be back home soon."

"What has he told you about this sudden friendship with Ed, encouraging us to get married? His explanation about Ed coming from such a good family and me getting older…

he's never been interested in my personal life. It just doesn't add up."

"The Millers are a good family," Faye offered.

Lauren was incredulous. "Are you taking his side?"

"No. It's just…never mind."

"Mom, what is it?"

"Let's talk about it tomorrow, Lauren. It's been such a wonderful day."

Lauren reached for the remote and muted the TV. Suddenly the segment airing about the fashion show didn't matter as much as she'd thought. "Mom…"

"You can't breathe a word of this to your father. He's such a proud man. But given how this could impact your future, you have a right to know."

Taking in the seriousness mixed with sadness that was her mother's expression, Lauren's stomach dropped. She may have the right to know, but did she want to?

"I know how hard your father worked to keep his business going, how much he struggled."

"I think we were all aware of it," Lauren said softly. "At one point he was working seven days a week."

Faye nodded. "What I didn't know is that he took out a few loans during that time."

"From Ed?"

"Not initially. Lauren, he mortgaged the house."

"Oh, no!"

"Twice."

Lauren covered her mouth to stifle a gasp. Furnishing and decorating the five-bedroom, three-bath home in Maryland's upscale Brandywine neighborhood had filled up those early months and eased Faye's dismay about leaving friends and family on the West Coast behind. Being forced to leave the home would be devastating. The sadness she saw in her mother's eyes took on new meaning.

"I still don't understand Ed's connection."

"I'm getting to that. Paul had known his banker for years

and was assured that they'd work with him until he'd paid back the money. But a little more than six months ago Liam, the loan officer who was also Paul's friend, got promoted. The new officer was not as lenient as Liam had been and demanded the long-overdue loan be immediately repaid in full."

"And Ed lent Dad the money." The sickening scenario became crystal clear. It was about that time that Ed had called and tried to get back together. He'd obviously used the loan as leverage to get her father on his side. Except her mother's tortured expression suggested there was more to the story.

"Oh my gosh, Mom. You look so worried. How much did he borrow?" Lauren asked this despite the fact that she doubted the five-figure amount in her savings account would cover what her dad owed.

"I don't know exactly, but given that our home is now worth half a million I'd say it's a sizable amount. And like the new banker, Ed wants all of it now unless you two get married."

Several minutes passed as Lauren digested the news. "There's got to be another solution. I mean, I know how much you love your home and I'd hate for you to lose it, but... I can't be with Ed. He's not a nice guy."

Faye's eyes narrowed as she studied her daughter. "Did he hurt you, Lauren?"

"No, not in the way you're thinking. Ed was never physically violent. But sometimes it's the verbal and emotional abuse that leaves the bigger scars."

Faye reached over and placed a comforting hand on Lauren's arm. "Nothing is worth your unhappiness, sweetheart, and nothing is worse than being in a loveless marriage."

"But that home means everything to you. What if you lose it?"

Faye sat back, her lips a thin line of determined strength. "I'll regret it, but I'll live."

The conversation didn't last much longer. Totally drained,

Lauren stumbled into the bedroom, stripped naked and fell into bed. In the dark quiet came the drone of a vibrating cell phone, the one that she'd earlier silenced. Fumbling for her purse on the nightstand, she pulled out the phone and checked the messages. Three of them were from Christian, the last one a question that for Lauren was a total surprise.

Will you come with me to Djibouti? Your fluent French will be an asset and not only was Mom's suggestion right on, she's already approved your time away from the foundation.

With Faye's latest revelation fresh in her mind, Lauren knew what her answer would be. She needed money, and a plan, to help dig her parents out of their financial troubles. Perhaps this trip would give her time to think one up. She replied without hesitation.

Yes.

It would be morning when she'd see Christian's simple response. A smiley face and a thumbs-up.

# Eleven

When off work, the average worker rushed to get away from their job. But when employed by the best hotel in the world, with the finest accommodations and entertainment in the city, there was often no hurry to leave. At 9:00 p.m. on a Wednesday night, Christian was still at CANN, entertaining a high-rolling client and prince from Brunei, along with his brother Noah, who worked in international sales, and Greg Chapman, the department's VP. They'd dined at Chefs, the über-exclusive restaurant that catered to their high rollers and other 1-percenters. It held only twenty tables and boasted menus without prices. The unspoken rule was, if you had to ask, you couldn't afford it.

Now that the meal was complete, the group relaxed in the members-only club near Chefs, where corporate executives took businessmen wanting to be away from the commoners' prying eyes, drink vintage liquor and enjoy stellar entertainment. They sipped pricey cognac from crystal snifters and listened to a band playing a folksy kind of neo soul, fronted by a woman whose voice reminded Christian of the singer Sade. He checked his watch and signaled the bartender to put the table's bill on the company tab.

Standing, he stifled a yawn and leaned toward the prince. "Gentlemen, it is a pleasure doing business with you, but I have an early-morning international flight, so I will take my leave." He addressed the other men at the table. "Noah, Greg, good night."

It wasn't until he neared the door that he realized someone else he knew had been enjoying the room's heady ambiance. Chloe stood with the look of someone well aware of her beauty, but for Christian, she wore a dress too revealing, boobs too surgically enhanced and a smile too seductive, especially in this room. When she'd asked for a card key to the private lair, he'd given her one without a second thought. Now he wondered whether or not that had been a good idea.

"Hey, handsome."

He allowed a light hug. "You know that coming in here alone isn't wise. Women who do so usually have an agenda. The men might get the wrong impression."

Chloe wriggled her eyebrows. "Or the right one."

"All right, then. Good night."

"Wait up. I'm leaving, too."

*Lucky me.* Christian headed toward the elevator, the private one that would take him directly to the executive lot and his car. Chloe stayed beside him.

"Where are you going?"

"What, no time to drive a friend to her car?" she purred.

"You're not valeted?"

"Yes, but that shouldn't matter."

"Not tonight, Chloe." Christian pushed the button. "It's been a long day. Once in my car I only want to stop for traffic lights or an opening gate."

The elevator arrived. Christian stepped in, standing near the door to block Chloe's entrance.

"In that much of a hurry to get home to your latest toy? It's been a couple weeks. I'd have thought you would have tossed her away already."

Christian knew what she wanted. Info. Details. From the time he'd met her when they were ten, it was her world and those around her were blessed to be in it. But just like she knew he could see through her fakery, had gotten that lesson in the very worst way, she should have known that like all of the other Breedloves, Christian kept it real. And private. Behind the bedroom door.

"Good night, Chloe."

He stepped back so the door would close, then thought

about her comment regarding Lauren. *Discarded?* Hardly. That precious plaything hadn't even been unwrapped. But soon.

Back at the Breedlove estate, Lauren walked into the guesthouse's master suite closet and tried to act as though it were every other day that she flew to the other side of the world on a private plane with the handsomest man in the Western US. Aside from meeting with Victoria for most of the day, this was the first time her thoughts went to anything other than what she'd learned from Faye's visit. Her father, cornered. Her mother, quietly distraught. Her nemesis, determined. Her life, upended.

Oh, how she wished she had a million bucks lying around, or whatever amount was needed for repayment. She'd have the money converted to pennies, placed in a dump truck and delivered to Ed so that he could be buried in them. Lauren had never been a gambler but more than once since she'd left home she'd had flights of fancy involving slot machines with million-dollar payoffs or driving to purchase a lottery ticket just beyond the state line. If Lady Luck was going to strike, it had better happen quickly. Faye had tried to make the truth less foreboding, but Lauren had known Ed for a decade. He was ruthless and selfish. Dad was in over his head.

She had no doubt that Ed was ramping up the pressure, turning the screws, forcing a decision to be made quickly. No matter how her mother tried to paint a rosier picture, the truth of the matter was that only a wedding ring stood between her dad and mom losing their forever home, maybe more. Lauren wouldn't put it past Ed to threaten her dad's livelihood. A man she detested held the ring, and the finger he wanted to place it on was hers.

Faye had assured Lauren that a house wasn't worth her unhappiness, but could she live with knowing her decision resulted in her mom losing that dream home, and her dad maybe losing his job?

Trying to force back the thoughts that had led to pounding headaches two days in a row, she pulled several items from their hangers and reached for the handle of her luggage. After tossing the items she'd chosen on the bed, she walked to the beautifully crafted armoire that anchored the wall opposite her bed and gathered her sexiest lingerie.

Instead of her usual attempts to push away thoughts of Christian, tonight she welcomed a flood of them into her mind and allowed herself to imagine ignoring good sense and being with him. Tomorrow, they were boarding his private jet and flying to Africa! While not sure of what phase they were in with the project, she doubted they'd be traveling alone. Most likely there'd be a few other executives, maybe an assistant or two, other investors...who knew? Maybe one roll in the hay with the guy and Christian would be out of her system. With that in mind, she picked out her naughtiest undies in case a spontaneous seduction occurred. After returning back to the States would be soon enough to contemplate her nightmare. But for the next several days, while traveling with Christian, she'd allow herself to dream.

The phone rang. She checked the ID.

Dad. Great. Dream over.

Lauren started not to answer. But her curiosity about what was being cooked up between her dad and Ed trumped her desire to leave all of her problems behind and head straight to the plane. She pressed the speaker button and continued to pack.

"Hi, Dad."

"Hello, Lauren."

He sounded formal, official, the same as he would while addressing a client. The history was different, but when it came to personality, Ed and her father were a lot alike.

"Faye said you wanted to speak with me regarding my

project with Ed. I was disappointed to learn that she'd divulged my personal business. It is none of your concern."

"Good, then I expect you to stop campaigning on Ed's behalf. I will not marry him."

"Ed loves you dearly, as do I, and wants to build a solid foundation that will benefit generations for both of our families."

"There doesn't have to be a marriage for that to happen."

"But Ed is in love with you. It's what he wants."

"What about what I want?"

"And what is that?" Lauren bit her lip to remain silent. Given that there were few secrets between her parents, her dad most likely knew about Christian. "Promise me you won't do anything stupid, Lauren."

"I've got to go. Bye, Dad."

"Lauren!"

It was the first time in her life she'd ever defied him. But Lauren wasn't about to make a promise that she wasn't sure she could keep.

An unexpected knock at the door caused her to flinch, a sign of just how badly the conversation with her father had put her on edge. She hoped it was Frankie, always good for a laugh or lending a compassionate ear. Her smile was faint yet hopeful as she peeped through the hole.

"Hey, you," she said after opening the door, batting away frustrating tears.

Christian stepped inside and took her into his arms. A diversion was just what she needed.

# Twelve

It wasn't what he'd intended to do, but Lauren looked as though she could use a hug. He would have ended it there, but when she glided her arms around his neck, wearing a skimpy top and boy shorts, reminding him of a butterscotch bar, what could he do but accept the invitation to cuddle? Then when she pressed her body into him and thrust her tongue into his mouth all Christian could think was...*well, damn!*

Christian deepened the kiss. He loved kissing, always had. It was an art he'd purposely perfected and growing up had practiced every chance he got. Lauren's kisses were magical, and the thought of her becoming proficient the way he did made him want to punch every guy she'd ever dated. Their mouths fit together as though hers had been made especially for him. But had it? Were those delectable lips now sliding down the side of his face to his neck a gift...or a weapon?

He slowly pulled away from her. "That was some greeting."

Lauren stepped back to let him in. "I won't apologize for it, but I got carried away."

"Are you all right?"

"Not really." Lauren reached for the crutch leaning against the wall, crossed to the bar counter and perched on one of the stools.

"Do you want to talk about it?"

"No." She looked at his lips.

"Is there anything I can do to make you feel better?"

"You can use that irresistible mouth of yours for something besides talking."

Without a word, he swept Lauren up into his arms and walked them into the bedroom.

He gently laid her on the bed and followed her down. Lauren's movements were urgent, but he slowed the pace, kissing every exposed piece of skin. He felt pebbling beneath his chest and rose up just enough to lift up her top and give a nipple a nibble. Laving the darkened circle barely discernible in the darkness, he thought of truffles and bonbons, only Lauren was sweeter. She moaned, and he kissed the other peak, a mere flicker really, a promise that he'd be back. Then he was back at her mouth, and this time he meant business. He pressed his tongue inside her warm, moist cavern. Their tongues danced and dueled and got to know each other.

"Chris." His name floated on a whisper into his ear. She moaned again, pulled off her tank top and reached for his belt. Christian felt himself harden and lengthen, and no longer cared to slow things down. They'd take their time on round two. And there *would* be a round two. He'd make sure of that.

Placing a knee on each side of her, he sat back and stared at her perfectly shaped, weighty globes, then gripped the waistband of her shorts and began to pull. Lauren rose up, her eyes dark with desire. She ground her hips a little.

*Sexy-ass minx.*

He eased the shorts over her hips, smiling at the patch of curly black fur covering her treasure. Some guys made a big deal of a girl being shaved, but for Christian that was overrated. If that was the woman's choice, cool, but sometimes a mass of soft ground cover meant she hadn't recently prepared it for anybody, that she hadn't been ravished in a while. Lauren said she hadn't recently dated, and not that it mattered, but he believed her. The thought of a snug welcome and rhythmic friction lengthened Christian's erection even more.

Propping his hands on her knees and careful of her ankle,

he coaxed her legs apart and took a long, slow dip into her dewy valley. The long moan emitted from the back of her throat let Christian know he was onto something that Lauren liked.

A lot.

That meant he couldn't half step. He needed to do the job right. So he shifted them until he could lie comfortably between her legs and spread apart her folds with his tongue. Licking, lapping, he tasted her essence, massaged her into a hardened pearl. He spread her wider, tasted deeper, raised his hands and cupped her breasts. She ground her hips against his face. Encouraging his direction. The move made him so dizzy with desire, he was about to burst. Sliding off the bed, he shimmied out of his pants and reached for his wallet in one smooth motion. He quickly tore open the foil packet and sheathed his engorged member. He climbed on the bed and held his body aloft.

"Are you ready, baby?" he whispered.

"I'm so ready," she replied.

"Then let's do this."

He aimed his ample appendage at her entry of ecstasy and connected with her in the deepest way possible with one…slow…continuous thrust.

Then the party started for real. Him plunging, retreating and plunging again. Her lifting her arched body, wanting him again and again. And when she squeezed her inner walls, tightly, it was Christian's turn to moan. He eased his hands beneath what could only be described as the juiciest booty, squeezing her softly as he branded her core.

"Oh my goodness," she gasped as her hip motion increased. Then more sounds, high-pitched, unintelligible, until her nails dug into his back as she went over the edge. Just in time, too, as Christian was also at his zenith. He plunged harder, faster, backward, forward, then shouted his release before collapsing on the bed beside her.

"What just happened?" Lauren asked in wonder, still catching her breath.

"Whatever it was," Christian muttered as he reached over and pulled her against him, "I cannot wait for it to happen again."

He didn't have long to wait. The second time was slower, languid, like blue-lights-in-the-basement, straight-ahead jazz. They showered together, and Christian received an unexpected treat. Turns out that kissing wasn't the only thing Lauren did well with her mouth.

Later, clean and sated, they cuddled beneath a sheet, watching the candle Lauren lit between rounds one and two flicker against the wall.

He stroked a finger across her shoulder, kissed her temple. "Do you feel better?"

"Infinitely so," she murmured. "You?"

"I'm not sure, to be honest. I might need rehab."

He felt Lauren's head rise off the pillow. "Rehab? Why?"

"Because your love is addicting and I could get hooked."

"Oh, Lord."

They laughed, hugging, before Lauren perched against the headboard. Christian rose up, too.

"So you haven't been with anyone in a while, huh?"

Lauren chuckled. "How could you tell?"

"I could tell."

"What about you?"

"Nothing serious, not lately. I have a few friends with a clear understanding. We're casual, getting together to have a good time. That's about it."

"Have you ever thought about getting married?"

Christian ran a hand over the sheet as he pondered the question. "I did, once."

"What happened?"

"Someone I'd dated but no longer dealt with came back and messed it all up."

She arched a brow. "You cheated with her?"

"No, but that's how she made it look."

"Wow, that's jacked up."

"Totally."

Lauren could feel his eyes searching for her in the darkness.

"What about you?"

"What *about* me?"

"Ever thought about getting taken off the market?"

"Taken off the market? Ugh! What am I, an egg?"

"Well, technically speaking…"

She hit him with a pillow. Talk lessened after that and then ended altogether. They fell asleep, spooning, Lauren clutching Christian's big, strong arms around her. They woke up, hours later, the very same way.

# Thirteen

Las Vegas was known for attracting the world's finest in the art of illusion and wizardry. Christian had sat in premium seats and seen the best of the best. But he'd never experienced the kind of magic that had happened last night between him and Lauren. He didn't want to overthink it or ruminate on what had happened before he arrived last night.

She'd pulled back a bit this morning, more guarded, less carefree. Clearly she didn't want to put a label on what was happening. Heck, he didn't either. But Christian knew one thing for sure. Even with the level of heat between last night's high-thread-count Egyptian sheets, the passion between them was just beginning to burn.

After a quick trip to Dr. Burman's office, Christian and Lauren headed straight to the airstrip. Their luggage had already been loaded, the plane had been checked, and they were ready for takeoff. Most of their time together had been with each of them handling last-minute business before leaving the country—Lauren on her tablet, Christian on his phone. But now, as they settled into the first two seats with Lauren's ankle propped up on a padded stool, a light breakfast ordered and the Gulfstream taxiing down the runway, Christian reached over and squeezed her hand.

"You okay, beautiful?"

"I'm fine, especially since speaking with Victoria this morning. Frankie is going to work in my absence so I don't feel that I'm leaving her in a lurch."

"And your ankle? There's really no pain?"

"None at the moment, thanks to this functional yet ugly thing."

Lauren lifted the leg that the doctor had outfitted with a sleek black bionic ankle brace and wriggled her freshly painted toenails.

"I don't know," he replied, his voice as silky as the leg he now squeezed, peeking out from the thigh-high slit in Lauren's maxi. Knowing that heaven awaited mere inches beneath the fabric almost made him go hard. "Your boot is kind of sexy."

"Frankie would kill me if he knew I'd matched this dress with such plainness."

"I'll take care of it." Christian reached for his phone.

"Who are you calling?"

"The other passengers coming on this trip."

"I thought you said it would be just the two of us."

"I said it would be only you and me in Djibouti. But we've got a couple slackers wanting to bum a ride to London."

Lauren frowned, obviously confused.

Just then the captain—not Jesse but an equally capable and more formal young pilot named Dennis—came over the intercom.

"An official good morning to you, Mr. Breedlove, Ms. Hart. You've picked a great day to fly across the pond. We've reached our cruising altitude of forty thousand feet. All the way into Hayward there's nothing but golden sunshine and blue skies so sit back, relax and enjoy the ride."

"Hayward?"

"Northern California, near San Francisco."

Lauren's eyes lit up. "Ace and London are coming with us?"

"They are indeed."

An hour later the plane descended and scooped up Mr. and Mrs. Montgomery. While London and Lauren settled on the couch and Christian gave Ace a tour of the plane, the ground crew loaded their luggage.

London reached into a designer tote and pulled out a sock dipped in crystals. "Voila!"

Lauren laughed out loud. "You've got to be kidding! Frankie made the glittery bootee I wore to the show. I didn't know they could actually be purchased."

"They can't be. That's an original, darling. Whipped up just for you."

"No way. Christian just called you, what, half an hour ago?"

"How long do you think it takes to dip a piece of apparel in fabric glue and roll it in Swarovski?"

"Is that what you did?"

Now it was London who chuckled. "Hardly. Ace called one of the guys at the shop who worked his magic and met us here."

"Wow, that makes me feel really special. Thanks."

"No, thank you. A version of what you're holding will be in our next collection. Hey, maybe we'll use you as the model." London lifted her chin as Frankie would. "You'll be fabulosity, sweetness."

"Oh my goodness, the moment Frankie sees this he'll expire on the spot. In fact, you should get him to model for you. Wait! I just thought of something."

"What?"

"Where's the baby?"

"Our little princess left with her nanny and the staff last night. They'll be there and have the house ready when we arrive. Speaking of, how long will you be in London? We've got some great friends there that we'd love you to meet."

Christian and Ace joined them in the sitting area. The plane took off and the party started. That London and Ace were on board with them could not have made Lauren happier. She didn't regret what happened last night. In fact, she couldn't wait for it to happen again. But having sex with Christian couldn't help but complicate a situation that the conversation with her dad made even more convoluted. A situation that no matter how much she wished, seemed to not be going away.

*Later*, she told herself, as the flight attendant brought out mimosas made with freshly squeezed orange juice and a ridiculously expensive bottle of Krug vintage brut.

For the next ten hours they ate, drank and, for Lauren, experienced shoptalk at a whole other level. She marveled at how London, Ace and Christian discussed billions and trillions the way average people talked about twenties and tens. The slackers, Lauren learned, would play an intricate role in the playground of the rich that Christian envisioned in Africa, with a designer house of Ace's fashions anchoring a sprawling mall and London's A-list celebrity connections purchasing properties and making the man-made islands like pricey, limited-edition baubles that only the wealthiest and luckiest could attain.

She watched the ease with which these friends did business together and couldn't imagine the same relaxed camaraderie between Ed and her dad. The pilot announced the plane's initial descent. The couples returned to their seats and buckled up for landing, and Lauren snuggled into the comfort of Christian's warm embrace.

"Good idea, baby," he whispered, his breath hot and wet against her ear.

"What?"

"Getting your rest. You're going to need it."

She shifted her head to look at him. "Is that so?"

"That's *so* so."

"Why? What's going to happen later?"

He pulled her closer to him. "It involves getting you wetter for me tonight than you were last night, and then taking my time to lick you dry."

His plan was already working. Lauren squeezed her thighs together against the pulsating flesh.

"Stop being a bad boy," she cooed, nestling deeper into his arms.

He kissed the top of her head. "Not a chance."

For a second her shield slipped, and Lauren wondered how it might feel to spend a lifetime in this luxury, night after night in the protection and passion of Christian's strong arms. Just as quickly the fantasy dissipated, replaced by a vision of Ed's cocky smirk and the memory of her dad's somber plea. Christian was a stellar deflection from what she faced once back stateside. But Lauren held no delusions that he'd ever be anything more than that.

They touched down at London's Luton Airport in the wee hours of the morning. After customs personnel had boarded the plane and quickly cleared them, the foursome dashed through a steady drizzle to a waiting car. As they neared the driver hopped out, opened the door and ushered them inside before handling their luggage. London nestled her head against Ace's shoulder and closed her eyes. Then, in a universal man move, Ace and Christian settled into a conversation about the car transporting them, a Rolls-Royce Phantom with seats that faced each other and leather so soft it cupped the body like a blanket.

Lauren was glad to not have to engage in conversation. The plane had landed but parts of her still floated above the clouds. Remembering Christian's naughty plans for the night ahead, her core quivered and her nether lips pulsed. Just thinking of his tongue once again inside her made every part of her body react. Nipples pebbled. Nub engorged. She was shaky and dewy and out of control, and even though bouts of drowsiness and jet lag accompanied the time change, all she wanted was Christian, demanding and hard.

A half hour later, the driver pulled up to the Sanderson Hotel in Berkenshire. Ace and London had invited them to stay at their home, but considering that they'd been on a plane for ten-plus hours and her namesake city was ninety miles away, Christian declined the invite. Lauren believed there may have been another reason, that he wanted what she wanted.

She was right.

Within minutes of the driver bringing in their luggage before tipping his hat and wishing them good-night, Christian and Lauren tumbled into bed. She wore nothing but her sexy bionic brace, which was covered by London's thoughtful gift, on the ankle Christian thoughtfully propped up with pillows before sheathing himself, sliding behind her and thrusting himself into her waiting warmth. He moved slowly and rhythmically, branding her soul, his fingers keeping the same pace sliding over her nub. Her orgasm was deep and delicious, intensely satisfying, and just as her eyelids fluttered shut she decided soothing sex with a master beat melatonin any night of the week.

# Fourteen

A text Christian received when he and Lauren awakened Saturday morning necessitated a change in plans. He'd been invited to meet the following day with members of the president of Djibouti's administration and a small group of businessmen. Knowing the importance of establishing and maintaining excellent relations with the country's political structure, he cancelled their plans for joining Ace and London for dinner at Restaurant Gordon Ramsey, and had their pilot make flight plans that would put them in Djibouti in time for a good night's sleep before the business meeting.

It would be his first return to the country since purchasing his own island, one of the smaller, more pristine in the Indian Ocean, his first time seeing the home he'd designed, with a mini golf course as the backyard and a pool on the roof.

Their flight arrived in Djibouti around one a.m. and instead of nonstop lovemaking as had happened in England, Christian and Lauren got a good night's sleep. After his business meeting later that morning, the couple toured the capital, Djibouti City. Christian loved introducing Lauren to the local cuisine and sharing what he'd learned of the country through extensive research and his many visits there.

The Republic of Djibouti, located in the Horn of Africa, bordered by Eritrea, Ethiopia and Somalia, was not the type of country most would consider as a possibility for a vacation paradise. But it fit Christian's vision perfectly, especially the islands off the coast of Djibouti in the Gulf of Tadjoura. The paradisiacal enclave of the Indian Ocean boasted an abundance of pearl oysters, extensive coral reefs and privacy. Before, he could only imagine the love nests that could be created for the rich and famous craving discretion. Now, with Lauren beside him, what he'd envisioned had come to life.

He looked at her now, golden body shimmering against the water, bathed in the light of a waning sun. Curly wet hair splayed across her shoulders and down her back. The rounded ass he loved so much bobbing out of the water like an apple ripe for biting. But he resisted and instead took in her pensive expression, and broached the subject that had bugged him since Wednesday night.

"Who is he?"

"Hmm?" she asked without glancing his way.

"The guy who had you frowning when I came by on Wednesday, and now."

Her hazel eyes pierced him and narrowed. "How do you know what I'm thinking?"

"Because you have that look of a woman irritated by a man. Trust me, I know that look. I've seen it many times."

This made her laugh. She became less defensive, turned her body and reached for a float. "Tell me about that."

"No way, Ms. Avoider," he replied. "We're talking about you right now."

He watched her nibble her plush lower lip and formulate an answer. "It's complicated," she said at last, her lips moist and swollen and looking so tasty that he wanted to nibble them himself. He ignored his twitching member.

*Down, boy.*

"Do you love him?" He refused to admit how much her answer mattered. She shook her head. "Then what's hard about it?"

"He's an ex who wants another chance. Our families are close. My dad likes him, and is the CFO of his father's company."

"Ah. That's complicated. Though I can understand the guy is probably kicking himself, trying to figure out how you got away."

"He'd be better served learning how not to be a jerk."

"Ha! Ready to get out of the water?"

"And do what?" She looked at him with suggestive eyes.

"Definitely that," he said with a knowing smile as he hoisted himself from the pool. "But later, after I run something past you."

Lauren floated over to the steps and climbed out, or tried to, as she tested putting weight on her ankle. He watched for a while just to drink in all that beauty as she slowly rose up from the pool like a nymph, water cascading off her hair, down her back and the long legs that had gripped him in the heat of passion. He saw her wince and went into action, closing the distance between them in two strides and lifting her out of the water as though she were made of glass.

"Hey, I can walk!"

"You can hop. There's a difference."

"Ha! Put me down, smart-ass."

He did, but ran his hands down her back and squeezed her butt, enjoying a juicy kiss before letting her go. She reached for the sarong made of bold animal print fabric that lay across a lounge chair and tied it around her hips. He took a towel from a nearby table, ran it over his hair and draped it across his shoulders. They entered the two-story great room that framed the pool. The tile floor was cool beneath their bare feet. Lauren hobbled over to one of a matching set of bamboo chairs covered in a lavish, water-resistant silk and sank into the plush cushion. She placed her legs on the ottoman nearby. Christian sat across from her on the couch and eyed her thoughtfully.

"So…what's up? What do you want to talk about?"

He cocked his head to one side. "How would you like to work for CANN?"

"I already do."

"Not the foundation, the corporation."

"With you as my boss? No, thanks."

Said with such mock seriousness, Christian laughed out

loud. "There could be benefits to sleeping with the boss, you know."

"Yes, and even bigger disadvantages."

"Are you speaking from experience?" he asked.

Her brow rose. "Are you?"

"I learned early on that the old cliché was true. Business and pleasure do not mix well. I also believe that there can be exceptions to every rule."

Lauren nodded, her eyes intent as she waited.

"When Dad named the corporation after us boys using the CANN acronym, he purposely stayed away from campaigns using the word. Too obvious, he felt, and a bit corny. But not long ago a guy you may have heard about used it fairly successfully in a presidential campaign—" he paused as Lauren smiled "—and there was something about how you used it in the social media campaign that made common phrases sound oddly refreshing. I think that approach might work for this launch."

Christian thought this revelation might shock Lauren. Her surprised expression proved that he'd been correct.

"You want me to work on the marketing for your trillion-dollar baby? A campaign to bring the rich, famous and infamous running to these shores?"

"Yes."

She pursed her lips. "Why?"

"Because of what I've seen, on your website and the internet, and even more by what I feel. It takes time for me to build trust with people, and while I generally don't trust women, I trust you."

"Why don't you trust women?" she queried.

"I've been lied to."

Lauren gave him a look. "Join the world of relationships."

Christian's smile was bittersweet.

Her tone turned serious. "That bad, huh?"

"In the eyes of my then-eighteen-year-old self it was worse."

"Care to share details?" she asked.

Christian looked away from her then, and out toward the pool. "Someone tried to trap me into marriage by saying she was pregnant."

"And she wasn't?"

He shrugged. "If she was, she didn't have it. I guess I'll never know."

"Did you ever see her again after that?" He nodded. "When was the last time?"

"Wednesday night. It was Chloe, right after breaking up with her once and for all."

"Judging by her reaction to me, she has yet to get over it." She shot him a look. "Are you over her?"

"Totally." He stood and walked over to where she sat in the chair. "I'm also done with this conversation, and have a much better idea for how we can spend the rest of the day."

"Great! What's that?"

Christian held out his hands to help her up. "Remember the promises I made on the airplane, the ones that involved your getting wet?"

Lauren nodded, the sweet blush on her skin proof that clearly she remembered.

"Well…it's time to be a man of my word."

The next morning, Monday, Christian was awakened by a shard of sunlight piercing his left eyelid. He squinted and ran his arm across the sheets in search of soft skin. Instead his fingers encountered a pillow and a part of the bunched-up sheet on the empty side of the bed. He reached for his phone, opened one eye fully to read the time. It was early, just eight o'clock. Considering the horizontal cardio they'd engaged in for hours the previous night, it was much too early to get up. But the custom king-size was lonely without her, so he rolled out of bed, slipped on a pair of shorts and went in search of Lauren.

She was in the kitchen, barefoot except for the ankle

brace, wearing the skimpy negligee he'd removed last night. He slid up behind her, squeezed her luscious booty before pulling her back against him and nuzzling her neck.

"Hey," she cooed, moving out of his grasp.

A subtle move, but Christian noticed. Last night she only moved toward him, not away.

"Was it something I said?" he asked lightly. "Morning breath?" He cupped his hand and blew into it.

"No, silly."

The teapot sounded. He watched Lauren pour the scalding water over a tea bag.

"Want some?"

"Sure, why not?"

He walked over to a bar chair and eased into it, content for the moment to watch Lauren looking all kinds of sexy in the domestic scene.

"Black or green?"

His eyes narrowed. "Definitely black."

She smiled, licked her lips. "You're talking about the tea, right?"

"I'm so *not* talking about the tea, but I'll have that black, too."

She fixed the tea and brought the mugs over to where he sat, along with lemons and agave she'd found in the fridge. For several seconds they sat side by side, the only sound that of silverware clanking against china, soft blows and tiny sips.

Whether a personal or professional matter, Christian believed in the direct approach. So he turned to Lauren, tucked a strand of hair behind her ear and allowed his fingers to linger in her gorgeous curls. "What's going on in there?"

"A lot of thinking."

"About?"

She glanced at him. "You. This. Everything between us—the attraction, the hot sex, the family dynamic with our mothers being friends, me working for Victoria…potentially working with you."

"So you're considering my offer."

"You made an offer?" she murmured. "I don't recall."

"I asked the question of whether you'd consider working with me, or more specifically, working on the CANN Island campaign." He caught her gaze. "Are you?"

"I'd be interested in working under contract. I'd rather do that than become an employee right now."

"That could happen."

She nodded. "Which is why I woke up thinking that while the fireworks we create in bed could probably be declared illegal in a few countries and several states…"

He ran his fingers up her arm and watched goose bumps pop up in their wake.

"Like that," she breathed, and moved her arm. "I think it's probably best for now that we go back to just being friends."

"No benefits?"

"Well, maybe every now and then," she murmured with a face that made him laugh. "Seriously, though. There's a lot happening stateside that I need to sort out, and that's what I need to focus on right now."

"The complicated ex?"

"The series of major events by the foundation over the next few months," she clarified. "It's a short contract, but I want to do my best. Hopefully the situation with…my personal issues…will require very little of my attention."

"Good. Because I'd like for us to work out the details of your proposed contract with CANN as soon as possible, and put you and that brilliant mind of yours right to work."

"Have you forgotten that I'm under contract with CANN Foundation?"

"Yes, but without the continued success of CANN International, there is no foundation. Don't worry. I'll talk to Mom. We'll work something out."

One of the hosts called and a short time later Christian and Lauren were picked up and whisked away to have lunch at the president's palace. He was led into another meeting and as was often the case in Muslim countries, only the men were invited. He not only felt bad but, considering the intricate role Lauren might play in the Island brand, was a bit miffed that she'd been excluded. Later he learned that one of the wives had taken her "shopping," a limited proposition, and to enjoy local cuisine—oven-baked fish, chapati, *mukbassa*—at Mukbassa Central Chez Youssouf.

On Tuesday, once business was done for the day, he and Lauren joined a French businessman and his wife for a turn in the canal in a glass-bottom boat. They were taken to where the magic of the coral reefs below the water was clear and brilliant to the naked eye without having to go underwater. They went farther out and watched dolphins play.

The following afternoon they left Djibouti and, remembering Lauren's suggestion to be "just friends" once stateside, took full advantage of their remaining time together. They'd barely reached cruising altitude before he pulled her into the jet's swanky bedroom and initiated a different kind of high, one where he thrusted, plunged and branded her insides. Lauren matched his enthusiasm and gave as good as she got. He rewarded her efforts with a final push that took her over the edge and into the status as a climax-carrying member of the mile-high club.

An hour before landing in Italy, an impromptu side trip before heading home, they showered and dressed and returned to the main cabin. Lauren read a magazine, leaving Christian to pick at his dinner and be alone with his thoughts. He replayed what Lauren had said in Djibouti about why their sexual escapades needed to end and found irony in how closely her reasoning actually matched his own. At least it had when it came to other women. But with Lauren, all of that logic seemed to fly out the window. He didn't want what started last week to be over, and the fact that she worked with his mother? Well, at the moment, he just didn't give a damn.

# Fifteen

Lauren felt like a jet-setter. On Wednesday, she and Christian had left Djibouti for Rome. When asked why they were going there, Christian had answered, his tone sincere, "I'm hungry and in the mood for Italian." They'd eaten at the only restaurant in the eternal city with three Michelin stars, enjoying delicacies Lauren had never imagined, like rabbit tortellini with carrot and chamomile, white asparagus with seaweed pesto, and fillet of John Dory with almond cream and lemon shrimp. The view was glorious and afterward they'd toured the famous ruins, thrown coins in the Trevi Fountain, and walked off dessert by testing out the strength of both the bionic brace and her ankle by climbing a few of the Spanish Steps.

Since Italy was one of the world's most romantic countries, she was glad her "no sex with Christian" rule was not yet in effect, and that she'd agreed that there could be occasional benefits to their friendship. She couldn't picture herself being here, especially with a hunk like the eldest Breedlove boy, and not making love.

Earlier today they'd left for Las Vegas. The whirlwind trip had left her exhausted, and she awoke to find her head on Christian's shoulder, his arm comfortably around her. She jerked upright and looked around. The plane was about to land.

"Sorry, I didn't mean to use your shoulder for a pillow."

"Baby, you can use any part of me anytime you want to."

"Come on now. We talked about that already. What happened in Djibouti is going to stay in Djibouti, right?"

"What about what happened over the Atlantic Ocean

and in Rome?" Lauren made a face. "Is that really what you want?"

"No, but I think it's best."

Christian exhaled roughly. "Being that you work for my mother, you're probably right."

"So you agree with me?"

"I wouldn't go that far," he replied.

"Working for Victoria is one reason, but not the only one."

He reached out and gently tilted her face toward his. "You sure it isn't the ex?"

"It's everything we've already discussed. Let's leave it at that, okay?"

"If that's what you want." Christian's phone rang. "Excuse me."

Lauren was grateful for the interruption even as she reached for her own phone, rarely used while in Africa. She'd become more and more uncomfortable with Christian's probing questions about Ed. The fewer people who knew about the "arranged marriage" that her father desired, the better.

She turned on her phone and while it powered up looked out the window at the familiar Las Vegas skyline, the hotels along the Strip, CANN the most grandiose—a gleaming mass of steel and glass jutting into the sky—and was surprised to feel as though she were coming home. Although she'd only been in Vegas a short time, she already felt like she belonged there, more so than she'd felt after years on the East Coast.

That revelation was much too complicated to mentally process, because she knew that the feeling had everything to do with the man beside her. The man she could see herself easily falling in love with, and also the last man she should date. At least now, while her life was in such turmoil.

The plane touched down just after noon on the West Coast. She said goodbye to the crew and the pilot while

Christian was preoccupied, and then began checking a slew of text messages and noting missed calls. Was there something wrong? Her brow furrowed as he assisted her down the stairs.

"Back to the real world," he said.

"Yep." She continued scrolling her phone.

"Is everything okay?"

"I hope so."

They reached Christian's car. During the short ride to the guesthouse she was quiet, listening to messages left by several people, including her friend Avery and her mom. He pulled into the drive, put the car in Park and jumped out to get her luggage from the trunk. He wheeled it up to the door and after she'd entered the code, rolled them inside.

She turned to him with a genuine smile. "Thank you."

"Where do you want them?" he asked.

"Here is fine," she replied, with a wave across the living room area.

"Sure you don't want them in your bedroom?"

She shrugged. "I guess that would be better."

"Sure you don't want to join me in the bedroom?"

"Stop it, Christian. We've already had that discussion, the outcome of which does not involve bedrooms."

"You can't knock a brother for trying."

"No, but I can knock a brother *out* for making the attempt."

They laughed. He pulled her into his arms. "I forgot, the wildcat."

"No, a bear."

"Dangerous either way." After a tender squeeze, he released her. "Thank you for joining me in Djibouti. Your presence made the trip infinitely more pleasurable, and not just physically. Your beauty is only outshone by your intelligence."

She rolled her eyes.

"This isn't bullshit," he said. "I'm serious. You're an

amazing woman and I'm lucky… CANN International is lucky to have you on our team. So I'll say it again. Thank you…for everything."

His words were so heartfelt and tender, they almost drew tears. Lauren covered the emotion by reaching for the crutch and heading toward the door.

"You're very welcome, Mr. Breedlove," she said as she opened it for him to walk through. "The pleasure was totally and completely mine, but from now on, it's back to work."

Lauren closed the door and leaned against it, willing herself not to cry at what could never be. The missed text messages and phone calls she'd read upon landing were the sobering reminder needed to snap back to reality and get a handle on what was going on. She walked into the bedroom, tapped the phone's screen and called her mom. The familiar message of Faye not being available encouraged her to leave a message at the sound of the beep. She didn't. Instead she ended the call and scrolled to Avery's number. She put the call on speaker and peeled off her clothes, donning a short silk robe when Avery answered.

"It's about time!"

Lauren laughed. "I just got home."

"How dare you send me a text about exotic travels and private planes and then be unavailable for the next week!"

"I guess I should have waited."

"No, then I would have been angry that you'd left me out. But I'm here now. Tell me everything!"

Lauren gave a condensed recap of her trip to Djibouti. "I can honestly say I've never felt so happy, yet completely conflicted at the same time."

A flood of emotions poured through Lauren, making her mind roil and her heart ache. But obsessing over what it all meant would have to wait, she realized, checking the face of her cell phone as the text indicator pinged.

"Avery, listen, I've got to go."

"You've got to be kidding!"

"I'll call you later, promise."

Lauren meant every word. She was sure that later she'd need someone to talk to. She tapped her cell phone's face again and read the text her mom had sent. The second one after explaining she couldn't talk because she was at the library doing research. She read it again, slowly, mouthing the incredible words.

Honey, your dad is in Vegas. And Ed is with him.

And just like that, the dream of a week she'd just spent with Christian crashed into the nightmare that she'd briefly escaped. Lauren sat stunned. What were they doing here? There was only one way to find out. She called her dad's cell phone. Paul must have been sitting right by it. He picked up on the first ring.

She was exhausted from all the travel and all the love-making and belatedly realized that maybe she should have waited to make the call. But there was no getting around it. A face-to-face showdown with both Dad and Ed was inevitable.

"Lauren, where are you?"

"Dad, why are you here?" She felt her question was the one that mattered. "And why is Ed with you?" The answer to that mattered even more.

"Lorrie, we need to talk."

No, not the term of endearment he'd used since she was a child, the only one allowed to call her by that name. It came out in the rush of a relieved breath, and wafted through the phone to her heart, gripping it gently.

She tapped the speaker button, sat on the edge of her bed. "Dad…"

"I have been worried sick about you."

"Why?"

"First you take a job without my knowing about it, then flee the East Coast with barely a goodbye. Now I hear you're traveling to God only knows where with that Breedlove character, a playboy from what I hear, who seems to go through women the way an omelet maker goes through eggs. This type of behavior is so unlike you. You've never acted this way before."

"I've never felt pressured into marriage before!" The words, delivered with missile-like precision, were regretted within syllables of their leaving her mouth. But they were true, and while she'd never want to hurt her father, his actions had caused her heart to bleed.

"Lorrie, I need to see you. Tonight."

"I'll talk to you, but not him."

A long silence and then, "All right. Should I come to you?"

"No. I'll come to you. Where are you staying?"

"The CANN."

*Of course.* "What room?" He told her. "Okay, fine. I'll be there in an hour. And I mean it, Daddy. You'd better be alone."

An hour later she pulled into the valet area. This was the first instance she'd entered through the main lobby entrance. She was struck by its vast grandeur and elegant style. At once modern and classic, with Victoria's imprint everywhere.

She reached the elevator and pushed the button, trying to forget why she was here. Each time she remembered her heartbeat quickened, and a sickening knot began to form in her gut. Who knew? Maybe this visit was about the business project between Ed and her dad and had nothing to do with this arranged marriage nonsense. That thought brought a good feeling, so much so that when she reached the fourteenth floor and headed toward the room number her father had given, she allowed herself to get just a little excited about the upcoming visit. She was going to see her dad!

Lauren arrived at the room and announced her presence with a rhythmic *rat-ta-tat-tat*. The door opened and there stood Paul Hart, eyes bright, mouth taut, a little slimmer than she remembered.

"Hi, Dad." She stepped into the room and into his embrace, her eyes misting unexpectedly at the familiar woodsy fragrance of his cologne. She held him at arm's length and looked him over. "Have you lost weight?"

"Perhaps a pound or two," he said. He smiled and crinkles appeared at the sides of his eyes. He stepped back and eyed the blinged-out sock London had given her. "Faye told me about your ankle. How is it?"

"Better every day."

"A horse threw you, correct?"

"Yes. She got spooked by a snake and I couldn't hang on. First time I'd handled reins in years."

"I remember how you used to love it, though. You learned on Robert's old nag, remember?"

Lauren thought about the ramshackle farm in Georgia, the one owned by her dad and her uncle Robert's father. The one that left the family's hands when Robert ran into financial problems and her father refused to bail him out. Lauren was saddened at losing the family land but couldn't blame her father. He'd bailed out Uncle Robert a lot.

"You look beautiful, Lorrie, though a little tired around the eyes. Are you being overworked?"

"I'm fine." With a limp barely noticeable, she took in the room as she walked over to the sitting area by the window—two high-backed chairs framing a round metal table covered with glass. The king-size bed looked grand and imposing, its brass-studded headboard with tufted black fabric covering a mattress that seemed to promise a heavenly night's sleep. It was a comfort her hardworking father deserved yet one that, given his sensible spending, surprised her. This single king-size room went for an average of two thousand dollars a night.

"I can understand why you chose the CANN but given the room rates, I'm surprised that you did."

"The company's paying for it, honey. My money doesn't stretch this far."

"So this *is* a business trip."

"Yes and no." Paul reached for a tumbler on a minibar counter Lauren just realized was there. She frowned slightly as he came over and sat down. Her father enjoyed a good, neat scotch and cigar as well as the next guy but usually only once in a while, after dinner, late at night. That it was midday and no food had been served caused a slight nervous flutter to return to her stomach.

"Dad, why are you here?"

"As I said before, we need to talk."

"What is so important that couldn't be discussed by phone?"

"Your future and making sure the choices you make are the right ones. When Faye told me you'd left the country with that notorious playboy, well, I knew you weren't thinking clearly."

"I'm a big girl, Daddy, a grown woman in fact. My mind is clear. I can take care of myself."

"Men like Breedlove are dangerous. You need someone sensible and grounded, who'll keep you safe in a loving home."

"And you think that's Ed?" Lauren snorted.

"Yes, I think that's Ed. And before you use my predicament as an excuse, this is not just about the money I owe. Over the past several months, I've had time to make my own observations. Ed is pragmatic and responsible, and he has loved you for a very long time. He believes that you two can be a power couple, that together our families can create a dynasty of generational wealth. Now, I don't know what happened years ago when you dated, but I think he's deserving of another chance."

"Dad, you've never cared one iota about who I've dated," she scoffed. "How can I not assume that your taking a loan from Ed has something to do with this new glowing view of him?"

"That I've never cared is not true. I've always been concerned, you just didn't know it. Ask your mother. She'll tell you. A secure future for my girls is all I've ever wanted. Thomas is a good man. Perfect for Renee."

She suppressed the urge to roll her eyes. "And you think Ed is perfect for me."

"Ed has become like a son to me. The one I've always wanted."

"Then I suggest you work something out with his dad, some kind of bilateral adoption so that he can join the family. An annoying older brother? Now that I can imagine. But a power couple, or any couple, Dad, that's not going to happen. When it comes to Ed Miller I couldn't be less interested. I am not going to date him. I am not going to marry him. There is nothing you can say that will make me change my mind."

A slight *click*, and then movement caught the corner of Lauren's eye. Ed was coming toward them, obviously from an adjoining room.

"I think there is something that might sway you, dear," he said with a sickening smile. "Paul, do you want to tell her? Or should I?"

# Sixteen

Christian knew there were several issues that required his attention that day but decided to work from home. He reached for the vibrating phone on his desk, looked at the number and sighed. Evidently the word had gotten out about Lauren joining him in Africa. He hadn't told her during their trip, but his phones had been blowing up with calls from half a dozen other women he'd casually dated in the past. Females who'd agreed to no-strings-attached friendships but had secretly hoped they might become Mrs. B.

That his private life hadn't remained private was extremely annoying. When it came to promoting the business, Christian lived for the camera, searched out chances for positive PR. Which made him even more guarded when it came to his private life. The less anyone outside of his family knew, the better.

No doubt Chloe was behind the leak that could only have led to rampant gossip. She always managed to know his business. If Christian ever discovered her source, that person would be fired immediately.

He leaned against the back of his chair, locked his fingers behind his head and turned to stare out the window at the peacocks dotting his backyard. He watched a pair of peahens walk by the three peacocks he'd personally chosen from a breeder in California. Similar to their human counterparts, when females were about, the cocks immediately began strutting their stuff, spreading their plumage in all its glory.

Christian smiled as the peahens continued across the yard to a fountain designed to not only provide them continuous water but to power an Old West water wheel churning into a koi pond. The age-old dance of court and conquer continued. The game had changed, he mused, thinking of the calls he'd ignored. These days, it was sometimes the woman shaking her tail feathers in hopes of attracting the man.

His thoughts drifted to the past couple years and the types of women he'd dated. And the years before that when he'd been the peacock, when his trust had been tested and broken.

Chloe. Who'd claimed to be pregnant, and wasn't. Pamela, who'd been snapped by a tabloid wearing a huge diamond ring and had hinted it was an engagement ring from Christian. It wasn't, and the lie led to the breakup with Erica, a Bahamian beauty, who at that time he thought was the love of his life. Natalie, who'd filed a felonious police report in an attempt to extort five million dollars from his family.

That nonsense with Natalie was the final straw that caused Christian to declare he'd never trust a woman again. Moreover, it had propelled him to set very clear boundaries with the women he dated, and brought on the need for confidentiality and nondisclosure agreements and women being vetted before they could enter his world.

His phone vibrated again. He didn't want to answer the call but pulled himself away from the window and crossed to the desk. Lauren. He smiled. The peahen who'd made him once again want to stick out his chest and spread his feathers, the one who not once had made him think about contracts and vetting.

A while back he'd wondered what it was about her that he found so intriguing. In this moment the answer came clearly: Lauren wanted nothing from him. He pressed the speaker button and answered the call.

"Hey, beautiful."

"Hey, hubby."

Her voice was sexy, seductive, made his manhood throb and reminded him of...wait. Did she say hubby?

"Sorry to bother you. I know you're working. But I'm here with my dad and he doesn't believe we got married."

Christian pulled the phone away from his ear and re-checked the name. Yes, it was the number he'd locked in the night of the fashion show, with a picture he'd snapped of Lauren lounging at his home in Djibouti, smiling from the screen. To say he was confused was an understatement. Was she trying to play a joke?

"Ed is here, too." *Ed? A former boyfriend?* "Ed Miller, my ex, the one I told you about in Djibouti."

The words made Christian's heart squeeze, along with the sound of subtle panic in Lauren's voice. It was high and bright and overly girlie, not the low, sometimes monotone quality he'd grown to love.

And she'd called him hubby. Said they'd gotten married. Something was going on. But what?

"Where are you?"

"At the ho—"

"Lauren?" He looked at the screen. It was black. The call had dropped. Or had it been disconnected? Was she okay? Why had her father come to town and brought her ex with him? His mind reeling with all the possible implications, he impatiently hit redial. The call rang and rang and finally went to voice mail. He hung up and tried again. Same thing. He called the hotel.

"Thank you for calling CANN, America's first seven-star hotel. My name is Zena. How may I help make your day amazing?"

"Zena, this is Chris Breedlove. I need to be connected to..." In this moment he realized he didn't know the name of Lauren's dad. "To a Mr. Hart."

There was a long pause. "His first name, please?"

"I don't know."

"I'm sorry, but I'll need his entire name to connect the call. We can't provide any information on our guests."

"Did you hear me? This is Chris Breedlove. As in the president of the hotel that employs you. As in your boss."

"I'm really so sorry, but how do I know this is you? We have very strict policies regarding the privacy of our—"

Cursing under his breath, Christian hung up the phone. It may have been the first time in his life he was pissed at someone for explicitly following the rules and being great at their job. And why hadn't Lauren called him back? Suddenly more concerned for her welfare than aggravated at the abrupt disconnection, or her call, he left his office and headed toward the hallway that led to his garage. He paused just briefly in front of the rack of keys beside the door, grabbed the one to his sports Lexus coupe and pushed the button to open the third garage door.

Seconds after he'd backed out of the space and headed down the long driveway, his Bluetooth announced a call. He hoped it was Lauren. It wasn't.

"Mom, has Lauren called you?"

"I'm well, son, thanks for asking. Good afternoon to you, too!"

"Sorry, but I don't have time for formalities right now. I just got a weird call from Lauren. She might be in trouble."

"What was weird about it?"

"For starters she lied to her father, told him that we got married in Djibouti!"

"Oh, dear."

"I told her about how Chloe tried to trap me and here she goes and does the same thing!"

"Lauren isn't manipulative like Chloe, honey. For her to do what she did, there had to be a very good reason. Something concerning her safety, or that of someone she loves."

"Do you know something?" he demanded.

"I probably have an idea."

"Well?" A frustrated hand ran through his tightly curled

coils as he navigated the roadway. "Do you want to let me in on it? Wait, did you already know about this?"

"About her saying you two were married? Of course not. I do know she left the East Coast to get away from an annoying, determined ex, the one who is probably at the hotel right now. If that's true, then I'm sure she had a very good reason to do what she did, and an explanation that will make everything make sense. For her to take such drastic action, her back had to be against the wall. Just let her explain, okay?"

Christian had heard enough. He shifted gears and gave the sporty luxury vehicle the chance to live up to its claim of zero to sixty in seconds. Victoria wouldn't tell him what was happening. Christian didn't care. All he knew was that Lauren had better do the right thing. He couldn't get to the hotel fast enough.

# Seventeen

The unexpected, insistent knock at the door caused all three in the room to jump. Conversation ceased mid-sentence as Lauren, Paul and Ed looked toward the door. Lauren's first thought was that someone had called security. Their talking had grown heated, and voices were raised. Perhaps, like her, a guest in one of the adjoining rooms had heard enough.

After sharing a brief look with her father, Ed walked to the door. He peered out the peephole.

"Who is it?" Paul asked.

"I don't know," Ed said, still looking.

"Security?"

Lauren's dad had voiced her thought.

"I don't think so," was Ed's curt reply.

Another knock came. It was louder this time, as though done with the meaty part of the hand and not with the knuckles.

"Lauren," the person outside of the room said. "I know you're in there. Open the door."

*Christian!*

She moved toward the door.

Ed spun around with his arm out. "Stay back."

"Open the door," Lauren said, feeling as though Christian were the cavalry come to save her. "Let him in!"

Another banging from the other side of the wood. "I'm giving you three seconds to open this door. Do it, or I will."

With one final glare, Ed opened the door. "Who are you?" he demanded. "And what do you want?"

Two seconds after the door to the hotel suite opened, Lauren knew what a knight in shining armor looked like. Christian took the cliché of tall, dark and handsome to a whole other level, and with his shoulders squared, eyes darkened with fury and his panther-like movements, he looked like a superhero. He pushed past Ed, who turned as if to attack him from behind.

"Don't even think about it." Delivered in a voice that was deadly quiet as the person behind it, Adam stepped through the door.

"Who are you?" Paul demanded. "What are you doing in my room?"

"Not quite the way I envisioned meeting my father-in-law," Christian drawled as he crossed the room, reached Lauren and slid a possessive arm around her waist. "But Mr. Hart—I assume you are Mr. Hart—I've come to collect my wife."

Paul's gaze shifted from Christian to Lauren. Her heart broke at the look of hurt in his eyes, and something else that seconds later she realized was abject fear.

"Do you want to stay here?" Christian asked her.

"No," she replied softly, as the gravity of the situation and of her knee-jerk declaration began to sink in. She moved toward her father. "Come with me, Daddy, so we can talk."

"You'd better take her up on it," Ed snarled. "It will be one of the last times you'll get a chance to do it without a sheet of Plexiglas between you."

Christian turned to Ed. "Is that a threat?"

"What's it to you? Mind your business. As for you—" Ed pointed an accusatory finger at Lauren "—know that whatever happens to Paul from now on lands squarely on your shoulders. Your father is getting ready to take a fall and you're the one to blame."

"Not if Gerald has anything to say about it. Unlike you, your dad is an upstanding man with character and integrity. He'll give Dad time to pay back what he owes. So save your threats for someone they'll scare."

"Do you think this is about money? No, it's about you. And if this marriage actually happened, you'll regret it, mark my words. There's more than one way to bring a man down. And his entire family along with him."

"That's enough." Two words delivered with such quiet authority that the room quieted in an instant. Christian stared at Ed for several heated seconds before speaking to Lauren.

"Sweetheart, why don't we give your father some time alone? I think everyone could use a break, a chance to calm down and…" Lauren felt his body stiffen as he turned to her ex. "A chance for you to get your things and get the hell out of my hotel."

Christian turned to Adam. "Can you handle that for me, baby bro?"

"Wait a damn minute," Ed snarled, clearly unaccustomed to being told what to do. "I'm a paying guest and this is a public space. You can't throw me out."

Christian took a step toward Ed. Adam blocked his path. "Take care of Lauren, brother." He slid his eyes toward Ed with quiet determination. "I've got this."

"Dad…" Lauren began, but Christian's grip suggested she had one choice, and that was to go with him.

"Your dad will be fine, Lauren," Adam said. "You have my word."

Lauren hugged her father. "Everything will work out," she whispered, having no idea given what she'd heard how that could be true. She reached for her purse without so much as a glance at Ed.

"This isn't over," he told her.

"It's over," Christian said.

He opened the door and led Lauren out of the hotel room without looking back.

"I can explain everything," Lauren whispered, mere seconds into the hallway.

From Christian, not a word, but the hold on her arm relaxed.

"I'm sorry," she offered.

His silence was loud.

They reached the elevator. He pushed the up button.

"Where are we going?" Lauren asked.

The elevator arrived. Christian pulled out a card and slid it into the slot. A panel opened, revealing six unmarked buttons. He pushed the top button on the right. Pulled out his card. The panel closed. He leaned against the elevator wall and stared straight ahead.

"Are you going to say anything?"

A sigh underscored his annoyance. "We're going where total and complete privacy is guaranteed. Once there, the only one who will be talking is you."

The suite they entered was beyond luxurious. The first thing Lauren noticed was the pool on the balcony more than a hundred feet in the air. She knew this wasn't the day for a guided tour, though. As soon as the door closed, Christian laid into her.

"Speak."

Lauren was immediately affronted but calmed herself down. He'd been blindsided by her the way she'd been bushwhacked by her father. He had a right to be angry and right now, she did not.

"Ed is blackmailing my dad."

She expected a response. When it didn't happen, she looked up. Christian stood waiting, arms crossed, clearly wondering what Ed and her father's issues had to do with him and marriage.

"It's a personal situation involving my father. What's happening between him and Ed is not my problem, or secret to share. To do so could get my dad in trouble. I know it sounds crazy and I want to, but I can't."

"You have no choice. Obviously your father coming here made his problem yours, one that caused you to lie and say we were married. Which now makes me involved in whatever's happening and that, darling, gives me a right to know all."

Lauren watched Christian cross the room and take a seat, as if to underscore the fact that without some type of answers they weren't going anywhere.

"You're right." She took a deep breath and joined him on the couch. "First of all, I'm so sorry for involving you. I'm not prone to lying and obviously don't do it very well, especially when in a state of shock. Finding out that my dad was here was enough of a surprise, but learning that Ed was with him only added to my angst."

"While this is all very interesting, sweetheart, would you mind cutting to the chase?"

"Okay…fine." Clenching her hands together on her lap, she finally blurted, "I thought Dad borrowed money from Ed. He didn't. He embezzled from the company and Ed found out. Ed threatened to file criminal charges on Dad unless he and I got married."

"And you thought to get out of marrying Ed by saying you were already married to me."

"The words jumped out before I could catch them. I didn't have time to think about the repercussions or you even finding out. It was just so I could buy enough time to help my father pay back what he owes Ed. But he didn't believe me so I was forced to call you and prove it was true."

"To prove that your lie was the truth."

Christian's brow furrowed. Even in her dismay Lauren couldn't help notice that she'd never seen a finer scowl.

"Basically."

"Why did your dad steal from the company?"

"That was the hard part of what I learned, the piece of the puzzle Dad kept from everyone, even my mom." Lauren paused, her heart breaking with the thought of how her proud father would never want anyone to know of the depths gone to because of his financial plight.

"He was deeply in debt and never told us, had taken out

a huge bank loan with their beautiful, forever dream home as collateral. He borrowed the money to repay that loan."

"He embezzled company funds to pay off a loan?"

"Yes, one that a friend at the bank set up to be repaid over a longer time than was usually allowed. That friend left. His replacement demanded the repayment be made immediately and in full. Dad is one of the most honest, upstanding and loyal men I've ever known. He fully intended to put back what he borrowed without anyone knowing what happened."

"But Ed found out," Christian surmised.

"Unfortunately, yes, which means Gerald, Ed's father who not only owns the company but is my dad's good friend, could also know the truth if Ed carried out the threat to tell him. Or worse, to call the police. Having Gerald think less of him would kill my father, and having the embezzlement made public would be like a tombstone on the grave. His name and reputation mean everything."

"How can a father use his own daughter as a pawn in a business deal?"

"I'm sure Dad didn't see it that way, at least not at first. Ed can be convincing. He had my father thinking that his intentions toward me were honorable. His true nature and threats of blackmail came only after I refused to go along with the plan.

"For the past few years it's been one blow after another, with my father treading water while trying to right a sinking ship. The moment Ed decided to check those books, his luck ran out."

"How much money are we talking?"

"Well into six figures. Enough to make what my father did a felony that, if Ed goes through with his threat, could get Dad locked up for a very long time."

"So Ed threatened to have your father charged if he couldn't have you. Sounds like a man obsessed, and after our trip to Africa, I can understand why."

The sudden tenderness in Christian's voice made Lauren's eyes misty and produced a slight smile. "I appreciate your saying that but trust me, the only person Ed is obsessed with is himself. He's used to getting what he wants and can't handle rejection."

"Ah, so you rejected him."

"Not fast enough," she confessed. "As you may have guessed, he's the ex I've mentioned several times when we've talked about dating."

"I did. The ex who now wants you back."

"The ex who wants to save face. Apparently he found another girl like I'd been, young, naive, and told everyone they'd be married. When their relationship ended, he needed another bride. That's when he tried to get back with me. My answer was no, unequivocally.

"His anger at the rejection and potential embarrassment turned into obsession. I had no idea he harbored these feelings, though, not until my dad did what he did and Ed felt he finally had a way to make me obey him. He's obsessed, but he doesn't love me. He wants to have his way. He wants control."

"That's why he's trying to force you into marriage, to keep your dad out of jail."

"Yes." Lauren turned toward Christian, her eyes angry, determined. "But I will not be manipulated. I just need time to figure out a solution. That's what I was thinking when I did what I did."

"But why me, though? You could have said you married anybody, even made up a name."

"I told you why. It was a reflex. I didn't have time to think."

Christian stood and walked over to the window. Lauren could only imagine how he felt. She'd given him a lot to process, and that while still being in shock herself.

Christian began speaking, still gazing out the window. All traces of tenderness were gone. "If what you said is true, it's a horrible story."

"What do you mean, if?"

He turned around. "I think you know the meaning of that word. And you know I've been lied to before."

"You think I'm lying, that I've made all of this up?"

Lauren got up and walked toward him, sure that he had to be speaking in jest. One look at his face, however, and she knew he was as serious as a brain surgeon in the operating room.

"Women have made up more for less."

Lauren was speechless. Not that it mattered, as Christian had much more to say.

"You show up suddenly and out of nowhere to work for my mother and within what, days, are in my bed."

"With a sprained ankle!"

"You push your way," he continued, voice raised, "into the company and the next thing you know you're heading to Africa on a private plane."

"You came to me with the idea of traveling to Africa."

"Only after my mother campaigned on your behalf."

"And I somehow manipulated that? I somehow put her up to having me take a trip I knew nothing about?" She shot daggers at him. "I didn't invite myself to Africa. You asked that I join you. And now that's my fault? Are you *kidding* me right now?"

"Do I look like I'm joking? My life is not a game, but I've been in it long enough to know that people will go to all sorts of lengths to get what they want, and I believe anybody is capable of doing anything."

Lauren was beyond livid. She couldn't think, could barely feel. Did he know how hard it had been to share the shame of her father? How he was being blackmailed and her back was against the wall?

"Somehow, this just got twisted. The only way that could have happened is for you not to have understood what I said."

"Oh, I understood you," he bit out.

"So you don't believe me? Is that it?"

Christian spun away from the window and stalked toward the door. "I don't know what to believe, but I know this. If one word about this fake marriage gets made public, you're going to have much bigger problems than you do right now."

# Eighteen

Lauren hadn't thought it possible to get angrier than she already was when Christian arrived in her father's room. But after their private conversation? She was surprised flames hadn't burst from her head. She could understand his being upset. She'd lied about their relationship, put him on the spot and involved him in a family matter much messier than she'd thought. But to think she'd done it on purpose? That there may have been an ulterior motive all along? What a blatant show of unmitigated gall!

*Really? You lied to a man and he called you on it. And you're mad at him?*

Lauren shrugged the devil off her shoulder and gripped the wheel. She hadn't planned to involve Christian in her drama. It had just happened. A small but necessary fabrication that would never be uttered outside of that hotel room. She hadn't had time to contemplate Christian's reaction, but couldn't have imagined he'd go ballistic.

All she wanted, and what she'd planned to tell him before the proverbial feces had hit the fan, was for Ed to think she was unavailable just long enough for her to sort everything out. She only thought to pretend she was married, and then only when she felt backed into the corner by the man she loved most in the entire world. A man who embezzled from his company, she thought, and the realization made her die just a little.

And then another thought rushed to the surface, one she had previously refused to consider no matter what, but now topped her very limited list of options. Marrying Ed would keep her dad out of prison.

Which brought her to the true crux of the matter—could

she turn her back on her father and watch him go to jail when she had the power to keep him out?

One thing was for sure. She could not, would not, remain in Nevada. Whatever happened with her dad and however she helped him navigate the future, it would be far away from the man who thought her a liar, a manipulator and a conniving fraud.

By the time she reached Breedlove and the estate, Lauren had formulated a foolproof plan. She tapped her Bluetooth to call Victoria. She wanted to be packed and out of there by morning. There wasn't a second to lose.

"Lauren, how are you? Is everything okay?"

"I've been better. Are you busy? Something's come up and I need to speak with you. Can I come by?"

"Certainly. Bypass the circular drive and come around back when you get here. Nicholas and I are enjoying drinks by the pool."

"Okay, but can we speak privately?"

"Of course."

She reached the estate and instead of turning left toward her guesthouse after being waved through by the guard, turned in the direction of the family mansion. A profusion of color from the tall trees that lined the drive bathed Lauren's chilled body in their majestic warmth. The peacocks that roamed the estate and that she had come to love strutted around proudly, roaming over the expansive front lawn. The pond stocked with fresh fish glimmered in the distance, and beyond it the orchard of pomegranate, apple, fig and plum trees dotted the countryside in perfect alignment. The estate was breathtaking, a veritable paradise. Lauren acknowledged a feeling of sadness. She was going to miss this place.

She drove past the circular drive as Victoria had instructed and followed it around the house and to a guest parking lot across from a side entrance, hidden from view by a wraparound fence, a gate and trees. She reached for

her purse. Her determination faltered a bit, but she had to
see this through. Taking a deep, energizing breath, she exited the car and hurried over to the backyard as fast as she
could manage with her still-healing ankle, now throbbing
from overuse.

Nicholas and Victoria were seated in one of several outdoor living spaces. Lauren hadn't seen this one before. Even
in her anger, she could see the beauty showing through.
Stone tile in deep, rich colors flowed from the back of the
house to the pergola anchoring the far side patio. The pergola held intimate seating, glass-top tables and a fireplace.
Next to it was an outdoor kitchen and to the right an infin-
ity pool. She approached Christian's parents with a tentative
smile. His father, Nicholas, debonair and incredibly handsome at fifty-five, stood as she approached.

"Hello, Lauren."

"Hello, Nicholas."

Something about his baritone voice and the fatherly way
he hugged her almost caused Lauren to burst into tears.
But she dug her nails into her palm and clamped down
the emotion. She was in a predicament at least partly of
her own creation, and while breaking down and losing it
would be totally understandable, she donned her big-girl
panties, squared her shoulders and leaned down to give
Victoria a hug.

"Hi, Victoria."

"I know you want to have girl talk," Nicholas said to
Lauren. "But I spoke with Christian on his way back from
Djibouti. He told me about you possibly coming on board
for the CANN Island project and drawing up a contract to
keep you with us for a while. Given how successful you
were with the fashion fund-raiser, I'm extremely excited
about that."

Lauren sat down as Nicholas walked away, glad he hadn't
waited for the response informing him that a contract between her and Christian would never happen. Nor would

anything else. Before the sadness in her belly could rise to her throat, she cleared it and began speaking.

"Victoria, something has come up and I want my contract terminated. Wait." She held up a hand. "Before you think this is déjà vu, please let me explain."

She provided a recap of what happened with Ed, with her dad and with Christian.

"In retrospect, *terminated* wasn't the right word. The day has been crazy and I can't think straight. I should have said modified.

"I will still do everything required in the agreement, but I'll do it from Maryland. Frankie and I have a great working relationship. He's talented and capable, and I trust him completely to carry out every detail. I can also fly in as the events approach and stay for several days until they're completed. I'm willing to do that at my own expense."

Victoria was quiet for a long moment. "First of all, darling, I'm terribly sorry for what you're going through. It's horrific, and criminal, and I think you should fight to not be dragged down in the mud. But running away is rarely a good answer." She reached out and squeezed Lauren's hand. "You ran here, right? And trouble followed. It is difficult but necessary to separate personal from business. For that reason I will not allow the agreement to be voided. This may sound harsh, Lauren, and I truly do empathize very much with your situation. But I will not aid in you abandoning your responsibilities, the foundation or me. The agreement must be honored."

Christian pulled into the circular drive but instead of going through the front door he walked around the backyard outdoor space where his mom often worked. He was mildly surprised to see Lauren's car there, extremely angry at the version of events that she was probably spinning to try to get Victoria on her side. He bounded out of the car and up to the door, took a breath to try to compose himself before walking inside. The effort was only partly successful. Fortunately it took him several minutes to find the two women. By the time he'd discovered them seated on a marble bench among vibrant exotic flowers and gurgling fountains, he'd gained control of his anger.

Lauren, apparently, had not.

One look at Christian and she rose from the bench, barely concealing what to Christian appeared to be an expression of disgust. "Victoria, I appreciate everything you've done for me. But I ask that you reconsider your decision and call Frankie."

"Seriously?" Christian called out after her. "You fabricate a marriage and then act like I'm the bad guy?"

Lauren wheeled around. "No, you're the guy who called me a liar!"

"Oh, my bad. I thought someone told her daddy that I was the husband, the man she'd married while in Djibouti."

"You know what I mean," she spat through gritted teeth, walking back to him with a finger aimed at his chest. "Yes, I lied and said I was married. I also told you why. I felt I had no choice! I laid all my cards out on the table, shared confidentialities because you'd accept nothing less, and what do I get back? Your cynicism and disbelief, your haughty, self-absorbed accusations. On the worst night of my life I learn that you've been living with the delusional premise that I've hoodwinked your mom, moved across the country and flipped my world upside down all because of you."

Her next step placed the finger she'd pointed squarely in his chest.

"There may be a line of women from here to Hong Kong who have that intention. But I—" *poke* "—am—" *poke* "—not in it."

She stepped back, spent, her chest heaving. Even in his anger he had to admit that her argument had been eloquently delivered, and having run frustrated fingers through her hair, she'd never looked more beautiful. Her eyes were fiery, bringing to mind the things he did to make them look that way. But then he remembered that it was those moments of weakness that had led to him letting down his guard in the first place.

"Are you finished?"

Lauren telegraphed her answer by spinning around and walking away.

"Lauren, wait!"

She increased her speed. He watched as what had been a disappearing limp became more pronounced. He ran after her and clamped a hand on her shoulder.

"Baby, please, be careful! You'll reinjure your ankle."

She shook off his hand. "Oh, now you're concerned about me being in pain?"

"You act like I don't have a right to be angry!" He stopped himself. "Look, let's just both take some time to calm down, okay?"

"We can do more than that. During the remainder of my contract, we can both take steps to see each other as little as possible."

The comment stung, but Christian shook it off. He took a step toward her. "What about CANN Island?"

Lauren's chuckle held no humor. "Clearly, working together is out of the question."

Another step and then, "Don't be so hasty to throw away the chance of a lifetime. Even enemies can come together if they've a mind to."

"What, for the Breedlove business?" she hissed as she reached the driver's side of her car.

He pinned her against it. "No, for this."

The kiss was hot and hard, possessive and intense, so good it took both of their breaths away. She pushed him back and got into the car. He watched her drive away, his lips still sizzling from the intense oral exchange. Deep in thought, he hadn't realized that Victoria had walked up and joined him.

"A smart man never makes a decision without having

all the facts," she said as the two continued to stare in the direction Lauren had driven.

"Are you saying that I should ignore the possibility of her planned duplicity after what I've gone through with others?"

Victoria placed a gentle hand on his arm. "No, son. I'm simply reminding you to be the smart man your father and I raised."

# Nineteen

"She refused to allow me to abandon her. She actually used the word *abandon*!"

"You did say you wanted out of the contract, did you not?"

"Yes, but not without a way to ensure plans continued to run smoothly," Lauren huffed. "My leaving would have led to your promotion. Whose side are you on?"

Hours had passed since the meeting with Victoria, and Lauren was no less angry now than then—resentful at Victoria's insistence she stay here, outraged at Christian for kissing her and furious at her own body for its betrayal. Even now her skin longed for his touch. She'd called Frankie and asked him to come over. She wanted help moving but now, even more, could really use a friend.

"Girl, lower your pressure before you have a stroke."

Lauren threw up her hands in exasperation. "My blood pressure is fine, okay?"

"Ooh, girl, watch it!" Frankie hurried toward her.

Lauren waved away the concern. "Don't worry about my ankle. It's basically healed."

"I'm happy to hear that, but it's not your injury I'm worried about. It's that vase you keep walking by, flailing your arms all around. When I came by that first time, I thought it looked familiar so I looked it up online."

"And?"

"It's from the Song dynasty, darling, that's the bougie folk in China." At Frankie's insinuation that she was culturally clueless, Lauren rolled her eyes. "That piece right there is a gourd from the 12th or 13th century, so if you don't have six figures and a ticket to Shanghai, you might not want to break it."

"So it's not my health you're worried about, but a pretty piece of porcelain?"

"Absolutely." Said with not one ounce of shame.

With Frankie's help, packing went quickly. It was her clothes mostly, and what she'd bought to create a home office in the dining room. She was thankful for his constant chatter. It helped keep her mind off the fact that her and Christian's…whatever it was…was in tatters. She'd been angry that he hadn't believed her, but more, she'd been hurt at the thought of their friendship coming to an end. That was the real reason behind her jumbled feelings and the hole in her heart.

Later she'd think about temporary housing, but for now she went online and secured a hotel room in Henderson, Nevada. She rented a car, and Frankie drove her to get it. After helping her load her things in the trunk and promising he'd meet her at the foundation offices tomorrow, he left for a rendezvous with a guy he'd met online. There was only one thing left for Lauren to do. She sat at the counter, opened her tablet and, after gathering her thoughts, began to type.

Victoria,
Please accept my apology for this afternoon's outburst. It's been a very challenging day. Despite the version you may have heard of what happened, I never meant to involve Christian in the drama. I have no ulterior motive for working with you. I am not out to trap your son. I respect him too much to ever do that and as much as I've tried to deny it, have developed true feelings for him, a fact that I hope can remain between us. That he thinks I've deceived him breaks my heart.

While I admit to wanting to immediately cut all ties with Breedlove, Nevada, I respect your insistence that I be a woman of my word. I enjoy working for the foundation, and with you, and will do my very best to make the remaining events not only successful, but the talk of the town.

Thank you so much for the generosity extended in offering one of your guesthouses for my stay. However, as of the writing of this note, I will no longer be here. I have made arrangements to live elsewhere, have secured a rental to get around and for the duration of the contract will work from the foundation offices. Considering the events that transpired today, and now knowing my true feelings for Christian, I'm sure you can understand. I remain eternally grateful for all you've done to help me and for the wonderful friendship you share with my mom. Until tomorrow...

Lauren hesitated only briefly before pressing Send. She closed the tablet, placed it in her tote, then took one last walk through her temporary home. It was the most beautiful residence in which she'd ever lived, and she was thankful to have stayed here. She'd miss it as much as or more than she'd miss the land itself. Most of all, she'd miss Christian, and would cherish the love affair that began within these walls. But life went on, and she had to move with it.

With a wistful sigh, she placed the card key on the counter, walked out of the front door, closed it softly behind her, and headed out of the Breedlove utopia and into the world where normal people lived.

The next day Lauren rose early, determined to get back to the business of the foundation and not deal with either her conflicting feelings for Christian or the drama involving her father on company time. It wouldn't be easy. Christian's kiss had seared her heart, branded her soul to the point that, except for dreams about him, she got no sleep at all. It wasn't just the sex she missed, she thoughtfully admitted. It was the man. A man whose absence left a void she doubted could be filled.

Fortunately for her, at least she'd be busy. It was roughly six weeks before the foundation's spring gala and there were a thousand details to handle between now and then. After showering, she blew dry and flat-ironed her hair, taking more care with her overall appearance. No longer working from home, and heading into halls undoubtedly roamed by upper-level millionaire executives, Lauren wanted to look the part, to fit right in. So after studying her options she'd decided on an ivory-colored wraparound dress, a strand of iridescent coral pearls she'd purchased in Djibouti, and even though she'd probably pay for it later, paired her braced sprained ankle with a three-inch ivory pump.

As with everything connected with the business of Breedlove, the foundation offices were located at the CANN, smartly appointed facilities of varying sizes and configurations on the building's fifth floor. There were meeting rooms and establishments that catered to the hotel's corporate customers including an office supply store; a print, mail and shipping company; a luxury car rental; and a travel agency booking everything from first-class flights to private planes and helicopters.

Entering her office, Lauren was pleasantly surprised to see that Frankie had beaten her there. They hugged and she walked through the bright, airy, contemporary space and sat behind her desk. She probably should have come here sooner. Setting up in an office made her feel better and ready to work.

"You want something from the coffee shop?" Frankie asked. "I had a one-eye-open cup of java and I need another one to open the other eye."

"A caramel latte sounds delicious. And a bagel if they have it. Multigrain. Thanks."

Lauren moved a stack of files from her desk out to Frankie's. She stopped at the stereo panel, found some smooth jazz and returned to her desk. The silky saxophone notes that oozed into the room conjured up pictures of Christian, naked and sated, his eyes half-open, watching her. With a huff, Lauren pulled out her laptop. She'd just fired it up when she heard the door open. Not long enough for Frankie to have gotten the coffee already.

"All right, girlfriend. What did you forget?"

"To listen, maybe?"

*Christian.* Lauren slowly turned around as he strode toward her, looking like a cool drink of water on a hot summer day. She tamped down emotions and kept her face a mask.

"Maybe yesterday I judged you too harshly. I've been burned a lot, and it's made me cynical. I hope you understand."

"Is that an apology?"

"Did you offer me one?"

They stared each other down, eyes blazing. Lauren blinked first, turned back to her computer. "I've got too much to do to deal with you right now. But just so you know, those listening skills still need work."

"Lauren, I'm sorry."

She could hear the effort that apology cost him, and turned back around. "Me, too. And while I've apologized before, I could also be more understanding. It was a terrible position to be in. You had every right to be angry."

"You're not the kind of woman who'd have to use any underhanded tactic to get a man, me or anyone else."

"Are those Victoria's words, or did you come to that conclusion on your own?"

"They're my words, but I'm sure Mom would agree with me. Dad, too, for that matter."

She watched him take a step toward her, saw his eyes darken and braced herself. "I missed you last night."

"Yeah," she whispered, barely audible. "Me, too."

"It's crazy. I dreamed of you."

"You did?" She swallowed the truth that tickled her throat, that she'd dreamed of him, too.

"Want to know what we were doing?"

Her smile matched his. "I think I can guess."

"We were back in Djibouti, in the glass-bottom boat. You were naked. And there, with some of the finest beauty in all of the world, all I saw was you."

Lauren's legs threatened to buckle beneath the sensuality of his dream. She abruptly sat and changed the subject. It was either that or close the door and take him on the desk.

"Thanks for stopping by, Christian. There's a ton of work to do in the next couple weeks, but I promise to get all the matter with Ed, and your part in it, straightened out."

"If you don't, I will."

"You won't have to," Lauren countered. "This is my business. I said I'd handle it, and I will."

"Okay."

They looked at each other. A second passed, then two. Their eyes conveyed words that didn't need to be spoken. Lauren inwardly admitted what she'd too long denied. She not only loved Christian Breedlove, she was falling in love with him.

He cleared his throat. "Speaking of business, listen. You've got skills that the company can use, and from the sound of things your being in Vegas is beneficial to you, too. So let's try to focus on work when we're working and handle personal affairs when we're not on the clock. Fair enough?"

"That's fair."

Just then, Lauren noticed a leather-bound portfolio Christian carried. He held it out to her.

She reached for it. "What's this?"

"A proposed contract for you to work on CANN Island. Look it over, run it past your attorney, make any changes you desire. After that we can meet and hammer out the official version for your signature."

Lauren flipped through the pages. "When do you need this back?"

"The sooner, the better. While part of CANN International, we want the island project to have its own special branding with a cool tagline, such as what you designed for the jewelry video. We want to get brochures done and videos shot. Collateral for both investors and visitors, too."

"Sounds like a lot of work, especially on top of what I'm already doing for Victoria and the foundation."

"I understand, and when working on major events, the foundation will still be your priority," he reassured her. "What I'm asking for should come during the foundation's downtimes, depending on how much time you'll need for the projects I'm proposing. It'll take a bit of adjusting on both our parts, but I believe we can work it out."

"I do, too."

Christian nodded and headed for the door.

"Christian."

"Yes?"

"Thank you."

His eyes darkened as they slid from her eyes to her lips. Quivers traveled from her core to her nether set. For several seconds neither spoke, but again, messages were communicated.

"You're welcome."

He left. Lauren let out the breath she didn't know she'd been holding. How could she work beside that man and not be intimate when her entire body craved his touch? It was a question she mulled over all day long but even after midnight, as she crawled into bed, she didn't have the answer.

# Twenty

"Big brother!" Said in stereo by Noah and Nick as they burst through the private entrance to his spacious office without bothering to knock.

"The dynamic duo," Christian said drily. "Ill-mannered and uninvited. Just what I need."

"You'll take back those words in a minute." Noah plopped into one of two chairs facing Christian's desk, with complete irreverence for the superlight gray cashmere Enzo D'Orsi original that had set him back almost six figures. "We've got an idea that will blow your mind!"

"And some great news to go along with it!" Nick added. He reached into a crystal bowl of mints, unraveled the plastic wrapper and popped it in his mouth.

Great news? He could use some. Lauren's betrayal had left him in a serious funk. Even now, days after he and Lauren came to a tenuous truce and with him finally believing the story about why she lied, the deception had put an unsightly mark on a woman he thought could be the missus. If he were looking for such a thing. Which he wasn't.

*You're married to CANN, remember?*

With all of the other women, this line had worked. He'd said it, and he'd meant it. But not today. His heart literally ached at the thought that the possibility of a lifetime with Lauren had been destroyed. But this was a personal matter, and he was on the clock. So he took a deep breath, forced his mind back on business and hid his angst beneath a casual smile.

"I have a feeling I could live to regret this but, all right, what's this bright idea?"

"CANN Isles," Noah began dramatically.

"Oh, like the one being planned in Djibouti? Were it not for the fact that Noah sat in on the quite extensive sales presentation, I'd say great minds think alike. Instead I'll just say…get out."

"Not so fast, thundercloud," Nick said. "We know you're proud of that latest baby, especially since our phones are blowing up with interested investors from all over the world."

Noah sat up and leaned forward, fixing Christian with a laser stare. "So, check this out. CANN Island is the deluxe version, in Djibouti, right? And on private islands dotted across the country, smaller versions of your grand idea will become known as… CANN Isles. Off of the most scenic coasts of every continent. Genius, right?"

Christian looked between the twins, searched for the twinkle in their eye that would tell him they were joking. They were not.

"You do know that isn't a novel idea, that people buy islands and build mansions on them."

"Right, mansions. Not hotels. And not like us."

"There may be a reason," Christian countered. "Like not wanting to sink a building of high-paying guests into the big blue."

He looked at his watch, fired up his computer and began going over notes for a meeting taking place in an hour.

"You're not getting it," Nick said. He hopped out of the chair and paced the room. "We're talking boutique hotels—limited number of rooms, very exclusive."

"With perks and amenities unparalleled," Noah said, counting on his fingers. "Butlers, private chefs, complimentary top-shelf drinks and a bottle of premium Dom on arrival."

"Isle to land service via a customized private plane."

Christian harrumphed with a slight headshake. *Offering my plane as part of guest perks? Kids… I swear.*

"I was in New York over the weekend," Nick said, following his brother in typical tag team fashion. "And a unique opportunity presented itself. A private island, ten square miles, with a view of Manhattan."

"What was the opportunity?" Christian asked.

"It was for sale, just came on the market," Nick replied. "And I bought it."

This got Christian's attention. He leaned back in his chair, watched as the twins shared a cocky smile between them and felt a little burst of pride in his chest. "Okay, duo dudes, tell me more."

For the next thirty minutes the twins shared their vision. When they finished, Christian was more than intrigued. "Put something together for Dad and me," he told them. "Do either of you have something pressing in the next hour or so?"

They both shook their heads.

"Good, I think it would be beneficial to have you two in this meeting."

He reached for the office phone, a sign of dismissal. The twins took the hint and quietly exited the room. Christian wanted them gone but there really was a call to make, to one more person who should be in the meeting. Lauren.

She arrived just moments before the start of his presentation and took his breath away. Her look was simple sophistication, impeccable. He never dreamed a tailored business suit could look so sexy. Her hair was still straightened, but today it was pulled into a high ponytail that emphasized her almond-shaped eyes and high cheekbones. Red lipstick boldly brought attention to her succulent lips. He watched the men pause as she walked into the room and VP Greg Chapman become a bumbling idiot as he rushed to pull back her chair. Noah sidled over with admiring eyes taking her in, leaned down and said something that made Lauren laugh.

Christian wanted to kiss her and choke him.

"All right, gang," Christian began a few minutes later. "Let's get started. Some of you have met Lauren Hart." He gestured toward her. She nodded, a pleasant, professional look on her face as she made eye contact with the eight people at the table besides Christian and her.

"Lauren relocated from the East Coast to help Victoria Breedlove with a series of CANN Foundation fund-raisers, an important component of the overall organization and one that helps thousands of people live better lives, both here in the state of Nevada and around the world.

"Two weeks ago the foundation held its annual fashion show and tea, and thanks to Lauren's uniquely creative marketing expertise, it became the most profitable fund-raiser in the ten years the foundation has been in operation."

He waited a beat to let that fact sink in, and watched respect and admiration be added to the subtle look of lust in their eyes.

"I had a chance to view part of Ms. Hart's campaign and got an idea of why the event experienced record-breaking success and immediately thought that skill set could be advantageous to CANN International as we move forward with several new ventures, the first of which is CANN Island.

"As some of you know, Ms. Hart and I recently traveled to Djibouti for a series of meetings, all of which went quite well. The government is well aware of what a business like ours can do for their economy, and they've been extremely welcoming and helpful. I also met with several investors and potential partners for the retail and entertainment aspects of the overall plan, all of which I've condensed into a report that by the time you return to your offices will be in your inbox." He cleared his throat. "However, for right now I'd like to formally welcome Lauren to the team and ask her to say a word or two regarding her thoughts on the visit and our future in African tourism." He watched her eyes flare briefly at the unexpected request, even as she scooted her chair away from the table. "Lauren?"

Lauren stood and joined Christian at the front of the

room. "Do we have any Boy Scouts?" she asked, holding up her hand.

A couple men held up a hand or a finger.

"I was a Girl Scout, and those of you who were Boy Scouts know the motto that was drilled into our learning experience. Be Prepared. That advice has served me well throughout the years, as it does now in being called upon for an impromptu presentation." She looked at Christian with a deceptively kind smile. "I'm prepared."

The men laughed and even the couple she saw who for whatever reason were clearly not happy seemed to loosen up a bit. She was confident and well-spoken as she gave a brief bio that included personal information such as her western roots, her college education and awards, and her professional history that included work with Fortune 100 and 500 companies.

"I believe there are some things that can't be taught," she finished, "or even learned. And while I appreciate both my higher learning and the experience I've gained, my uniquely creative way with words, as Christian put it, I believe is a gift, something that's always come naturally. I was thrilled to learn that the ideas put forth for the Valentine's Day fashion and tea resulted in a record-breaking fund-raiser. I look forward to working on the for-profit side of CANN and breaking even more."

Christian scanned the room as Lauren spoke, his coworkers, peers, in the palm of her hand. He was no exception. It was the first time he'd witnessed her in a corporate environment. He'd been enthralled, smitten, while watching her effortlessly navigate the high-ticket fashion show's rarefied air. But here, on his boardroom turf, she was just as natural and even more impressive. Beautiful and smart, a winning combination. Even for a woman he couldn't marry. He ignored the errant thought, focused on her lips and remembered the long moments he'd gotten lost just kissing them.

When he knocked on her office door an hour later, kissing was still very much on his mind.

"Hey, beautiful," he said when she beckoned him in. Lauren made a face. "Sorry, I forgot. It's business hours. Hey, Lauren."

He was rewarded with a smirky smile. "Mr. Breedlove, how can I help you?"

"By joining me for lunch."

"I wasn't planning on taking a lunch. Being at the meeting and learning more about CANN was very beneficial, but it took a chunk out of my workday."

Lauren came out from behind her desk to place a book on the history of casinos and the Las Vegas Strip back on the office's well-organized shelves. "I think I'll go online, check out the restaurant menus and have something delivered."

When she turned, Christian was there, a hair's breadth away. "It's not good to work on an empty stomach," he whispered. "I think we should…eat."

He leaned over and removed the inch of distance between their mouths, capturing the lips that back in the boardroom had driven him insane. Lauren responded as he'd hoped she would, stepping closer, her hands running up his chest to encircle his neck. He brought his hand up to the delicious peaks that he loved to swirl with his tongue, slid his hand beneath her top and under her bra. Lauren moaned. His manhood swelled. She began grinding against it, undid his belt and reached for his zipper. The movement made him as hard as a rock. Then she stopped.

"No," she mumbled, stepping away from him. "We can't do that. I can't. Not here, not now. There's still so much uncertainty, so much to work out."

"I'm sorry."

"Don't be. I wanted it. I still do."

"Lunch, then…" Lauren shook her head. "No private room. I'll even do fast food in the main casino, surrounded by hundreds of tourists and clanging slot machines."

"Somehow that's impossible to envision. You being handed a hot dog and fries in a paper bag."

"If it meant spending more time with you," he drawled, "I'd eat the paper bag."

Lauren returned to her chair behind the desk. "You're not making this easy."

"I hope not."

She walked around the desk and reached for her purse. "Where are we going?"

His smile was as bright as sunshine. "That's my girl."

They bypassed the upscale food court and settled on a restaurant boasting American fusion cuisine and run by a celebrity chef. They ordered their meals and in a mutual yet unspoken agreement climbed above the touchier matters to safe, innocuous subjects.

Lauren stopped eating a scrumptious salmon salad and wiped her mouth. "Did you ever want to do anything else?" At his genuinely confused look, she added, "You know, besides working for the family business?"

Christian smiled and shook his head. "No, never. From my earliest memories, I worshipped Dad, wanted to be just like him, do everything he did. I vividly remember getting my first suit—three piece, navy—an exact replica of one that he wore. I cried when it was time for bed and Mom said to take it off. She had to threaten me with a spanking before I obeyed her."

"Oh my gosh! How old were you?"

Christian rubbed his chin. "Three, almost four."

"I can only imagine. You were a handful."

He fixed her with a look. "I still am."

The atmosphere shifted. Both tried to ignore it. But when they simultaneously reached for the salt and their fingers touched, the truth couldn't be denied. The attraction was still there—strong, powerful and hotter than ever.

# Twenty-One

Strained didn't begin to describe the next few weeks. Lauren saw Christian more than ever. They worked out a deal for her participation in the Djibouti CANN Island project. Not much work, really. Christian made her an offer she'd be a fool to refuse. She'd earn twice the money that she'd made anywhere else while putting in fewer hours for CANN International and enjoying the perks of a full-time employee.

Only once had he asked about her father and Ed, and if she'd told them about the fake marriage. He was constantly traveling and immersed in plans for CANN Island. Work seemed to have pushed what happened to the back of his mind. For Lauren, however, the situation remained at the forefront and continued to loom large over her happiness. Ed continued to harass her, threatening to out her father's dark deed and calling her marriage to Christian a sham. "Why can't I find anything online?" he'd asked. This weekend he'd have his answer. Lauren would tell the truth and let the chips fall where they may.

As the plane neared the airport and began to descend, she looked out the window. The gray skies and raindrops sliding down the small windows seemed appropriate as they mirrored her feelings exactly. Conflicting emotions warred inside her, and it was hard to know what to feel. In the moment, she was numb, feeling nothing at all as thoughts chased memories, bumped against each other and then melted together, becoming one endless scenario of despair and ecstasy, frustration and chaos.

The pressure in her ears increased as the plane continued lower. She worked her jaws to pop them, watched as the silvery ribbons turned into highways and the green swaths became lawns and trees. Was it really less than two months ago that she flew to where Christian's jet had been customized, and then touched down in Vegas on his birthday to escape her old life and search for a new one? Where her preteen crush turned into the greatest whirlwind romance of her life only to dissipate in an equally short time? And the biggest question of all: Could they rise above the drama, have their lust turn into love, and have their flickering desire become a lasting flame?

Unlike Thanksgiving or Christmas, Easter travel was the same as any regular weekend in the nation's capital. Lauren had only brought a carry-on for the long weekend she'd be at home and made it through Washington National rather quickly. On the way from the Jetway she'd texted her mom, who pulled up curbside within minutes of her nearing the exit. She withstood the steady drizzle sans umbrella, threw her carry-on into the back seat and gave her mom a hug.

Faye hugged her back tightly. "It's so good to see you, honey."

"It's good to see you, too. Although honestly, I was less than excited to come back home."

"Given the circumstances, I'd feel the same way." Faye checked her rearview mirror and eased away from the curb. "I'm so sorry about everything that's happened. So is your father. After what happened in Las Vegas, he took a good look at Ed, asked around about him. The coworkers didn't hold back."

"What did they say?" Lauren asked.

"That he's a jerk, basically, the same as you said. Paul went to Ed and told him that he no longer supported his desire to marry you. Despite what may happen to him, Paul demanded he leave you alone."

"That couldn't have been easy."

"No, and it didn't go over well."

"What happened?"

"Ed reiterated his threat to tell Gerald about the embezzlement. That's when your father turned the tables."

"How?"

"Just yesterday, he called a meeting with Ed and Gerald and told him everything."

Lauren whispered, "Oh my God."

"From what transpired after that, the man upstairs was definitely present. Gerald isn't going to press charges, honey."

Lauren dropped her head in her hands. "Thank God!"

"He was hurt, very hurt, and disappointed. But Paul told him the whole story without holding back—about the fledgling business, even after Gerald's investment, the mortgages on the house and Ed's threats. Gerald was really angry about that. He couldn't believe his son would try to blackmail someone into marrying him. I think that's what really gave Gerald the compassion to forgive Paul and accept restitution instead of pressing charges."

Lauren sat silent, too stunned to react. This news changed everything! With Ed's threat no longer a cloud over her head, she could reveal the sham to him and then go on with her life. She could think about a future in Breedlove, Nevada. She could think of a lifetime with Christian.

"Did Dad lose his job?" she finally asked.

Faye shook her head. "Paul offered his resignation but Gerald refused it, again showing what kind of true friend he is. It's hard to believe an apple like Ed fell from that tree. He did order a full audit, though. And there will be financial oversight from an outside company for the next five years. Paul will have to pay for that. But all in all, given what could have happened, this is an outcome beyond what we could have dreamed."

As the conversation shifted to other topics, Lauren's mood lifted. She took in the city with brighter eyes. She noticed the last of the cherry blossoms on thin, bobbing branches and appreciated the blending of old and new in the

city's regentrifying neighborhoods. They reached the wide
avenues of Brandywine, with its large manicured lawns and
white oak and Virginia pine trees. The Harts' home on the
corner lot anchored their block. Tall, white and imposing
with black shutters and gleaming glass, multicolored flowers against the wrought iron fence, and a red cobblestoned
drive made it stand out, a fitting tribute to what the upper-
class builders had in mind when development of the tony
area began. Lauren's heart swelled with gratitude. The threat
was over. Her parents would not lose their home.

After placing her luggage into her old bedroom, now a
guest room, Lauren called Ed. She put the call on speaker,
pacing as she waited for him to answer the phone.

"Hello?"

"Ed, it's Lauren."

"Lauren. To what do I owe the pleasure?"

Lauren ignored the attitude in his voice and responded
as pleasantly as she could. "I just talked with Mom. She
told me what happened, that Dad told your father the truth.
I wanted to share a truth as well."

"What, that you'll marry me?"

Lauren plopped on the bed she'd slept in for years. "Ed,
you don't want to marry me. You just don't like to lose.
There is someone out there for you. Someone who can do
more for you and your image than I ever could. I know you
love moving and shaking in the tristate area, and I've extended my contract in Nevada. I'll be staying out west. You
need someone here, a socialite, someone who'll look good
on your arm and wants to be there."

She waited, hoped for a civil exchange. No matter how
she felt about Ed, his father, Gerald, was a man she greatly
respected. Not many in his position would have forgiven
her father and kept him employed.

"What if I'm not ready to let you go?"

"You can't hold on to what you've never had. There is

no chance of a romance between us. We need to end this madness, now."

"Or what?" Lauren could hear Ed's rising anger through the phone. "You going to sic the Breedlove brothers on me? Well, let me tell you something, baby. I'm not afraid of those effeminate dudes. And if they ever come east, on my turf, they'll find that out."

She ignored the jab, refused to take the bait. "Speaking of the Breedloves, I have a confession to make."

"You're not married to that asshole," he hissed. "I already know."

"I lied because I felt pressured, like my back was against the wall."

"Lies can get you into trouble."

"I know, which is why I wanted to clear everything up."

"Consider it cleared."

"So this is it? The harassment's over?"

"You have nothing I want," he said.

"I wish you the best, Ed."

"Have fun out west."

The cordiality in his voice was obviously fake, a tone that gave her the chills. She tried to dismiss the foreboding feeling. But as she ended the call, she couldn't deny the truth: *that was much too easy.*

A veritable feast was being prepared at the Breedlove estate. The family gathered for a down-home cooked meal on the northwest side of the property at Papa Will Yazzie and Grandma Breedlove Yazzie's rambling single-story farmhouse. It was one of a few times of year that Grandma Jewel forbade "chef anybody" or "catered anything" to darken her door. Christian knew that Easter was one of his grandmother's favorite holidays. It reminded her of childhood—frilly dresses, colored Easter eggs and speeches at a small Methodist church.

For Papa Will, Grandma's second husband who had Native American roots, the holiday held less meaning. But he'd do anything to make "my Jewel" happy. And so would she for him, which is why the following weekend they'd head to New Mexico for the Gathering of Nations annual powwow.

Today, extended family from both sides had traveled from as close as California and as far away as Texas. Inside, the women ruled and in the kitchen, Grandma Jewel's domain, she was the captain of a mountain of sides—dressing, salads, macaroni and cheese—and it was all hands on deck. Even Victoria, who rarely stepped into any of the three kitchens located in her home, sat at the table, chatting with her mom Sylvia, dutifully and daintily separating the yolks from the whites of hard-boiled eggs for her sister's famous deviled eggs.

Outside, the brothers enjoyed hanging out with their cousins and friends. Nick and Noah played touch football with a group of their peers while Adam and some of the others attempted polo a short distance away. Others sipped beer and other libations on the wraparound porch. That's where Christian sat, keeping company with Papa Will, watching as he carefully basted a slow-roasting pig on a spit and listening as he spilled secrets on how he and Jewel kept the home fires burning and the love alive. "Humor and humility, mostly," he crooned, while basting the beast.

Cuts of beef and whole chickens sat on the grill; a whole turkey set dressed for the fryer, the smell of hickory and burning wood filling the air. His gaze drifted from Papa Will to the mountain in the distance, the one where after visiting their childhood cave Lauren had been thrown from the horse. He allowed the truth of the matter to fill his mind. He missed her, desperately. Reaching for his phone, he walked a distance into the yard as he hit the speaker button.

"Hey, beautiful."

"Christian, hi!"

"Wow, you sound happy. The East must be agreeing with you."

"I've never felt better." She gave Christian an update of what had happened over the past few days. "I can't believe that it's over. I'm so relieved."

"So am I."

"I know I've said it more than once but again, I'm really sorry for lying and putting you in such an awkward position."

"You did what you had to do. That's behind us now. Let's have it stay there. When are you coming home?"

"My flight leaves at seven and arrives at McCarran just after eleven," she answered.

"Text me the itinerary. I'll pick you up."

"You don't have to."

"I want to. And just so you know, you're coming home with me and spending the night. No argument. No excuses."

"I wouldn't offer any because there's no other place I'd rather be. I'll see you later, then?"

"You can count on it, beautiful."

Christian hung up the phone and joined the rest of the family gathering on the porch as dinner was served. There was more food, drink and laughter than he'd seen in a while. He was happy, almost giddy. There was one reason. Lauren.

At a little past nine, he hugged everyone goodbye and headed home to shower and change to meet Lauren at the airport. He was pleased to see her smiling face within moments of reaching the passenger pickup lane. Before he could exit the car she'd opened the back door and thrown her carry-on inside.

"I was going to do that for you," he drawled, soaking her up with his eyes.

She leaned over. "I know. I'm in a hurry. It's time to get wet."

The verbal nod to their earlier encounters was all the encouragement Christian needed to test his car's horsepower. He didn't have to check the speedometer to know that night he broke the law. Conversation was minimal during the short drive to Breedlove. They exited the car, giggling like teenagers as they pulled at clothes and each other from the garage to the great room. That first coming together was urgent, almost frantic, Lauren splayed across the back of the leather couch, urging him to take her from behind.

He pressed his tip against the wet entry beckoning him forward, then stopped.

"No!"

"Wait, baby. I need a condom."

"I can't wait," Lauren panted as she turned and reached for the massive hard shaft that was hot to the touch.

Her pleading was something he couldn't deny. He placed his hands on her hips, spun her back around and sank into paradise. The unfettered rawness of skin against skin drove the relentless pounding, along with Lauren's moans and growled commands. He squeezed her cheeks and slowed the rhythm to match the swivel of her hips. It was a perfectly executed dance for which they hadn't rehearsed, yet performed as though having done it a thousand times. When he reached for Lauren's silky folds, slid a finger between them and massaged her pearl, she came undone. He wasn't far behind. The reunion was super climactic, but they were just getting started.

"Come here," Lauren whispered when she'd regained her breath.

"Where are we going?"

She didn't answer, just reached for his hand and headed to the master suite. Once there she continued to the customized shower, stared at the various knobs and showerheads.

"How do you work this thing?"

Christian laughed. "What do you want? A single flow, duel pumps, a rain forest effect?"

"Definitely the rain forest."

Christian turned on the water and joined Lauren beneath the flow. She poured bath soap into her hand and then, forgoing a sponge, used her body as the friction to unleash the bubbly scent. That done, her eyes locked with his, she began a trail of kisses. His neck, pecs, abs, hips, until taking his hardened heat in her hands and stroking its length as she stuck out her tongue and outlined his perfectly mushroomed tip. Over, and again, before taking him in, her warm cavern causing goose bumps all over his skin. She lavished him from head to toe. Then he returned the favor. As trails of orange, purple, pink and blue announced the dawn, Christian and Lauren climbed into his bed, wrapped themselves around each other and fell into what was for both the first night of dreamless sleep in a while.

# Twenty-Two

Lauren awoke with a smile on her face. She looked over at Christian, who was also awake, also smiling and looking at her.

"Hey."

"Hello, beautiful."

She rolled into his arms. "Did last night really happen?"

"All the way into the morning."

"Ha!" Lauren sat up and stretched. "I feel amazing! Oh, but wait a minute."

"What?"

"What about our stateside rule?"

"What about the friends-with-benefits exception?"

"Right. It's kind of like having our cake and eating it, too."

Christian shifted his body and kissed her breasts. "Speaking of...are you hungry? Because I could definitely eat again."

"Something tells me you're not talking about a dish that the chef can cook up."

"Naw, you rule this particular kitchen."

Lauren slid down alongside Christian. Just as they began to kiss, his cell phone rang. He looked over, saw that it was Adam and declined the call with one of the prepared messages. Busy. Call you later. Within seconds, his text and email notifications began going off like crazy. He frowned, reached for the phone and placed his finger on the fingerprint scanner to unlock it. Figuring that the texts and emails could be part of a scam, he instead tapped the screen to return Adam's missed call. He put the call on speaker and pulled Lauren into his arms.

"What's up, bro?" he asked.

"There's no easy way to tell you," Adam replied. "But

you need to brace yourself. Because your fake wedding is all over the news."

"What?" Adam's words sat Lauren straight up.

"Is that Lauren?" Adam asked.

"Hey, Adam. Yeah, it's me. What's going on?"

"That's what you need to tell my brother. Christian, I sent one of the links to your phone. You need to check it out... ASAP."

The line went dead. Christian turned and looked at her. His expression was confused, yet cold. She could tell he fought to stay calm.

"Well?"

"Christian, I swear I don't know what's going on."

He got out of bed, donned a pair of shorts and reached for his phone. He scrolled the face, reading whatever Adam sent him, she presumed. His jaw clenched in anger. She got out of bed.

"What does it say?"

"You didn't talk to anyone back east?"

"Only the conversation with Ed that I told you about. Where I admitted to having lied about being married."

"Where did the conversation take place?"

"Over the phone. What are they saying in the article?"

"Not what you said you told Ed. Put on your clothes. This party is over. I'll take you back to your place where you can read it for yourself."

Lauren went in search of her clothes. By the time she'd slipped into them Christian was dressed, too, with keys in hand.

"Christian, wait." She whipped out her phone, did a quick internet search on Christian's name and clicked on the first link that appeared.

"You can't possibly believe I had anything to do with this," she said, after reading the first damaging paragraph.

"You told me the conversation with Ed was cordial, that he agreed to leave you alone."

"He did, but…" Lauren's words trailed off as she remembered the feeling that came over her when their call ended. "He said everything was fine and I desperately wanted to believe it, so I convinced myself that saga was over and done. But I felt something was wrong, off, about his demeanor. Like the resolution was almost too easy. This had to have been Ed's doing, Christian. He probably had it planned all along, as revenge if I told him no."

She looked at Christian, her eyes filled with regret. "Baby, I'm so sorry."

"I am, too. Let's go."

"I don't want to leave you, Christian. Not like this. Why don't I stay so that we can work through this together?"

"Maybe later," he said. "Right now there's work to do—conferencing and strategizing with attorneys and publicists. We've got a few fires to put out."

The drive from his house to the hotel was done in total silence. He pulled into the circular entrance and waved away the valet coming to greet them. Christian put the car in Park and after a long moment, held out his arms. Lauren fell into them and fought back tears.

"I'm sorry, baby," he said, moving his hands from around her and placing her away from him "I know this leak isn't your fault, but I can't help thinking that the lie you told Ed was the basis for this story." He held up a hand to stop her protest. "I'm not saying that what I'm thinking is right or even rational. What's happened in the past affects my present. And because of that, I can't be with you right now."

"So this time it's you putting the brakes on our making love?"

"I guess so." He put the car in Drive, a sign that their conversation was over. "But tomorrow it will be business as usual. I'll see you at work."

Lauren maintained her composure until she entered her room, then allowed the tears to flow. She pulled out her phone to call Avery and was surprised to see missed texts and calls. Only then did she realize she'd been so excited to see Christian that she'd never taken her phone out of airplane mode. When she did, she wished she hadn't. The sham marriage wasn't the blogger's only news. Her father's indiscretion had also been exposed.

Lauren called home. Faye answered the phone, distraught as Lauren imagined she'd be.

"Your father is holed up in the study," Faye finished. "I'm worried about him, Lauren. He's totally broken."

"Mom, I'm so sorry," Lauren cried, tears falling again. "It's all my fault."

"Ed Miller is to blame for this. I'd bet everything I own that he was behind this article. Your dad stood up to him, and he couldn't stand it."

"Should I come back home? Do you think Dad would feel better if I talked to him?"

"Nothing can help right now, dear. Except prayer. Will you do that?"

It had been a while since their last conversation, but when Lauren ended the call with Faye she closed her eyes and asked God for the biggest favor in her entire life.

The next day Lauren and Victoria met in the Breedloves' home. Victoria was gracious, as usual. She could afford to be more objective than her son. The family had endured greater scandals, she assured Lauren, and said no doubt there'd be more. She even offered the guesthouse back for Lauren's extended stay. But Lauren moved out of the hotel in Henderson and found a condo to sublet not far from the Strip and threw herself into work for the foundation.

When at the hotel working with Christian, she hid her heartache at his distance behind a professional veneer. Did she miss making love with him? Absolutely. Did she think it was possible for them to have a relationship? No idea. Lauren couldn't figure out her own feelings, much less try to meld them with someone else's. She was worried about her parents, who'd indeed retained legal counsel, even though

Gerald penned a response that blasted his own son. Fortunately for her, the foundation's second major gala—a Saturday-night concert during Memorial Day weekend—was taking place in just three weeks. Between overseeing that project and working on CANN Island, she had precious little time to think of Christian, how much she missed him or if she would ever feel his arms around her again.

The following Monday, her second week back in Nevada and first full day in the office at CANN, Lauren worked twelve hours. She was exhausted but felt immense satisfaction from being in control of something she was good at and getting things done. Being the last person in the office, she turned off the lights, locked up and headed to executive parking, dreaming of Chinese takeout, a long, hot shower and a good night's sleep.

"Hello, Lauren."

Lauren turned toward the voice, where the private elevator doors had just opened. Even without turning around she would have known it was Christian. He looked good enough to eat and as tired as she was, she still wanted to.

"Hey."

"Trying to avoid me?" he asked.

"No."

Lauren continued toward her car.

Christian fell in alongside her. "Just another day at the office, burning the midnight oil?"

"I got the email about the meeting next week and was getting a head start on my presentation. With the upcoming concert, this was one of the only days I could focus on CANN Island."

"Your work is impressive. Even my haters have taken notice."

"Phillip Troutman and Wally Long?" she guessed.

"Ha! You figured them out already?"

"I pay attention." They reached her car. "I also saw the retraction by the blogger who released that initial article about my dad and our supposed marriage, and the article your publicist wrote stating the facts. Your kind words were a boost to my father's spirits, and while you could have raked me over the coals, you didn't. That was very kind of you, and I appreciate it."

"I hate that Ed told the blogger I actually got married and other papers reported the lie. Scandal can affect business. But as Mom has so eloquently pointed out several times recently, it comes with the territory of being a Breedlove. Back then you did what you felt you had to do, and what subsequently got leaked was not your fault."

"Thank you."

Lauren reached for the door handle. Christian blocked her.

"Where are you headed?"

"Home, thank God."

"Where's that," Christian asked, "since you turned down Mom's offer to return to the guesthouse?"

"Not far," was Lauren's evasive answer.

"Listen to you, trying to sound all mysterious."

"That was a polite way to suggest that you mind your business."

"Ha!"

Lauren smiled. "I'm kidding."

"No, you're not. But that straightforwardness is pretty sexy."

"Hmm."

"Come with me."

"Where are we going?"

Christian gently took her arm and led her a couple cars down, to a pearl-white sedan.

"To get something to eat."

Christian pulled out a key fob. Lauren heard a *click*. He held the door open.

"This is you?" He shut her door, then went around to the driver's side and got in. "You got another car?"

"I'm thinking about it. Trying it out."

Lauren looked at the steering wheel and saw a symbol she'd seen before. Not in person, but in magazines, and on television a time or two.

"This is a Bentley?" He nodded. "No wonder the leather feels so amazing. But look how it's streaked. They must have used the cheap stuff."

Her jab did as intended and caused Christian to flash his flawless smile. The beauty of those pearly whites against his dark skin, framed by those nice lips, was like a cup of caffeine straight into her core. That fine brother gave her life!

"It's a way of treating the leather that retains the hide's natural essence."

"It's beautiful, but so not politically correct."

"Definitely not for everyone."

So focused on the car's interior, she didn't pay attention to where they were going until Christian pressed on the gas, and the power generated by the twin-turbo engines forced her back against the seat. They'd merged onto Interstate 15, headed toward Breedlove.

"Are we going to the estate?" Christian shook his head. "Where then?"

"We're going to hang out with the Breedlove locals."

She arched a brow. "Isn't that what I've been doing for the past two months?"

"You've been in the inner circle of the town's elite. We're going to hang out with regular folk."

Lauren relaxed against the headrest, watched Christian's strong, capable fingers work the stereo system until the soft sounds of neo soul filled the air. She remembered the last time those hands had touched her body, the night she'd returned from Maryland and they'd made love all night long. Aside from music delivered so crisply it sounded as though the artist was in the back seat, there was no other noise. No sound of tires rolling on cement, no hum of engine, no sound of wind. Before, she'd felt it a complete waste of money to spend as much on a car as some did on their houses. But

now as the beast quietly ate up the highway, she understood
why some did. Riding in the Bentley was like floating on a
cloud. That Christian was beside her made it feel a bit like
heaven. But Lauren knew that, sadly, there was no reclaiming that paradise. Even though he knew that Ed leaked the
story, Lauren owned her part in the matter, that had she never
lied in the first place there wouldn't have been a story. Could
Christian ever truly forgive her for that? And did she want
to be with a man who couldn't forgive, forget and move on?

They drove past the estate and into the town of Breedlove,
population 2,137. The main street, called Main Street, was
straight out of a movie, Mayberry in the twenty-first century.
A bank anchored one corner, with a small grocer on the other.
Lauren glimpsed a doughnut shop, an insurance company, a
consignment store and a dollar mart before Christian turned
the corner onto Sixth Street, the second main drag. Several
cars lined this street. Young people mingled between them.
Two guys tossed a neon football. Loud music played. She
tried to imagine Christian as one of these kids. She couldn't.

"So this is where you grew up, huh?" Lauren murmured.

"Yes and no. I went to a private high school in Las Vegas,
so my interaction with kids my age here in Breedlove was
limited. Plus there was the whole 'rich kid' stereotype, and
people thinking I thought more of myself than I did." He
exhaled. "Add to that the other guys' girlfriends always
coming at me and you end up with someone the other guys
would rather not have around."

"Sounds rather lonely."

"Hardly. Who needed them? I had my brothers. Those
who were welcomed into our gang were the lucky ones."

Lauren would have called him cocky or conceited, except she knew what he'd said was true.

They pulled up to a '50s-style burger joint with two huge
*B*s outlined in neon lights.

"What's that stand for?" Lauren asked, after Christian
had come around and opened her door.

"Breedlove Burgers."

"Another family business," she teased. He nodded. "Really? I was just joking."

They entered the noisy establishment, which smelled of caramelized onions and grilled beef. Private school aside, Christian seemed to know everyone in the place. He spoke to them all on the way to a booth at the back of the room. A server came for their order, which he placed without asking what Lauren wanted. "Trust me," he said, to her raised-eyebrow question.

She did. "You guys really own this place?"

"Not us. My brother Adam. This is his baby."

"I never would have taken him for a restaurateur."

"It's a way for him to show off the beef he raises."

Lauren shook her head. "You lost me."

"Adam's a cowboy, and a rancher. You've been to his place and didn't figure that out?"

"I saw dozens of cattle that day out running but it didn't occur to me that they belonged to Adam. Is there anything your family can't do?"

"No."

Over double burgers on toasted buns and home-cut fries, Lauren learned about the history of Breedlove and the part Christian's dad, Nicholas, played in founding the town. It was quite a backstory, which left her even more impressed with the family than she already was...which was a lot.

"Do you think we could work together?" Lauren hadn't meant to ask the question aloud and even as she had, knew he'd misinterpret its meaning.

"We do work together, Lauren."

"Not professionally, but personally. Do you think you and I could have a successful relationship, or do you think our personalities are too explosive for it to ever work out?"

"Wow, what brought that on?"

"The decision to be honest with myself, and to be as honest with you as I was with Ed when I told him I didn't want to be with him." She rested a hand on his arm. "I do want to be with you, and if you feel the same, I would love to see where having a real relationship might take us. Is that possible?"

"I don't know."

His smoldering look seared her insides even as his answer squeezed her heart.

"I'll admit that what we have is special. You're an amazing woman who's caused me to consider things I've never thought about before. Having just been promoted to the helm of CANN, I had no plans to get into a relationship. Yet even though we've never said it, that feels like what this is."

"I feel the same way, too," she whispered.

"But the truth is, everything that's happened recently makes the matter more complicated. I'm already high profile and don't know that I'm ready for the spotlight that would come with dating the woman named in the blog that went viral, exposing deception. I've forgiven you," he quickly added. "What I'm saying isn't personal, but viewed strictly from my position as president of a company where profile matters. It may sound cold to hear me put business before love, but I have more than myself to think about. I have my family, hundreds of employees, their families, investors…" A look of aching regret crossed his handsome face. "What happens to me reflects on the company, for better or worse. Any scandal in my personal life is seen by my professional peers. Maybe later, after the CANN Island launch, when the rumor mill has tired of the sham marriage story, I'll feel more comfortable taking the chance. But right now is not that time. Can you understand that?"

Lauren nodded, squared her shoulders and placed a shield over her heart. "I can totally understand it."

He held out his hand. "Friends?"

She slid her hand into his and braced herself against the jolt she knew would come, and did.

"Friends."

# Twenty-Three

For the next two weeks, Christian and Lauren didn't see much of each other. Outside of meetings or the occasional room or hallway encounter, she was MIA, busy working on the concert, she'd said when asked.

But Christian knew that it was more than that. Whenever they met she was polite, poised and professional. She laughed when he joked with her and smiled on cue. No one could have accused her of being anything less than a standout, the kind of person any corporation or organization would be lucky to have working on their team. But he knew something was missing when he came around. Desire. Heat. He found himself remembering how they blazed in the throes of passion, found himself wanting to experience it again. But was it fair to reopen a door that he'd closed, especially for a brief visit instead of a longtime stay?

It wasn't fair to her. He knew this. But it didn't change the fact that he wanted her, that without the real Lauren, all of her, days weren't as bright as they used to be and nights were much too long.

After wrestling with his thoughts and feelings a couple more days, he called his father.

"Morning, son."

"Good morning, Dad. Have you left for the office?"

"I'm not going in today."

"Everything okay?" Christian asked.

"More than fine. Now that you're president, I'm a thumb twiddler. Promoting you pushed me right out of a job."

"That's such a crock."

"But it made you feel good, didn't it?"

"A little bit." Christian headed toward the shower. "Is it

okay to stop by before heading into the city? I've got a situation and could use your advice."

"I'll be here."

A short time later, he pulled his Bentley into the circular drive. Lauren's reaction to it had convinced him to buy it. If things worked out the way his mind had been headed, maybe he'd buy her one, too. Just beyond the foyer, he ran into Sofia.

"Where's Dad?" he asked, after greeting her warmly.

"In his study, waiting on you."

"Thanks, Sofia."

"Chris?" He turned around. "Are you hungry?"

"I'll grab something when I get to the office."

"Gabe just made cinnamon rolls. They're still warm."

"How can I say no to Gabe's gooey rolls?"

"I'll bring it down," Sofia said, smiling. "With milk."

Christian reached his father's study and after a light tap, opened the door. Where the rest of the house mainly had Victoria's aesthetic, this room was pure Nicholas Breedlove. Christian took it all in as he crossed over to where his father sat on a love seat by a corner fireplace. The dark walnut walls, floor-to-ceiling bookshelves, rich leathers, antique desks and tables radiated pure masculine elegance.

Nicholas's dedication to family was evident in a grouping of portraits—him and Victoria, all of the sons. A small one of Nicholas's father, Jewel's first husband Bobby, and his group, the Soul Smokers. And Christian's favorite, the only one in color, of Nicholas's mother—their grandmother Jewel—which was prominently displayed in a rectangular gilded frame. She was at the center of a line of showgirls, adorned in fishnet stockings and sequins, with a feather headpiece at least three feet tall. He remembered visiting her home as a boy. Even then, in her fifties and sixties, no one could tell Christian that his grandmother wasn't a star!

In the boardroom Nicholas was all Rolex and Armani but here, in the study on his vast estate, one caught a glimpse of the foundation at the base of the man. His foundation was family, and owning one's own.

"What's going on, Pops?" Christian asked, settling down in a chair.

"That's what I'm about to find out," Nicholas said.

"Sofia's bringing in cinnamon rolls, just so you know."

Nicholas patted his stomach. "I've got a brand-new tuxedo for the next charity ball. That cummerbund has got to lie flat."

Christian nodded, totally understanding. He got all of his style from his father. But he hadn't come by to talk about fashion. And not having much time, he got right to the point.

"How did you know Mom was the one?"

Nicholas's eyebrows rose in obvious surprise. "Whoa, that wasn't the question I expected."

"Thought this was going to be about work?"

"Why, yes, I did, son. Don't mind your asking, but can I ask you something first?" Christian nodded. "Is this about Lauren?"

"It is."

There was a light knock at the door and once given permission to enter, Sofia brought in a tray of rolls and wheeled it over to where Christian sat. The smell of cinnamon, sugar and butter wafted under his nose. His stomach growled in delight.

"I brought coffee and tea, along with the milk."

"Thanks, Sofia," Christian said. "You're the best."

He reached for a saucer, picked up a roll and took a hefty bite. "This should be illegal," he said around the mouthful.

"For me, right now, it is," Nicholas replied.

Christian took a couple more bites before reaching for one of a stack of linen napkins, dipping it in a small crystal bowl filled with water and wiping his hands. "When Mom hired Lauren, I didn't remember that we'd met before."

"I don't know why you didn't. Faye and Vic have been friends for over twenty-five years."

"Lauren reminded me that it was her older sister Renee that I'd checked out."

Nicholas smiled, nodded. "Time brings about a change. She's a beautiful woman. But then, I'd imagine that's why you're here."

"Ah, Dad. I don't know what to do. We became close during that first trip to Africa and dated a couple times once we returned. But then she decided that mixing business with pleasure wasn't the best idea."

"Sounds like somebody I know," Nicholas replied, with a pointed stare toward Christian.

"All right, I admit to sharing that same viewpoint. I agreed with her, especially given that her mom and mine were friends."

"So what's the problem, she wants more now?"

"She did, but I messed it up."

"How?"

Christian stood and slowly paced the room. "By not being able to get over what happened. That's not exactly what I told her, though what I did share was the truth as well."

"Which was?"

"That perception is everything and that considering the fake marriage scandal, I wasn't sure dating her wouldn't mar the CANN image, have the public more focused on my private life than the next public offering.

"But that was only part of it. The other part is that she lied, big-time. I know there was a reason. I know it went further than she intended. I know she came clean. Intellectually, I get all that. I've forgiven her. But Dad, I just can't seem to forget."

"Did you tell her that?"

"At one point I did, right after reading the blog. She wasn't happy and not long ago came straight out with what she desired…for us to be together." Christian ran a hand through his curls and plopped down in a chair.

"Then I'm not sure I get your dilemma, son. According to Vic, Lauren is by far the best assistant she's ever had. Just the other day she told me that she could resign tomorrow and feel totally confident in her ability to lead the foundation on her own. Is she not producing the same level of work with the Island project? Is her attention to the gala interfering with what you need?"

"Not in the office," Christian mumbled.

Nicholas leaned against the back of his chair. "Earlier, you asked what it was about your mama that made me know that she was the one. It's when I started to think more about her than I did about any other woman, or even the business. It's when I started feeling lonely whenever she wasn't around. Let me tell you something, Christian. All the money in the world doesn't compare to the right woman warming the other side of your bed. You hear me?"

"I hear you, Dad. Thanks."

Christian gave Nicholas a hug and headed toward the door.

"It's good that you hear me," Nicholas said. "But the real question is, what are you going to do about it?"

It was a fair question, Christian thought as he headed to the car. He was determined to figure out the answer.

# Twenty-Four

Lauren felt like pinching herself to make sure she wasn't dreaming. Partly because in preparing for the concert she'd gone nonstop, and sleepwalking was a real possibility. But mostly because her entire family would be attending before they continued to California for a long-overdue visit with some of their West Coast friends. Even Renee and hubby Thomas, always tied to their children, had left them with a sitter to spend some alone time in Sin City.

Lauren had balked at Victoria's suggestion that they all stay at the CANN but then she pulled the "it's my gift to Faye" trump card, putting her parents, sister and brother-in-law into a two-bedroom suite.

Lauren was staying at the CANN, too, along with most of the Breedloves. The concert and dance finished at twelve, but a private party for VIP guests would likely last well into the night. Staying there only made sense. As she sat perfectly still, letting the makeup artist Frankie had insisted on getting for her work her magic, Lauren thought of a third reason the night felt like a fairy tale. Her gorgeous couture gown, a gift from London and Ace, which was part of his latest HER collection.

As the makeup artist was finishing up, there was a knock at the door. One of the assistants went to open the door. It was Frankie, his pose regal, as he leaned on the jamb.

"The party can start now, darling," he cooed. "Fabulosity has arrived!"

He floated in on beaded Louboutins, his long legs clad in sequined skinny pants, paired with a feathery top and long drop earrings. His makeup was perfection and his hair had been cut, gelled and slicked back. He was drop-dead beautiful, and Lauren told him so.

"Please go and check on the rooms for the silent auction. Make sure all of the tablets are set, working, with styli and paper backup below. I feel fairly confident with the team we've assembled but with the extravagant donations we've received, we can't take any chances."

"I'm already all over it, girlfriend. The proceeds from tonight are going to be huge!"

There were collector's items being auctioned of Las Vegas greats—from Liberace, Jerry Lewis and the famous Rat Pack to more current headliners like Jennifer Lopez and Celine Dion. In an act of total selflessness, London donated her wedding dress. The bidding started at $250,000. Two interested parties had already phoned in.

A quick look at the clock said she needed to hurry. On cue, the hairstylist put down the rattail comb she'd been using to arrange Lauren's curls. Her hair had been pulled up and piled high into a burst of curls on top of her head. After viewing her jewelry she'd decided none was appropriate to go with the masterpiece Ace had designed. The dress alone would have to be enough.

Now it was time to become Cinderella. Lauren carefully stepped into the skirt, layers of deep red silk organza and gold tulle. She held her breath as the corset was laced, and figured the next time she breathed would be sometime tomorrow. Shimmering crystals accented the waist even more, and a boatneck bodice showed just the right amount of cleavage. After stepping into red satin pumps, she looked into the mirror. Indeed, she looked on her way to a ball. All she needed was a prince to complete the tableau.

There was a knock at the door.

"What has Frankie forgotten now?" Lauren asked the room. Although she'd given her family the suite number. It might be Renee.

It wasn't Renee. It wasn't family. It was her prince. *Christian.*

He stepped inside the door and stopped, his eyes drinking her in like a camel gearing up for a trek through the Mojave. Little did she know but her eyes mirrored his as she took in the deep red velvet tuxedo jacket, made more striking by being paired with a black shirt and slacks. His eyes caught and held hers, and she could swear the earth tilted. Everyone, everything in the room disappeared. Her heartbeat increased. She felt light-headed. Either the boning in the corset had cut through her windpipe or this sister was falling even deeper in love!

Seconds passed, and neither spoke. And yet an entire conversation passed through their eyes.

*Yes. Me, too. Later. Can't wait!*

"…Lauren!"

Someone was calling her. The name cut through a haze of emotions, softly at first and then louder.

She gave her head a slight shake to pull it together. The stylists had been forgotten. "Huh, um, what?"

"Do you need us for anything further?"

"No, but my family might." She gave them the suite number. "I'll let them know you're on the way."

The group scurried away, as though feeling like interlopers, suddenly unwelcome. Christian's eyes never left Lauren's as the door clicked in place.

"Hi," Lauren said shyly.

Christian visibly swallowed. "You take my breath away."

"I know the feeling. You look—" she licked her lips without meaning to do it "—really good."

"It's from the HIS collection."

"And this is HER."

"Ace did his thing with the summer line."

"Oh, I almost forgot. My family. The team. Let me call and give them a heads-up."

Lauren walked over to where her phone sat on the dining room table, next to a square gold clutch. After alerting her mom to the glam squad's arrival, she turned back to Christian.

"Shall we go down, then? I assume you're here as my escort?"

Slowly walking toward her, Christian said, "That's only one of many reasons why I'm here."

He stopped mere inches from her face. "The other is to give you this."

So caught up in his gaze, Lauren hadn't seen the box he held. Now she did, and looked at him again.

"What is this?"

"A peace offering."

"For what?"

"For telling you no when I should have said yes."

"Christian, I…"

"Shh." He placed a finger on her lips. "Let's talk later. For now we have a beautiful concert and a wonderful dance to enjoy."

Still staring at him, she lifted the lid and revealed another box inside, silver, with intricate designs. She let the cardboard box fall to the floor as she slowly lifted the silver box lid.

Her mouth dropped.

"No."

Christian chuckled. "What do you mean, no?"

"No, Christian! These can't be for me."

"They're absolutely for you, and now that I've seen how you're wearing that dress, baby, this present is perfect."

"They're beautiful," Lauren said, tearing up. "I've never…thank you."

"You're welcome. Here, you handle the earrings. I'll help with this."

Lauren turned, felt the coolness of the gem against her warm skin as he clasped the teardrop yellow diamond held by a thin gold chain. She put on the matching earrings and looked in the mirror. Now her ensemble was complete.

She looked at her watch. "I've got to go."

"Don't throw away that box. There's something else in there."

Lauren reached for the box and saw what lay at the bottom, what had been hidden by the intricately designed box that held the jewels. A hotel card key...to Christian's private suite.

He didn't know if she'd show, but Christian made the obligatory rounds at the VIP party, sent Lauren a text and then slipped out as quickly as he could. He entered the suite and looked around. His butler had staged the room to perfection, had followed every instruction to the letter. The candles, rose petals, champagne perfectly chilled, food flown in from Rome and Djibouti.

It had been so long since he'd been nervous about anything that at first he didn't recognize the feeling. Once he did he walked over to the bar, poured a finger of scotch and knocked it back. He walked over to the wall panel and pushed a few buttons. The soft sounds of neo soul floated across the room. Fifteen minutes passed, and then fifteen minutes more. He took off his jacket. Ten more minutes went by. Christian finally got the message. She wasn't coming. He walked into the bedroom, eased out of his shoes, and heard the soft *click* of the lock.

His heart thudded against his chest. There was another reaction, several inches below, as his sex twitched with anticipation. He walked into the living room. Lauren stood still, staring. She looked ethereal, like a goddess, the beads glittering, candles flickering off her golden skin. He walked over and pulled her into his arms.

"Thank you," he whispered.

He stepped back. She looked around. "This place looks amazing."

"It's all for you. Can I get you something to drink or eat? I've got some special dishes I think you'd like."

"Maybe later," she said softly. She perched on the sofa arm and slid off her pumps. "Right now I'd very much love it if you'd assuage another appetite."

Christian didn't need to be told twice. He pulled her up, turned her around and undressed her, everything but her thong, right there in the living room. While she was still standing he went to his knees, gently spread her legs and pressed his mouth against her heat. As his tongue snaked its way under the thong's silky fabric, his fingers splayed her cheeks and teased the star of her moon. Lauren groaned and joined him on the floor, using the $20,000 dress she'd just worn as a cushion against the cool marble.

Christian covered her naked body with his fully clothed one, took her face in his hands and kissed her deeply, her essence like nectar as he licked, nipped and teased. He stopped just long enough to pull off his shirt. As he worked with the buttons, Lauren handled his belt, button and zipper, and pushed down slacks and boxers in one fell swoop. It was a take-charge move that said "I want you now." The plans for a slow seduction went out the window. He reached for the condom in his slacks, rolled it on, and slid home.

Coming together again was heavenly. For a moment they lay still, barely breathing. He basked in the feeling of being fully sheathed inside her, of feeling the muscles of her inner walls flex and tighten, heightening his desire beyond what he thought possible. He eased out to the tip and sank in again slowly, deeply, smiling as the increased friction made her moan. He increased the pace—plunging, thrusting, squeezing, grinding—branding every part of her insides with his hot iron. He made love until a thin sheen of sweat covered his body and still, he could not get enough. His tongue and hands were everywhere. No part of her body, no crevice, no cavern, was left untouched. He poured himself into her, body and soul, and his mind whispered... *I love you*.

After the second orgasm and a leisurely shower, round two began and Lauren returned the favor. She licked and tickled his long, thick shaft, savored his tip, followed the line of hair with her tongue and drove him wild when she pulled him inside her warm, wet mouth. Over and over, until the sun rose. Until there were tears, as both of them recognized and acknowledged that what started as lust had deepened to a soul-mate love. They heated the food and conversed about trivial, mundane things. No one talked about the past. No one talked about the future, although later they'd realize that at this time they both saw the other in it. For right now, however, they only focused on the present, and each other.

# Twenty-Five

The weeks between Memorial Day and the Fourth of July passed by in a blur of love, laughter, family and fun. Lauren and Christian spent quality time with Renee and Thomas, and dazzled them by scoring tickets to some of the best shows in Las Vegas—Cirque du Soleil and front-row seats to Criss Angel and MJ Live.

Afterward, Lauren traveled to California with her parents and marveled at the change in her dad. Or was it her just seeing him differently? Either way he seemed happier, his spirit much lighter. He still owed Gerald Miller a boatload of money, but hearing her dad's hearty laugh at a warm-up comedian made Lauren feel that the worst may indeed be behind them.

Paul and Faye came back for the Fourth of July celebration. Victoria had insisted on it, and on them staying in one of the guesthouses on the estate where the party was held. Thousands of mini lights—red, white and blue—were strung around and between three large white tents, with paths of slate laid between them, perfectly smooth and evenly laid in order to accommodate the Choo, Blahnik and Louboutin heels that would walk over them.

The best foods had been flown in from around the world, along with several renowned chefs in charge of a menu featuring Breedlove beef, Maine lobster, Alaskan salmon, Nova Scotia bluefin tuna and organic everything. Not a hot dog or potato chip in sight. One tent had been arranged with intimate seating for the one hundred or so guests who'd been invited. The third tent held additional seating, a lit dance floor and a massive bar that would attract a crowd all night.

Christian and Lauren arrived, hand in hand, a standout

couple among a crowd of jewels. They spotted their parents at about the same time, sitting at a round table of ten, chatting with another couple and among each other. The lovers headed that way.

"Don't they make the cutest couple?" Victoria exclaimed after pleasantries. "And can you imagine their babies?"

"Victoria!"

"What?" Victoria held her ground while taking in Lauren's shocked expression. "You do know that's the end result of…hand-holding."

The table chuckled. Lauren swore her dad blushed.

"Sit down, you two," Nicholas said.

"Yes, do sit," Victoria said. "We have news to share."

Christian pulled out a chair for Lauren and sat down beside her.

"More specifically, Paul and Faye have news."

Lauren looked at her mom, then her dad.

"I wouldn't call it news, exactly," Faye began, her eyes twinkling. "But your dad and I been talking this week about how much we love Las Vegas. Years ago we joked about moving here when we retire and—"

"What?" Lauren's screech attracted more than one head turn. Who was this adventurous couple before her and what had happened to her parents?

"When did these conversations happen, because I've never heard the two of you talk about moving anywhere. In fact, Dad, you told me once that you were fine with coming to visit wherever I am but for you Maryland would always be home."

"I've learned that one should never say never," Paul said. "Life happens, things change, and so can perspectives. Sometimes we get so caught up in the year-in, year-out routine that we don't take the time to consider something different."

"And now you're considering a move across country? Okay, Mom." Lauren turned her attention to Faye. "I can totally imagine you wanting to move here. How did you bribe him?"

"That would be me," Nicholas said, raising his hand. "With CANN, there'll be major expansion over the next ten years and along with that the need for an increased workforce. We're always looking for skilled, dedicated people to join the team and considering the person you are, a talented force with creative ideas that are ingenious and progressive, I figure Paul had at least a little influence in how you turned out, and that's amazing."

"Nothing's official," Paul said. "I'd have to convince Gerald to let me go and then help find a suitable replacement."

"The truth, dear," Victoria continued, "is that this is all one big conspiracy to keep you here. The foundation is flourishing, the philanthropists love you, and so does everyone who works there. So with only a short time until your contract expires, we've had to put our heads together and work really fast."

It wasn't often that Lauren was speechless, but now was one of those times. She'd never been a weepy woman, either, but right now she could flat out boo-hoo. Looking between her mom and dad, they seemed so happy! And for the dad who not very ago lost his reputation, almost his freedom, and had been ready to resign, a job opportunity? Who knew?

"I really don't know what to say. It's not often my parents shock me, but I didn't see this coming.

"I know the holiday is over but you know what? This is truly a special gift and whether or not I stay past the contract, Nicholas, thank you. Despite everything that happened, when it comes to finances, you really couldn't hire anyone better than Dad."

Lauren waved over a waiter carrying champagne flutes. "It's time for a toast, guys." Christian reached for a flute as the parents raised their glasses. "To fateful endings, new beginnings and wonderful, amazing, astounding friends."

"I know I'm all that," Nicholas deadpanned. "But what about Vic?"

"On that note," Christian said with a laugh, pulling up Lauren, "I think it's time for us to hit the dance floor and get our party on."

"Don't make me have to hunt you down for my kiss of independence," Victoria chided.

"Are you kidding? You're my good-luck charm, Mom," Christian said. "I'll find you wherever you are."

As they headed toward the dance floor, Christian reached for Lauren's hand. He squeezed it and raised it to his lips. Their eyes met. He winked. A smile coasted from her face to his, lifted and brightened at an unspoken message of love, one that changed the atmosphere ever so slightly.

For years, he'd brought women to this annual gala, the brightest, most beautiful, rich, famous, all of the above. But he'd never felt that he was attending with the right one, the forever one…until now.

They reached the dance floor and as if on cue, the music shifted to a slow song. He slid his hand around Lauren's waist and pulled her into his arms.

"You're pretty amazing," Lauren whispered, sliding her hand across his butt. "Did you know that?"

"It never hurts to have the fact confirmed," he said.

Upon hearing those words, Christian's manhood swelled. He smiled, revealing a heart containing a giddy happiness he'd never felt before, exposing a soul reveling in complete contentment. It made him more convinced than ever that whatever happened, tonight was exactly how life was supposed to be.

"So are you going to tell me?"

Christian twirled her on the dance floor. "Tell you what?"

"How you talked your dad into hiring mine."

"That was all Nicholas. Nothing about me."

"I find that hard to believe."

Christian shrugged. "It's true. Besides, you heard my mom explain what this is really about. They're trying to keep you."

"And you have nothing to do with that, either?"

"Nothing about me."

They settled into the dance and the night, mingling with employees, patrons and friends, and taking advantage of line dances to boogie with everyone. By eleven o'clock the twins were feeling no pain and in a move right out of the movies, brought twins as their dates. Adam sat with a harem, literally, clustered together at a table for ten, nine beautiful women and him.

They ate, drank, partied down, and as day turned to night, he kept his promise and made his way toward the family. They all gathered in the open area, ready for the fireworks. Amid a flurry of colorful, fiery explosions, Christian turned to Lauren. "This is pretty impressive, but you're all the firecracker I need. I love you, babe."

"I love you, too."

The kiss was soft, teasing, a quick swirl of tongue before they ended it, shared a heartfelt embrace and hurried over to the Breedlove tables to watch the fireworks show. Amid the rockets' red glare and Roman candles bursting in the air, there were two people who were ready to give up their independence.

Noah and Nick assaulted their big brother. "Man, you're lame,"

"I thought you were going to go for the big one!" Noah said, frowning.

"What in the heck are you two talking about? For the rest of the night both of you should just say no."

"We're talking about the pro-pro, bro."

"The diamond ring, the knee bend thing. What are you going to do? Let a good one get away?"

Christian was amused, and touched, at the knuckleheads'

banter. They must have really liked Lauren, as they'd never given two hoots about his women before. They needn't worry. Christian had no intention of letting Lauren leave Las Vegas. Even now, a ring design that he'd worked on with Ace was in the hands of a jeweler to the stars. He wanted the ring to be original, like Lauren, one of a kind.

As for asking Lauren to be his wife? That would be a moment not shared with the masses. He lived enough of his life in the spotlight, and with the expansion of CANN that would happen even more. When the time came to declare his forever love, Christian had a plan. He would offer up a private proposal, for her ears alone. And Lauren's answer would be for just the two of them.

All she had to say was yes.

* * * * *

# SON OF SCANDAL

## DANI WADE

This book is dedicated to everyone
who helped me through one of the hardest times
in my life, also known as January 2018.
My sister, Ella (as always!). My mother.
My husband and children. My coworkers.
The Playfriends. My editor.
And all the readers and author friends
who reached out to me on Facebook to offer
encouragement and prayers.

This book would never have been
finished without you!

# One

"Dance with me?"

Ivy looked at the outstretched hand, surprised and nonplussed at the same time. Her own fingers clenched over the itch in her palm. The itch that told her to reach out, to take what she coveted.

After a year and a half of carefully keeping Paxton McLemore at arm's length, did she dare step in close for a waltz?

They were at a masquerade ball, after all. The most glamorous charity event of the year, planned by her sister Jasmine Harden, Savannah's most noted event planner. Dancing with Paxton would be a natural action. One that wouldn't be judged by those around them, even though he was her employer. But she would know. Could she successfully hide how she felt when she was that close?

Though he wore a traditional black mask, she'd recognize his brilliant amber eyes anywhere—not just because of the intense color, but also the ever-present flash of intelligence and intuition she observed every day as his executive assistant.

It was just a dance... Why did she hesitate?

Suddenly he wiggled the fingers of the hand she had left dangling by her indecision. She smiled; the silly gesture was a charming reminder of the lighthearted moments they shared every day at work.

Ivy finally reached her hand out to his.

"You know, there's been a change in my office," Paxton said as his warm fingers curled around hers. "This new assistant came to work for me, and she makes me smile every day."

A glow warmed Ivy's core as he lifted her hand to graze her knuckles with his sculpted lips. She glanced down at their clasped hands as Paxton led her toward the dance floor in Keller House's renovated ballroom.

Though she should be focused on doing her part to make sure the incredible masquerade ball her sister had orchestrated ran smoothly, Ivy let thoughts of caterers and fundraisers and responsibility fall away. But with a single touch, the struggle to breathe became real. It took her a moment to realize the truth—Paxton had never touched her before this.

Oh, she went out of her way to make him smile at the office, to soften the strain of his intense focus on work. Though her crush had intensified since she'd been working for him, she'd kept her actions and words strictly professional.

No touching. Until tonight.

Before she could register what was happening, they'd moved onto the dance floor and Paxton had turned to face her. He opened his arms, inviting her in. Ivy blinked—once, twice.

*This is dangerous.*

She chose to ignore her mind's warnings. Ivy stepped forward, and they took the waltz position, but didn't move. Instead Paxton's eyes widened at the initial contact, as if he, too, could feel the electric shock as they embraced.

Then his eyelids lowered to half-mast, taking on a slumberous, sexy look. A look she'd only seen in her fantasies.

Her heartbeat sped up, thrumming at the base of her throat. He took the first step, leading her in a modern-day version of the traditional dance.

Even though the warning bells she'd been silencing for a year were back full force, Ivy let his arms close around her, pull her closer. As they danced under the crystal chandeliers, amid dozens of other couples in the impeccably restored ballroom, the moment felt surreal. Out of time. His black tux was classic. The striking contrast between it and her emerald-green ball gown caught her eye as they glided past the wall of ornately framed mirrors.

The decadent illusion was dangerous—just like him.

She'd tried hard since her parents died to be practical, independent. But a small, hidden part of her still clung to the fantasy of fairy tales and Prince Charming.

Tonight, that part of her refused to be denied.

So she let him lead her, turn her, bend her to his touch. The touch that she'd fantasized about for the last year and a half she'd worked for him. During their daily routine, she'd resisted the pull of attraction, attempted to distract herself with clients and travel arrangements and meeting preparations. She'd thrown herself into the busy schedule of the head of the manufacturing division of his family's shipping conglomerate. But at the most unexpected of moments, she'd find herself immersed in far more intimate thoughts than she should have about her boss.

Tonight, he was that dream come to life. His touch and the intensity of his gaze made her feel beautiful, wanted.

Her body tingled whenever he pressed close. This far surpassed her simple fantasies. The feelings were intense. Impossible to ignore.

They moved through the sea of people as if alone. The way her heart raced and her skin tingled with every brush of his hand was pure magic.

Every time logic attempted to assert itself, the intensity of his stare pushed it back. She wanted nothing more than to be his entire focus and let reality melt away.

He drew her closer, cocooning her in his arms. His gaze turned hungrier. His body grew harder.

Somewhere in the intensity, Ivy's resistance evaporated and she knew she'd go wherever he led her.

Even when the song was over and she had left him to do her hostessing rounds for her sister, she caught glimpses of him nearby. No matter how close or how far away, she could sense exactly where he was in the crowd. And it wasn't long before they found each other again in the muffled quiet of the front foyer.

Ivy held her breath, uncertainty washing over her. "Paxton…"

"I know," he said, reaching out to rub a finger over the velvet ribbon that held her mask in place. "I didn't expect this either. But I can't deny that I want you…very much."

He leaned into her, his mint-scented breath making her mouth water.

"We shouldn't…" she whispered, though her eyelids were already fluttering closed.

"I know…" He groaned.

Then his mouth covered hers and all protests were lost.

His kiss was just this side of demanding. Her body melted in acquiescence. He pressed closer, as if to absorb her surrender and claim his victory.

She knew how the night would end, and couldn't find an

ounce of hesitation in her mind or body. Not even when he had paused, giving logic an opening to fracture the fantasy.

"I know I shouldn't ask you, that I have no right," Paxton said, the intensity of his stare making her shiver. "But, Ivy, will you go home with me?"

In that moment fantasy ruled. Though she'd denied it for over a year, Ivy had never wanted anything more than she wanted to spend tonight in Paxton's arms. "Yes. Yes, I will."

The happiness and excitement Ivy felt left her in a very surreal place, as if she couldn't quite grasp the reality of the decision she'd made.

Still she forced herself to be practical for one moment and made a quick call to her sister Jasmine. Hunting her down in the throngs of people would take too long. As she waited for Paxton to get the car brought around, Ivy heard the hesitation and concern in her sister's voice. Her tone escalated to alarm as Ivy told her where she was going but Ivy couldn't bring herself to care.

She'd spent the past year ignoring her family's secret connection to Paxton's. She justified taking the position with him by telling herself that he never had to know who she really was. Becoming his assistant had been a dream job for someone her age. With her drive to stand on her own two feet, there was no way she could have passed up such an incredible opportunity to advance. Or the temptation it had presented. Yes, it was a foolish hope. But maybe, just maybe, this was the right thing.

She glanced at the teardrop emerald on her right ring finger, swearing it actually twinkled in the subdued lighting on the front stone steps, where she waited. The piece of jewelry handed down to her and her sisters through generations of their family, who believed its magic would guide them to find their true love.

The professional Ivy wanted to scoff at the notion that

the ring had anything to do with what was happening tonight. But the princess wannabe she hid deep down inside regarded the ring with a smile before she glanced up to see Paxton step out of the back of the company limo.

"Come with me?" he asked, reaching his hand out to her.

She knew what was happening. Knew he was giving her a way out at the same time that he made his preference known. He was a gentleman, through and through. Tonight, she wanted him to be hers.

He quickly handed her into the dim interior, which got even darker as he closed the door behind him. The driver pulled away from the curb right away. Paxton wasn't wasting time on niceties. His urgency mirrored hers—much to her relief.

Paxton immediately distracted her from thoughts of rings, sisters and the fact that he was her boss. In the private world of the back seat, he embraced her without hesitation. Their decision was made.

He cupped her head in his large, warm hands, holding her steady for his kiss. In the tight space, every breath, every gasp, every moan was amplified. Then his hands traveled downward, heating up her neck, collarbone and the tops of her breasts. The air stuttered in her lungs as she ached for him to slip his hand beneath the edge of her dress. Instead his mouth followed the trail, creating a heated path of sizzling nerves. She arched into the pull of his lips and tongue and teeth against her skin.

Then he was slipping away from her, pulling back from the grip of her fingers around his upper arms. But the disappointment was quickly replaced by a thrill of both fear and need as he insinuated his big body between the V-shape of her thighs.

The thickly layered skirt of her ball gown proved no match for Paxton. She felt his long fingers close around her ankles in a firm grip, tight enough to let her know he was there without leaving a mark. Her thighs clenched as everything inside her tightened. She needed to surrender to that touch, to let him do with her what he chose.

His fingers traced down over her four-inch heels, a rumbling groan rolling out of his chest. A half smile escaped her, one he might see in the occasional streetlights they passed. They were nearing the city now.

Slowly his palms traced upward, beneath the layers of material. Cupping her calves. Rubbing her knees. Massaging her thighs. Ivy panted as she grew wet with need. Would he touch her there? Or would he leave her to wait?

His fingertips found the line of her garters. "Heaven help me, Ivy." Without warning, he bunched up the heavy skirt and disappeared beneath it. His hands curled around her knees and pulled her forward. She felt open and vulnerable. She swallowed hard, wishing now for just a hint of the logic that had made a brief appearance earlier.

But it was nowhere to be seen.

His mouth met the tender skin right above the top of her thigh-high stockings, sucking hard as if he could swallow her into him. Her muscles tightened as if to push him away, but the move was merely instinctual. Truthfully, she wanted him to taste her there…wanted him to taste her more. His tongue flicked firmly along the upper lace edge, then along the garter, until he buried his face in the crook between her thigh and hip. She felt the breath he drew with every nerve ending in her body.

Abruptly the car halted, the brakes applied with a little more force than necessary.

But it was enough to bring Paxton to his senses. Thank goodness, because any mindfulness she had was long gone. Paxton made quick and careful work of returning her skirt to its original modest position. Then he opened the door and stepped outside. She heard him speaking with the driver, but when he reached in to help her out, the man was back behind the wheel. The car was speeding down the drive before Paxton had her halfway up his front walk.

Now they were alone together. No audience. Just the night and the two of them. The perfect ingredients for her own incredible fairy tale.

Paxton woke to incredible warmth.

The sun shining through the half-closed curtains heated the cool room. The tangle of his legs with the woman asleep beside him heated his skin. His body was alive with urgent need.

Then his brain kicked into gear.

Where it had been last night, he wasn't sure. His body tightened as images rose from his memory. The full impact of what they'd done hit him in a rush.

His assistant. He'd spent the night with his assistant.

An incredible night…

He breathed deeply, attempting to mitigate the odd mix of desire and panic. To slow his racing heartbeat, cool his body's ardor. Because they couldn't do this again.

He'd been such a fool.

Paxton glanced over at Ivy. She faced away from him, but the smooth curve of her shoulder and waterfall of tangled blond hair drew him. Her beauty made him reach out to touch, but he clenched his hand into a fist instead to stop himself.

Last night he'd been blindsided by the need to bury his hands in that silky blond hair. He licked his lips as he remembered the taste of her skin last night, of her full lips, plump breasts and soft thighs. And that garter!

A flash of fever heated his bare skin.

But as he watched the sun flirt with her as she slept, the

panic lurking in the background simply wouldn't go away. What had he been thinking?

Well, he hadn't been.

He urgently needed coffee; it would be a welcome distraction. He eased from the bed, careful not to rouse Ivy, reminding himself that she must be exhausted. She'd spent the last week working her full-time job with him, then helping her sister out with the charity ball. Then she'd spent all day Saturday preparing for the event, and Saturday night splitting the hostessing duties.

She had every right to be tired…and to sleep in.

Leaving her asleep had nothing to do with not wanting to face her…not wanting to tell her this could absolutely not go any further than it already had.

As he headed to the kitchen, he heard the faint noise of his phone vibrating against the foyer table. Instinctively he made a detour for it. One glance at the display told him his executive VP was on the other end of the line—and weekend calls were definitely not his thing. Paxton's senses geared up for whatever emergency was coming his way.

"What's up, Mike?"

"Where the heck have you been? I've been calling since 5:00 a.m."

Paxton clenched his jaw. "I'm here now," he said.

"We've got a problem," Mike said, ignoring his tight tone. "Remember how we took a chance on not replacing the old super engine?"

Paxton groaned. His manufacturing plant in Virginia had been a buyout that they were in the process of refurbishing and upgrading. He'd had a tough time convincing his grandmother, who was still chairwoman of the board, that it was a worthwhile endeavor. This could be a major setback.

Mike went on. "Yep. It blew during the night. I'm gonna need some help out here."

Which meant catching the first flight out to Virginia ASAP. Paxton would need to be on site to formulate his plan for the repairs or replacement, while still keeping the plant functioning. He signed off, then sighed. Not a good morning for this. The only thing he wanted was coffee, and the chance to figure out what he needed to say to the woman whom he'd had the most inappropriate skin-to-skin contact with ever in his life.

Well, maybe not *the* most…but he didn't want to think about the past mistake that made him believe the present situation could end in doom, too.

Knowing he needed to get a move on, Paxton headed upstairs to the master suite to shower and then pack his bag. He felt a moment of relief when he remembered how he'd rushed Ivy into one of the downstairs bedrooms last night because he couldn't wait to get her undressed, and because that was simply his MO with women.

At least he wouldn't be haunted by memories of the passion they'd shared every night when he would lie down in his own bed.

He quickly finished dressing, then threw some clothes into a duffel bag. A few days at the plant in Virginia, then he and Ivy could have a nice long talk about what had happened between them last night. And what should happen between them now. Paxton had his future mapped out to a *T*. And his family was fully behind him. Marrying his assistant was not in his life plan.

Paxton hoped Ivy was on the same wavelength.

On his way out, he paused in the shadowy doorway of the downstairs bedroom. Ivy still slept, oblivious to his dilemma. He felt the urge to crawl back into that sun-kissed space beside her. He even took a single step forward.

But duty called.

His phone started vibrating in his pocket, warning him

time was of the essence. In a quick scrawl, he wrote a note, letting Ivy know that he'd had to run, but she could call the car to take her home. He'd be back soon…and they would talk then.

Still he carried the memories of her sun-warmed skin and everything they'd done to each other in the dark of night as he rode to the airport, paced the VIP Lounge and then boarded the first standby flight he could get for Virginia. He thought a few times about texting her…but it just seemed like such an impersonal, lousy thing to do.

Maybe after a few days away, they could both gain some perspective on what they wanted, how they could return to their steady, professional relationship. Right? He rubbed his palm over his face. Hell, what if this blew up in his face big time?

He remembered the sun glinting off her loose mane of golden hair this morning. Why had she been hiding it in a severe ponytail all this time? Oh, he knew. His buttoned-up executive admin was the utmost professional. Hair always pulled back. Business suits, but only with skirts. He'd always been grateful that she didn't cover up the smooth curve of her calves with dress pants. Instead she accentuated it by wearing smart, sexy heels.

He gulped the last of his hot, black coffee as the plane began to descend.

Of course, he'd been careful to only look when she was walking away from him. Still she'd caught him looking a time or two. Just like he'd found her doing the same. And even though there'd been definite sparks in the air every time they'd locked gazes in the office, neither of them had been willing to break the status quo. Until last night.

They'd been playing with fire, not realizing just when it would blow up.

Paxton forced himself to pick up his bag from the luggage carousel, and then headed outside to flag down a taxi. Mike had his hands full right now, so Paxton had told him not to worry about sending a car. As he settled into the back seat, he read the half dozen text messages waiting for him from Mike. Each one was worse than the next. Paxton may have gotten his start in industry through his family name and his grandmother's owning the umbrella conglomerate, but his diverse interests, determination and leadership skills had earned him the success he enjoyed today as the CEO of an international shipping parts manufacturer...with his eye on running the entire conglomerate one day.

So why was his mind on the woman who was still asleep in his house, instead of the major issues awaiting him at the factory?

# Two

*Two months later...*

"Paxton. You there, big brother?"

Paxton snapped to attention to find Sierra frowning at him. She had every right. He'd stepped in to take her to the obstetrician today, toddler in tow, while her husband was out of town. He should be present in mind and body, but thoughts of Ivy and all that had happened since his return home yesterday kept distracting him.

Marshalling his powers of concentration, he stepped out of the car and circled around to free his niece from her car seat in the back.

Just when he'd thought he and Ivy would be okay, that their professional life would move forward just as he'd wanted it to, she'd sent him her resignation via email. It had arrived while he'd been on the plane home, so it had been the first thing to catch his eye when he'd landed.

"So, what kept you away so long?" his sister asked.

"I was only supposed to be gone a few days. A week, tops." The reality had been a nightmare. "One mechanical problem led to another, then another. At one point we actually had to shut down production for over twenty-four hours."

"I bet Grandmother was thrilled," Sierra said with a conspiratorial smile.

Oh, she'd been none too happy to hear it, reminding him she wasn't cutting him any slack just because he was her grandson. He still had to justify every expense and setback.

At least it had distracted him from thoughts of Ivy. And as the days rolled into weeks, neither of them had mentioned their night together, even though they spoke on the phone almost every day and emailed even more than that. Their conversations had been strictly business, and Paxton had been perfectly happy with that.

He'd thought Ivy had been, too.

By the time he'd made it back to his house and dropped his luggage in the master suite, Paxton had convinced himself her resignation was for the best. Obviously she hadn't wanted to face him in person. He could understand that. Their night together had been a bigger mistake on his part. As her boss, he bore the weight of responsibility and should be grateful she hadn't accused him of sexual harassment, despite their intimacy being mutual. He should probably reach out with a severance package to keep her from bearing any burdens while she looked for another job. Would she accept? Or was she angry that he'd stuck strictly to business all this time?

Still he couldn't stop thinking about her. A woman he should be grateful was gone.

He needed his head examined.

"You must be living on another planet today. Did you

leave your brain in Virginia?" his sister demanded, her normally calm demeanor showing strain as she pulled her daughter from his arms.

Paxton took a deep breath, trying to regain his equilibrium. "I just have a lot on my mind."

Sierra led the way across the parking lot, toward the office building. "Just so long as it's work and not a woman. Grandmother would have a fit if you didn't keep your priorities straight."

The bitterness in her voice immediately caught Paxton's attention. He stared at her in surprise.

His family members were founders and high-ranking business leaders of Savannah society. They'd been taught to marry well, aim high and value family over all else. He'd grown up looking forward to starting one of his own, and he'd been groomed to marry the woman who would best enhance his professional and personal profile. Just like his sisters, who'd chosen their husbands from elite Savannah families.

That was the plan—one that didn't include Ivy. Yet he'd wanted her since he'd first laid eyes on her. And nothing had prepared him for the ecstasy of actually having her.

Except, according to the map he'd laid out for his life, he couldn't keep her. He'd stepped out of his comfort zone in the name of romance and knew it was a mistake.

But that wasn't something you said to a woman over the phone.

"What?" Sierra demanded.

Her sharp tone had him looking closer. Paxton couldn't miss the strain in his sister's expression. Some people might attribute it to the fatigue of her being in the second trimester of pregnancy while taking care of his very active niece, but Paxton knew better. The tight muscles around her eyes and tart tone weren't normal for her.

He slowed her down with a hand on her arm, easing her over to one side of the hallway outside of the doctor's office. His niece had gotten sleepy, laying her heavy head on her mom's shoulder.

"Are you okay?" he asked in a quiet tone, pulling himself forcibly back to the here and now. "What's up?"

As if realizing just how much she'd revealed, Sierra glanced away. But Paxton didn't miss the rapid blinking of her eyes against the sudden tears. "Nothing. It's probably just the hormones."

While that could definitely play a part, his big-brother instincts told him something more was going on. "Is everything okay?" He thought back over her words. "Is there a problem between you and Jason?"

"I wouldn't know," she sniffed, then reached up to stroke her sleepy daughter's hair. "He's always at work. Though I guess that's what I married him for…right?"

She turned back to him after only a few steps. "Take it from me, Paxton," she said in a low tone. "Just because the whole business-before-pleasure thing worked for our parents and grandparents doesn't mean it's the wonderful life they told us it would be. Marrying for money is just as complicated as marrying for love."

Then she quickly changed the subject. "Let's check in," she said, almost too nonchalantly. He knew she was trying to hide from him as she reached for the door.

He'd never known her to keep secrets, but her stoic facade worried him.

Following Sierra and his niece into the doctor's waiting room, Paxton felt that familiar surge of protectiveness that he often got by just hanging out with his siblings. They'd always been close. Add in the gaggle of girl children his sisters had given birth to, and Paxton found himself to be a hands-on uncle. His grandmother often prophesied that

Paxton would be the first to give the family a male heir, something he definitely looked forward to. But until then he would protect and love the women in his life as much as possible.

If he only knew what Sierra needed protecting from...

"Here," he said, reaching out for his niece, "let me take her while you sign in."

He snuggled the droopy toddler in his arms and stood behind his sister as the receptionist opened the window that separated her from the waiting room. Small talk floated around him as Sierra signed the check-in list; he wasn't really paying attention. He glanced over the women's heads, farther into the little box the receptionist occupied. Behind her, at the exit window, a woman in scrubs was speaking to a patient who was checking out. At first Paxton couldn't see her. Then she turned toward him.

*Ivy.*

Without a thought, Paxton leaned closer to the opening. He knew he shouldn't eavesdrop, but it was if his hearing was tuned in specifically to her voice. Luckily for him, his hearing was excellent.

"Here are your vitamins," the woman in scrubs said.

Ivy had a nervous expression as she glanced down at the box on the checkout counter. Paxton's gaze followed. He swallowed hard. The words *prenatal vitamins* seemed to jump out at him.

The woman continued, oblivious to the audience behind her. "And this is a prescription for nausea medicine. Take it when you need it, which will hopefully only be for another month or so. You and the baby need good nutrition right now, so we don't want you too sick to eat. Got it?"

Ivy nodded, swallowing hard enough for Paxton to see her throat working. Nausea? Prenatal vitamins? Baby? The words floated through the fog clouding his brain. He blinked, trying to process. He knew what the words meant, but he couldn't get the significance to register.

Just then, Ivy looked across the tiny room and spotted him. Her eyes went wide. Her lips parted, but no words came out. He didn't need any. Panic spread across her features like a wave, putting the final piece in the puzzle.

A baby. They'd made a baby?

No sooner had he blinked than she was gone. He couldn't see which way she went through the receptionist's window.

"Paxton, what is wrong with you today?" his sister complained.

He glanced down to realize the way he was leaning had her blocked in against the check-in counter. "Sorry," he mumbled. "Here."

He handed his niece over to her mother, then murmured, "I'll be right back."

Remembering the office layout from the few times he'd been there before, Paxton knew the exit let out on the other side of the clinic, but then patients had to come back up the front hallway to get to the parking lot. He rushed back out the way they'd come in, hoping to intercept Ivy. Not that he knew what he'd say. His only thought was to find her. Now.

The hallway was empty. He backtracked down the hall to the adjoining one, but still didn't see her. Maybe she'd already gotten outside? But he couldn't find her in the parking lot either. He cursed himself as he realized he wasn't even sure what kind of car she drove. After a good five minutes—and one missed call and exasperated text from his sister—Paxton returned to the doctor's waiting room.

But Ivy's panicked features remained foremost in his mind.

"Paxton McLemore saw me at the obstetrician's office." The heart-pounding panic as Ivy spoke the words to her sisters was almost overwhelming. She forced herself to breathe in and out slowly. This intense upset couldn't be good for the child she carried. Even if it was justified. She'd spent a month second-guessing herself, only to have all her plans smashed with one doctor's visit.

"What happened?" Jasmine asked, her voice hushed with expectation. Jasmine was the epitome of the older sister, fulfilling her role with wisdom and the same matter-of-fact tone she used on unruly clients in her event planning business.

"I looked up from the counter, and there he stood. Watching me." Ivy swallowed. So tall. With a baby sleeping in his arms, he'd almost seemed like her fantasies come to life. Only it wasn't their child. And the realization that she was truly seeing Paxton in that moment had been more like a nightmare.

One that mocked the dreams of happily-ever-after she'd been rudely woken from that fateful morning, two months ago.

"He recognized you, I hope?" Auntie asked, her frown deepening the wrinkles on her beloved face.

Oh, he had. "Yes. There was recognition in his eyes. Then shock." Her finger traced the interlocking pattern of the tiger wood on the dining room table.

Ivy had watched Paxton's gaze drop to the box on the counter with the paralyzing realization of what was to come…and knowing she could do nothing to stop it. Luckily the nurse had wrapped things up quickly.

She imagined her disappearing act would not go over well with Paxton once he got over the shock. "I panicked. I didn't know what to do, what to say." She looked around, shame burning her cheeks. "So I just grabbed my stuff and ran."

A little giggle sounded to her left. Ivy cast a quick glance at Willow. "What's so funny?" she demanded.

Willow pressed her lips together, but it didn't help since her amusement was evident to everyone. Their middle sister had always marched to her own drum. "Well, all I can imagine is you running down the hall, pushing people out of the way, like one of those victims in a thriller movie. In heels, no less." She giggled again. "Not your normal modus operandi."

Auntie started to chuckle, then Jasmine. In less than sixty seconds, they were all giggling until the tears started. Even Ivy. She drew in a deep breath. Man, that felt good. No one could make her laugh when she needed it like her sisters.

"Maybe he won't care?" Willow asked, sober once more. How could she sound skeptical and hopeful at the same time?

Ivy forced herself to wipe away the last of her tears. She'd been reliving that awful moment when she'd looked up to see Paxton staring at her from across the little office for hours now. She'd finally realized his sister had been with him. At least his being there made some sort of sense now.

Even though it was still disastrous.

Auntie cut into her thoughts, offering the same steady wisdom she'd handed out to the girls since she'd taken them in as orphaned teenagers. "Oh, he will care. The question is, what will he do about it? Men like him never quit."

As Ivy felt her stomach tighten in protest, Jasmine admonished, "Auntie, that's not helping."

"Doesn't make it less true," Auntie insisted.

How could she have gotten herself into this mess? With Paxton McLemore, of all people? "Why did I wear that ring?" She moaned, letting her head drop into her hands. "Why did I think it would bring anything but bad luck?"

"Because it produced miracles for Jasmine and me?" Willow asked.

This was really not a good moment for both of her sisters to remind Ivy that they'd found their happily-ever-afters while wearing the ring. She hadn't been so lucky.

Ivy glared at Willow. "Too bad I didn't get the same treatment."

But she couldn't truly blame the ring. She'd let fantasies overtake her since the first day she'd started working for Paxton McLemore, at the expense of her true mission. Keep her head down, work hard and get ahead—all without him discovering who she really was. Playing with fire had gotten her burned. Now her family could be in as much trouble as she was…if Paxton pursued her too closely and discovered who they really were.

"He hasn't called, even though he has your personal cell number," Jasmine said, obviously trying to change the subject. "Even though it's only been a few hours, that's a good sign, right?"

"I don't know," Ivy said and then moaned.

"Will he realize the baby is his?" Auntie asked.

"There's no way Paxton McLemore won't put two and two together." They'd used a condom, but mistakes happen.

Ivy worried the inside of her bottom lip with her teeth. She didn't doubt Paxton would contact her at some point. He might not care anything about her—he'd made that clear over the last two months. But a baby… Paxton was a family man through and through. She doubted he would ignore her pregnancy, no matter how much of an inconvenience it was to him. "I have no idea what to say to him."

A banging on the front door startled them all. "Geesh," Willow exclaimed. "Take it easy."

She headed down the hallway. Jasmine's hand covered Ivy's, warming her chilled skin. "Everything's gonna be okay," she murmured.

Why didn't Ivy feel the same way?

They heard Willow open the door and say something, followed by a deep, smooth male voice.

"Where is she?"

Ivy's eyes widened, her gaze locking with Jasmine's. There was no mistaking Paxton's voice or the forceful tone that she'd heard time and again in business meetings. The panic from earlier returned full force, drumming in her chest. She and Jasmine scrambled from their seats.

Together, they peeked around the door frame of the dining room, straight down the hall. Paxton stood in the front doorway with an angry expression on his face. In that moment he glanced over Willow's shoulder and saw Ivy.

He didn't bother asking for permission. Instead he shouldered past Ivy's sister and stomped down the hallway, causing the wooden floors to creak in protest.

"Paxton," Ivy exclaimed. "What are you doing here?"

"Hunting down what's mine."

A small part of her was thrilled at his words, but the anger in his expression told her in no uncertain terms that he wasn't here for her. At least, not the way she wanted.

"Get out!" The words escaped her mouth just as Auntie murmured, "I told you so."

A hint of amusement passed over Paxton's face before he turned grim again. "If I'm understanding this situation correctly, you turned in your resignation and walked away, knowing you were pregnant with my child?"

A chorus of feminine "oh dears" filled the air and guilt struck Ivy hard. Yes, that's exactly what she'd done. But his blunt recitation of the facts didn't truly represent the whole picture: her loneliness and fear and anger over the past two months.

"Ivy," Paxton said, his timbre low and menacing. He stopped directly in front of her, looming just enough to inspire a touch of fear. "It seems we have a problem."

# Three

"Do I get any kind of explanation?"

"Do you deserve one?" Under other circumstances, Ivy had plenty of reserves to pull from to keep herself diplomatic. But Paxton's appearance here had her off guard and on edge.

She needed her sisters. A glance toward the doorway from the kitchen showed that it was empty. Ivy licked her dry lips. When Paxton had asked to speak with her alone, they'd reluctantly left for the front parlor. Not that they wouldn't come running if she yelled, but still…she couldn't stop herself from wrapping her arms around her middle.

Facing him alone made her stomach hurt even more than when she'd just been worrying over him showing up.

"How'd you find me?" she asked.

"Human resources was nice enough to help with an address."

She licked her lips again. "Why?"

"Seriously?"

Ivy was genuinely surprised as Paxton's eyes widened and his tone deepened with more anger. She wasn't sure why. Paxton was passionate about kids. But the knowledge that he was here for that reason alone made her own anger surge.

"I could have been at the doctor's office for any number of reasons..." she insisted.

"Like getting a prescription of prenatal vitamins?"

"That was none of your business, Paxton."

"Don't even go there..." he growled.

He leaned closer, his height giving him the advantage. His intention might not be intimidation, but it sure felt that way. Even in her heels, she'd never come close to his height. In her current flip-flops, she didn't stand a chance. But at least she was still on her feet. Sitting down felt like giving him too much of an advantage, so she continued to stand, even though her body swayed under the continuous onslaught of pregnancy hormones, nausea and exhaustion.

Paxton wasn't through throwing his weight around. "If you simply wanted to walk away from your job, that's your prerogative. But with my child? No way."

The possessiveness in his words sent a scary thrill through her. "*My* child," she insisted.

"Your words earlier already told me it's mine, too." He smirked. "You can't deny it. I was listening at the window. I heard it all."

*How would it feel to be able to wipe that smirk off his face?*

If she'd known he was listening, she'd have been careful not to give so much away. *Eavesdropper.* But then, Paxton was used to having his way in life. She'd seen it time and again when she worked for him. It would be best to set some boundaries up front. "A little beneath you, isn't it?"

"I could say the same. Sneaking around. Running away. You could have just told me."

In that moment it felt like Ivy's blood turned to jet fuel and someone set a match to it. Heated fury instantly engulfed her. She stomped forward. "At what point? You made it clear you weren't interested in hearing anything personal. And you certainly didn't seem to be interested in any consequences before today."

He shook his head. "This is a child we're talking about here."

Obviously that's all that mattered. "I see. The only consequences of note are the ones that affect you."

He stalked away, steps heavy on the kitchen's tile floor, and raked his hands through his blond hair in a familiar gesture she'd seen so many times in his office. Frustration. Anger. It took a lot to push Paxton that far. When those emotions overtook him in public, he simply went cold in his expression, movements and words.

Not in private. That was the part she already missed—all the emotions she'd been privy to that Paxton rarely showed anyone outside his family.

Unfortunately, now the emotions were directed at her. And not the fiercely tender ones she remembered from their one night together.

After several rounds of pacing, he settled in a chair at the table, then gestured for her to do the same. The stubborn part of her that wouldn't rest today wanted to insist he wasn't her boss anymore. She'd sit when she was good and ready. But the invitation rather than demand in his simple motion made her stubbornness seem petty.

*Damn him.*

She sat across from him, uncomfortably reminded of the many business negotiations she'd seen him participate in, sitting just this way. Facing his opponent dead-on. He didn't let them know they were opponents. Oh no. He greeted them with a charming smile and handshake. Otherwise he'd be giving too much away.

She unconsciously braced herself as he leaned her way.

"Why?" he asked, his voice soft but with an undercurrent of steel. "Were you ever going to tell me?"

She bit her lip, feeling heartless. But what could she say? She hadn't truly decided what she was going to do. Right now, every day was about survival: submitting résumés for another job, getting enough food in her so she didn't pass out, but not so much that she threw up.

Not an easy balancing act.

Finally she sighed, then attempted to put her thoughts into words. "Eventually..." She swallowed, studying the intricate pattern of light and dark wood pieces fitted together to create the handmade table where so many big family discussions had taken place in her life. "Once I had things figured out and stable, I would have let you know."

"And what needs to be figured out?" His voice had gone low again, this time with warning.

Surprised, she glanced over at him. She'd known that Paxton was unusually devoted to his family and doted on all of his nieces. Every bit of that protective instinct was alive and well in his expression right now. But not for her... never for her. "Obviously a new job," she said, hurt clipping her words.

"Obviously?"

"Yes, Paxton." Her exasperation left her breathy. "Regardless of what happens between us or with this pregnancy, working together after this would not be pleasant... or professional."

"Why not? Can't you separate your emotions from your job?"

*Not that much.* "Don't be ridiculous, Paxton."

"What happened between us—"

"Was a mistake."

He froze for a split second, as if he couldn't believe her words. "Says who?"

"You—" she erupted, slapping her palm on the table with more force than she had intended. How dare he act like she was overreacting. "You did. With every phone call and email that contained plenty of instructions but a whole lot of nothing." She couldn't control the rise in volume. "You did this, Paxton."

"You never said anything."

"I slept with my boss!" She struggled for breath in the midst of her raging emotions. "When he leaves without waking you up and then never mentions it again, there could only be two explanations—he's either too drunk to remember what happened or refuses to acknowledge what happened. There's not a whole lot I can say to address either of those situations."

"I wasn't drunk," he said quietly.

"Which leaves only one alternative." Turning away, Ivy pressed her hand hard against her stomach. The chaotic emotions rushing through her did not help her morning sickness at all. Though why they called it that, she'd never know. Hers was more like morning, noon and night sickness.

"Are you okay?" Paxton asked, his voice sounding closer. Sure enough, a quick glance confirmed he was on his feet and halfway around the table already.

"No," she snapped. She breathed slow and deep, in through her nose, out through her mouth. So far the only things she'd found that helped when the nausea hit at its random times were to keep very still and stay calm. This situation wasn't conducive to either.

"Besides, there are other issues to consider."

"Like what?"

She realized he wasn't going to let her get away with not answering that question. But her brain was seriously on strike right now. Thinking things through wasn't her strong point. All she knew was that anything she said about her family could potentially do a lot of damage.

Not just for herself and any custody battles she found herself in, but also for Jasmine. Even though her sister had a fiancé with clout now, the news of the Harden sisters' true heritage could break her event-planning business if the McLemores decided to go after her.

"I can't... I can't talk about that right now. My stomach—" She hated to use illness to get herself out of this discussion, but at least this overwhelming sickness came in handy for something.

"Okay," he conceded.

But she had a feeling she wasn't getting off easy. Suddenly he stood before her with his legs braced and his arms crossed over his chest.

"But remember," he said, "I can't fix what I don't know."

"I'm not sure this can be fixed." Ivy gasped against a wave of nausea. "I just... I need time."

"We don't have an infinite amount of that left."

She glanced up to find him facing her, big body braced, arms crossed over his chest, causing his dress shirt to strain over smooth muscle. He opened his mouth. Then closed it. All while staring at her.

"What?" But she was almost afraid to ask. Paxton wasn't the type of guy to be at a loss for words.

"Did you do this on purpose?"

*Wow.* Ivy swayed. Or did she? Maybe it just felt that way with her mind reeling. She really had been delusional to think he might feel anything for her...hadn't she?

Her chest was too tight with hurt for her voice to come out more than a whisper. "Is that really how you see me?"

His answer was too matter-of-fact for her liking. "No. But people can hide a lot."

Just like he had. He'd hidden a lot of suspicion behind caring, hadn't he? "There's nothing I can say to convince you that I didn't deliberately get pregnant, Paxton," she said with more resignation than conviction. "That's gonna be a problem, isn't it?"

"Probably."

*She doesn't look so fierce in her sleep.*

Paxton stared down at Ivy as she rested on the sofa in the Hardens' front parlor. Her tousled hair looked the same as it had on the morning that he'd left her in his bed, but her face was thinner now. A slight frown rested between her brows, as if she couldn't get comfortable, even in her sleep.

Uneasy with the softening of his emotional defenses, Paxton forced his gaze away from her to the surrounding room. He took in the antique furniture mixed with a few well-worn pieces and lots of soft feminine touches. The living space seemed well used and designed for comfort, while respecting the past.

"She's plumb tuckered out all the time," the older woman the sisters called Auntie said as she came up beside him.

Paxton glanced over at her, unease filtering through him. "Is this level of sickness dangerous? I don't remember either of my sisters having this problem."

Sierra rarely got sick at all. Janine had spent the first three months throwing up every morning, then she was fine the rest of the day. But they were both very emotional— conversations could turn into minefields without warning.

"Oh, it isn't dangerous," Auntie said with a wave of her hand. "As long as we keep enough food in her, she and the baby will be fine. Not comfortable, by any stretch of the imagination. But safe."

Paxton suppressed a smile. "Good to know."

"It's all been rough on her—" Auntie went on, shifting slightly "—between the sickness, how this all came about and getting used to the idea of bringing a new life into the world. That's a lot for a girl to take in."

Paxton was well aware. "I bet."

"She'll be a good mama, though. You'll see."

Finally Paxton let his gaze return to the sleeping beauty. He knew Ivy to be capable, efficient, eternally prepared for any number of clients' demands. The night of the masquerade, he'd discovered just how passionate she could be. The last thing he'd wondered about her was what kind of mother she'd be.

Guess he better start considering the possibilities.

*That's not why I'm here.* Paxton shook his head slightly. He'd spent the night vacillating between sheer panic and endless questions. Not the joy that he'd felt each time his sisters had announced their pregnancies.

He'd realized immediately after leaving yesterday that he'd taken the wrong tack. Letting their emotions take control wouldn't get them anywhere. Especially not him. It was the first time he could remember his emotions overtaking his logic so completely. A scary place for him to be.

So he'd returned this afternoon for a bit of reconnaissance. His best option for moving forward and answering his own questions about this whole situation was information.

Information about Ivy outside of their professional exposure to each other. Information about her family and the environment the child would be born into. That way he could make decisions and plans based on what he thought was best.

This situation wasn't ideal. It was what it was. He just needed a plan of action.

He forced his gaze away. Focus on the plan. Not on the woman.

"Thank you for having me," he said, turning up the wattage on his smile as he glanced back at Auntie. Just as he had yesterday, he'd noticed her limp as she'd led him from the front door, into the parlor. She had the pinkish complexion of health, but also the slight droop of exhaustion in her expression. Even this early in the evening.

"Oh, these girls keep me busy," she said, "but it makes life happy, you know?"

"I do, indeed. My family is a big part of my life also."

And he was not looking forward to hearing their thoughts when they found out he'd gotten his assistant pregnant. Definitely not what they'd had in mind when they urged him to start a family. Of course, it wasn't what he'd had in mind, either. Family had been the last thing he'd been thinking about when he'd taken Ivy to bed that night.

"I love having a big family," Auntie was saying, "Even though they came to me later in life. Do you have a big family?"

Paxton smiled and chatted about his two sisters and all his nieces. He truly loved his family, even when they were driving him crazy. He'd always been close with his siblings and his parents and grandmother. As the only grandson, they had high expectations for him and his future family. Almost as high as he had for himself.

Having a baby with Ivy didn't fit into the plan. His stomach twisted as he imagined their disappointment. But regardless of whether this baby fit his stringent requirements for having children, the baby existed. Paxton was not the kind of man who could simply walk away.

It wasn't just about responsibilities, either. He'd spent

a lot of time with his sisters and nieces. He didn't know where this was going, but those joyful thoughts of welcoming a child into the world and watching it grow were already taking hold.

Only a day, and he'd already been sucked in.

"Thank you for taking care of her," he said, in a sincere effort to show his appreciation, despite what Ivy would have thought if she'd heard it.

The older woman's smile was kind. "Ivy insists she's handling it, but it is wearing her down, I believe. She doesn't want anyone else to feel responsible, but that's what family does."

She leaned a little closer and lowered her voice. "I even postponed a trip with her sister Jasmine because I just don't want her alone. And she needs her own bed right now, her own space. Not to be out at Willow's place, away from her comfort zone."

Paxton stared for just a moment, his brain kicking into overtime. Something started to take shape, but before he could analyze it, a soft voice drifted across the room.

"Somehow I knew you'd be back."

Paxton was unsettled by Ivy's resigned tone. Without thought, his chin went up and he said, "You shouldn't doubt it. We'll be a major part of each other's lives from here on out."

Inwardly he winced. Probably not the right approach at the moment. Unlike Ivy, Paxton knew he needed to keep his emotions out of this situation. He wasn't sure how he felt about Ivy. About her being the mother of his child. He'd attempted to put every spine-tingling moment of their night together out of his mind…and had succeeded until the moment he'd returned home. But he didn't want to think about it. Right now, he needed to focus on the child.

The one thing he refused to walk away from.

Not wanting to hover over her, Paxton crossed to the sofa, where she lay, and eased himself into the far corner. Ivy's eyes widened before she pushed herself into a more upright position and pulled her feet closer to her. But not before he caught sight of her delicate feet with their bright pink toenails.

Once more he struggled to push back the memories.

"I'll leave you youngins alone for a bit," Auntie finally said, winking at Paxton. "I'm sure you have a lot to discuss."

Indeed they did.

Paxton turned back to Ivy, then winced at her cynical expression.

"Any particular reason you're trying to charm my aunt?"

*Busted.* "What are you talking about?"

"I've been watching you in action for a year and a half now. I've seen that same smile a hundred times. What are you trying to prove?"

*That I'm not the bad guy here.* "How are you feeling?" he asked, instead of answering her question.

She pushed the heavy fall of her hair back behind her ear. "Okay."

He could spot the lie from a mile away, even without her grimace.

"Medicine helping any?"

She glanced down at the floor as if she was uncomfortable with the attention. "It helps me not be sick, but doesn't take away the nausea altogether."

She'd lost weight, he noticed again. Her high cheekbones stood out more than they had, creating a hollow beneath. There were dark shadows under her eyes, too. She was indeed having a rough time of it.

"The doctor says only about a month more…" she said, her voice weak. "Then we should start to see some improvement."

As much of a jerk as it made him, he was about to use that little fact to his advantage. The idea that had teased him earlier now fell firmly into place.

As he looked into her cautious gaze, Paxton kept his expression serious. It would be all too easy to slip into charming-businessman mode, like he had with Auntie. That realm he could navigate easily. But Ivy would feel like she was being played.

He needed her on board. Not on edge.

"Ivy, I want to come stay with you."

The shock that widened her eyes reverberated inside of Paxton. He couldn't believe he was saying it out loud. But this made the most sense to him…and he hadn't been able to come up with a better option to get the amount of information he needed.

Thankfully she didn't mock his motives, or rage about the time they'd spent apart. Instead she seemed almost sad as she whispered, "Why?"

"We're having a baby together."

"Not really," she countered. "I mean, we have created a child together. But we aren't really together, are we?"

She had a point. Paxton stood, the need to clarify his thoughts pushing him to pace. "No," he said. As uncomfortable as it might be, they needed to get this point out in the open. "For now, we aren't together." He pivoted to face her. "But we will always be tied to one another. And right now, I'd say I know as little about you outside of work as you know about me."

She was already shaking her head. "I just can't deal with this right now, Paxton. Maybe later—"

"That's just it. I've had a lot of experience with pregnant women. You know that." After all, she'd watched him go to appointment after appointment with his sister last year, when her husband was away on business. "Auntie says Jasmine wants her to go on a trip with them. Let me take care of you. It will be easier on you, and on—"

"How's it going in here?" Auntie asked as she came back through the door with a tea tray. She set it on a little table near the couch. "Here's some ginger tea, sweetheart. Sip this slowly."

She handed a delicate teacup to Ivy, who raised it to her lips for a little sip before saying, "Thank you, Auntie."

The older woman limped over to a recliner, then lowered herself into it gingerly. Ivy frowned as she watched, the questions obvious on her face.

"Actually, Auntie," Paxton said, taking a chance despite the growing horror in Ivy's expression, "I'm trying to convince Ivy to let me stay here for a while. Let me take care of her. Take the burden off you so you can go on the trip with Jasmine."

Auntie glanced at Ivy with an almost-amused expression that he didn't understand. "Now, young man, don't you use me to put pressure on this young lady. She's carrying enough guilt as it is."

"I didn't mean to—"

"Then you don't know women as well as you think you do," she said with a smile. "Most women feel guilty for something or other. Ivy has had to take a step back lately, let other people do the work while her body handles the process of creation. That's not what she's used to...but I do think you have a point."

"You do?" Paxton hadn't thought she'd come onboard without some persuasion.

"This isn't really about me," Auntie chided him with a soft smile. "It's about you and Ivy. And you can't figure out anything about you and Ivy without working it out together." She transferred her smile to the woman looking pale and panicked on the couch. "It's hard to do that with distance...and a chaperone."

A stubborn expression took up residence on Ivy's face. "So you want to let someone you don't know live here while you're gone?"

"But you know me, don't you, Ivy?" Paxton prompted.

"So why did you accuse me of getting pregnant on purpose? Obviously you don't know me."

Paxton gave in to the renewed desire to pace. He didn't want to get into the particulars of his doubts, his accusations. But he wasn't seeing a way out. Especially not with Auntie's and Ivy's gazes trained directly on him. The pressure to explain warred with the desire to be defensive about his mistakes. "It was a long time ago."

"Did someone try to trap you into marriage?" Ivy asked, her wide eyes a sign of surprise he didn't believe.

Auntie made a soft clucking sound of comfort.

"No," Paxton assured her. Veronica hadn't trapped him into anything. "I have simply been deceived in the past by women who want more than I care to give. While I don't think that's what's happening here, the question had to be asked."

Auntie laughed. "Son, if someone is scamming you, I doubt they're just gonna admit it when you ask directly like that. But I can assure you, my niece is on the up-and-up. Besides, I doubt she was the one who brought the birth control to the party. Right?"

"Auntie!" Ivy cried, her pale cheeks flushing rose-red.

Paxton would normally have chuckled, but he was too lost in the memory of grabbing a condom from the bedside table. The box of condoms he'd bought. She was right. Birth control was always something Paxton handled himself. Only this time it had failed him.

He felt a low throb in his body, as if reminding him it had all been worth it. Too bad his body lied.

Then Ivy pressed a hand to her stomach and grimaced. As she lifted the teacup back to her lips, Paxton decided to give her some breathing room. Normally, he pressed hard when he wanted something. Pressed until he received the answer he wanted. But now wasn't the time for that...and he had a feeling Ivy wasn't a woman who would take it.

"Look, just think about it. I think it would be good for us." Even if maintaining his distance would be harder under those circumstances. But he had to remember his life plan. This might be a detour, but he refused to be derailed from his own goals. Or his family's expectations. "I'll come by tomorrow."

"Why don't you just call?" Ivy asked.

Maybe he would press...just a little more. "Because regardless of your decision, you're stuck with me. Yours is only a choice of location."

# Four

"Auntie, why didn't you tell me?"

Ivy hated the whine in her voice, but couldn't seem to suppress it. Every minute that brought her closer to having Paxton staying with her, in her house, alone together...well, her nerves were definitely on edge. She'd just found out that he was due to arrive in a few hours and would be staying for the duration of Auntie's trip with Jasmine.

"Unlike Paxton," Auntie said with a small smile, "I know how women work emotionally. There's no need for you to feel responsible for my decision to have him stay here."

Ivy glanced at Jasmine as they crowded around her bed in the far upper room of the house. "Really?" Ivy said. Jasmine had been just as bad, keeping their plans quiet until the last minute.

Her sister shrugged. "Not my place to tell you we were going, either," she said. "Stop with the grumpy face."

"Don't I have a say?" Ivy asked, throwing her hands up

in a futile gesture. "I'm a grown woman, perfectly capable of taking care of myself."

"Not right now, you aren't," Auntie said. As she walked through the door, she threw back over her shoulder, "And guess what? That's okay."

No. It never was, in her book.

The energy drained from her, causing Ivy to plop down on the bed. "Am I doing the right thing?"

Both of Ivy's sisters paused in sorting the laundry on her bed to stare at her. Unable to handle the astonishment in their looks, she turned away. She let her nervous fingers trace the hand-sewn stitches on the quilt Auntie had made for her for her eighteenth birthday. "I'm not myself, okay?"

"You must not be," Willow said with an astonished tone. "Because I've never known you to ask us what the right choice is."

"Ever," Jasmine agreed.

Willow chuckled. "You keep this up, we might start to think you're human."

Ivy grimaced. It wasn't so much that she thought she knew everything. She simply hated to burden other people with her problems, or her upkeep, or her needs or wants. She preferred to give rather than receive...ever since her parents had died and she'd found herself as the youngest child with everyone else struggling to support her.

As her brain entered yet another round of asking, *What am I going to do about Paxton*? She wilted. No nausea so far today, but her entire body felt drained. Hopefully the doctor had been right and she only had a little over a month of this to go. Then her hormones would calm down and the nausea would subside.

She could feel her sisters' gazes on her, their concern, which was why they'd come over to help Auntie pack and get some things straightened up before their trip. But she wasn't sure how to express herself right now. This baby seemed to have sucked the life from her brain, as well as her body.

She also suspected they wanted to check out the situation firsthand, make sure she wasn't being forced to do something she didn't want to do. Or that Paxton wasn't even more volatile than the last row they'd seen, even though Ivy had assured them that that was unusual for him.

Jasmine tried to reassure her. "You don't have to do this if you don't want to. Even if he's already at the door. We'll figure it out."

And leave Auntie disappointed that she couldn't go with Jasmine and her daughter, Rosie, on this special trip. "I'm scared not to," Ivy whispered.

That had them dropping the laundry and closing in. "Why?"

Jasmine grabbed one of her hands. "We'll simply stay home if this is too much. You know we'll do everything in our power to take care of you."

Which was exactly what Ivy didn't want. Her sisters both had their hands full these days. The last thing Ivy wanted to be to anyone was a burden.

She rubbed her palm over her lower belly. As much as this little booger was giving her fits, she loved it already. Sight unseen. "I know that. But I need to do this… There's a lot at stake."

Her sisters scooted closer. Jasmine draped an arm around her shoulders. "Are you gonna tell him?" she asked.

Ivy knew what they meant. The secret history their family shared with Paxton's. The history he didn't even know about. Oh, he'd heard the story, of course. Probably many times, considering it was one of his ancestors who had died when her family allegedly sabotaged one of his family's most impressive cargo ships several generations ago.

It had sunk off the coast of Savannah, with the family's heir inside.

Her family had been accused of destruction of property and murder. There wasn't any proof, but that hadn't stopped the McLemores from destroying her great-grandfather's life anyway, until he'd had to move away to protect the safety of his wife and daughter.

Only, he'd been innocent all along.

Jasmine had thought she was safe. After all, the family name had died with their mother. Their return to live with Auntie after their parents' deaths went unnoticed by anyone aware of the tragedy. There had been no reason for Paxton to ever know his employee was hiding her true identity from him.

Now she was tangled up in a web that felt deceitful, even though she'd never meant it that way. Despite the beliefs of Paxton's family, her great-grandfather had been a good man. But she had no way to prove his innocence at the moment. Ivy raised her gaze to Jasmine's worried expression. "What are the odds of us raising a child together without him ever finding out who I really come from?" she asked.

Well, they wouldn't be truly together…not in the way she'd dreamed of before that magical night. But they would still talk, interact with each other, make decisions together, right? Now that she knew for certain Paxton would be a part of her child's life, Ivy knew it would be important to stay on good terms with him.

As much as that was within her power.

Her stomach lurched for the first time today. This was not how she'd imagined having a child, nor how she'd imagined being with Paxton.

"I'm sorry," Willow said. "Maybe soon I will have the proof we need. That's why I went to Sabatini House, to see if I could find proof that the Sabatini pirates were actually responsible for sinking that ship, but I got a little distracted."

Willow rubbed her own belly then. Her sister had found herself pregnant only a few weeks after Ivy. But her circumstances were much different…and happier. Ivy reassured her, "What you found there was far more important than family history."

"Hopefully we'll have the pieces we need to prove our family's innocence soon enough," Jasmine said.

"Should we have a plan?" Willow asked.

Ivy frowned as unease drifted through her body. "That seems wrong…devious, somehow."

"Why?" Willow asked. "It's called contingency planning. There are certain things you can't control, but we need to decide ahead of time if there are circumstances where you need to give the details of our family history. Otherwise, the best plan is silence. For now."

"I can't think of any reason you would bring this up yourself," Jasmine said with a shake of her head. "I think the plan should just be silence, unless he brings it up himself."

"How would he find out?" Ivy asked.

Willow snorted in a very unladylike fashion. "Who knows? Then again, you don't really know Paxton very well outside of work, do you?"

Ivy was ashamed to admit that she didn't, although she had felt like she did. Day in and day out in each other's company had given her a false sense of familiarity. But she'd kept it that way on purpose. While she'd fantasized about more, she'd never planned on getting closer to Paxton than watching him from across his desk. For this very reason. She'd needed a good paying job…and he was never supposed to know who she really was.

"No, I don't," she mumbled. "I definitely can't tell him anything until I know more about him and his family."

"Then focus on that," Jasmine said. "Besides, connecting with him on a deeper level will be very valuable if his family disapproves later on."

Ivy really didn't want to think about that. Paxton's family had never been very friendly when she'd seen them in the office. They pretty much pretended she wasn't there unless they needed something. It didn't take a genius to realize that her past wouldn't be the only problem with that crew. Her present circumstances would throw up just as strong of a roadblock.

Willow added as they stood to go downstairs, "That will give me time to do my thing. I'll see if I can find any more connections as we work on cleaning out the attic, too."

That would be good. The attic at Sabatini House had yielded the first answer the girls had looked for about their past. The sisters grinned at one another. Ivy's stomach settled once more. Though she worked really hard to be independent, her family was the best support a woman could ever ask for.

As she made her way downstairs with her sisters, she felt calm for the first time since she'd known Paxton was coming to stay with her.

"See," Willow went on. "I think this is a very solid contingency plan."

Paxton's voice shot at them from the doorway at the other end of the hall. "And why would you need one of those?"

Paxton hadn't been expecting a landing party when he'd shown up at the Harden place to take care of Ivy. The sea of people now crowded into the front parlor would have been intimidating for anyone not used to addressing groups like he was… In truth, he found himself energized by the challenge.

He recognized Ivy's sisters from the pictures that used to be on her desk at work, along with the sweet little toddler with dark curly hair in Jasmine's arms. Ivy's niece, Rosie.

The sole man in the group he recognized for a completely different reason. His presence was a bit of a shock. Ivy had never mentioned Royce Brazier to him. He'd heard through the grapevine when he'd returned home that Royce had recently become engaged to his event planner, but he'd had no reason to look into the details.

He'd only vaguely remembered Ivy's sister was an event planner. She had never been very forthcoming about her family at work.

As if drawn to the only other male in a sea of femininity, Paxton held out his hand. "Good to see you again, Royce."

"Long time, no see," Royce agreed.

His handshake was firm—firmer than usual. Though it had been almost a year since he'd interacted with him, Paxton didn't remember Royce as the type to pull macho power plays. But the look that accompanied the move assured Paxton that Royce was the person in charge here.

"All right," he said as he released Paxton's hand. "Let's give the man some room to breathe."

Auntie waved her arms around in a shooing motion to disperse the crowd from the front room. Suddenly the rapt audience began fiddling with luggage and discussing itineraries. The noise faded as they finished their last-minute preparations.

Only then did Paxton realize that Ivy wasn't there. Had she not been in the room all along? Had she snuck out while the rest of the family was piling in?

Nobody mentioned her absence as they rushed into last-minute preparations for their trip. In the sea of scurrying women, Paxton and Royce stood still.

As he continued to watch the strangely coordinated movements, a tingle of panic rose inside Paxton. Where was Ivy? Was something wrong?

Oblivious to the other man now, Paxton took a step toward the doorway, determined to find out where she'd gone. Only to have Royce move directly into his path.

Paxton took a deep breath, forcing himself to relax, not to let the other man see his hackles rise at the move.

"Is something wrong?" he asked.

"No," Royce said, though his deliberate stance belied the casual denial. Arms crossed over his chest. Legs braced. Definitely in charge. "Not at all."

Paxton raised a brow in inquiry, waiting to see where Royce wanted this conversation to go. He didn't have to wait long.

"I just thought it would be a good idea to make sure we're all on the same page before most of Ivy's family travels across the country, leaving her alone with a man none of us know very well."

The suspicion in his voice was blatant. Not that Royce was attempting to hide it.

"Royce, that's not really necessary." Paxton reminded himself he would probably issue his own warnings over his sisters and pushed down the rising need to fight for the alpha-male position. "You've met me before. You're aware of my reputation. Do you really think I'd hurt her?"

"This isn't professional—it's personal. And each of these women has come to mean a lot to me." Royce's gaze didn't waver from his for a minute. "I think every woman deserves someone to look out for her, to back her up."

"I agree."

Royce continued to study him for a moment longer than

was comfortable. "I see you do. Just don't forget that Ivy's not alone in this. She might not like the idea, but we are here for her nonetheless."

Regardless of that last cryptic sentence, Paxton totally got that Ivy now had the backing of not just any man, but one of the most powerful men in Savannah. As much as Paxton liked to think of his family as loving, they were also business people, who more often than not made decisions based on logic and profitability, rather than emotions.

It was a reputation they'd carefully cultivated; it was also the truth. Looking at it in that light, Paxton saw clearly Royce's need to protect Ivy.

"I understand."

"I don't think you do," Royce said, for the first time breaking into a grin. "But you will." He patted Paxton's shoulder as he urged him toward the hall. "Just remember—I've been there. The learning curve is steep, but oh so worth it."

*Huh?*

As the two men headed into the hall that ran the length of the house, Paxton thought back to the swirling rumors he'd paid little attention to at the family dinner when his sisters had tried to catch him up on all he'd missed while he was out of town. The only reason he'd listened was because he never knew when a bit of gossip could lead to a business breakthrough.

Had the stone-cold businessman finally grown a heart? From what Paxton could read, he had—at least for the Harden sisters.

But Paxton had always had a heart, hadn't he? Even when he chose to work strictly based on logic instead.

"Where did Ivy go?" he asked as they moved into the long hallway that ran the length of the house.

"I'm pretty sure she's back here," Royce said as he led the way to the kitchen.

Sure enough, Ivy sat at the table, surrounded by women who chatted and filled the room with last-minute admonishments to take care of herself.

Auntie beamed as they walked inside. "She ate some broth."

"Now, if I can keep it down," Ivy said in a snarky tone that Paxton wasn't used to hearing from her.

But she seemed to shake it off as she stood up for hugs all around and an extra kiss for Rosie. "Y'all have a good time," she said.

Though her expression was cheerful, Paxton suspected it was forced for their benefit. If he hadn't been watching her instead of the mass exodus going on around them, he would have missed the momentary droop, the dropping of her guard that allowed him to briefly glimpse the exhaustion underneath the facade. Luckily her family didn't seem to see it.

He knew in that moment how very important it was to her that her family see her as strong. Capable. Had this ordeal been difficult for her? Forced her to concede a weakness she would rather have kept hidden? Required her to lean on them?

Her discomfort about being dependent probably extended to him, too, considering the speed with which her mask reappeared. Almost before he could even blink, he faced a sphinx instead of the warm, professional woman he was more familiar with.

He was even less prepared when she turned immediately back down the hall after closing the door behind her family. "I'm going to lie down now," she said.

Paxton trailed after her as she made her way slowly up the stairs. To his amusement, that seemed to make her pick up her pace.

"Is there anything I can get you?" he asked, while doing

his level best to ignore the firm curve beneath the soft pants she wore.

She didn't pause before opening a door about halfway down the hall. Paxton had a brief glimpse of silk and lace and a mixture of pastel and vibrant colors. No halfway for Ivy. He felt like it was a momentary glance of the woman behind the professional facade.

Very quickly she turned back to him, pulling the door closed until he could only see her face. "I'll catch you later," she said, then shut the door almost on his nose.

So much for reconnaissance.

# Five

Ivy jumped at the sharp knock on her bedroom door.

"Dinner."

Paxton's tone brooked no argument. After Ivy had refused lunch, it wasn't surprising. She'd been locked in her room all day—napping, reading and completely ignoring Paxton. Even if she did pause at every noise, her throat tightening as she wondered if he would try her door.

Guess he reached his limit.

So had she. Though worried it would make her nauseous, she knew she needed to eat.

Just walking into the kitchen made her mouth water. She couldn't tell what it was exactly, but the heavenly smell seemed to make her feel warm and cozy all by itself. Paxton looked up from the pot on the stove.

"Hungry?"

Her stomach growled as if it knew she wouldn't answer honestly if left to her own devices.

Paxton gave her a half grin that made her heart feel funny. "I'd say that's a yes," he said.

Anxious for something to distract her from his golden good looks, Ivy moved toward the cabinets to get plates. Then she noticed bowls already sitting on the counter. "Soup?" she asked, awkwardness stiffening her movements.

He nodded. "Have a seat."

"I can do—"

He didn't argue, but simply stepped into her path. "I said, sit."

She wanted to be angry, but he wasn't being rude. Just firm. Her treacherous body complied, melting into the nearest chair.

His busyness gave her the chance to admire his agile movements as he dished up the food and brought bowls to the table. Paxton had always moved with an almost languid lack of speed. He was never in a hurry, no matter how urgent the cause, but he always got the job done.

Steam rose from the bowls that he set on each of their place mats, tempting her to inhale. They were joined by perfect slices of cornbread. Could this man do anything wrong? This meal couldn't have been better designed to settle her stomach. Carbs and more carbs.

Not that her admiration sat well with her. She wished she could ignore how capable he was, both in business and with people. Feeding her anger and resentment would make this situation a whole lot easier. Those emotions helped her keep him at arm's length, whereas admiration just made her want him more.

To hide her conflict, she leaned over the bowl and breathed deep. Potato. She remembered it as one of his favorite options this past winter from one of the local restaurants where she ordered his lunches. Paxton also set a tray on the table with little bowls of cheese, bacon, sour cream, ham and scallions.

"This is very domestic," she said. Almost immediately she winced, because she hadn't meant to sound petulant.

"Man cannot live by restaurant alone," he joked, ignoring her tone and flashing that grin again. "Not even the single man."

Ivy knew her mouth had fallen open, and she struggled to close it even though the surprise remained. "You made this?" she asked, remembering all the lunches she'd provided to him over the last year and a half. Paxton didn't believe in brown-bagging it.

He raised a brow. "Your extreme surprise is not very flattering."

She met his expression with a lifted brow of her own. "I think I have a right to be surprised. I used to order all your takeout, remember?" She gestured toward the steaming food. "I just assumed this came from a restaurant."

"No restaurant. Just these two hands." He raised them, palms facing her, as if that alone would prove the truth.

She knew just how capable those hands were. In the office. With his family. In the bedroom. But she'd never guessed that they were also talented in the kitchen. Deep down inside, she was ashamed that she hadn't known this about a man whom she felt so deeply for. What other things about him did she not know outside of work?

For lunch, he ate at his restaurant of choice. Either there or had it delivered to the office. It never occurred to her that he was cooking like this at home. She stared down at the creamy concoction in her bowl.

"Though I do admit," he went on, as if conceding her point, "I had the groceries delivered."

Man, that grin was so hard to resist. As if sensing that she might be open to conversation now, he quickly changed the subject. "I've been looking around the house this afternoon."

There was a subtle accusation in his pointed glance that she chose to ignore. "This house has excellent craftsmanship. Have you always lived here?" he continued.

Without thinking, Ivy answered, "Auntie's family built it. Then she and her husband lived here during their marriage."

Paxton's brow furrowed…the first sign of her mistake. "I'm confused," he said.

Shoot. How much could she say without saying too much? "Oh, Auntie isn't really our aunt. She took us girls in when my parents died."

"Wow." Paxton looked impressed. "She went from no children to three girls? That's a very big sacrifice. I assume she knew your parents well?"

Certainly Ivy was aware of the dangerous waters she was swimming in. Any discussion of her family or Auntie's family could move into dangerous territory very quickly, so she'd keep her answers short and sweet. "She was my mother's nanny."

She took a couple more bites as an excuse to not talk.

"I didn't know you were an orphan. How did your parents die?"

Ivy's stomach twisted. Her parents' deaths were not something she was comfortable discussing, even after all these years. "It was a car accident," she choked out.

The flash of grief, memories of a young child devastated at the sudden loss, made her antsy. She found herself crumbling the last bite of cornbread on her plate between her thumb and forefinger.

"Were y'all from here? Originally?" he asked.

The questions seemed so innocent, but were they? Ivy's

emotions coalesced into a distinct unease. Until she found the right path, she had to protect her family.

Oblivious, Paxton went on. "There definitely seems to be a sailing theme around here." He pointed to some of the memorabilia in the china cabinet, a few ships in miniature that had been passed down to the girls. "Was your family in the shipping business?"

Alarm sped through Ivy with the speed of a wildfire. She stared deep into her empty bowl, wishing she had more of the yummy goodness. Not because she was hungry, but just to have something to occupy her hands. "I'd really rather not talk about this right now," she mumbled.

Then she forced herself to her feet and carried her bowl across to the stove.

"Let me do that," Paxton insisted, rising from his seat.

"I can do it."

It was ridiculous how often she had to repeat that these days. She was capable, though some days she needed to convince herself that she *could* do things, even if it was something as simple as fixing herself a bowl of soup.

"I don't mind," he said. "Let me do it for you."

Helplessness washed over her, but she refused to give in. *Stubborn.* It's what her family had always called her. Through clenched teeth, she repeated, "I can do it, Paxton. I'm not an invalid."

The strength of her emotions washed away any desire for more food. Embarrassment filtered into the mix. But she hated anyone thinking she was weak, hated how much she had to rely on other people these days.

But most of all, she hated how out of control everything felt...

*This reconnaissance mission is going nowhere.*

Frustration sharpened Paxton's nerves as he stared out

the window late that night. He couldn't even focus on the laptop open before him. Concentrating on work had never been a problem. This situation was just unusual enough to cause a simmering mixture of unease and frustration that blocked his usual productivity.

His purpose in coming here had been thwarted by one prickly blonde woman. Instead of hanging out together, or even sitting in the same room, Ivy had retreated to her bedroom not long after dinner—and he'd counted himself lucky that she'd hung around that long.

Though they had technically been in the same room, she'd pretended to sleep between lunch and dinner. She might actually have slept for a bit in front of the television, which was tuned to a marathon of a crazy reality show she hadn't seemed to be watching. He'd wondered more than once if she'd chosen it on purpose just to annoy him.

But what annoyed him more was that Ivy had refused to ask for anything to drink, had refused to let him fix her another bowl of soup, had refused to let him make her cookies.

What pregnant woman refused cookies?

But it was as if she had to prove to him that she didn't need him there at all. That she could get what she needed herself, rather than let him lend a hand.

Finally Paxton gave in and retired to the guest room for some sleep. He wasn't getting any work done, so he might as well call it a night. But the resolve wasn't enough to allow him to fall asleep. Instead he stared at the pressed-tin ceiling, wondering how to break through Ivy's insistent need for independence. About fifteen minutes passed before he heard footsteps upstairs. Slow steps, then running.

A door slammed. Paxton sat up to listen. Water rushed through the pipes overhead. The sink? A toilet? He couldn't be sure.

That was the only sound for a few minutes, then he heard

a loud thump. He jumped out of bed, his body preparing for action. What was that?

But the water continued to run, long enough that he wondered if she was taking a shower. His muscles relaxed as the water finally ceased.

Then the barest creak of a door. No footsteps. He cocked his head to the side, listening hard. Was she just standing there? Or tiptoeing down the hall? Then another heavy thud came. Almost directly overhead.

After that, nothing. Silence descended, aside from the normal household hum. What was she doing up there?

His heartbeat sped up a notch. A lot of *what-ifs* sped through his mind... But the fact that he couldn't distinguish between the normal household sounds and what could be a serious situation made him angry.

He didn't care if she wanted help or not. He was going. It only took a second to pull a pair of sweatpants over his boxers and make his way up the stairs two at a time, turning on lights to illuminate the dark of the house along the way.

The first thing he saw in the upper hall as the light flicked on was tangled blond hair spread across the green floor runner. For a moment time froze.

"Ivy!"

She lifted her head a little as he knelt beside her.

"I'm fine," she said, but her voice was thready. Though she normally maintained the gorgeous porcelain skin of a Southern belle, right now she had the sickly-gray cast of someone definitely under the weather.

"Obviously." For the moment, his fear was easier to handle as sarcasm. But beneath the coping mechanism, he could feel rage building. "So, lying on the floor is just more comfortable than your bed?"

She patted the runner beneath her. "Just looking for a change of scenery."

"You know my room is directly below this spot, right?"

She closed her eyes, but he wasn't letting her ignore him this time.

"All you had to do was call my name. Heck, say my name and I would probably have heard you." Heat slipped into his voice without permission, but dammit, why hadn't she just called him for help?

He didn't think any further, didn't ask what she needed. He simply swept her up in his arms. She shrieked, but he ignored her.

"Put me down!"

Pretending to comply, he let her legs sweep down until her feet touched the floor, then lifted his arms in a hands-off gesture...until she swayed. "Sure that's what you want?" he asked.

A whimper was the only answer he waited for, before he picked her back up and strode down the hall to her room.

It wasn't until he set her onto the bed that he registered the bare skin against his palms. As he stepped back, the disheveled covers and hair reminded him of a much more titillating scenario. Something that shouldn't be registering at this point. He quickly pulled his mind back from the brink and focused in on his anger. That seemed the safer, easier option.

"Are you really so angry with me that you'd rather sleep on the floor than ask for help?" He exploded, giving the frustration free rein. "And why were you on the floor in the first place?"

Ivy covered her face. At first he thought she was simply avoiding his demanding questions. "This resistance to any bit of help is getting very childish, Ivy."

Then her shoulders started to shake. Paxton realized she wasn't blocking him out. She was crying.

"No—wait."

He held out both hands as if to pat her shoulders, but pulled back at the last minute. He wanted answers, but not like this. Upsetting her was the last thing he wanted. He hated for his sisters to cry. It made him feel helpless. But when Ivy lifted her face, *helpless* didn't begin to describe his emotions.

"You don't understand!" she spat out. "Two months ago, I was a fully functioning, fully capable woman. Now I have no job. No life. And apparently no ability to walk, either!"

Paxton could only stare as tears continued to rush over her cheeks.

"I'm just tired and weak and disgusting. Half the time, I can't fix myself something to eat. I'm too exhausted to work. I haven't done my nails in weeks. I mean, look at my hair!"

It was a genuine feminine complaint in the midst of bigger issues. Paxton understood. Her words painted a better picture of the loss of control she was feeling right now. His brain latched on to the details as something he could finally fix, something he could do to actually improve her feelings about this situation, as opposed to simply covering the basics.

But he had a feeling she wasn't going to like his next move, either.

# Six

The feelings washing over Ivy were even more out of control than her usual pregnancy doldrums. *Why had she been cursed with hormones?* Though that was probably a common female lament at various times in life, in this moment it was her truly heartfelt cry. Without consent, tears overflowed her eyes and trailed down her cheeks, even as she cursed her weakness.

This time she didn't protest as Paxton once again lifted her into his arms and retraced his steps down the hall. His destination: the bathroom where she'd just gotten sick. Her ill-fated attempt to make it back to her bedroom on her own, even though she'd known she was weak, had ended with her collapsing on the floor.

Even now her limbs felt weighted with the heaviness of fatigue. Her eyes refused to open. She was too tired to fight, too overwhelmed to keep her emotions under wraps. The roller coaster of the last three months was now running off the rails.

Heat burned beneath her skin as she remembered her whining complaints. At least, that's probably how Paxton heard them. Without comment he set her on the stool they kept in the good-sized room, then moved away. It wasn't until she heard water running into the tub that she started paying attention. Her soggy eyelashes took an effort to lift. "What are you doing?"

He didn't even look up from his task. "You'll be more comfortable if we wash you up."

"We?" she squeaked.

"You just collapsed on the floor. Are you gonna do this alone?"

She felt her mouth open to defend herself, but nothing came out. She glanced at the water, able to almost feel the heat with the rising steam. Then she looked back at the larger-than-life male pulling fluffy towels from the cabinet. Tendrils of sensual awareness shimmered through her exhaustion—familiar even though distant.

*No. No. No.*

She was not getting naked in front of him again.

Then he poured some of her favorite bubble bath into the running water. The soft sent of bourbon sugar filled the air. Her muscles started to ache, as if demanding to be immersed in the liquid warmth. Her body desperately wanted to relax, to rest…along with her brain.

Paxton used her distraction to his advantage. With a rush of fabric, her oversize T-shirt was whisked over her head, leaving her clad in nothing but her underclothes. Only then did she realize just how much of the lower half of her body had been on display. Even more was on display now.

"In you go," he said like a nursemaid, urging her to her feet so that she was facing the tub.

At least she didn't have to watch his expression while he undressed her. But that didn't stop the worries from rushing in. Unaware of her runaway thoughts, he popped open the clasp on her bra, and part of her wondered if he was just no longer interested in her...sexually.

Why couldn't she shut down these distressing thoughts?

Especially when his warm fingers brushed her hips as he pushed her panties down. Almost immediately a towel was draped over her shoulders.

*He's protecting my modesty, not ogling.* Why did that thought depress her? Contrary tears prickled the backs of her eyes. She didn't want to be wanted just because she was a naked woman.

Any naked woman.

But his practical touch reinforced the fact that he no longer saw her as desirable—just as the mother of his child. Someone he would take care of, but not cherish the way she'd dreamed of months before.

Ivy squeezed away the tears and focused on the warmth of the water as he guided her gently over the edge, into the tub. As she sank beneath the bubbles into sheer bliss, she heard him close the curtain.

A weird mixture of disappointment and relief shimmered through her. She saw his shadow lower as he sat on the stool. Trying to ignore the intimacy of the moment, she let her eyes close once more and focused on the sweet-scented steam in the air, the lap of water against the sides of the bathtub, and the loosening of her muscles in the liquid heat.

"Any more nausea?" Paxton finally asked.

Ivy did a quick self-check and realized her body was settling down, even if her mind wasn't. "No," she answered simply.

"Okay... Just give me a little warning if need be."

That was funny. "I'll give you as much warning as I'm given."

"I completely understand," he said with a chuckle.

Ivy lay cocooned in steamy warmth, lazily watching the bubbles float with her subtle movements, hyperaware of Paxton on the other side of the curtain. His silence. His vigilance.

"You've been pretty sick," he said, his tone deepening. "That must make the idea of motherhood pretty daunting."

"Not as much as doing it all alone." She immediately tensed, knowing she probably shouldn't have said that... but it was at least honest.

"You don't have to."

His quiet voice was steady, but could she trust him? If only it were that simple. She couldn't hold back her answer. "I'm not so sure about that."

Outside the curtain, he shifted, causing the stool to squeak. "Look, I'm here. I'm staying."

Maybe it was time for her to address the elephant in the room. At least this situation helped her feel secure, facing him but not really having to see him through the curtain. First she took a deep breath; then she let it out.

"So, why didn't you stay before?"

No good deed went unpunished.

Paxton had simply assumed Ivy would avoid any kind of deep discussion now, the same way she had since he'd gotten here. Her question came out of the blue.

A dozen excuses ran through his head while his lungs struggled for air in the steamy space. *I'm not ready. I wasn't prepared for what happened. I wasn't sure I wanted this to continue. I don't want to know if what I'm feeling is more than lust...*

He couldn't say any of that...but she deserved something real. Paxton wasn't sure if it was the warm air, the soft scent of vanilla or the sounds from the bath that brought to mind images of Ivy's soft skin and even softer curves—whatever the cause, it loosened his tongue.

Maybe it had been the same for her, the intimate atmosphere prompting something deeper.

Without permission, he heard himself say, "I was afraid."

The silence that engulfed the room seemed to echo in his ears. His throat clenched in a belated attempt to hold the words inside. Why had he said that? What was he thinking?

He wasn't. In an attempt to cover up the truth, he rushed into speech. "I just didn't want to ruin our working relationship."

Yes, that sounded perfectly logical.

"We work—worked—so perfectly together, and I could trust everything was taken care of when I wasn't there. I didn't want to risk losing that."

Ivy wasn't buying it. "Since when do you run instead of facing problems head on?"

Ah, the joys of arguing with someone who knows you all too well.

"I wasn't running." *It was more of a strategic retreat.* "I had a business issue to attend to, and felt we should talk about it face-to-face."

"Sure, in a week or two… Not two months later."

Funny how he could picture her slightly affronted expression just from her tone of voice. "So, why didn't you bring it up?" he asked, not willing to accept all of the blame.

"And risk losing my job?"

He couldn't argue that. Though he did lose sight of it from time to time, he was very aware they were in a situation where he was the one with the power. And a lot of Ivy's choices had reflected that same knowledge.

"But didn't you walk away from it in the end, anyway?"

Her sigh sounded sad, defeated. "Yes," she conceded.

"And it was one of the hardest decisions I've ever had to make."

While Paxton had simply avoided making any decision at all...until she'd forced him to with her actions.

"Do you know what I think?" she asked.

He wasn't sure he really wanted to know.

"I think you couldn't figure out how to handle me or what had happened between us. You had no perfect plan."

He grunted as her words hit home, but he wasn't ready to concede just how much their night together had impacted him. Not yet. Maybe a distraction would get him off the hook. "Let's get your hair washed before the water gets cold."

"I don't need help—"

"Right." He'd heard that a time or two. "Exactly how long do you think you can hold your hands over your head right now?"

Suddenly it was her turn for silence.

He couldn't suppress a grin. Victory, even a small one, felt pretty good. He let himself rub it in, just a little. "I thought so. And I know I heard you say your hair was driving you crazy. Don't worry... I've washed my nieces' hair plenty since they were babies."

Which was a load of bull, because he knew touching Ivy in any way would be nothing like those innocent experiences. Paxton sucked in a deep breath, bracing himself for wet, naked skin. When he pulled back the shower curtain, he found Ivy shifted forward, her arms wrapped around knees covered in bubbles.

The pose shouldn't have been provocative. All major erogenous zones were thoroughly covered by her arms or the thick bubbles drifting on the gentle current of the water. It was the bare curve of her spine, so vulnerable, so sexy, that had his breath catching in his throat. Not to mention the wealth of golden waves that spilled over each shoulder as if to frame the intimate sight.

He held up a shampoo bottle. "This one?"

She looked up briefly to confirm, then nodded at him. He picked up the large plastic cup nearby and used it to douse her hair with water. The long, tangled locks flattened instantly, spilling across her back to shield him from the tempting sight of her skin.

Paxton braced himself against the side of the bathtub. His body's response to seeing her like this was swift and immediate, like a kick in the gut. But instead of intense pain, intense pleasure shot through him.

Eager to avoid this response, he let it drive him into action. Though not the type of action he craved.

The liquid shampoo was cool and thick as he squeezed it into his palm. Another sweet vanilla scent, but it didn't quite match the bubble bath. He rubbed his palms together, spreading the mixture as he studied her hair and formulated a plan of attack. Finally he aimed for the wet mass right around her shoulders. He could feel the tangles as he rubbed in the shampoo. Even when wet, her hair was thick and heavy.

Not at all like the children's. Usually with them it was a couple of quick strokes and they were ready to rinse. Even when his oldest niece's hair had started growing in for real. Not this time.

His hands instinctively worked the shampoo into the thickness, down to the tips and then back up to the top. The mass seemed to grow under his attention, forcing him to corral it, rub it, scrub it.

That's when he heard the first tiny response. Small noises at first, slowly growing into deep moans as he worked his fingers against her scalp. So very similar to the sounds he had heard one special night before.

Rivulets of foamy shampoo bubbles spilled down onto her glistening skin, making it look slick and oh so touchable. Dangerous territory, his mind warned.

Inadvertently his thumbs pressed down the length of her neck, easing the tension in the muscles along her spine. A soft sigh of satisfaction had him freezing in place.

He didn't realize his hands had gone still against her head until she lifted it slightly. She didn't open her eyes, probably to keep the shampoo from getting into them. Regardless of the reason, he was relieved.

"Everything okay?" she asked, her voice now husky.

*No!* "Almost done."

He forced himself to view the task logically as he rinsed the soap from her hair, then added conditioner and ran a wide-tooth comb through the mass to remove tangles at her instruction.

But the wild feeling of satisfaction—the peace that stole over him, telling him there was nowhere else he'd rather be—wouldn't be washed away.

# Seven

Consciousness came slowly to Ivy the next morning. She woke in a much more leisurely manner than her usual "shocked opening of her eyes, rush for the toilet" ritual of the last two months. Even so, she lay perfectly still, evaluating her body for any concerns. No nausea yet, but she was still hesitant to move. Often that would start the cycle in the morning if she didn't already feel like tossing her cookies.

After a good ten minutes, she lifted one eyelid to peek at the clock. Nine o'clock in the morning. The house around her was silent, but it wasn't the normal silence of people still sleeping. It was more of a feeling of emptiness, as if she were the only one in the building.

Paxton had let her sleep in? But was he still here somewhere? She had a feeling that he was a consistently early riser, despite the middle of the night interruption he'd had.

Hopefully he had no idea just how she'd responded to his touch last night. The morning sickness of the last two and a half months had certainly done a number on her libido. But her body had forgotten all about that when his hands had been in her hair. She'd attempted to keep her outward response to an absolute minimum out of embarrassed modesty. After all, it was clear from his smooth touch and strict attention to her hair alone, not to mention his leaving after making sure she could safely get herself dried off and dressed, that he was no longer interested in her naked body. She just hoped she had adequately hidden the telltale tightening of her nipples and the ache that surely must have shown on her face.

It wasn't even just a desire for sex. The awakening realization that his touch alone was just as powerful had shaken her. Before last night, she hadn't been conscious of just how much she'd craved the comfort and care of his touch. The feel of his fingers working against her scalp. The gentle pull of the comb as he released the tangles in her hair. The press of his thumbs along the muscles of her neck, releasing the tension, easing the stiffness.

It had been the stuff of both nightmares and passionate dreams. And she had no intention of letting him know just how intensely she'd felt every brush of his fingers.

The sudden sound of a door closing downstairs forced her to finally sit up. Though she had no desire to face Paxton in person with all of these emotions running rampant inside of her, she refused to let herself cower behind her fears.

Ivy's hormones might be making her slow at the moment, but she was still a smart woman. She knew deep down that ignoring Paxton here in her house was not going to help her or her baby. Acting off emotions was not going to get her anywhere. Or at least not anywhere she wanted to go.

Time to wise up.

Her emotional side wanted to return Paxton to the role of lover. But that was not the reality of this situation.

She needed to think about the baby. And the future. Not the past.

Besides, she was just becoming aware of the stirring of hunger deep in her belly...miracle of miracles. Now that she knew he could cook—and cook really well—she had to wonder what he might have made for breakfast. Memories of his potato soup were like a warm, comfy blanket.

Getting dressed and the trek downstairs went well enough. She reached the bottom of the steps without feeling any nausea rising up the back of her throat. She sighed in relief, mentally tallying how many days she had until the doctor said she'd be out of the woods.

Of course there were no guarantees, but she sincerely hoped she was one of the lucky women who left morning sickness behind in the first trimester. Since she obviously hadn't been lucky enough to not have it at all, like Willow.

Just the thought had her crossing all of her fingers and toes.

She found Paxton at the kitchen counter. She paused just outside the doorway so she could take in the sight of him chopping vegetables, the muscles in his shoulders rippling beneath his polo shirt as he moved. Inwardly she sighed in regret that nothing about this gorgeous picture would ever truly be hers, but she refused to let any of that show on the outside. Instead she forced herself to step through the doorway and say a quiet good morning.

"Good morning!" he replied over his shoulder.

Man, would she ever reach the point where she didn't have to steal herself against that charming grin? Or ask herself if it was really meant for her or just an automatic reaction to the world around him?

"I wasn't sure how you'd feel this morning," he said.

He gestured toward a small plate of crackers on the table, and the tea cozy nestled next to it. "I picked up some more ginger tea for you."

Ivy eased into the seat, his thoughtful errand softening the armor she'd slowly been rebuilding since last night.

"I feel pretty good this morning, but better safe than sorry."

Pulling the cozy off, she lifted the warm cup to hold between her palms. The spicy ginger scent teased her senses. She watched him as she took a few cautious sips, then a couple of nibbles of the crackers.

Paxton expertly transferred the vegetables he was chopping to a frying pan without spilling any. Even the sizzle sounded delicious as the scent of butter filled the air. Then he began to crack eggs into a bowl.

The silence between them felt awkward after the intimacy of the night before. Though the words they'd spoken hadn't been comfortable or exactly what she'd wanted to hear, they had been honest. Only, now she didn't really know what to say to him face-to-face. How did she start rebuilding a bridge when she wasn't even sure what it looked like? How did one go about turning someone from a lover to something different? Something practical, like a co-parent.

Especially when everything inside of her ached for what might have been.

Finally she looked down at her plate and noticed a small tin next to it. "What's this?" she asked.

"I got those for you at the health food store this morning. I remembered one of my sisters mentioning how she swore by them when she was pregnant with her daughter. I figured it was worth a shot."

Inside the old-fashioned-looking tin, the little ginger lozenges were lined up in neat amber-colored rows. She lifted the tin to her nose. They smelled good. "Like you said, definitely worth a try."

"So, you seem to have learned a lot from them," she said, searching hard for that first plank on the bridge.

He nodded as he poured the egg mixture into the pan. "Watching them. Listening to them talk with my mom and grandmother. Reading articles about women and pregnancy. It helps to pay attention for those moments you can help... to make up for when you do screw up."

Ivy ignored the implication and let herself laugh as memories of his many internet searches came to mind. "You just love to learn about anything, don't you?"

He smiled sheepishly. "It doesn't matter if it's production or people—but my sisters deserve the best. I've been determined to give it to them."

She refrained from pointing out that that was probably the job of their husbands. Though she'd seen his sisters many times in his office, she'd never met their significant others. And she wouldn't have asked about them, even if given the chance.

Paxton's family, which he seemed to love to no end, was not necessarily a friendly lot. They rarely talked to her at work beyond the necessities of getting into Paxton's office, though by far Sierra was the most personable.

None of them seemed too big on seeing their employees as people, or at least not nearly as much as Paxton did. He was well loved within the company, and could often be found chatting with various employees in the hallways. Not just the upper management, but anyone from his secretary to an intern in the mail room.

He was rarely too busy for anyone.

"What will they think?" she asked cautiously.

Though they were just feeling their way now, eventually the news would spread. There would be no getting around that if Paxton planned to be a full-time part of the baby's life.

He didn't seem to catch her drift. "My sisters both love kids. Sierra has two. Alicia one. They'll be thrilled to have a cousin."

All her thoughts of allies and families pushed Ivy to ask, "What about me? Is that going to be a problem?"

Though Paxton paused to deliver a fully loaded omelet onto a plate and then place it on the table in front of her, Ivy knew there was a bit of a delay tactic in play. It took him more than a minute after setting the plate in front of her to actually meet her gaze, but to his credit, he did.

"I honestly don't know," he said.

Family was a complicated subject. How his family had treated her before wasn't something that was a credit to them, though his sisters were a bit more personable than his mother or grandmother. That woman scared the pants off Ivy.

But this was different.

Facing them alone scared Ivy. And her own family couldn't go with her everywhere, not even her new, overly protective big brothers in the form of her sisters' fiancés. She thought of her sisters' words from before…about the need to learn more about Paxton, learn how they could work together…so that she did have some form of buffer between her and his family.

She needed an ally. She looked at Paxton, who was across the table from her, digging into his omelet and toast. *A platonic ally.*

The words made her want to cry, but she forced herself to sit straighter and brace herself. No more attitude. No more overly emotional actions. The thought in and of itself brought sadness, not because she wanted to be ugly to him, but because she knew those emotions were just the flip side of the passion she'd felt before he'd abandoned her.

But for her baby's sake, she now needed someone who would stand by her side, help raise their child and form a united front against anyone who chose to tear apart their alliance.

Just no sex.

This isn't about romance, she reminded herself. This is about a joint effort to create an unconventional, but supportive family. She couldn't have the happily-ever-after, so she'd settle for whatever it was they were building right now.

"You're what?"

"We aren't coming home tomorrow."

Though Jasmine enunciated her words pretty well on the other end of the line, Ivy still wasn't comprehending. Maybe she didn't want to. Her time spent with Paxton had become more and more enjoyable. They had taken to playing games from the overcrowded wall of bookshelves in the front parlor, and talking about books and movies and plays. Subjects they'd never explored well within the confines of the office. Though part of it was Ivy doing her best to keep discussions of family and personal subjects to a minimum so she didn't accidentally give away anything she wasn't supposed to.

It was good. A good way to become allies, to get to know each other deeper than they had in their business relationship. But it had been hard on her personally. With Paxton right here, there was no break to nurse her feelings of sorrow and grief over the dreams she'd been forced to abandon.

"We want to add a little side trip," Jasmine was saying. "We're having such a good time, and we thought we would travel down into wine country and spend three or four days. Auntie is having so much fun, but she's really worried about you. Worried about leaving you for longer than we already have."

Well, that made Ivy feel good. *Not.* The last thing she wanted was for her family to worry over *her*.

"And it's so exciting, because Royce is giving up business to do this with us as a family. You know what a big deal that is."

Ivy did. Royce had been very much a button-down businessman before Jasmine got a hold of him. For him to just blow off business at the last minute? That would've been unheard of six months ago.

But deep down Ivy felt panic rising. She couldn't stay here for another week with Paxton. That wasn't fair to him. And she wasn't sure if she'd be able to keep her feelings to herself under those circumstances. He might spend an hour or two in front of the computer each day, but the rest of his time he devoted his attention to her. Under different circumstances it would have been a situation made in heaven.

But her current circumstances were not heavenly at all.

She drew in a breath, long and low. "Well, you can tell Auntie that I'm definitely improving. Between the ginger tea and the medicine from the doctor, and these little magic lozenges that Paxton brought me, I'm actually feeling great, keeping food down and regaining energy. I'm even feeling better enough to want to start sending out résumés again."

"Now Ivy, don't take on too much, too soon."

Ivy hated when her sister got that caretaker tone in her voice. Like she was too much of a child to make sound decisions. "I'm not. I'm just trying to do what I can, when I can."

The anger building in her chest was hard to suppress. So many people telling her what to do with her life was getting more than a little annoying.

Especially with all the uncertainty and unfavorable variables that kept popping up.

Digging deep, she forced a cheerful note. "But look, I'm thrilled that you're going to stay for a while. I don't want Auntie to worry. Everything is great." She hesitated for just a moment, then asked, "But can we just keep this information between ourselves?"

Caution entered Jasmine's voice. "What do you mean?"

"I mean..." she said, irritation quickly returning over the need to spell this out to someone she thought would understand. "Could we keep this between us? As in, could you please not tell Paxton about this?"

She'd handle that herself...once she figured out how.

"Don't tell me about what?"

Ivy whirled around to face Paxton, who had come in without her noticing. In his hand he held his phone at chest level, display facing her. The image showed a series of text messages with Royce's name at the top. The accompanying irritation on Paxton's face told her she'd made the wrong move. Again. She quickly said her goodbyes to Jasmine, along with even more assertions that everything would be fine.

Then she laid her phone on the table with a very careful movement and met that accusing gaze once more. "I'm sorry—"

"Is it really that horrible hanging out with me? Letting me take care of you? Why wouldn't you want me to know that your family is planning to stay gone another four days?"

She honestly hadn't been thinking about hurting his feelings. Just about handling this herself instead of imposing on Paxton even further. "When you put it that way, I know it sounds pretty bad."

He shook his head, some of the emotion draining from

his expression. "No, I'm sure you have good reasons. It's just upsetting to know that we haven't come to a place where you would discuss them with me first."

That's actually what she'd wanted—after she'd had the chance to think through all of her reasoning. Guess she'd just have to wing it.

"Look, Paxton, I've used up a lot of your time and energy. Of everyone's, really. I just don't feel right taking up any more. You need to return to work. And to your family…"

Paxton looked away. Ivy knew exactly what he was thinking about. His mother had called several times during lunch on Sunday, until Paxton had finally answered. Apparently she had been extremely unhappy that he was not at the weekly family dinner, and he hadn't been willing to give her an excuse.

He'd been quiet and unsettled the rest of the afternoon.

Paxton paced back and forth, as if trying to get his thoughts gathered through movement. Such a familiar action that made her heart ache. "What if I could continue to help you and still do all those things?"

Ivy frowned. "What did you have in mind?"

She was already hiding out from his family and the world she'd known when she'd worked with him. How much more could she disappear?

Ivy wasn't very comfortable with how those thoughts made her feel. Selfish and jealous and just a little bit angry. Not pretty at all. And not necessary. She would never play a prominent part in Paxton's life again—she needed to get used to that idea.

Still she said, "I've used up everyone's time and energy—yours, my family's. That's hard for me. You need to return to work…to your life… I need… I don't know," she mumbled.

"Is there something I should be doing that I haven't?" The surprise in his voice was almost amusing.

"Paxton, what I need, neither you nor my family can give me." She might as well start being honest.

He just looked confused.

"I know it's hard to tell sometimes, especially right now." Her behavior had been less than exemplary. "But I'm very grateful for all the care and concern that everyone has given me. That doesn't mean it isn't hard for me to accept."

"Why?"

Though he'd asked, she thought she saw a glimmer of understanding in his gaze. Accusation was gone from his tone, leaving a genuine curiosity that she couldn't resist.

"Since my parents died, my sisters and Auntie have worked hard to keep our family afloat. We didn't always have much, but they worked hard for what we did have. I was little when Mom and Dad died. There wasn't much I could do to contribute. It made me feel...helpless."

The sounds he made were noncommittal, but his attentive gaze urged her to keep going.

"I've always pushed to be responsible for myself. I got my first real job when I was twelve years old. And now..." She gestured to her tummy. "I've made a stupid mistake," she whispered, closing her eyes against the welling tears she didn't want. Her push for independence had made her take the job with Paxton in the first place. She hadn't been able to resist the opportunity to make a good living. In a single night she'd jeopardized her ability to support herself and her family's reputation. "A mistake that's affected everyone. And I have to fix this."

"Not alone." Paxton's voice was closer than she'd expected.

Ivy opened her eyes just in time to see his arms enfolding her. It was the first time he'd held her since their one night together, and her treacherous body melted against him immediately.

He felt so good, warm and solid. Though she knew the security was an illusion, she couldn't resist it.

"You did not make that decision alone," he insisted. "You will not carry the consequences alone."

Paxton backed up to look down at her face, hands on her shoulders. "I know how capable you are. How driven. You're excellent at your job. That's why we work so well together." He shook his head. "But your work right now involves something you can't really see. Growing the baby inside of you—getting this pregnancy off on the right foot. It's a very special project—which means your other work has to be delegated for right now." He squeezed her shoulders gently. "Do you understand?"

For the first time, she really did. "But that doesn't change the fact that you still have other responsibilities, and family…" One she really did not want to know anything about her at the moment.

"You're right. I do." He paced away, leaving her feeling chilled without his touch. After a moment he swiveled back to face her.

"What if I could take care of you and the baby and still do all of those things, too?"

"And run yourself ragged?" She shook her head. "I don't understand how that would work for either of us."

He turned to face her squarely, with that familiar posture she'd seen in the office many times. Arms crossed firmly over his chest. Legs wide and braced. She felt like she was being warned.

"It wouldn't require nearly as much effort…if you moved into my place."

# Eight

Paxton took a deep breath as he circled the car to open Ivy's door. At least this was one part of their normal interactions that had stayed the same. Though she'd worked for him, any time they'd left the office together, he'd always made a point to treat her like a valued person and a lady. In the South, men opened doors for women as a courtesy. Though in truth, he'd often had women do the same for him.

But whenever possible, Paxton had always held the door for Ivy. Today the gesture felt familiar, a touchstone in a sea of constant changes. Paxton knew he was swimming out of his depth, even if he was convinced this was the right move.

He held out his hand, steadying her as she stood up. Luckily there'd only been a small hint of nausea on the ride over to his house. He hadn't been sure how she'd do in the car, even as smoothly as his car drove. But she seemed to be having a good day.

He smiled as he thought about the little ginger lozenges

she was never without these days. At least he'd gotten that right.

She stared up at the stone facade and white trim of his two-story custom-built house as if dazzled.

"You've been here a couple of times before, right?" he asked.

Ivy glanced sharply in his direction before dropping her gaze. "Just once during the day. I dropped off some papers about a year ago, I believe."

And her other visit had been in the dark of night. That one, at least, Paxton wasn't likely to forget.

"We'll need to show you around when you're feeling up to it. I want to make sure you feel as at home as possible."

Her small smile was a weak concession. Her every hesitation, every refusal to meet his gaze broadcast her nerves. Paxton wished he knew how to break the ice better than this. Then again, he'd never brought a woman who was pregnant with his child home to live with him.

What could be more awkward under these circumstances?

He tried to view the surroundings from her perspective. The house was impressive, yes, but he'd bought it with the idea of raising a family in it. Not as a showcase of his wealth. It had lots of bedrooms and he'd ensured there was plenty of comfortable space. The gray stone blended perfectly with the wooded acres the house was situated on. A good many mature trees surrounded it for climbing and tree houses.

He'd imagined the pitter-patter of little feet on the antique maple-wood floors. Thanksgiving dinner in the dining room, which overlooked the pond. He wasn't set up for kids yet, so his family rarely visited him here. It was easier to meet at their houses. But he would still dream about it. Just not like this...

So why did it feel so right when he took Ivy's hand and led her into the house and around the lower floor? He tried to tell himself the gesture was necessary in case she was tired or feeling sick. But the truth was that he had an overwhelming urge to touch her once more.

Especially in this moment. Inside his house.

Attempting to pull his mind away from their one night in this house and back to the consequences, Paxton led Ivy down a short hallway to the one downstairs bedroom. "I thought we'd put you in here."

It wasn't until he noticed her staring at the bed that Paxton realized what he'd done. He was thinking of her comfort…not the fact that this was the room where they'd spent the night together.

*Bluff it out.*

"I figured this would be more comfortable for you than having to climb the stairs to the other bedrooms."

"I'm not disabled, Paxton," she murmured.

He couldn't tell if her tone held hurt or pain or maybe even relief.

"I realize that," he conceded. "I just wanted to make things easier."

Where was that ready charm that usually came so easily to him? Normally he was in and out of an embarrassing moment quick as a wink. Today he felt as paralyzed and awkward as a schoolboy.

So he might as well get the other awkward conversation out of the way. "I also want you to know…you don't have to worry."

"About what?"

"I haven't told anyone you're here, per your request. Including my family."

He'd been surprised when she'd made that a condition of her decision to move in with him, but upon reflection he could understand. It was for the best, for now. The last thing this volatile situation needed was his grandmother's involvement. And her demand was easily accommodated, since his family didn't usually come to his house.

"Do you regret having me here already?"

The unexpected question pulled his gaze to her. Something in her still, small voice compelled him. But he couldn't see any condemnation in her eyes...just genuine concern. For him.

"No..." he said. "I should, but I don't."

As soon as the words were out, he regretted them. Honesty wasn't always the best policy. He didn't want to hurt her, but he was also leery of giving away too much. There were reasons he needed her at arm's length...in another room...on another floor. He needed to remember that.

"Besides, keeping quiet makes my life—with my family—a lot less complicated. As long as we both agree to keep it that way." Why he felt the need to add that caveat right at this moment, he wasn't sure. But he knew immediately he'd given too much away.

"Have I ever given you a reason not to trust me?" she asked, startling him.

He didn't like the idea that she could read what he was thinking. "No, of course not," he answered readily. "Well, until you disappeared without telling me."

"I told you I was leaving. I just didn't tell you where I was going. But I have a feeling that's not all that's going on here."

Paxton looked away. He wasn't sure he'd be able to keep the past where it belonged. Under lock and key. The last thing he wanted to talk to Ivy about was how gullible and vulnerable he'd been as a young man. He'd taken many steps to protect himself since then.

Lessons learned.

She went on, "Well, I think maybe we need to come up with a plan. Don't you?"

As if his body recognized the way out, his muscles relaxed. Now she was talking his language. Paxton grinned. At the office, he asked about "the plan" first thing every morning. Every meeting ended with a review of "the plan" going forward.

They'd certainly jumped into this situation without one. Maybe a more businesslike approach would get them both back on track.

"What is the purpose here?" she murmured. "We're in this for the long haul, I guess." She glanced at him before her eyes widened. "I mean, not this." She gestured to the bedroom before them. "But this." Her slim hand then motioned between the two of them. "Oh dear." Her cheeks were now beet red. "I mean—"

"It's okay," Paxton reassured her, though he couldn't hold in a smile. "I know what you mean. A goal would make it easier to know when we've arrived, right?"

Her glance flickered back toward the bed before she averted her gaze. "Definitely. And I think if we focus on getting to know each other, building a strong base so that when the baby comes, we can make decisions together."

He nodded. That's where the focus needed to be...not on the bed they'd spent the night in, or any bed at all. "No matter what, we'll be working together. This is just a different arena than it was before. This is personal, not professional."

Just not too personal.

"So, how are you feeling today?"

The awkward question was not at all how Ivy had imagined starting off dinner tonight. She'd hoped to serve something really nice to celebrate Paxton's first full day back at work and her ability to actually handle raw food without feeling sick. Instead they were sitting down to dinner two hours late to dried-out fettuccine Alfredo and grilled chicken that had gone from raw to the consistency of cardboard.

"Well, I was able to handle raw meat today," she said hesitantly, grabbing the first thing that came to mind.

"That's a plus." He seemed happy, but his smile was strained around the edges.

She hadn't cooked since right before she found out she was pregnant. The smells were simply more than her queasy stomach could handle. But she was fast approaching the threshold that the doctor had told her about, and with each day the nausea retreated. She was actually close to having true morning sickness, instead of all-day sickness.

Miracle of miracles.

"Your kitchen is incredible," she said, searching for a new topic of conversation.

When Paxton had finally come through the door, Ivy wasn't sure what to think. Instead of the easygoing boss she was used to seeing in the office, or the laid-back caretaker she'd dealt with over the last couple of weeks, Paxton seemed highly stressed and irritated at the moment. Even though he didn't show it much beyond his tightened mouth and overly bland expression, Ivy could somehow sense it in the vibrations coming off him.

But he seemed to relax a little more with the compliment. "It sure makes cooking a pleasure," he said with his trademark grin.

Ivy had marveled over the difference between their dated but charming kitchen at Auntie's and the miles of stainless-steel appliances and natural Italian tile in Paxton's.

She'd been afraid of messing something up, but quickly pushed the fear aside because she wanted to do something nice for Paxton. He'd been extremely attentive when he'd been home, and had waited to go back to work full-time for over a week. He hadn't had to do that, but she was more than grateful for the chance to get back on her feet.

Her family had been, too, when they'd returned from their trip. Ivy and Paxton had gone over there for a slightly awkward lunch, during which stories of her family's travels distracted them from thoughts that none of them said out loud... Too bad it was written in almost every expression. They'd been surprised to find Ivy staying with Paxton, and even more surprised when he mentioned packing some of her stuff. But other than a few quietly whispered questions to make sure she was okay, they hadn't meddled.

Which was kind of shocking, in and of itself.

Still, even after the intimacy they had shared at Auntie's, and upon their arrival here, Ivy couldn't handle tonight's unspoken conflict. The stiff, arm's-length business. As though they had regressed to strangers who had never worked together, never slept together. He'd been like this since yesterday. Maybe that's what she'd been trying to break through with this dinner.

Which was a complete disaster.

Paxton's phone dinged, and he rose to retrieve it from the bar countertop. He glanced at the screen, then sighed, running fingers through his blond hair as he stomped back to his chair. The careful mask slipped, and Ivy could more clearly see the frustration in his expression.

"Is everything okay?" she asked, unable to ignore his distress.

"What?" He glanced up as if just remembering she was there. "Oh, sure." He picked at his food again.

Well, this wasn't going according to plan. But then again, nothing in Ivy's life in the last three months had gone the way she'd wanted it to.

As she watched him shuffle his food around on his

plate, Ivy remembered all of the wonderful meals he'd cooked for her. Guilt reared its ugly head. "I'm sorry," she blurted out.

Paxton froze, glancing around the table as if trying to find the source of her regret. "About what?"

"That dinner isn't very good." She shook her head. "I can cook, I promise. I just don't know how to fix it when it dries out."

Paxton shot her a sad grin. "After several hours, I don't think there's much you can do. Don't worry. I didn't bring you here to cook for me." He held her gaze, as if trying to convey a meaning he didn't know how to say out loud. "But, Ivy, I do appreciate the thought."

His weariness truly registered. The stress that had seemed to build under the surface the last few days was out in the open. And he was checking his phone during a meal when he would normally have left it until later. Maybe this wasn't really about her?

"Is work going okay?" She wasn't sure if it was her place to ask, since she wasn't his wife or his secretary, but she couldn't *not* ask.

He rubbed at his forehead. "Honestly, no." Another ping from his phone. She couldn't imagine who would be texting him from the office at this hour, unless there was a major incident. After-hours communication, outside of emergencies, wasn't a habit that Paxton had ever developed.

"Oh, for Christ's sake!" Paxton dropped his phone onto the table, then got up to pace.

Watching his trek back and forth increased her worry. She fiddled with her cloth napkin. What could've gone so wrong?

"Is there anything I can help with?" she asked.

He froze midstep. "Not unless you're willing to come back to work for me."

Her eyes widened, and she shifted back in her chair in surprise. Was he kidding? Or serious?

But before he could follow up, his phone rang. He swiped to connect the call, his expression tense. His lips were tight as he said, "Hello?"

His grip on the top of the kitchen chair grew tighter and tighter as the minutes passed, until Ivy could see the strain in his knuckles from across the table.

"Yes, Mrs. Holden. Yes, we probably need to get that straightened out."

Realizing that his new assistant might be the source of his irritation was actually a relief to Ivy, though she wouldn't be petty enough to admit it. She quickly retrieved the bottle of wine and refilled his glass while he finished the call. He gave lots of clipped responses before he signed off, none of them seeming to relate to an accident or emergency. Just some kind of mix-up. Then Paxton sank into his chair and took a large swallow of wine before letting his gaze meet hers.

"This is not going to work," he said.

"But she did so well when I was training her," Ivy said. "What went wrong?"

"It's the scheduling. She's great with most of the paperwork and greeting people and all of that stuff, but she can't keep my calendar for anything. And I end up with texts like this—" he lifted his cell phone so she could see the displayed lists of texts from tonight "—at the end of the day because things didn't appear in my calendar. And even though I now know it's for tomorrow, I can't plan at the last minute. Everything I've already put in place for the next day has to be rearranged. It's just a mess."

Knowing how important it was to Paxton that he be in places on time and prepared, and add to that the set amount of hours he dedicated to working in the office every day, told her just how annoying this would be to him.

"I feel like I should fix this," she said.

"Why?" he asked, cocking his head to the side. "It's not your fault."

"Well, I am the one who helped put her in that position. I even gave a recommendation to HR."

Paxton studied Ivy from across the length of the table. It wasn't huge, but it wasn't small either; there was just enough distance between them that she couldn't read his expression in detail. Mostly she saw curiosity. Concern.

"I'm serious," he said.

She swallowed hard, feeling like some of the dried pasta was stuck in her throat. "About what?"

"Would you consider coming back to work for me?"

Ivy was surprised by how much she wanted to do just that. During her time as his assistant, she had excelled. She felt far from excellent at the moment.

But she shook her head. "I don't think that's a good idea. Someone could find out..." Not to mention her own personal pull toward her boss. Though she didn't want to talk about sexual attraction with him, she knew for a fact it was alive and kicking...for her, at least.

"We don't have to advertise anything at the office," he said, enthusiasm growing in his expression. "I promise not to make any casual personal comments. Heck, I would even be happy with you working from home. Part-time. Full-time. I'll take whatever you want to give me."

He couldn't know how good those words sounded. If only he meant them in a different way.

"But as things become more obvious," she said with a gesture toward her still flat tummy, "what will you tell people?"

He shrugged, a desperate light in his eyes. "For now, it's

the perfect excuse for you quitting, then coming back full time. No one would guess who the father was." He glanced away, as if realizing how dismissive that might sound. After a moment, he looked back. "I realize this is selfish of me to ask. But I promise, we will work out the details. You know my family…they aren't the most observant of—"

"The help?" She supplied the word for him, only letting a little of her judgment seep into her tone.

He grinned. "Yeah. I'm not saying it's right. It's just who they are. Even if they notice your pregnancy, they wouldn't be interested enough to ask."

Ivy knew that was the truth, from her own experience of them. But that didn't keep her unease at bay. Just to clarify, she asked, "Is she really that bad?"

"Not really. But I just… I like how we worked together. You ran my office smoothly. I had absolutely no complaints. And I just want that back."

Ivy never thought she'd be so tempted by a job offer. But was it really wise? Were there complications besides the obvious that she was missing?

"I know I'm putting you in an awkward position," Paxton said. "And I don't mean to. But desperate times…" He shook his phone at her. "Please, Ivy. We worked so well together. Let's just try it. There's plenty of time to figure the rest out. We'll tackle that when it becomes an issue."

Again, the best laid plans…

There were probably some parameters she should put into place, but her brain wouldn't comprehend what they were at this moment. She simply knew that she herself would love to return to the rhythm of her days from before that fateful night three months ago. She couldn't resist. But would she find later that she'd made a deal with the devil?

# Nine

This was not going according to Paxton's perfect plan.

He watched from the doorway as Ivy handled a phone call at the desk that she had occupied for so long before her pregnancy. Simultaneously she input information into his schedule with smooth key strokes. After a few moments, he felt the vibration of his phone in his pocket as he was automatically notified of the change.

It sure was good to see her there. But not in the way that he had expected. She was great at her job, but he was seeing so much more that he hadn't when they had worked together before—the small curling tendrils that brushed her neck when her hair was up, the electricity that accompanied every accidental touch or the way she nibbled at her lips when she was concentrating.

Why had he never noticed how red and kissable that made her mouth?

Her poise, her ability to defuse potential problems, even

how she handled things with a calm facade when he could tell she wasn't really feeling well remained the same.

But she seemed to be better lately. The morning commute was a little iffy, and occasionally he would notice her slipping one of the little ginger lozenges into her mouth during the day. She was only working part-time…three quarters of the time when she felt up to it, but it was enough for him to start relying on her again.

He was grateful that she was doing so well, but they hadn't addressed the baby lately. Maybe tonight, though. He needed to ask about her next doctor's appointment. Even though they'd returned to being boss and assistant, he wanted her to remember that he was first and foremost there for her and the baby.

Things between them had changed more than he'd wanted to admit. Before he'd seen her exclusively as an employee. Well…maybe not. He'd tried. He'd known there had been an attraction there, but they'd both steadfastly avoided it.

Somehow the knowledge that his assistant was pregnant with his baby added a feeling of intimacy to their time here together, no matter how focused they were on business. He was grateful that she was so good at her job, but the atmosphere between them was completely different. He liked that.

More than he wanted to admit.

Watching her hands, her mouth, reminded him of that night together so long ago. It seemed like forever since he'd touched her. But he wished that he could touch her again. More than just the briefest of brushes that he experienced here. Even more than the intimacy of washing her hair in the bathtub.

He even found himself wondering if there was a way he could make it work outside of the office. For real.

The temptation grew with every day they were together. He knew he should run away fast. But he simply couldn't. Neither his feeling of obligation as the baby's father nor the fact that he actually cared what happened to Ivy, and that she not feel her life had been waylaid, would let him get too far away.

The phone in his pocket buzzed again, this time announcing that he had a phone call. Which meant it was family…

With a last long look at Ivy, he turned back into his office. Then he swiped to answer the call from his mother.

"Hello," he greeted her simply, wondering why she would call him during the day on his cell.

She didn't make him wait for long.

"Well, if it isn't my long-lost son," she said, sarcasm heavy in her words. "I was beginning to wonder if you would answer the phone if I called."

Paxton felt the unexpected urge to snap at her, but reined himself in. "What can I do for you, Mother?" His tight control couldn't stop the formality from creeping into his voice.

"For starters you could tell me if you're coming to Sunday dinner. Or are you going to skip again this week… with no excuse?"

"I have every intention of being there," Paxton assured her.

And he did. Things had been kind of hectic until he had gotten Ivy settled in. But he'd kept his promise, and hadn't mentioned her to his family. They had too much to decide first.

Still he couldn't keep ignoring them. So Sunday dinner was the minimum he could do.

"See that you are," she said. "Otherwise we might start to think that you have a secret that you're hiding from us."

The muscles along Paxton's back tensed up, creating an ache at the base of his skull. That was the last thing he needed them thinking.

"I don't know why you would think that, Mother," he said, anxious to deflect her attention from anything that might lead to snooping. "You know things have been hectic since I was out of town for so long. It's just taking a lot to get back on track."

"And that's why I've tried not to bug you," she said. "But I can only put this on hold for so long."

"Put what on hold?"

"Why, dinner with the Baxters." Her tone indicated she expected praise for this announcement.

Paxton frowned. The name sounded vaguely familiar. "I'm not sure I follow." Socializing was a regular requirement for both their business progress and social standing, but what was so important about this particular family?

"I can't believe you don't remember me mentioning this before you left. Where is your brain, Paxton? I would think you of all people would be excited."

"About what?" He glanced out the window of his office to see Ivy studying a file. Guilt and need mingled inside his gut. He wished his mother would just spit it out. But sometimes she truly enjoyed stringing the conversation along. It made her feel more in control.

"I told you that the Baxters' daughter has moved home. She was off at one of those fancy colleges, getting another degree, and now she's back here, interviewing for jobs. Not that she would need to work if she got herself a successful wealthy, business-minded husband. Goodness knows all that learning is a bit much."

*Oh man.* He could not handle matchmaking right now. It was the last thing he needed. "Mom, I'm not sure—"

"She would be perfect for you. Pretty, poised and able

to handle the circles that you socialize with, network with. Obviously she's smart, so she should have plenty to talk about. You should at least give it one dinner." Her tone brooked no argument.

Thankfully she wasn't there to see him roll his eyes. How could he admit to his mother that the last thing he wanted was another woman in his life right now? He had enough going on at the moment, and he had enough conflicts over this thing with Ivy to keep his psyche occupied for quite a while.

"We can talk about it later, Mother."

"We can talk about it at Sunday dinner. I even have pictures."

At least Paxton got his stubbornness honestly. He and his mom had clashed throughout the years, but he still loved her. She reminded him of his grandmother in force of personality, even though she was a daughter-in-law, and she'd be a solid leader for their family once his grandmother was gone. He loved her, but sometimes her desire to lead her children where she wanted them to go was more than a little heavy-handed.

But after he rang off, Paxton felt guilt settle into his gut. His family had always come first in his life, business second. They were often intertwined. He hated lying to his family, even when he knew his mother was trying to manipulate him.

He should be thrilled that his mother wanted to introduce him to a woman who fit into the plan *he'd* talked about for so long. A wife raised in his own social circles, able to understand the subtleties of high-society conversations and interactions, a woman able to step into high-pressure situations with poise and ease. A woman who already knew many of the people he dealt with on Savannah's social landscape.

As his office door opened and Ivy came through, Paxton felt that conflict build. Ivy could do many of those things with a little training, but he couldn't change the circumstances of her birth, her upbringing. He might want to overlook her station, explain away her occupation by saying that she would soon have a high-profile brother-in-law. But he knew the truth.

His family would never accept her...and neither would she fit into the plan he'd laid out for his life.

His thoughts were interrupted by the big smile she offered him as she reached his desk. "Thank you," she said.

Her comment caught him off guard. "For what?"

"For giving me this chance. It's so good to be back. Thank you for overlooking the issues..." She gestured between them. "I'd been trying to find another job, but deep down I knew that I really enjoyed working here and I missed it."

"I didn't know you'd been looking for work."

"Well, I was, between bouts of morning sickness." She shot him a rueful grin. "I've always had a big need to support myself. You know, it's one of those control things."

They shared a glance full of knowledge.

"Anyway," she went on, "I know it will be complicated later. But I do love my job. I think I'm damn good at my job. I just wanted you to know that this means a lot to me."

In a rush, Ivy put her arms around him for an all-too-brief moment, then hurried back to her desk.

Paxton wanted to follow her. Her happiness and enthusiasm drew him. She was passionate about her work, and he could have all that passion directed toward him—he remembered that experience all too well. All he had to do was give up his perfect plans for his future.

And his family's support.

\* \* \*

"You seem awfully calm for a man about to babysit a toddler," Ivy said as Paxton drove them to Jasmine and Royce's place near the historic district of Savannah.

"I have plenty of experience," he said, utter confidence in his words and body.

It was the same confidence with which he drove his luxury sports car, which still had that new-car smell despite being several years old. Paxton's grip on the steering wheel was loose and easy.

Ivy wished she felt the same. She loved her niece and had always enjoyed spending time with her...before. Now between the thankfully still-rare toddler tantrums and her own impending motherhood, Ivy was beginning to wonder if she was cut out for the day in, day out stresses of being a mother. It just all seemed so complicated, with every little decision fraught with the potential to scar her child for life. Something she became more aware of with each passing day.

How in the world had she gotten signed up for that?

They rode the elevator to the top floor of Royce's building in silence, with Ivy still feeling jealous of Paxton's quiet confidence. She tried not to show her nerves as Jasmine let them in, holding a little girl with dark curly hair who had a cherubic smile that could turn to tears at the least sign of resistance.

Sure enough, her birthday was right around the corner, and she'd be two.

"Thank you so much," her sister rushed to say. "With Auntie sick and Willow restricted from lifting anything, I was in a panic about tonight."

"Not a problem," Paxton said.

Jasmine sent him a questioning look, but didn't say anything as Royce made an appearance. They looked like the perfect high-society couple—Royce in his black tux, Jasmine in a sparkling floor-length gown and heels.

Ivy felt grubby beside them in her jeans and T-shirt, even though she knew it was the most practical choice for playing with a toddler.

Rosie came straight to Ivy when she held out her arms to the little girl, settling comfortably against her while eyeing the stranger in her house with suspicion. Rosie was more used to being around girls than guys, and it definitely showed. Jasmine pulled them both into a hug as Royce shook Paxton's hand.

"I'm so glad you're feeling better," she whispered against Ivy's ear.

Then off they went, glamour personified. The opposite of all the nights Ivy hung out at home in her sweats these days.

Not that she was jealous or anything. She settled the toddler onto her feet. "Rosie, let's show Paxton your toys."

She led him into the gorgeous main room of the suite, which constituted half the floor of the renovated building. Royce still had the brown suede furniture from when this had been his bachelor pad. A large flat-screen television and entertainment center sat in one corner. Several oversize rugs were strategically placed to help soften the polished plank floor for Rosie's tender feet, and one corner now held a play kitchen and shelves of toys for her. Toys and children's DVDs were something Ivy would never have imagined seeing in this room the first time she'd walked into it.

But the main attraction and focus of the room was still the glass walls that looked out over the city of Savannah. It was absolutely gorgeous, especially on a night like this, when soft lights decorated the dark panoramic view.

The view gave the room an air of sophistication despite the new family-style touches.

Paxton was obviously impressed, but quickly turned his attention back to Rosie and her toys.

"Whatcha got, pretty girl?"

In the way that only children can, Rosie went from giving Paxton the side-eye to being his best buddy in record time. Ivy found herself relegated to helper status throughout dinner and Rosie's bath, but it was Rosie's insistence that Paxton alone put her to bed that was the kicker for her fragile self-image.

Left alone, Ivy stared out the window as she waited in the living area, worries whirling around in her brain. Without thinking, she crossed her arms tightly over her stomach, as if hugging her body to comfort herself. Maybe the stance would hold in all the stupid emotions that kept washing over her, but Ivy couldn't hold back the few tears that slipped down her cheeks. Disgusted, she wiped her face to erase the evidence of her weakness.

"Are you okay?"

Ivy jumped. Of course Paxton would come back into the room at right that moment, instead of granting her the dignity to hide her emotional response to something that shouldn't affect her at all. She mumbled about stupid hormones to brush it off as easily as the tears from her cheeks.

"They are the bane of a woman's existence, from what I've been told," Paxton joked.

Ivy couldn't help giving a tired laugh. "You smooth talker, you."

She watched his approach in the reflection from the windows until he walked into the shadows directly behind her.

"I do my best," he said. "But I wouldn't mind knowing what's going on with you. You've been awfully quiet tonight."

"I've been replaced, apparently," she said, then instantly

felt embarrassed by the confession. Her niece was just a toddler, after all.

Paxton moved in close, as if he wanted to hug her but was afraid to... Would he reject her if she leaned back against his chest? Would he welcome that kind of intimacy these days? Or would he turn away from her, embarrassed that she'd presumed too much?

"Toddlers are fickle creatures," Paxton said.

Ivy tightened her arms around her torso. If no one else would hug her, that's the only comfort she had. She knew her fears were unfounded, but still... "What if I'm not a good mother?" she mumbled.

Paxton was silent for a moment, as if he hadn't heard her clearly, then he asked, "Why would you think that?"

More than anything, Ivy wanted to pace back and forth before the windows, to expend the energy driving her emotions, but she also didn't want to face Paxton. Or move away from him. Instead the energy went into tapping her foot against the plank floor.

Her stomach cramped, but it wasn't nausea this time. It was stupid nerves. "I'm not one of those women who has spent a lifetime dreaming of marriage and family."

At least, not the family part. All of Ivy's daydreams had focused on the romance leading up to the happily ever after. She shrugged. "What if I'm just not good at it? The chores I can handle. But what if I do something really stupid and screw him or her up?"

Paxton chuckled, finally moving in close and wrapping his arms around her this time. She went still with shock, her foot going quiet. He was heated comfort, with that edge of sizzle.

"Don't worry," Paxton said. "I have plenty of money for therapy if they need it."

Ivy jolted. *They?*

Paxton squeezed a little tighter, bringing the front of his body into delicious alignment with her back. It should've been a platonic move, but it wasn't. Not for Ivy.

"You know what?" he asked.

"What?"

He rested his cheek against her hair. A gesture that made her heart ache. "We made a baby together," he said softly, his reverent tone surprising her. "How awesome is that?"

"I've been so focused on keeping food down and not being terrified that I forget sometimes," she said in a hushed voice that matched his. "Is that terrible?"

"No, it's coping the best you can. That's all any of us can do, Ivy," he reassured her. "Trust me—if you didn't care enough about the baby, you wouldn't question whether you'd be a good mother or not."

"I don't want to screw this up. For the baby, for me... for you."

"You won't. Besides, I'll be there to help."

"So this baby can love you more, too?" Ivy realized she was only half joking. Paxton had lived up to his words, playing hands-on daddy all night to a kid who had loved, loved, loved it.

Could she really live up to someone like that?

"Oh, I doubt my child will find me as much of a novelty."

The only reason she could think of for that was if he was rarely there. How hard would it be to watch Paxton only visit on the weekends? Would his commitment to his child wain? Would he get tired of trying to share and decide to go for full custody?

"I hope not," she murmured.

# Ten

"Hey, Willow. How's life on the island?"

Ivy fiddled with the cord of the phone on her desk as she answered the call from her sister.

Willow had moved to one of the outer islands off Savannah's coast to be with her significant other. Tate had been one of the biggest secrets in Savannah, and still lived the life of a semi-reclusive author. But being involved with one of the Harden sisters had given him a much-needed social life. He was a man who had interesting ties to their family history—just as they had ties to his future. Willow was currently pregnant with his twins.

"I've got a surprise," Willow said.

By her excited tone, it must be a really good surprise. Of course Ivy had always known bookworm Willow to get excited about the strangest things. "Well, spit it out!"

Willow chuckled before launching into her subject. "So, the ledger we found in Sabatini House's attic, the one from Tate's ancestors that had the contracts in it for all of his illicit business, well…" She paused for dramatic effect, a tactic Ivy was more than familiar with Willow using. "Tate found the man's family. The one who was contracted for the night the McLemores' ship went down."

One of Willow's deciding factors in going to Sabatini House to work for Tate as a housekeeper had been to find evidence that their family was not responsible for sinking the McLemores' ship. She had found a ledger in a dusty room on the abandoned third floor with contracts between Tate's great-grandfather and various disreputable men in Savannah. There was a contract for the night in question, with not nearly enough details. What they really needed to know now was what it meant.

Could they use it to create reasonable doubt of their family's involvement? Or even to prove their innocence?

"Really? Is it a family that still lives around here?"

"Only a couple of hours away. We're going up there on Thursday, just to see what they can tell us."

Ivy wasn't so sure about this plan. "Do you think they'll actually appreciate you accusing their ancestor of sinking a ship? Murdering people?"

"Don't you know this is the South? We don't hide our crazy people in the attic. We bring them right out onto the front porch."

Having heard the expression before, Ivy smiled. It faded fast as she realized once more where she was…and what they were discussing.

"But the man was a murderer," Ivy reminded her, lowering her voice as she glanced toward Paxton's office.

"Some families enjoy talking about their notorious relatives," Willow reminded her, not concerned in the least. "We will see when we get there… For someone who has avoided people so much, Tate has done a lot of interviews for his books. He says it will be fine. Trust him."

"I'm trying," Ivy said, squeezing her eyes shut. While she wanted to trust that the future was going to work itself out, she was having more than a little trouble with her faith at the moment.

"This could be the evidence we need to prove Tate's family hired the person who sank that ship. How do you think Paxton would feel if we could prove our family was actually innocent?"

Ivy shook her head. "I honestly don't know." She'd never considered the fact that her family was thought to have damaged his when contemplating her feelings for him. Mostly because she'd never thought those feelings would be returned. On the night they'd been together, her family history had been the last thing on her mind.

Would he embrace her if she confessed, with the evidence that it wasn't really an issue? Or would there be other things that stood in the way? Who was she kidding? Of course there were other issues, some she could only guess at, since Paxton had retreated from her way before he knew the truth of who she was. She had no idea how he would feel when he found out how notorious her family really was.

Ivy murmured, "I don't know."

But she desperately needed this back-up plan, because the truth would come out eventually, and she needed to mitigate the damage as much as possible. Parenting would be awkward enough without his relatives shunning her child over something her family had not been involved in.

"How exciting will it be to know what really happened?" Willow enthused, her love of history and family fusing into one explosive firework over this subject. "I can't wait!"

Ivy chuckled. "You're such a nerd."

"You know it."

"Thank you, Willow. And thank Tate for me, too. I don't know what I'd do without all of your help."

Ivy ran off before she could get too emotional. She took a deep breath, trying to regain her equilibrium. "Everything will be okay," she murmured under her breath, then got out of her chair. Only to find Paxton watching her from his doorway.

She shot a panicked glance at the phone. How much had he heard?

"Everything all right?" he asked.

She pasted on a bright, forced smile. "Isn't that my line?"

His shrewd gaze narrowed; he wasn't buying the brush-off as quickly as she'd have liked.

"Is something wrong?" He glanced down at the hand she'd unknowingly rested on her still-flat tummy. "Everything okay with the baby?"

The genuine concern in his amber eyes was almost more than Ivy could handle. She raised a hand as if swearing on a Bible. Though it was a good thing she wasn't. All the secrets she was keeping would surely send her to hell in a handbasket.

"Absolutely nothing. I was just talking to Willow about a new plot of Tate's. You know, supersecret author stuff."

The look in Paxton's eyes slowly morphed from concerned to questioning. *I'm not very good at secrets.* He advanced on her carefully, step-by-step from across the room. Each move made her heart pound.

How could a simple walk be sexy enough for her body to react?

"Are you lying?" he asked, drawing out each word.

Nerves caused her throat to close up, refusing to let out the words. She shook her head. She couldn't let Paxton find out about her family. Not yet. The fallout wasn't something she was ready to face.

"I think you are." His voice deepened, taking on a sexy, teasing tone that she'd thought she'd never hear again. "What do I need to do to get to the truth?"

He couldn't ever know the truth. Then again, if he kept walking like that, she might break her resolve in a heartbeat.

Paxton's eyes widened as he reached the halfway point, awareness suddenly flaring in his eyes. Awareness of the game he was playing. Danger seemed to shimmer between them. Ivy knew she shouldn't mess with the undercurrents she felt, but this game wasn't in her hands anymore.

Paxton kept moving forward, holding her gaze, until he came close enough to bury his hands in her hair.

His husky voice sent shivers over her body as he asked, "Are you sure there's nothing you want to tell me?"

"What's going on in here?"

For a moment Paxton thought he'd only imagined his sister's voice—a figment of his guilty imagination. But no. One glance to the side showed Alicia staring wide-eyed at him from just inside the door to his office suite.

*Caught with his hands in the cookie jar...*

Sierra would have been far preferable, as she was the more forgiving, tactful sibling. He jerked back, only to have Ivy cry out and press a palm to her scalp.

"I'm sorry, Ivy," he murmured, but there was no time to lose in diverting Alicia's attention. He turned fully toward his sister in order to block her view of Ivy.

"Alicia, what brings you here?" he asked, forcing himself to appear calm and collected, when inside his body was instantly primed and ready for a fight.

Actually, he realized it was primed and ready to *protect Ivy*. Which was not how he would have imagined this same scenario six months ago. Then everything would have truly been calm and collected. Actually, this entire scenario would never have happened.

His sister raised her blond brow, a typical expression of hers that matched her slightly acerbic personality. "Apparently I'm not coming in often enough," she said.

In an attempt to derail her from having this conversation in front of Ivy, Paxton crossed to his sister and marched her to his inner office with a hand on her arm.

"What I do in my office isn't any of your business," he stated under his breath, hoping to spare Ivy any embarrassment.

His sister didn't share his qualms. She used what his mother would have called her "outside voice" to say, "Since Grandmother still controls the board of this company, I think she'd be very interested in what happens in this office."

Paxton shuffled her inside the inner sanctum and closed the door with a little more force than necessary. Alicia had always been the more difficult sibling. They had butted heads many times over the years, though he would say that overall their relationship was a good one.

"Don't start with me," he warned.

She adopted a *who me?* expression. "I'm just trying to figure out if this is the 'work' that's been keeping you so occupied."

"Let it go," he growled.

Alicia wandered around the room, trailing her fingers over his bookshelf. "Why?" She tossed him a mischievous glance over her shoulder. The kind that had always spelled trouble for him when they were teenagers. "Torturing you is so much fun."

"This isn't a game, Alicia."

Certainly not one he wanted to play. If his grandmother got wind of any involvement with his assistant, it would go very badly for Ivy. Not that Paxton couldn't protect her, but his grandmother would make her life miserable in the meantime.

"I think it might be, especially since Mother is trying to set you up with that Baxter chick."

How did that get around? Paxton settled into his chair with a creak of leather and a sigh. "Nice to know my, um, professional life is so interesting to everyone."

"Your recent absence—and how unusual that is—has made you a very common topic…just among family, though."

*That's reassuring.* Paxton leaned back to stare at the ceiling. "Ah, the joys of a close-knit family."

His sister crossed over to rest her hip against his desk. "Any information you'd like to grant me permission to share would definitely up my credibility with the old lady."

"Well, this—" he waved his hand toward the window, where they could see Ivy working at her desk "—is not something anyone needs to worry about. A complete non-issue. Now—" he gave her a stern look "—what did you come by for?"

In an unusual move, Alicia turned her attention down to her impeccable manicure. "I just wondered if you had noticed anything off with Sierra?"

Paxton thought back over the cryptic words Sierra had spoken to him at the doctor's office and how often her husband had been absent lately. Paxton may not have been very involved with family matters since returning from his trip, but that was one thing he'd kept on the edge of his awareness.

"Not really," he hedged, not wanting to give a hint of what he suspected in case it caused problems for Sierra. "Why?"

"She's just been pretty emotional lately."

"She is pregnant," he reminded her. Alicia should know all about those strange pregnancy mood swings after two children of her own.

"Even so... I'd hate for her to do anything rash based solely on pregnancy hormones."

Paxton leaned forward, training his gaze on his sister and her unusually meandering conversation. Normally she was much more direct than this. "Because you think she might..."

Finally Alicia met his gaze. "She's made quite a few remarks about her husband being absent. How he lost interest in them once he knew this baby was also a girl. How when he is home, he's always locked up in his study. That kind of thing."

Now, that was news to Paxton. But then he thought back to what she'd said that day at the hospital. *Just because the whole business-before-pleasure thing worked for our parents and grandparents doesn't mean it's the wonderful life they told us it would be. Marrying for money is just as complicated as marrying for love.*

"If that's true, it sounds like she's got good reason to be unhappy," he mused, upset he was just now paying true attention to the signs.

"Feelings should not be a reason to make major changes," Alicia insisted. "Especially with her husband this close to sitting on the board." She held her fingers up an inch apart.

*Better now than later.* Though he didn't say it, Paxton had the uncomfortable urge to defend his sister's right to make decisions based on how she felt. He settled for saying, "No matter how logical it seems for the business—and Jason has done a great job in his position—that doesn't mean she has to be miserable for the rest of her life." He stood up, feeling the need to brace himself. "That's what the prenup is for."

"You're not helping, Paxton." Obviously that wasn't what she wanted to hear.

But he couldn't stop the thoughts from crowding in—thoughts contrary to everything he'd been taught his whole life. "Maybe it's time we started worrying about our sister more than we do the bottom line."

He stomped out his agitation as he walked to the door. He was more than ready for this conversation to be over. Luckily his sister went with him. He wasn't prepared for her to go back to the earlier subject, though.

"Is ignoring the bottom line going to protect you with the hired help?" she asked, nodding her head toward Ivy. "You know, when she gets herself pregnant and all."

Alicia probably thought she was being funny, but Paxton felt a flare of anger that loosened his tongue, just as it had when they were teens.

"I won't need a prenup," he said, frustration over his current situation and how his family would view it prodding him hard. "I'm smart enough to know my assistant isn't marriage material."

Only when he caught Alicia's smirk did he realize she had opened the office door before he spoke those infamous last words.

# Eleven

Ivy could tell from Paxton's body language that he was upset and quickly putting up his emotional guard. Only, she couldn't tell if it was to continue the confrontation with his sister, or because he'd been caught red-handed by Ivy. Of course, he could probably read the same emotions in her body, too…if he was paying any attention at all.

His sister left without a word. That was Alicia's usual exit when Paxton wasn't around, but it was even more pointed today, given what had transpired. He didn't watch her go. Instead he stood right outside the door to his office, those watchful eyes cataloging Ivy's every move.

She knew exactly what emotions she was telegraphing. Big. Time. Anger. *Not marriage material.*

Humiliation burned like lava slowly spreading over her nerves. To have Paxton talk about her that way with his sister dug deep into Ivy's insecurities. Having him reduce her to her job, her station in life, left her ready to explode, but she deliberately locked those emotions down tightly.

She'd suspected that his family viewed her as less than from the first, but not Paxton. Never Paxton.

Silence settled after the door closed behind Alicia. Ivy didn't rush to fill it. She wanted to choose her words carefully, but the emotions churning inside of her muddled the connection between her brain and her mouth.

Finally she just opened her lips and let loose. "So, I'm good enough to knock up, but not good enough to marry?"

She hated the way her voice shook, but this was a conversation she wasn't walking away from. Not if they were to have any future relationship at all, even just one that consisted of co-parenting.

In contrast, his voice was even as he said, "I would never describe you like that."

"Why not?" She paused to swallow hard, desperately trying to keep her voice a few steps down from a yell. "Even if Alicia doesn't know the whole story, we both know it's what you meant. Assistants are not marriageable material, right? I should have known that's what the disappearing act was about…"

Paxton gave a single sharp shake of his head. "No, Ivy." As if he couldn't resist, he braced his body in his typical boardroom stance—legs locked, arms crossed over his chest. "Look, I'm sorry. I was trying to extricate myself from an uncomfortable conversation by saying what my sister would expect to hear."

Ivy wasn't buying it. "Apology not accepted. Why would you talk about me with her in the first place?"

Paxton took a step closer, his movement tentative, as if too much pressure would make her go off like a bomb. "We are very close. There was no way she wouldn't ask about what she walked in on."

That earlier near miss wasn't something Ivy wanted to talk about. Not right now.

"Which you explain away by bad-mouthing me?" she asked instead. "What a gentleman you are."

"My family—" he ran his hands through his hair "—they don't see things the way most people do."

"You're right. I have plenty of experience with them, right here in this office. They see people as objects—in terms of what purpose they can serve. Not who they really are."

He shook his head as if to deny it, but she wasn't letting him off the hook with this.

"I thought you were different, Paxton. Is that really how you want to live? Giving credence to that type of thinking?"

She stepped closer, her brain working through all the implications. Horror filling her as she thought about the future. "What about our child? I don't want him to think that's okay. That I'm inferior because I was Daddy's assistant."

Paxton took a deep breath. "You know I see you as more than that."

"They don't. Do you honestly think I'd let my child be alone with them so they can bad-mouth me when I'm not there?" Though how she'd prevent that, she wasn't sure.

"I would not let that happen."

"I want to believe you, but somehow you always end up disappointing me."

"What?" Surprise opened up his face, but she wasn't sure if it was because of her opinion or because she had the audacity to say it out loud.

It was that surprise that did her in—unlocking the churning emotions deep inside of her.

"Yes, Paxton. I spent the night with you, gave you my body, and you walked out without a word. I try to make decisions on my own, trying not to bother you until necessary, and I get accused of keeping secrets.

"I finally believe we are building some kind of partnership—" she almost choked on the word "—to raise our child, and I overhear you belittling me to your sister. I guess I'm the lesser partner in this arrangement." Ivy struggled not to let tears make an appearance, but she was failing.

"I've worked here for almost two years. You're a great boss and I appreciated that enough to keep my distance. I never thought it would happen, but then we moved beyond business. And it was the most incredible thing I've ever experienced." A white-hot wave of emotion washed over Ivy, blurring her vision with a flood of tears.

"I should have known the magic wasn't real. You were too good to be true, and I'm left trying to find the good in this nightmare. Is it just something about me? Something that won't let me have anything good that's truly mine?"

Ivy doubled over, the only way she knew to hide the tears that fell. It took a moment for the haze of anger and pain to dissipate, leaving her head clearer.

Actually too clear.

Ivy knew immediately she'd said something she shouldn't have. The last thing she'd wanted Paxton to know was how much their night together had meant to her, how deeply his disappearing act had hit her.

As she straightened, she could tell by the shell-shocked expression on his face that he'd gotten that message loud and clear. It hurt, because that expression meant she'd done a better job of hiding her feelings since he'd been home than she'd thought…or that he was completely clueless as to how she'd felt when they'd been together.

Then his expression darkened, intensifying as he studied her. But his look was far from analytical. More like a deep, hidden realization coming to life.

It became even more focused as he approached her. Her heartbeat picked up speed, causing her to catch her breath. Was he angry? Was he panicked? Was he—

Then his hands were in her hair once more and his lips covered hers. Ivy's world went dark and she gave herself over to the ultimate rush. There wasn't a single ounce of resistance in her body. At least not until he pulled back.

"I wasn't trying to put you down, Ivy. I was trying to throw Alicia off the trail. To protect you and our child from my family.

"It's sad that I had to do that, but I in no way meant to hurt you. The things you've said...these feelings you have... they're a more precious gift than anything I've ever been given. Never, ever forget that."

Ivy was lost in the whirlwind as Paxton locked them in his office and closed the blinds. With no guarantees, no resolution, she should not trust him, trust this... But something deep inside would not let her deny herself the chance for one more taste.

Each step he took toward her brought out a pulse of awareness that she didn't want to face. They were in his office—the ultimate no-touch zone. A combination of guilt and excitement mingled inside of her.

But when he moved in close, cupping her face as if her revelations had opened his eyes to her true self, she melted. Her shoulders relaxed as she dropped her guard. Her head fell back, granting him access to her vulnerable neck. The move was instinctive, a surrender to both his will and the emotions that had brought her here.

He lifted her to the credenza against the wall, crowding close between her legs. Though her skirt still covered her, its flowing style left her feeling exposed. His commanding presence overwhelmed the lingering fears in the back of her mind. As she braced herself with her arms behind her, Paxton took full advantage of her position to press even closer.

She tightened her thighs, unconsciously embracing his hips, drawing him into her with her lower body. Fear held her back. Even though she ached to hold him close, Ivy could not get her arms to make the move. No matter how desperately she wanted him.

Then Paxton leaned in, resting his lips against the frantic pulse at the base of her throat. His mouth, his breath, were heated softness stroking her skin. He didn't rush or push for more. Instead he breathed deeply, inhaling her scent. A flash of heat shot through her, settling with a soft explosion between her thighs. Her soft cry echoed around them, a sound this room should never have heard.

Only then did Paxton open his mouth and cover the delicate spot. The sensations overwhelmed her. Soft, wet suction. The rumble of a groan deep in his throat. The tight grasp of his hands anchoring her on each side of her waist.

After long, heady minutes of his exquisite attention left her hot and edgy, he pulled back. His knuckles brushed the underside of her breast as he lifted his fingers to the two buttons of her suit jacket. He didn't move to open them, but instead held still.

Waiting. Then watching.

His head lifted. That intense amber gaze found hers and locked on. Mesmerized, she could not look away.

His fingers tightened as if it were all he could do not to rip the jacket open. Instead he asked, "Ivy?"

The questioning tone echoed in his expression. A need to acknowledge her permission; a desperation for it to be granted.

She wished she could ignore it, but the ache in his request hit her with a fierceness she hadn't expected, amplifying her own desires. She'd already laid herself bare. There was no denying him or herself right now.

So she answered simply, "Yes, Paxton," knowing there would be regret and pain further down the line. But his emotions and her own were a dynamic duo she couldn't walk away from.

It was short work for him to open her jacket, then the delicate blouse beneath. Her fuller breasts swelled over the cups of her bra, plump from the life growing inside of her. He brushed the creamy tops with his thumbs, followed by desperate sucking kisses. His attention to her breasts drew her deep into this moment, melting away any lingering fears for the future.

"Paxton," she murmured, wishing she had the courage to cradle his head in her hands.

Finally his palms pressed beneath the hem of her skirt, then squeezed the quivering muscles of her thighs. She felt a muffled curse against her breast as his fingers found the top edge of her thigh-high stockings, then another as they reached the damp material of her panties.

Ivy found herself slipping into a world of sounds and sensations as he worked his fingers around the barrier to explore her most intimate flesh.

Around and over and under until she wanted to weep in time with the pounding in her core. Then his teasing fingertips barely slipped inside of her. She couldn't stop the jerk of her hips, her body's attempt to draw him deeper. He eased in an inch more. Two fingers, then three.

At the same time, his whole body crowded closer. She found herself caught in his gaze once more, telling him things with her expression and movements that she would probably wish she had left hidden later on.

When sanity returned.

He worked her expertly, as if he knew just how to bring

her greatest fears and fantasies to life. She tried not to think about the last time they'd done this—pure, exquisite pleasure, followed by so much pain.

"Paxton, please," she cried, her body skating the edge of ecstasy without the key that would push her past the brink.

"I need you," he said, pulling back to fumble with his pants. "Heaven help me, but I need you, Ivy."

In a matter of seconds, he had freed himself, bared her and was pressing against her lower lips. Ivy tilted her hips, granting him access. Her core seemed to suck him inside, so great was her need.

Only then did she allow her arms to embrace him, her hands to anchor him to her. He filled her to overflowing. Her every nerve jumped straight to overload. Her entire world narrowed to the feel of him moving inside of her, the sound of his desperate draws of air, and the way only Paxton McLemore could overtake her body and her mind so completely.

His increasingly hard thrusts sent her into a tailspin and she screamed her release as he surged against her. In this moment, need, relief and love rolled into one, leaving no more room for the fear.

# Twelve

It took a moment for Paxton to realize that Ivy was quiet, not moving as he parked in front of Auntie's house. Despite the physical connection forged in his office last week, they'd tiptoed around each other and the heavy subjects neither of them seemed to want to tackle.

Paxton knew Ivy was afraid for the future, but he had no answers for her, despite their incredible attraction. So he left the emotions locked away, where they were safe. Where he was safe. She seemed content to do the same.

Still, every time they touched, those emotions made an appearance.

"Are you okay, Ivy?" he asked, a little worried by the way she stared out the window, toward her family home without making a move to get out of the car.

Then there was the way she worried her lower lip with her teeth. That little move told him something weighed on her mind. He wanted to ignore it, to avoid any deep subject that would upset their current intimate equilibrium. But he wasn't a coward, especially not with the women he cared about.

Ignoring the jolt of that thought, Paxton pressed harder. "What is it, sweetheart?" he asked.

She glanced his way with the weak smile. "Just hormonal, I guess."

"That doesn't make it any less valid," he reassured her, only to be reminded of his words to his sister last week. He'd forgotten in the upset at the office and its aftermath to check on Sierra. He needed to do that.

"I love my sisters," Ivy finally said. "I'm so excited that I'm finally feeling well enough to help Jasmine with this charity auction." She worried her lips with her teeth some more. As sexy as he found that...

"But..." he prompted.

"Sometimes it's hard to be with them." He caught a brief glimpse of a sad smile. "They're so happy. They have strong relationships. They're building families. And I have..." She frowned. "What? A business relationship? With an extra helping of sex?"

Her pain and uncertainty hit him hard. Hard enough to overcome his reluctance to go deeper. "No, Ivy." He cupped her worried face between his palms and struggled for honesty. "I'm not sure exactly what this is between us—yet—but the last thing I want is a business arrangement. Hell, especially not in the office."

The smile they shared was more intimate than Paxton could ever remember having with any other woman.

But the feeling faded as she asked, "So why are you holding back?"

He was. He knew that, knew it came not just from the obstacles with his family, but his own memories of being used by a woman in the past, something he wasn't ready to talk about. So he deflected. "Why are you?"

The knowledge was there in her eyes, even though he knew she didn't want to admit it. "We both have reasons for holding back, Ivy."

Leaving it at that, he got out of the car and went around to open her door.

He genuinely enjoyed dinner with her family, appreciating how open and welcoming they were to him and to each other. There was no strategy in the way they interacted, no subtle attempt to one-up each other. Paxton could relax and be himself.

After the meal, Royce left to attend a meeting, and the women got down to the business of planning the upcoming auction that Jasmine was coordinating through her event-planner business.

Paxton spent some time reading about the history of Savannah's shipping industry in the books on the over-crowded bookshelves in the front parlor. It was fascinating to learn more about the industry his family had been involved in since they'd settled in Savannah so long ago. Then he chatted with Auntie until she fell asleep in front of the television.

He was certainly living the high life tonight.

Finally he decided it was time to at least check in and see how much longer the women would be working. He headed back down the hall from the front parlor to the kitchen, Auntie's snores fading into the background. The women's conversation was muffled until he reached the doorway to the dining room.

Only then did some of Willow's muffled words take shape. "Oh, they were more than happy to talk...just not about that night."

Paxton paused, confusion running through him.

Willow went on, "He never said…never out right admitted his involvement. So while it's likely he was involved… ship, there's no proof…"

Icy shock jolted through Paxton's body. His brain struggled to catch up. He strained to hear more.

"But don't give up, Ivy. Tate will find something."

"What should I do in the meantime? After the…office, I'm afraid…if they find out before we have proof."

Willow sniffed. "I'd watch that grandmother of his… She hears the name Kane, and it's all over."

*Kane.* It sounded so familiar, but Paxton probably wouldn't have realized why if Willow hadn't paired it with his grandmother. *The ship.*

Kane was the name of the man who had sunk his family's ship.

Cold rational logic was the only thing to get him through this. He stepped into the kitchen to a chorus of gasps all around.

"Ivy, what exactly is it that you know about the Kane family?"

She swallowed hard, but then lifted her chin and replied, "That was my mother's maiden name."

Fury bubbled up from his core before Paxton shut it down through sheer will. "So, you deliberately kept this from me?"

She didn't answer, but her wide eyes remained trained on him as he stepped closer.

"Is this one of those 'things I'm going to hide from you because I don't have a direction yet' scenarios? The kind that keep me protected until you can decide exactly what *you* want to do?"

Ivy cast a quick, guilty glance toward her sisters before she slowly nodded. "Maybe. But, Paxton—"

He cut her off with a sharp, dismissive wave of his hand.

"You were talking about the sinking of a ship. The one that took the McLemores' heir and beloved son from them?" Paxton's angry words rang through the kitchen. He thought back over what little he'd heard. "That night is a scar on my family's heritage. My grandmother has never been the same since that night."

The rest of the earlier conversation slowly registered.

"What makes you think this man you were talking about was responsible?" he asked as he put two and two together. He ignored their shocked faces as he stepped farther into the room. "Even more, why would you care?"

"Paxton—" Ivy swallowed.

Ivy was part of the Kane family. The implications hit hard and fast. He stomped closer. "I want to know what's going on, Ivy," he said, pinning her with his hard stare. "Right now."

Her mouth worked, but it took a minute for words to come out. "Paxton, I didn't want you to find out—"

"Obviously. I realize you're not that familiar with my family, but the story of that ship is notorious. My grandmother tells it often. It was devastating to our family."

He circled around to get a better look at her face. "But to my knowledge, the family that was responsible left Savannah. The Kanes. Isn't that right, Ivy?"

She slowly shook her head. "It's not what you think, Paxton."

"Are you sure? Because it sounds to me like you are part of a family that attacked our company *and* our family."

Paxton knew he sounded overly emotional about something that happened generations ago. But that was just how sensitive his grandmother was over the same subject. It had shaped the McLemores' entire history.

Jasmine stepped in. "Yes, Paxton. We are descendants

of the Kane family that was accused of sinking that ship. But that's not—"

"No, I want to hear it from her." He leaned against the table, so heavily that the pattern of the wood grain registered against his palms. "Have you known this all along and hidden it from me, Ivy?"

"Yes," she said, finally meeting his gaze. "I have known all along, Paxton."

"And once again, you chose not to tell me?"

Willow answered. "You'd never have given her a job in the first place."

Another cold shock wave washed over him. "So, you knew *before* you came to work for me?"

"I did know, but it wasn't important because my family didn't do it."

"Like hell they didn't."

Both women took to their feet at that point, speaking over each other. Paxton waved it all away and focused solely on Ivy.

"You could have told me at any time, but you didn't because…why would you even come to work for me when you knew…"

He wasn't buying her broken expression or her silence.

"Did you think if I knew that I would have come within ten feet of you?"

Confirmation of what he'd said came in the expression on her face, in the crocodile tears that trickled down her creamy cheeks. "I needed a job…well, wanted a good job. Yours was a great opportunity. I didn't think you would ever know."

"Now I do," Paxton said, letting his anger free as he leaned in close to her face. "You're right… I wouldn't touch a Kane if you paid me."

He turned on his heel and made a beeline for the door,

his hard steps accompanied by furious whispers and quiet sobs. But he ignored it all as he shot back over his shoulder.

"There's something you might want to remember, dear Ivy—my family would be more than happy to run yours out of town for a second time."

"I don't know, Tate," Ivy said as she stared at the modern-fairy-tale facade of Paxton's house. "I don't want it to look like I'm throwing around my family's new connections."

She'd never seen Paxton so angry before, even when he'd learned about the baby. The very intensity of his emotions had frozen her in place.

He'd stormed out last night, leaving Ivy stranded at Auntie's house. Her sisters had consoled her with chocolate and ginger ale, since she shouldn't have wine, but she was determined to talk to him today, especially before he contacted the family lawyer about custody. It was a weekend, but she doubted the lawyer would refuse calls from him at any time. With as many connections as the McLemores had, they probably had their attorney's home number on speed dial.

But as she sat in the driveway, she second-guessed her decision to come here with Tate. Even after such a short time, the house looked like it was waiting for her. So perfect. And now everything had fallen apart. What good would convincing Paxton of her family's innocence do?

All she knew was that she couldn't leave things the way they'd ended last night.

Paxton didn't look any happier when he opened the door for them. "Have you come to get your stuff? Or just to spread more lies?"

Tate stepped into view. He didn't have to say anything, just stand firm.

Paxton glanced between them. "Back-up?"

Tate shrugged. "Call it whatever you want. But let's have a civil discussion before any decisions are made."

For a moment Ivy thought Paxton would refuse. But he finally stepped back and let them inside.

She followed him into one of the front rooms, staring at his stiff back. Then he turned to brace himself. Arms crossed over his chest. Legs locked. Anger closing off his expression.

Ivy struggled to clear her throat. "Paxton, this is Tate Kingston. Willow's fiancé."

Paxton arched a brow in recognition at Tate's name before closing his expression down tight. "Start talking," he said.

Tate grunted a protest, but Ivy held up her hand.

"I'm not going to apologize for not telling you about this up-front," she said, using all of her control to keep her voice steady. "It wasn't important when I first came to work for you. It was more important that I was good at my job and you needed help in the office. Besides, I didn't plan to get close..." She took a deep breath. They both knew how those first intentions had been derailed. "Then you left. There just wasn't time to address it."

"What about since I came home? There's no excuse for not telling me, Ivy."

"Really?" She took a few steps closer, her heart pounding hard enough to bring on a wave of nausea. "Knowing how your family feels about mine, would you honestly place a child in the middle of that?"

She could tell her question hit home, but he quickly shrugged it off. "That doesn't change the fact that your family is guilty."

"Maybe they aren't," Tate said as he stepped forward. "I want you to look at this."

Paxton threw her a quick glance she couldn't read, then focused on Tate and the worn ledger in his hands.

"Your family and the Kanes weren't the only successful shipping families in the area at the time. Mine was also around. The Kingston family was ruthlessly undercutting the competition in an attempt to take over the majority of the business in and out of Savannah's ports," Tate said. "Now, I don't know what evidence caused your family to focus on the Kanes, especially after the police cleared them, but I think mine is a little more compelling."

Tate laid the book on the coffee table and opened it to a page not quite halfway through. "Do you recognize this date?"

Paxton gave the page a quick glance, then paused for a longer look. "Yes." He drew the word out.

"This ledger is the place my great-great-grandfather kept record of all of his business transactions that were…let's just say, illegal. To put it mildly."

Paxton raised a brow, giving him a look as princely as his surroundings. "I'm surprised you keep this."

"Why wouldn't I?" Tate shrugged. "The Kingstons have always thought they were invincible. Every generation of them. All of the family records are stored on the third floor of Sabatini House, much to Willow's delight."

Paxton tilted his head in question.

"She's quite the history buff."

Tate's casual manner seemed to calm Paxton a little. Much to Ivy's relief.

His stance relaxed somewhat as he listened intently to the rest of Tate's story. "It did not surprise me to know that my ancestors were not very nice people. I knew from personal experience. I'm not exaggerating when I say they were ruthless in their business dealings. I can assure you, it was not much different in their personal endeavors."

"Are you actually proud of these criminals?" Paxton asked with an incredulous shake of his head.

"Absolutely not. They were bastards, by my standards. But it does make for interesting book fodder."

Ivy might have smiled if the situation hadn't been so tense. Only Tate, a famous horror author, would look at it that way.

Paxton looked a little dazed himself.

"Anyway, Willow found this in the attic and the date does correlate with the sinking of the McLemore ship."

Paxton crossed his arms over his chest again, closing himself off. "Well, this is quite convenient for her."

Fear pierced Ivy's chest. What if Tate's plan didn't work? She hadn't realized just how much hope had risen in her heart since Tate had started talking. Could she handle it if everything stayed sour between her and Paxton?

Tate didn't seem at all phased by the remark. "The investigation was purely an academic exercise until Ivy's, well, predicament came along."

Great, now Paxton was back to shooting daggers in her direction. Metaphorically, of course.

Tate just kept talking. "We knew it would be important to find out what really happened, if we could. For the baby's sake, if nothing else."

"That doesn't explain why I wasn't told."

Ivy stepped up, though her tight throat made speaking hard. "And I may never be able to explain it. I'm sorry, Paxton. I had to make a lot of tough decisions on my own. You might have made a different choice. But remember, it's easier from the outside, looking in."

He stiffened.

"Besides," Tate said, "we thought we'd have more proof of her family's innocence by now. I contacted the family of the man who signed the contract with my relatives, but they weren't able to offer more than confirmation of his shady character."

"But no specifics about the ship?"

"No. Not only would he never mention it, he left the room if it came up in any conversation."

That tidbit seemed suspicious in and of itself. "How would they know that?"

"Family legend," Tate supplied. "They passed down the story that on his deathbed, he tried to tell them something. The only word he could utter was *McLemore*. His surviving family members suspected he'd been involved somehow and remembered his odd behavior. But they were never able to get a confirmation from him."

Paxton turned away, but not before Ivy noticed a slight shake in his hands. Hope surged as she held her breath.

After several long, silent moments, he turned back to face them. "You have the most to lose, Tate. Do you believe this?" He waved a hand toward the ledger.

"Wholeheartedly. But there's nothing to lose for me. I don't care what people think of me or my family. My future wife and sisters-in-law are another matter."

Ivy wanted to hug her future brother-in-law, but she was too busy wondering if the actual evidence was enough to give her a fighting chance.

# Thirteen

Paxton could understand Tate's sentiment—all too well.

It would be easy to quit caring about his family and be led by his fascination with Ivy. He should have spent the night figuring out how to sue for custody of his child. Instead he'd spent the hours obsessing over losing the woman who had come to mean so much to him.

So much about Ivy had haunted his dreams. Her sexy lips and enthusiasm in bed. Her hard work and ability to handle all manner of issues in the office. Her love for her family, which rivalled his own. Then there was the incredible fact that his child grew inside of her, spawned by a night of passion he'd never forget. Not a single moment.

But he'd been lied to by pretty faces before. He wasn't sure he could get over that.

"So," Tate said as he gathered up the ledger. "This portion of the investigation is at a dead end. But we're still looking for clues."

"Have you thought about a private detective?"

Tate shook his head. "I don't know where they'd look except where we are already looking. And I don't want a stranger poking around my house."

The thought still niggled at Paxton. Maybe...

"So...can I leave you two alone, or do I need to go get some packing boxes?"

Paxton couldn't bring himself to look at Ivy just yet, but he noticed her body shift in his peripheral vision.

Did he want to do this? Was what they had together worth working this out for? Or should he walk away while he still could? Before he revealed more about himself than he felt comfortable with.

His body shouted *yes, keep her*. But his mind knew exactly where this conversation with Ivy would lead. She would be just as demanding for answers as he had been. He wasn't sure he was ready to reveal so much about himself or if he could handle how close it might bring them.

Again he noticed that slight movement out of the corner of his eyes as the minutes ticked by. What did he want? Then a soft feeling of contentment invaded his chest and he knew what he needed to do.

"Give us some time, Tate," Paxton said. "We can call if Ivy needs you."

Tate stared him down for a long moment. Clearly taking his measure. Paxton let him. He had to take into account that two pretty high-powered men had become involved with Ivy's family. Tate wanted to know if he could trust Paxton. He would want to know the same if they were talking about one of Paxton's sisters.

"Okay," Tate conceded. "Ivy?"

As Paxton turned his gaze in her direction, she nodded.

"You have my cell phone number." The front door closed after Tate, leaving behind the most awkward silence Paxton had ever experienced.

Ivy didn't hesitate to break it. "I'm sorry, Paxton."

"I know." And somehow he did. How he'd become this attuned to her, he wasn't sure. The connection wasn't always clear when his emotions got in the way. Still the certainty remained.

"I needed to protect myself. My family. But I realize now how selfish it was of me to hide this from you after we became…involved. I just thought I could fix it first."

The strained tone in her voice pulled his reluctant glance her way—just in time to see her tilt slightly off-balance.

"Ivy, sit down."

He ushered her into a nearby armchair. As soon as she was seated firmly in place, he forced himself to step away. He could see the hurt on her face, but couldn't admit he had to pull back before he pulled her close.

Instead he channeled all of his chaotic thoughts and resulting pent-up energy into a steady bout of pacing. "I don't know, Ivy. I don't know if I can get past this."

"The family thing—"

"The hiding. The secrets."

It was a long moment of silence. Paxton couldn't speak. His hypocrisy suddenly hit him hard, and his stomach dipped as though in anticipation of riding a roller coaster. How could he talk about her secrets when he insisted on keeping his own? Could he really do this? Expose his humiliating history to her?

"I'm only going to say this one more time. I'm sorry, Paxton." Ivy's voice was harder than he'd ever heard it. Justifiably so. "I should have told you what I knew."

"That seems like a running theme with you." Maybe he still had some anger lurking beneath the surface. Then again, emotions were rarely cut-and-dried.

"Look, I get that you're angry, but you also don't have

stories handed down from your parents of your great-grand-father being so terrified after someone runs his wife's car off the road with his baby daughter inside that he packs up their bags and flees during the middle of the night to protect his family."

That stopped his pacing in an instant. "What?"

"Guess your grandmother left that part out, huh?" Ivy's eyes were glistening. Her face scrunched up with emotion. Paxton couldn't look away. "That was just the last in a long line of terror that was dished out to him before they ran for their lives. I know exactly what your family is capable of."

He should, too. He'd suspected they had resorted to phys-ical violence, but the details were never shared. To hurt an innocent woman and her child was unthinkable.

"If there was an option for proving our innocence, I wanted to take it, Paxton."

And his family, the one he'd been trying so hard to serve, were the ones who had pushed her to keep the truth from him. Paxton felt all of his preconceived notions start to crack.

"I really do understand, Paxton," she said, pushing up from her chair and crossing the room to him. Each step had a hesitancy to it, as if she weren't quite sure she should ap-proach. "And I wanted to trust you. But I wasn't ready. At first it honestly didn't matter. But later, with the baby, there was too much at stake."

She laid a hand on his arm. "I know you were caught off guard. But I thought we were getting to know each other. Why wouldn't you even listen to me? Give me a chance to explain?"

In that moment his gaze lifted and he caught sight of those gorgeous blue eyes and the stunning amount of hurt they held.

"I will not live through that again," she insisted. "Paxton, I know I didn't tell you right away, but that's not lying. About this or the baby. I can't always tell you every single thing according to your timetable. I just can't."

He was already shaking his head, knowing his own secrets would have to be revealed. It was the only way to fix this problem.

"It's not about you. It comes from someone before you." His throat closed, as if urging him to keep his secrets to himself. To spare himself from reliving the humiliation. But she deserved something, even if it was only the bare facts. He had to look away from her fixed gaze.

"I was involved with someone, a long time ago." He couldn't tell her how infatuated he'd been, how naive. He'd grown up fast in the end. "I was young and stupid. I overlooked a lot of clues that I was being used before I overheard her telling her friends that she was with me for my money."

He expected a sympathetic look or maybe even a few tears, but instead anger transformed Ivy's face.

"Seriously? How could someone, anyone, get to know you and still only want you for your money? How pathetically shallow could she be?"

Her surprising outrage dissolved his embarrassment in seconds. That wasn't at all what he'd expected…though he might have if he'd been thinking with any kind of clarity. He was still uncomfortable with what he'd shared, but she deserved the truth after he'd been so judgmental.

"At least you're good for my ego," he said with a slight laugh.

She studied him as if she knew he wasn't telling her everything, knew there was something deeper behind his quip, but she didn't press for more.

Instead she shook her head. "Paxton, I'm so sorry. I

just didn't know when the right time was to tell you everything."

"Do I know it all now?"

To his surprise, she met his gaze head-on. "You know everything I know." Her sigh echoed his own exhaustion. "I just don't want to put my family in any jeopardy. They don't deserve that."

Immediate protests rose to his lips, but he held them back. As much as he didn't want to admit it to himself, she had a right to be afraid.

He wasn't sure what his family would do when they found out the truth. He still wasn't sure what he felt about it himself. He only knew that he couldn't turn his back on this woman for something that happened to his family several generations ago. Or for something that happened to him when he was just a kid.

Right then and there, he determined to get himself out of the past long enough to appreciate what might just be his future. But he had a feeling his family wouldn't follow suit.

Paxton listened intently to the shower running in the master suite, wishing he could join Ivy under the warm rush of water. Technically things between them had returned to normal on the surface, but the underlying strain of uncertainty kept them from truly coming together.

The ease Paxton had started to feel with Ivy had disappeared. He found he missed it, even though he'd told himself they shouldn't get close. There wasn't a clear way forward on their relationship after the revelations about her family. He should keep his distance.

But the deep, aching need for her didn't follow any logic. Listening to the shower running, thinking of joining her in it, was torture.

His moment of indecision was solved when the doorbell

rang. Paxton felt a brief panic. The house was in a gated community, so his visitor wasn't going to be a random salesman. His neighbors rarely came over. Those interactions usually came at unexpected moments, when they were out in their yards. It could very well be one of his relatives, though they'd rarely been here since he'd moved in. Then what would he do?

As the bell rang again, Paxton knew he couldn't ignore it. All the lights were on. No one would buy that he wasn't home. So he opened the door and found Sierra on his doorstep.

He hurried to relieve her of the heavy toddler draped over her growing belly. "Sierra, what are you doing here?" he asked, panic truly taking hold. What should he do about Ivy? He had no way to warn her.

His niece wrapped her arms around his neck and snuggled close. The drive must've made her sleepy. Then Sierra stepped inside and the light glittered over the tears on her cheeks.

"What's wrong?" Everything left his mind in that moment except helping his sister.

"I just don't know what to do anymore, Paxton."

A vision of Alicia in his office flashed through his mind. *I just wondered if you had noticed anything off with Sierra?*

"Tell me what happened," he urged her.

"It's like he's decided I'm invisible or something." She waved her arms around to emphasize her point. "I wake up and he's gone. He doesn't come home until after I'm in bed. Honestly, if it wasn't for the dirty dishes, I wouldn't even know he'd been there."

More tears spilled over.

"You haven't spoken to him about this at all?" He led her through the front hallway to the breakfast nook.

"I haven't seen the man in a week."

That wasn't good. What husband went a whole week without seeing his pregnant wife and daughter? This had to be something serious, or she was right: he'd completely lost interest.

He got Sierra settled into a chair, then eased into another one himself and leaned back so that his niece could lie more comfortably. It was well past the toddler's bedtime. What would Sierra's husband think when he came home to an empty house?

Paxton gave a heavy sigh, then jumped in with the most obvious question. "Do you think he's cheating?"

Sierra slowly shook her head. "I don't think so. Otherwise why bother to come home at all? I mean, yes, his clothes are there, but he could take them with him at any time. It's not like I do the laundry."

"Do you think maybe he's worried about something? About a project at work? His move on the board? What about his family?"

Sierra frowned for a moment, then shrugged. "Well, I don't know."

Though the McLemores made marital decisions based on logic, and what was best for the family and the company, that didn't mean that the relationships were cold or heartless. Sierra and her husband had formed a merger, but they got along well enough to produce two children.

"We never really talked about that," Sierra continued. "You know, problems or what's going on at work."

Hmm… "What do you talk about?"

"Her," she said, nodding toward her daughter.

"What about before she came along?"

"Well, we were building the house, and I guess mutual acquaintances. We went out to a lot of parties."

Paxton was beginning to see part of the problem. It

might not be the complete issue, but it was definitely a start.

"Maybe you should talk to him," he suggested, thinking back over his and Ivy's own issues. "If you haven't let him know that he can come to you if there's a problem, then why would he?"

His own words hit him with a jolt. Was that how Ivy had felt? Like she couldn't come to him because he wouldn't care enough? Because he would always side with his family over her? Especially after he'd left. He felt like such a dolt.

With a little frown, Sierra said, "I guess that's true."

Paxton leaned forward, but was careful not to jostle his precious bundle too much. "Do you want to stay? Or is this marriage not what you want anymore?"

Sierra glanced away, the frown becoming more pronounced. She absently rubbed her distended belly. "I guess I wouldn't be upset if I didn't really want this. Right?"

"So, this isn't just hormones? Or some kind of possessiveness thing rearing its head?"

"No." She looked up and held his gaze. "No, it's not."

As soon as the words were out, she raised her brows at him as if asking for his approval. But she didn't need it. He reached across to squeeze her hand, which had finally come to rest on the table. "If it's what you want, then maybe you should start fighting for it instead of just wondering and worrying."

She opened her mouth to respond, but suddenly her gaze snapped to the doorway behind him. "Who is that?"

It took Paxton a minute to realize what was happening. He glanced over his shoulder to see Ivy in the kitchen. She had a pretty cotton nightgown on and a towel wrapped around her damp hair as she looked into the refrigerator.

How on earth could he have forgotten about her?

"Is that a woman?" Sierra headed to the kitchen with a grin. Paxton was slow to follow, hampered as he was by the toddler hanging on him.

"Hey, there." But Sierra's voice trailed off as Ivy turned around, her eyes bright blue and wide.

"Paxton!" his sister said, her gaze darting between the two of them. "Are you sleeping with your secretary?"

# Fourteen

Over the next week, Ivy waited anxiously for the other shoe to drop. Though Paxton assured her he'd sworn his sister to secrecy, she knew it was only a matter of time before word got back to his family that a woman was living in his house.

That would probably be worse for them than just knowing that he'd slept with her. Living here implied some kind of permanency. How humiliating would it be to listen to Paxton explain the uncertainty of their current arrangement?

She was just thankful it had been Sierra who had walked in that night, rather than Alicia. The latter was a mini-replica of Paxton's mother, Elizabeth, neither of whom were the nicest women to deal with. Sierra, on the other hand, tended to be more personable. It helped that she usually had her little girl when she came into the office, which lightened things up quite a bit.

But Sierra's surprise, and referring to Ivy as Paxton's assistant, had left Ivy in no mood to talk that night. Not to mention being caught in her pj's. Startled, Ivy had rushed out of the kitchen and into the downstairs bedroom, staying inside until Paxton joined her almost an hour later.

Listening to him talk about Sierra's visit had made the lack of a heads-up much more understandable. Yes, Paxton could have excused himself for a quick trip to the bathroom and warned Ivy to stay upstairs. But her tears had tripped Paxton into big-brother mode, ready to help Sierra slay any dragons that she needed help with.

While Ivy hated that Sierra was having trouble with her relationship, she was more worried about what her little visit to Paxton's house would mean for Ivy. And eventually Ivy's baby.

It only took a week to find out.

The morning had been slow and smooth in the office. Paxton had no meetings he had to attend. They were making steady progress until Paxton had a conference call, so Ivy settled in to work up some notes he'd asked her for. The part-time assistant would come in that afternoon so Ivy could go home to rest. Paxton had insisted, because she hadn't been sleeping well.

She hadn't had the heart to tell him it was worry keeping her awake, not her pregnancy.

The quiet morning made Elizabeth McLemore's arrival all the more jarring. Her appearance was usually a no-brainer. Though she was a forceful woman, she understood having to wait while Paxton was in a meeting or on the phone. Her words to Ivy were always short and to the point, making their interactions easy, even if they were uncomfortable on Ivy's part.

Today was a whole other matter. Her march through the door and trained gaze set off a wave of nausea for Ivy. Still she pasted on a smile and said, "He's on a phone call, Mrs. McLemore, but I'll message that you're here."

"No need. I'm not here to see him."

"Excuse me?" Ivy was horrified to hear her voice come out as a squeak.

Paxton's mother raised a haughty brow as if that little noise just confirmed her superiority. "I just want to know if there is something you hope to gain by sleeping with my son?"

*Keep it a secret, my foot.* So much for Sierra keeping her mouth shut. Ivy raised herself slowly to her feet, even though her body suddenly felt like lead, in hopes it would help her project confidence. "Mrs. McLemore, what happens between Paxton and I—"

"Is of complete interest to me, since I serve on this company's board."

"Why?" For a moment Ivy didn't quite understand the correlation. "You're going to reprimand your son for being involved with his assistant?"

"No. Not my son."

Ivy had only a moment to absorb the panic that streaked through her. Thankfully Paxton opened his door. Taking a page from Alicia's book, Ivy asked, "Are you threatening me?" Petty, but she wanted Paxton to hear exactly what was happening. For himself.

"Ivy—Mother. What's going on here?"

Suddenly his mother was all smiles. "Darling, your sister was telling me about your new—well, I came down to meet her."

Ivy cocked her head to the side. "I've worked here for a year and a half. You've met me before," she insisted.

His mother ignored her, as usual. "Sierra tried to tell me, but I knew you would have told me first."

Paxton didn't seem as concerned as Ivy would like. Deep inside, panic tightened her every muscle.

"You wouldn't have listened," he said simply.

"I always have time for—"

"You wouldn't have listened, because you wouldn't like what you heard."

Startled, Ivy noticed a deepening of his tone, as if something hidden was slowly coming to the surface.

"Ivy was at my house by my choice. Our choice. And it's nobody's business but ours until we are ready to share it. I simply wanted to wait until I knew there was something to tell."

"Is there? Because Sierra seemed to think this person, your assistant, was living with you." Her gaze shot straight over to Ivy as if she could not believe that would be true.

"I believe so," Paxton said quietly.

The odd note in his voice had Ivy looking his way. He looked back, his expression oddly hopeful. Hesitant. In that moment it was as if all the recent distance between them had dissolved. The connection of their gazes suddenly had a sizzle, as if her psyche had just been waiting for his to accept what they both knew was happening between them.

"I'm sure Miss Baxter will be very disappointed," Elizabeth said sotto voce.

"Through no fault of mine."

"Yes, well…" Obviously she didn't agree. Her expression tightened, with tiny frown lines appearing, along with a slight curl to her lip. "We shall see."

She turned to the door, but Paxton stopped her. "Did you need to see me, Mother?"

Her gaze flicked to Ivy. "No. I got what I came for."

She was almost out the door when she turned back again, causing Ivy's stomach to lurch. She was definitely gonna need the afternoon off.

"I almost forgot, your grandmother expects to see you at the luncheon on Sunday. Both of you." Her eyes widened in an innocent expression that Ivy wasn't buying. "See you then."

"Welcome."

Alicia spoke with the appropriate formality, but the Cheshire grin was what had him worried. For the first time, he found himself on guard against his own family.

Protective instincts swelled inside him. Not for his child, as he would have expected, but for Ivy.

The unfamiliarity of it itched just beneath his Sunday suit. Still he couldn't deny what it was. Without hesitation he laid his hand at the small of her back—a move of both possession and solidarity. Beneath his palm, her muscles relaxed just a touch.

An echo of the heat he felt whenever he was alone with her flashed through him, pulling him even closer to her.

They moved through the grand foyer, with its strategically hung chandelier, skylights and oversize palm plants placed for dramatic affect. Paxton turned left into the library where he knew the rest of the family would be having drinks.

Sierra was the first to meet him. "I'm sorry, Paxton," she whispered as she slipped into his arms for a solid hug.

Leave it to Sierra to head a scolding off at the pass. She even turned to the woman at his side and said, "Welcome, Ivy," her voice much warmer than Alicia's had been.

Paxton shook hands with Sierra's husband, who offered a somewhat strained smile before slipping an arm around her. Paxton noted the move with surprise. One thing Sierra and Jason had never exhibited was any kind of affection in public. None whatsoever. But as he watched his sister slowly relax into the touch, he hoped this was a result of a much-needed come-to-Jesus meeting. Whatever brought happiness to his sister was worth it.

Determined to give the right impression immediately, he cupped Ivy's arm possessively and led her to where the elder McLemores congregated. They didn't bother to stand, which made him frown.

"Mother, you know Ivy. Father, this is Ivy Harden, whom I don't believe you've had the pleasure of meeting."

His father had the class to get up and bow over Ivy's hand. Father's manners had always been impeccable.

"Grandmother, this is Ivy Harden. Ivy, Karen McLemore."

Beneath his touch, Ivy stiffened as his grandmother nodded her head in a regal gesture, then returned to the conversation without any other acknowledgment. Paxton used his hold to pull Ivy closer into his heat, seeking to comfort her.

His grandmother knew exactly what she was doing. Her social persona was second nature; he'd seen it in action his whole life. Snubbing Ivy was her way of getting her point across—this person wasn't welcome, even though she'd been commanded to be here.

Paxton suddenly wished he'd followed his instincts and left Ivy at home, confronting his family on his own. Less collateral damage.

Because Grandmother had just made it clear she was up to something. But what approach would she take? Mulling it over, he guided Ivy over to the younger set and joined their conversation.

When dinner was served, Ivy barely ate under his grandmother's stare in the formal dining room. Paxton started to worry the nausea, which hadn't made an appearance in days, had returned.

Conversation was smooth for the first half of the meal, but his grandmother remained silent, upping the tension.

"So, Paxton—" Grandmother's voice echoed around

the walls when she finally spoke "—what can you tell me about this young lady?"

Paxton was startled by the question, but decided it was in their best interest to simply answer. "Well, Ivy has been my assistant for almost two years, and keeps the office running better than anyone before her."

Paxton noticed that Ivy simply gave up eating, and dropped her hands to her lap. But she refused to be cowed. Instead she kept her head high with a polite smile on her face.

"And your family, dear? I don't believe I've heard of them."

Paxton stiffened. There was no way his sister could've known who Ivy's family really was. And Paxton was not ready to start World War Three over it until he had more information.

Ivy answered the question with a simple, "I'm orphaned, actually."

"A secretary and an orphan. Well, isn't that just pitiful."

It should have sounded sympathetic, but it didn't. Paxton narrowed his eyes toward his grandmother.

"From what I understand of your family, you're solidly middle class."

Ivy turned her head slowly to meet Paxton's gaze, giving him a clear view of her resignation before she once again faced the head of the table.

"We make do… But if you knew that about my family, *Karen*, then why did you ask me about them?"

"A simple fishing expedition, my dear. A family like ours must keep protections in place."

"Protections?" Ivy shook her head. "Isn't that a bit melodramatic? You seem pretty well protected to me."

"Oh, one can never be too protected from people like you."

A sudden stillness invaded the room, causing Paxton's voice to echo off the walls. "Grandmother, that's enough."

"I'm sorry, Paxton. You brought this on yourself."

"What?"

"I never took you for being so gullible. Then again, pretty faces are your weakness. They always have been."

Anger shot straight through Paxton at the reference, pushing him to his feet. "I said, that's enough." The burn of regret flooded his chest. "Let's go, Ivy."

As he helped Ivy up from her chair, Karen said, "So, you would disregard your family's prudent warning in favor of a woman who will trick you into marrying her?"

This time the gasp was more collective. Paxton was glad to see some of his family had sensibilities.

"I have never demanded that Paxton marry me," Ivy insisted.

"But that baby gives you a pretty good meal ticket, at least for the next eighteen to twenty-two years, in my opinion."

Paxton froze for a moment. Ivy's soft whimper seemed loud in the room. How his grandmother had found out about the baby, he wasn't sure.

"She's pregnant?" his mother moaned.

A quick glance showed each of his sisters eyeing each other with raised brows. The rest of the audience was frozen in place, not daring to interfere, though his father did shoot him a look of sympathy.

He wanted to get Ivy out of there fast, but knew retreat would be seen as weakness by his family. He'd have to stick it out a little longer.

"Though I don't know how you know that, Ivy did not trick me into getting pregnant. I'm the one who provided the protection." If the situation hadn't been so tense, Paxton would have smiled as he remembered the illuminating conversation with Auntie.

His mother's face scrunched up. "Paxton!"

"Grandmother brought it up. I'm simply stating the truth."

But the elder Mrs. McLemore wasn't buying it. "I'm sure that's what she let you think. Regardless the result is the same." Karen folded her hands before her as if reinforcing her matriarch status. Her words were clear and even. "Despite how it came about, the first male grandchild will be a wonderful addition to our family."

"What?" Ivy said, confusion clouding her face. "I thought you didn't want anything to do with me?"

Paxton reached out for her arm. He had a feeling it wasn't going to be that easy.

"Regardless of whether we marry or not, Ivy and her baby will be a wonderful addition to the McLemore family," he said.

"Hardly, Paxton. I'm afraid we must maintain standards." She eyed Ivy. "But that's all right—everyone has a price."

Ivy's entire body snapped to attention. Paxton could tell by the hard look on her face that she'd had enough. He had, too. Unfortunately his grandmother spoke before he could get them moving toward the door.

"So, how much is it, my dear? I'm sure a lawyer will happily draw up an agreement for us to purchase your parental rights."

Ivy scoffed, even as her face went sheet white. "There isn't enough money in the world to separate me from my child, lady. Especially not after all I've been through."

The pain on her face shook Paxton to his core. Time to end this.

He stepped in close and secured her to his side with her arm through his; a look was all he could give her right now to assure her he understood. Then he escorted her to the head of the table, where he paused to look down at his grandmother, his body a barrier meant to protect Ivy.

"All I asked for was a number, Paxton," Karen said, an odd look of surprise in her amber eyes, so much like his own. How could she not know what she was doing was wrong?

He'd happily set her straight. "Since you obviously haven't realized this yet, let me make a few things clear. One. Ivy and I will make our own decisions in this situation. Not you. Not Mother or Father."

Then he leaned closer, dominating his grandmother's space in a way he never had before. "And two, if you think I'm the type of man to separate any woman from her child, you never knew me at all."

# Fifteen

Concern for Ivy exploded in Paxton's chest on the drive back to his house. When they got inside, defeat weighed her down, causing her to sag against the side table in the foyer, her head hanging forward. Paxton sympathized. She'd been through so much. His family's behavior had to be a body blow.

One he didn't know how to soften…even for himself.

Without hesitation he put his arms around her, pressing himself firmly against her back as if to protect her from another hit. "It will be okay, Ivy," he whispered against her temple.

Though he didn't know how. He knew his grandmother well. If her decision about Ivy was this firm, she'd just keep coming. She didn't back down. Weakness was a trait she'd never allowed to fester, not even at her advanced age.

Could he possibly find a way to change her mind?

Unbidden, he found himself swaying back and forth as

if to music only he could hear. Slowly Ivy's body softened, the tension leaching away. He drew her even closer against him, wishing they were skin to skin. But the lack of space in the foyer was almost symbolic to him—the two of them, together as one against the world. Most power struggles were simply a business game to him—a cat-and-mouse race to see who reached the prize first. Winning was a pleasure.

Now it was a necessity. For him. For Ivy. For their child.

"We'll get through this together."

*Together.* They would, but right now there would be no fighting. Only love.

Yes. That was what they needed.

He lifted her into his arms, savoring her gasp of surprise. Then he carried her up the stairs to the master suite. His room. Their room.

And he wanted nothing more than to have this princess in his bed.

It was a little reminiscent of a fairy tale, he had to admit. The thought made him grin, a return of lightness. Though she didn't come from an upper-class background, Ivy had always reminded him of a princess. It was just in the air about her and the way she held herself. As he laid her in the king-size bed, her golden hair spread across the burgundy-colored pillows, giving her a rich, royal air.

The impression didn't diminish as he removed her clothing, piece by piece. If anything, the white lace bra and panties gave her an even more noble air. How anyone could look at Ivy, with her classic bone structure and regal demeanor, and define her as something common was beyond him.

He wanted to tell her how gorgeous, how perfect she was. Instead he determined to show her.

Quickly Paxton stripped his tie and jacket, toeing off his shoes while he opened his shirt one button at a time. He held her gaze, letting the anticipation build.

Ivy had been the adventure of a lifetime.

Needing to be closer, he crawled up, letting the open sides of his shirt fall on either side of her naked body. His shadow overtook her. As the need to imprint himself on her grew, he made a place for himself between her thighs, resting the weight of his body on hers. He buried his hands in her hair, then leisurely tasted her lips, neck, down her collarbone to her breast. When this was over, he wanted Ivy to remember him with every part of her body. Never to forget his possession or the pleasure he made her feel.

Her hands closed over his ribs, and he felt her growing urgency in the desperation of her grip. His body reveled in her urgency, letting it feed his own. She lifted her hips against him, silently begging him to take her. Every single part of his body, down to his smallest cell, gathered the energy he would need to meet this incredible challenge.

He lifted up onto his knees. To his relief, she immediately unbuckled his dress pants. Slick skin greeted him as he pressed intimately against her. He savored the decadent feel of her naked beneath him, his still-covered legs rubbing against her delicate inner thighs. Bare chest to bare chest.

Paxton's drive, to take what he needed and leave her with even more, kicked into full gear. He pressed inside of her. Any logical thinking that remained at this point imploded, leaving him a creature of instinct and emotions. His inner struggle mimicked the rise and fall of their bodies until he pushed them over the edge, into the ultimate oblivion.

But in the quiet aftermath, when the only sound was their labored breathing and her whispered "I love you, Paxton," he found the word still wouldn't come in return. Instead he once again kissed her temple and whispered that everything would be okay. Then he wrapped his body around hers, and prayed he didn't have to make the choice he could see coming.

* * *

"I wish to see Paxton, please," Karen McLemore demanded as she approached Ivy's desk.

Without a word Ivy led her through, no longer feeling any need to bother with polite pleasantries. The elder Mrs. McLemore probably wouldn't appreciate them anyway. And Ivy knew, without it being said, that her days here were numbered.

There wasn't any reason to buzz him first. She knew Paxton wasn't in a meeting or on the phone. The last few days he'd spent most of his time staring out the window, trying to make decisions he didn't share with her. Ironic, considering how many times he'd judged her for the same.

She only knew he felt more distant every day, since the moment she'd made the mistake of saying *I love you*. Were the words too much pressure for a man like him? Was it only a matter of time before he decided to leave her? Decided that she wasn't worth fighting his family for?

Ivy wasn't able to ignore professional courtesy, so she opened the door for his grandmother, but didn't glance his way. Karen McLemore strode inside with the confidence of an imperial ruler surveying her domain.

Just as Ivy began to retreat, the imperious command rang out. "Stay!" Then a quieter but no less stern, "This concerns you, too."

That couldn't be good.

Was she about to be fired? Karen McLemore was, after all, the owner of the family corporation. She had the power to do as she wished. And the right to do so.

Even though Ivy had been anticipating this very thing, the thought of trying to find a job right now brought on a wave of nausea. She didn't imagine Paxton's grandmother would skimp on all the details she was sure to pass along to any potential employers who were looking for a reference. That would look good on Ivy's track record...not.

Would Ivy have to move away to be able to support herself and her child? Was history about to repeat itself?

As she froze in quiet panic, Paxton rose from behind his desk. "Grandmother," he said, acknowledging her in an overly-formal tone.

"Paxton, you have not returned my phone calls."

He stayed silent, keeping his gaze trained on the older woman. His expression was more somber than Ivy had ever seen.

Ivy wasn't even aware his grandmother had tried to contact him. Then again they rarely spoke these days, except for business. Instead they spent every moment outside the office in bed, as if desperate to savor the connection while it lasted.

"I can't really imagine what we would have to say to each other," he said.

"Well, I can."

Karen strode forward, pulling a stuffed file folder from her leather portfolio. "The final report from our private detective came in."

Ivy swallowed hard. *Our?* Had Paxton been aware of this? Involved in this?

He glanced her way, as if he could read her thoughts. "The company retains an investigator, but I've never used him to look into your background."

"You should have," his grandmother said. "They found something you need to know."

"That Ivy's family was involved in sinking our ship generations ago?"

That took his grandmother by surprise, something Ivy imagined didn't happen often. Karen stiffened. "You knew?"

"Of course." He shared a glance with Ivy. "We don't have any secrets from one another."

Anymore...*except how you really feel about me.*

His grandmother slammed the file down onto his desk. "Paxton, how could you consort with the enemy? We did not raise you to be led astray by good looks and a willing body."

His face hardened. "Ivy hadn't even been born when that ship went down."

Karen glanced her way. "There's murder in her blood."

"Really? The same way our family tried to kill an innocent woman and her child in retaliation?"

Karen's eyes narrowed. Ivy felt a moment of fear, even though the gaze wasn't directed at her.

But Paxton refused to back down. "We wanted revenge so badly, we would kill a child over something we had no proof of? You don't usually include that part of the story, do you, Grams?"

Karen raised her chin. "We did what was necessary."

"What was necessary was to find the real villain instead of victimizing the innocent."

She was already shaking her head in denial. "We did nothing of the sort."

"Really? I've seen the police reports. There was no evidence against her family."

Shock rippled through Ivy. Tate had spoken about police reports, but Ivy had never seen them. She'd imagined they'd been lost to time.

"And I've seen proof that another party might be responsible." Paxton crossed his arms over his chest. "Her family is innocent. But I guess your PI didn't dig quite as deep as mine."

As if sensing she was losing her grip on this situation, Karen changed her tactics.

"Paxton, we've always been close." She studied him intently. Ivy would have been squirming by now, but Paxton stood solid. "Your outright rebellion is cause for great concern."

"Maybe I'm starting to see what my family is really like. And it's not something I want to be a part of."

"That can be arranged."

Ivy gasped as the words hit her square in the chest.

Paxton leaned forward, bracing himself against his desk. "Are you threatening me?"

"No, I'm assuring you that I will terminate your employment here if you do not end this relationship immediately."

*No. No.* Ivy had known this might get rocky, but this—to take Paxton from what he loved, what he was so good at…

"I don't need our family background or name to be successful in business."

"You might. When word gets out that you were sticking it to your secretary."

Ivy gasped at the crude language, but the battle of wills continued without her.

"I've told you before, Grandmother. I will not separate Ivy from her child."

The words were a promise, one Paxton had given her many times, but still he offered no words of love.

"Nor will I condemn her for something neither she nor her family did. They've suffered enough."

He crossed his arms over his chest as if to say, *I can withstand anything you want to throw at me…*

"Clean out your desk."

Pain crossed his face, but his expression quickly smoothed out, hiding any further clues. Then he said, "Done."

"No."

Both of them looked her way. "Paxton, I know this isn't what you want."

His grandmother smirked. "Neither does she. I'm eliminating her meal ticket."

"How can you be so cold?" Ivy demanded, the woman's words crashing like a shock wave over her system. "He's your grandson."

"He needs to be taught a lesson. As do you—we don't need your kind in our family."

Ivy almost caved, but she couldn't. Not after seeing that flash of pain on Paxton's face. Besides, there was nothing to lose now.

"I'm not doing any of this for money. I love Paxton. The last thing I would want would be to separate him from the family that means so much to him."

"Too late."

She looked at Paxton—a man too proud to give in, but with each of his grandmother's words, his hurt pushed to the surface of his cracking facade. This wasn't what she wanted.

"I will not do this to you, Paxton," she said, surprised to see a touch of panic widen his amber eyes. "The last thing I want is to tear you away from the family you love. And we both know that's where this is headed. It has been for a week now."

That's why he'd been so quiet. And she understood. She truly did.

"Goodbye, Paxton."

Nothing could've hurt more than saying those words. Even the fact that he didn't make a move to stop her.

# Sixteen

Ivy put the finishing touches on the table containing the items Tate had donated to the auction at Keller House. Then she stood back and looked over her handiwork.

Not too bad, considering her heart wasn't really in it.

"Thank heaven for a busy week," Willow said as she, too, surveyed the display for tonight's auction. "It's the best thing to take your mind off a man."

Ivy wished it were that easy, but the reminders of Paxton seemed to be everywhere. From trying to find her hair clip in the few boxes she'd hastily packed while Paxton was at work one day—at least one of them still had a job—to her difficulty finding a dress for tonight that would accommodate her thickening waistline.

She couldn't get away from him as easily as he seemed to ignore her.

"Is Tate driving you crazy?"

Willow rolled her eyes. "He's near the end of a book.

Nothing like it to make an author grumpy, hungry and re-clusive. Kind of like a bear, from what I've heard."

Better to talk about her sister's man problems than her own. Ivy made a noncommittal noise to keep Willow talking.

"It was all I could do to drag him off the island for tonight's auction."

Ivy could fully understand. Before Willow, Tate hadn't had any kind of social life. His only trips off his island had been meetings with his editor. Now he came to family dinners and the occasional event. Not to mention rescuing future sisters-in-law when they needed it.

"Have you heard anything from Paxton?"

Ah, the one question Ivy did not want to face. But there wasn't any point hiding her humiliation from her sisters.

"No," she sighed, stepping back to survey her handiwork. "I would have thought I would at least hear from the lawyer by now. You know, some attempt at future custody arrangements, but…nothing."

The silence was driving her crazy.

"You feeling okay?" she asked as Willow pressed a hand against the base of her spine. "How's your back holding up?"

Ivy was under strict orders to not let Willow lift anything, though bending over the displays couldn't feel great, either. Her tummy was worthy of her maternity clothes, whereas Ivy was at the barely-bump stage. Her regular clothes were too tight, but maternity clothes hung like a sack.

Then again she wasn't carrying twins like her sister was.

"Doing good," Willow said. "Can't say I'm looking forward to more restrictions coming my way." She turned to Ivy and grinned. "Aren't you glad you didn't get the double blessing?"

Most definitely. But she was finally starting to connect with her pregnancy now that she felt better. Despite the struggles over Paxton, her energy was returning and she felt more physically capable each day. Rubbing lotion on the small mound of her belly, wondering when the child's first movement would happen, took her mind off her aching wish for Paxton.

Suddenly Willow gave a strange squeak that drew Ivy's attention. She glanced up to see Willow's gaze glued on the distance beyond Ivy's shoulder.

"What? Did the doors open early?" Ivy should've had another twenty minutes or so for a quick walk-through with Jasmine.

But when Willow didn't respond, Ivy turned to look for herself. Standing ten feet away was Paxton. Tuxedoed, freshly shaven, way-too-sexy Paxton.

Definitely squeak-worthy.

Willow mumbled, "I'll go let Jasmine know," and turned to leave, but Ivy stopped her.

"No, she's got enough to deal with. I'll handle this."

It was obvious he planned to speak with her by the way he patiently waited, gaze never leaving her. But why would he choose this public venue to confront her again?

Every step of his approach had her breathing harder and faster. Boy, had she missed him, even with all the uncertainty. Her heart wanted him just as much as it had that one magical night so long ago.

"What are you doing here?" she asked, unable to look away from his amber eyes.

He paused a few feet from her, but the way he shifted on his feet told her he wasn't as confident as he looked.

"I wanted to see you. And I thought this might be a good, neutral space." He used that charming grin to full effect. "Besides, I already had a ticket."

"You only now wanted to see me?"

"I had a few things to work out before I could."

She wasn't sure whether to push or ask or wait. It seemed like her every move through all of this had been the wrong one.

So she let him make the next move.

He did. One step closer, then another.

People started to mill about. The doors must have opened finally. "I'm sorry. I have a job today," she said. She needed to focus, not be distracted by Paxton's good looks and the mix of emotions clouding her judgment.

"Wait. Just a few minutes, okay?"

Ivy crossed her arms over her chest, wrinkling her gown, but didn't leave.

"You haven't come to get your stuff," he said. "At least not all of it."

"I've been a little busy." She waved a hand about the room. "Besides, you could always have it packed up and sent to me."

"What if I don't want to?"

His tone wasn't aggravated or even disdainful, but she didn't understand where he was going with this.

In her frustration she threw out, "Donate it."

The last thing she could imagine doing right now was going over there to pack. She simply couldn't.

The past few months had taken too much from her.

Again he moved closer, this time crowding into her personal space. She held her breath, not wanting to smell the unique spicy sent of him, but her lungs overrode her resolve.

So good. So warm.

She glanced up to see his gaze turned on her, as if he could see through her disdainful facade to the aching need underneath. "What if I'd rather you come home?" he murmured. "Where you belong."

"I don't belong there." Not without his love.

"I believe you do." He ran a finger over her cheek. A touch she desperately wished she could have every day for the next fifty years. "You must. Nothing is the same. The bed feels empty. The kitchen is too quiet. The—"

He swallowed hard, his gaze darkening. "I need you. I didn't realize just how much."

"What about your family?" She wanted this so badly, but… "I can't live like that, Paxton, under constant attack, and I won't allow my child to be exposed to that, either."

"I was wrong, Ivy."

Her eyes widened. That was definitely not what she'd expected to hear. "What?"

"I let my loyalty to my family color everything between us. And the truth is, they don't deserve the consideration."

*At the risk of sounding like a broken record…* "What?" This was so unexpected, she was having trouble taking it in.

"I knew it. But I didn't want to admit it. I had to work through that—you know."

"I understand." She'd spent too much time trying to work through her issues with Paxton before fate took a hand.

"I promise I will never let them hurt you again." He tilted his chin up. "I haven't gotten it all figured out, but I promise to protect you."

"But I know you love them, Paxton. I can't tear you away from that."

"You don't have to. I resigned my position the day you left."

"What? Why haven't I heard about this?"

"They're too busy trying to get me to return to make an announcement. I guess Grandmother didn't think of the things she would put into action with her little ultimatum."

Ivy found herself clutching the lapels of his tuxedo, her attention caught. "How will you live?"

Then realizing what she'd said, she covered her face. "I'm sorry. That's just what your grandmother would expect me to ask."

He gently uncovered her face. "And just what I do expect, not because you're mercenary, but because you're worried about me."

"You love your work."

"And I can do it somewhere else. Between my savings and investments, I'll be fine. If not, I'll sell my stock in the company. But I'll be fine until I figure out where I'm going. Maybe even start my own company—who knows?"

Ivy marveled at the excitement on his face before he sobered.

"It's for the best, Ivy. It really is. Regardless of whether you come back to me, I think this separation is important. Grandmother needs to understand that I won't be controlled."

He brushed Ivy's lips with his. "And I don't want the world's best assistant afraid to work for me."

She had so many questions, but as the crowd thickened around them, she knew this was not the time. Instead she let herself be swept away by his kiss until she heard her sister Jasmine close by. "Does this mean what I think it means?"

Ivy pulled back with an embarrassed giggle, but Paxton would not let her go far. He kept an arm fully around her.

"I certainly hope so," he said with a satisfied smile.

"I'm so sorry, Jasmine," Ivy said. "I got distracted—"

"I noticed." But Jasmine and Willow were both smiling.

She saw Tate and Royce talking, over near the display table. "We did finish—"

"And it looks gorgeous," Jasmine said as they all moved closer to the display. "Tate is very pleased with what you've done with his donations."

Paxton halted abruptly, jerking Ivy to a stop. "This is

from Tate?" he asked, the odd note in his voice causing Ivy to look up to him.

His startled expression quickly morphed into one of intense focus. He leaned forward.

"Yes, some memorabilia we found in the attic," Tate said. "I figured the local history buffs might bid on some of it."

Paxton seemed to study a watch in the middle of the table. He blinked, stepping closer. His face paled. "Tate—"

Then Paxton's grandmother's voice cut through the crowd. "Paxton, I figured I would find you here."

Paxton couldn't have been more shocked than when he surveyed the group that had approached. His entire family was here. That was a pretty important feat, even for his grandmother. He knew for a fact Sierra would have warned him if she'd had advanced notice, but then again he hadn't told any of them he would be attending.

He hadn't spoken to his family since breaking the news of his resignation during a brief appearance at Sunday dinner. He'd crashed it since he hadn't gotten an invitation. Not that he'd have been able to bring himself to eat. The memories had been too bitter.

Grandmother eyed his arm as he automatically pulled Ivy close. "Consorting with the enemy again, I see."

Tate and Royce also stepped close to their women, but it was Royce who spoke. "I'm going to have to ask you to remain civil, Mrs. McLemore, or you'll be asked to leave."

She drew herself even taller than her normally impressive height. "I'll have you know we bought tickets."

"Keller House is mine," Royce said. "This is my event. What I say goes."

Karen McLemore looked back at Ivy. "You have managed to gain some powerful friends."

"No, ma'am," Ivy said, her voice tight but respectful. "This is my family. Family sticks together."

Paxton felt a glow of pride engulf him. A slightly taken-aback look flashed on his grandmother's face before she recovered. "Only if that family survives. It's my job to see that we do."

"But for you it's only survival if you beat out everyone else on the block. When all is said and done, you end up alone."

The rest of Ivy's family murmured their agreement.

"Nevertheless—"

"Grandmother," Paxton interrupted, the truth of what he needed to do finally hitting him square in the chest. "There's something I think you should see…"

"Not now, Paxton."

"Yes now, Grandmother."

The Harden women parted as he led his grandmother to the display Ivy had been finishing when he arrived. He waited silently while she inspected the items on the table donated by Tate Kingston. Anticipation caused his heart to speed up.

He knew the minute she spotted it.

Her breath grew shaky. Out of the corner of his eye, he saw her hand reach out and grasp the man's pocket watch.

*The watch with part of his family's insignia engraved on it.*

That's when things started to fall apart. With a moan, his grandmother clutched the piece to her heart, and stumbled forward against the display, shaking the table and its contents. Paxton grabbed her, his heartbeat increasing to triple time. He hoped to steady her, but her weakness as she leaned into him alarmed him even more. The swarm of his family around them and the cacophony of voices added to the confusion.

"Grandmother," he said sharply, "can you breathe?"

He heard her draw in a shaky breath, then mutter, "Yes."

He glanced over to see his father on the other side, supporting her. He shot a quick, panicked look at Royce, only to find him already taking control.

"This way, Paxton," he said.

As one large group, they made their way through the staring crowd to a side room.

"I'll be right back. I saw Dr. Michaels in the crowd earlier," Royce said before retreating out the door.

Between them, Paxton and his father settled his grandmother into a chair. She looked awfully pale, with a high flush along her cheekbones. Deep inside Paxton panicked until he felt a hand on his shoulder. Then he saw Ivy reach out another hand to lay it over his grandmother's.

"It will be okay," Ivy said in a soft but firm tone. "The doctor will be here soon. Just breathe, Mrs. McLemore. Slowly in. Slowly out."

His grandmother seemed to lose all care for who Ivy was in that moment and simply held on to her like a lifeline, following her instructions to steady her breath and calm her instinctive panic.

No more than two minutes later, Royce returned with the doctor. Only then did Karen let go of Ivy's hand. They all retreated to give the doctor some space, crowding around the outer edges of the small room with quiet whispers.

Ivy stepped back next to Paxton, laying her hands softly on his arm. He turned and pulled her hard into his embrace, steadying himself with her heat and soft curves.

"I never wanted this," he murmured against her hair.

She lay her hand on his chest, directly over his fast-beating heart. "I know. What happened? Has she had this happen before?"

Paxton shook his head. "I'm not entirely sure."

Dr. Michaels thoroughly checked his grandmother over, conversing quietly with her and Paxton's father. Slowly her color became less stark, though she was still pale.

Paxton's father caught his eye and motioned him over. Paxton knelt beside the chair, but could sense Ivy standing at his back. Her presence steadied him.

"I think she's okay," Dr. Michael said, "just a bit of a shock to her system, but I would feel better if we ran a few tests at the hospital. Just to make sure there's nothing going on with her heart."

"Yes. Let's go," Paxton said.

"Not yet."

For a woman who was recently so weak, his grandmother's voice was surprisingly stern.

"Mother," his father protested.

"No, son. This must be done first." She patted his hand. "Then we will go."

Paxton braced himself, utterly sure his grandmother was about to go on the attack once more. Those in the room edged closer. Karen pinned Ivy with her gaze, causing Paxton to tense up. She lifted the watch fob. "Where did you find this?"

Confusion clouded Ivy's expression. "It was Tate's."

He stepped forward. "We found it in the attic of Sabatini House. It didn't have any significance to me, so I donated it to the auction."

"It may not be significant to you, young man, but it certainly is to me."

"I'm sorry, Mrs. McLemore," he said. "Does it belong to your family?"

Karen opened the fob, then glanced at Paxton. "You recognized it?"

Paxton nodded. "It's an emblem from the family crest."

"This belonged to my uncle. It disappeared the night he drowned on that ship."

A collective gasp echoed in Paxton's ears. "How?"

"We assumed it was lost with him. The divers never found it or any trace of the body."

Leaving behind a devastated family, including a grieving little girl. "I'm sorry, Grandmother."

"I was his favorite." She glanced up at him, tears watering down her normally strong amber gaze. "He would bring me candy. I would sit on his lap and he would let me play with his pocket watch—this pocket watch—while he talked with the grown-ups." Tears spilled over her well-preserved cheeks. "Then he was gone."

Which explained why she told the story so often.

Tate spoke into the heavy silence. "Ma'am, on behalf of my family, let me extend my sincere apologies. They were the type of people who got what they wanted and didn't care who was hurt in the process."

"So were we…" Karen murmured.

This time she looked at Jasmine, then Willow and finally Ivy. "And you were caught in the cross fire."

Suddenly Karen struggled with her breath, shuddering as she drew it in with visible strain.

"Grandmother, let's get you to the hospital," Paxton insisted.

She nodded, then held the pocket watch out to Tate.

"No, ma'am," he said with the shake of his head. "That doesn't belong to me."

The room quietly cleared as Dr. Michaels called for an ambulance. "They'll meet us at the east entrance," he said when he ended the call. "Easier and more discrete."

As she stood Karen grasped Paxton's arm. "Paxton, darling, please forgive me."

He could, but he wasn't sure he could ever forget.

Then she looked at Ivy, who was standing close behind him. "Young lady, I want you to know, I will welcome you into our family." Suddenly she looked shaken, broken. "I was wrong. I don't know what more to say."

"Nothing," Ivy graciously offered. "Just take care of yourself."

As the group moved to meet the ambulance, Paxton felt an almost painful pull to stay behind with Ivy despite wanting to be with his family. He turned to her, opening his mouth to speak, but nothing came out.

She hugged him close and repeated the same words he'd given to her in comfort. "It's going to be okay, Paxton."

Somehow he knew it would be. Even though he hadn't accomplished all he'd meant to tonight, his purpose was clear.

"I'll be back for you," he said, and he meant it.

# Seventeen

"Go ahead home, Ivy," Jasmine said. "It's been a long night. Or would you rather sleep in one of the guest bedrooms upstairs? I don't want you too tired on the road."

"I'll be fine," Ivy mumbled, "but thanks." Then she turned to go. Anything more and the waterworks would start.

She was just tired enough not to be sure she could stop them. Her body hurt more than it usually did after a long night working these events, probably because of her pregnancy. Her legs and feet ached, and she wanted nothing more than to sleep for twelve hours straight.

Unless it was sleeping for twelve hours straight in Paxton's arms.

She checked her phone on the way out—no calls.

Paxton had driven his parents to the hospital, behind the ambulance, with the assurance that he'd call later on, when he knew something more definite. But the hours had passed with nothing but silence. Now Ivy just wanted to curl up in a space of her own and recover from all the ups and downs of today. But she wasn't sure where that space actually was anymore—Paxton's? Auntie's?

She felt like she didn't belong anywhere. And even though Paxton had acted like he loved her, acted like he wanted her, still the words were missing. She needed the assurance of the feelings rather than just her assumption that they were there.

She should be thrilled that her family had been cleared of the accusations from generations ago. That Paxton had come back to her, but the future was no more certain than it had been five hours ago.

Except now her feet hurt.

Pausing beneath the tall lamppost illuminating the front steps of Keller House, Ivy reached up and loosened the pins that secured her updo from her hair so it could fall in waves around her shoulders. Her headache eased slightly. She sighed, wanting to melt into a puddle.

But not yet. Maybe after she got home and had a bath.

But that only made her remember the time that Paxton had washed her hair, and the tears welled once more.

She lingered at the top of the stone steps, in almost the exact same place she had waited for Paxton all those months ago. A long look at the dark navy sky, with its bright stars so clear this far from the city, steadied her.

At least the stars made her smile.

A real smile, not the professional one she'd pasted on her lips for the last few hours.

"Everything will be okay," she said aloud, echoing Paxton's words as she rubbed her baby bump through the soft chiffon of her formal down.

"Ivy."

She glanced down as Paxton's voice reached out to her from the dark, but her movement was too quick. The shadowy landscape around her swirled. She listed to the side, but Paxton caught her before she lost her balance.

"Careful there," he said, pulling her firmly against him. "I can only handle one ambulance ride tonight."

Ivy laughed, just as he'd intended, but let her fingers grasp the lapels of his jacket tighter than normal to steady herself.

"Guess it's been a little longer since I ate than I thought."

"Junior and I can't have that."

*What?* "Who says it's a boy?"

"Grandmother insists. She couldn't stop telling everyone at the hospital about it."

Out of respect, Ivy only gave a quiet harrumph instead of an insistent one.

"But right now, I'm less worried about him and more worried about you."

"I'll be fine—"

"No." He quietly shut her down. "I know you aren't, Ivy. And that's my fault."

She held her breath a moment longer than normal as he tucked a few loose strands of her hair behind her ear.

"But I'm ready to remedy that."

"What do you mean?" she asked, but wasn't sure she was ready for the answer.

"We've gone about this all wrong, you and I."

*Oh yeah.* "I'll agree with that."

He buried his other hand in her hair, cupping her head so that she couldn't look away. As if her aching heart would let her do that.

"Well, from here on out, I want to do it right. You deserve that, Ivy."

She shook her head. "I want it to be right for both of us. That's all I care about, Paxton."

He confirmed her words with a kiss, slow and slick, until

she couldn't think of anything but the taste and feel of him. Only when she lost all touch with reality did he pull back.

Then to her surprise, he knelt before her on one knee.

"Paxton!"

"Ivy!" He grinned—oh, that smile got her every time—then he reached into his pocket and pulled out a small jeweler's box. Her body went really still.

He popped it open so the light on top of the lamppost nearby glinted off a central princess-cut diamond. But Ivy barely glanced at it before looking back up into his strong, handsome face.

"Will you marry me, Ivy?" he asked. No bravado, no overconfidence, just a quiet question. "I need you."

As much as she hated to say it, she forced the words out. "I'm sorry, Paxton."

He cocked his head to the side, an unspoken question.

"I can't. Even though you're saying all the right things, it's not the things that I need to know."

Somehow she knew, if he never said the words, she'd spend her whole life wondering if he was willing to risk his heart for her. And he needed to know it, too. Know that he could put the past behind him and move forward with her.

Pulling her hand to his mouth, he pressed a kiss to her skin, then looked up and said, "I love you, Ivy. I love everything about you—you're strong, you're sexy and you stand your ground with my family, without losing your signature grace and poise. I know it. They do, too."

Then he stood. "I hope it's never an issue again, but if it is, know that I'm by your side, no matter what."

There was no mistaking his sincerity as they stood in the moonlight, having come full circle from where this adventure had all started.

There under the stars, he pulled the ring from the jeweler's box, then slipped the box back into his pocket before lifting her hand. The gold band felt cool against her skin as he slipped the ring on to her finger.

"You're stuck with me, Ivy, no matter what the world decides to throw at us."

She smiled at him, knowing that he deserved just as much from her. Not just her love, but… "And I promise, no more secrets."

He kissed the ring where it encircled her finger. "Except for one," he said.

She glanced up at him.

"The gender reveal. I think we need to keep that secret to ourselves."

Oh, he was naughty. "Your grandmother is going to have a fit."

"Well, we've got to have fun where we can."

# Epilogue

The Harden sisters stepped into the hallway at Keller House—Ivy and Jasmine on the outside, with Willow in the middle. All of them were dressed in their own versions of wedding white. Just down the hall, Auntie stood with Rosie and two of Paxton's nieces, each with a basket of flower petals.

Ivy nodded, and the wedding director got everyone underway.

"Whose idea was it to walk half the house to get to the wedding ceremony?" Willow asked with a lighthearted grumble. "I have to pee again."

"You just went," Jasmine exclaimed.

"Doesn't matter when you have two munchkins bouncing on your bladder."

Ivy sympathized. At thirty-eight weeks herself, she felt like there was definitely no more room at the inn. They'd wanted the wedding before all the babies were born, and this was the only time they'd been able to coordinate for everyone, but they were definitely pushing it a little.

They were lucky Willow had been blessed with an extremely easy pregnancy, despite the twins, and had only had to deal with a few limitations. Bed rest not being one of them.

"Just do your best," Ivy said. "It will be over and party time soon."

"And all you'll remember of your wedding is the urgent need for the bathroom," Jasmine teased.

Which was funny because it was true. So, that's how the Harden sisters arrived at the ballroom door for their wedding, giggling.

They walked into the crowded room as if they were royalty. A very limited amount of exclusive invitations had been given to attend the wedding of the year. Three of Savannah's most notorious bachelors were being wed after making a splash on the social scene with their brides-to-be.

The large room was understated elegance incarnate. The gilded panels and floor-to-ceiling mirrors along one wall were incredibly elegant. Jasmine had chosen antique-white chairs, with gold leafing to compliment the surroundings.

Enormous flower arrangements and tulle bows splashed a mixture of the women's colors in pastel versions of green, blue and rose on the gilded backdrop. The aisle to the altar had been set wide enough to accommodate the three of them as they made their way to the men waiting for them in dark gray suits.

They paused at the end of the aisle, allowing the photographer to take a couple of shots.

Willow sighed, then looked at each of her sisters in turn. "I'd say that ring did an incredible job, right, ladies?"

They shared a smile. Willow had been right all along. The ring had been magical…and it had unleashed a magic in their lives unlike anything they could have imagined. Even in all the fantasies that had gotten Ivy through her lonely teenage years.

"Mother knew just what she was doing when she passed that on to us," Ivy agreed.

Her heart swelled over Paxton's loving gaze as he watched her approach. To marry him with her family celebrating with them and his child nestled deep beneath her ribs was the most enchanted moment she could ever have imagined.

And she didn't miss her glimpse of his family in the front two rows, either. His grandmother had not been happy for her only grandson to share his spotlight on this special day, but she was definitely learning his boundaries…protective barriers he fiercely upheld against everyone, including his family.

Paxton wouldn't be held back, but lowered his head to brush his lips over Ivy's as soon as she arrived, drawing a ripple of comments from the crowd. He grinned, causing her heart to speed up and her body to ask for more.

"We're pretty good at making a splash, huh?" he asked.

"Oh yeah," she said, then glanced at her sisters, only to see the other couples watching them.

"We're ready when you are," Willow said. The crowd laughed.

"You look beautiful, princess," Paxton murmured.

With Paxton, she definitely felt like a princess. Every day he pampered her and cared for her, showing her exactly how much he wanted her and their baby. She was due in just a few short weeks, and they were so excited about the birth of their son.

Not that they had mentioned the gender to anyone…

including his grandmother. A fact that always made Paxton laugh.

As the officiant spoke a blessing over the couples, Ivy marveled at how far they'd come as a family. She looked past Paxton to her sisters and their soon-to-be husbands.

Each one unique. Bringing their own history, pain and strengths to their relationships. This year had changed the course of their family. Today they celebrated marriage, but it was also a celebration of family. Triumph. New life.

Then the pastor gave each husband-to-be the chance to speak as they placed the rings on their new wives' fingers.

Royce went first. "Jasmine, until I met you, my life was made up of numbers and spreadsheets. Now it's filled with color and laughter and joy. I promise to put you and our family above all else."

Then Tate. "Willow, you've shown me that life is truly worth living. Not in fear, but in full. I promise never to retreat from the world, or you, again. And to look up from my typewriter every once in a while…"

And Paxton. "Ivy, you are the strongest, most gracious woman I've ever known. You've taught me about trust and love and true connection. As the saying goes, I promise to never leave you nor forsake you. I love you."

As he slid the ring on to her finger to nestle against her engagement ring, Ivy felt a rush of tears that she rapidly blinked away. She met Paxton's gaze and mouthed, "I love you, too."

"I now pronounce you *husbands* and *wives*," the pastor said, his emphasis drawing a laugh from their guests. But Ivy paid no mind as she leaned in for Paxton's firm kiss, eager to seal all the promises they'd made to each other.

The standing ovation from the wedding guests finally pulled them apart. As Ivy stared into the amber eyes that mirrored her own happiness, she heard Willow say, "Well, I almost made it through the whole thing."

Suddenly all eyes were on her very pregnant sister. Jasmine and Ivy both rushed to Willow's side.

"Are you okay?" Ivy asked.

Ever the pragmatist, Willow grimaced. "I really did try to wait, but I think my water just broke."

Her sisters laughed. Jasmine joked, "I don't think that's something you can control."

"I haven't been able to control anything about this pregnancy."

Paxton looked from Willow to Ivy and back. "Honestly, the odds were against a labor-free wedding."

Ivy reached out to Tate, who had gone pale and shaky. "Are you okay?"

"Is this bad?" he asked. "Isn't it awfully early?"

Willow shook her head. "You know the doctor said this might happen. Everything will be fine. But we might want to go on to the hospital, instead of partying. You know, do the responsible-parenting thing."

"Yes, definitely," Tate said.

Royce turned to the crowd. "Ladies and gentlemen, please head into the reception room down the hall. Some of us will join you for the cutting of the cake, but I'm sure you can understand our sense of urgency."

The crowd obediently headed to the back of the room and out the ballroom doors to the dining hall, where the reception had been set up, but the swell of speculation echoed off the mirrored walls. Auntie followed the final trickle of people, holding Rosie by the hand.

"Willow did this just for me," Tate said. "Didn't you, wife?"

"I don't understand," Paxton said.

Willow gave a half grin that turned into a grimace as she bent forward to breathe.

"Contractions already?" Ivy asked, feeling her own face contort into a sympathy-induced frown.

Willow nodded. After a moment she straightened and said, "Tate didn't want to be stuck having to talk to hundreds of people at the reception…"

"Convenient," Paxton said.

Jasmine's event-planner persona kicked in. "Okay, hospital time. We will meet you after we've posed for some pictures with the cakes."

Thank goodness they'd taken all the other wedding photos earlier.

Paxton and Ivy followed the other couples out through the kitchen, where a driver was waiting to take them to the hospital. They watched as the car, with its cute Just Married banner on the back window, gained speed as it headed down the drive.

"Pretty soon it will be our turn," Paxton said.

"I know your grandmother can't wait."

"I can't wait." Paxton placed a quick kiss on Ivy's neck, sending shivers down her spine. "I'm ready for the adventure to begin."

Ivy smiled into Paxton's gorgeous amber eyes, wondering if their baby would be lucky enough to inherit them. "I think it already has."

\* \* \* \* \*

# LET'S TALK

*Romance*

For exclusive extracts, competitions
and special offers, find us online:

# COMING SOON!

We really hope you enjoyed reading this book. If you're looking for more romance, be sure to head to the shops when new books are available on

## Thursday 7th March

To see which titles are coming soon, please visit

**millsandboon.co.uk/nextmonth**